SEPTIMUS HEAP

✢ BOOK ✞WO ✢

Flyte

ANGIE SAGE

ILLUSTRATIONS BY MARK ZÚG

BLOOMSBURY

First published in Great Britain in 2006 by Bloomsbury Publishing Plc
36 Soho Square, London, W1D 3QY

Published in America by HarperCollins Children's Books,
a division of HarperCollins Publishers, 1350 Avenue of the Americas,
New York NY 10019

A CIP catalogue record of this book is available from the British Library

Hbk ISBN 0 7475 7772 2
9780747577720
Export pbk ISBN 0 7475 8392 7
9780747583927

The paper this book is printed on is certified by the © Forest Stewardship
Council 1996 A.C. (FSC). It is ancient-forest friendly. The printer holds
FSC chain of custody SGS-COC-2061.

FSC

Mixed Sources

Product group from well-managed
forests and other controlled sources

Cert no. SGS-COC-2061
www.fsc.org
© 1996 Forest Stewardship Council

Printed in Great Britain by Clays Ltd, St Ives plc

1 3 5 7 9 10 8 6 4 2

www.septimusheap.co.uk
www.bloomsbury.com

SEPTIMUS HEAP

✠ BOOK TWO ✠

Flyte

OTHER BOOKS IN THE
SEPTIMUS HEAP SERIES:

Magyk

For Laurie,
supplier of magogs.
This one's for you, with love

⊹⊦ CONTENTS ⊦⊹

Flyte

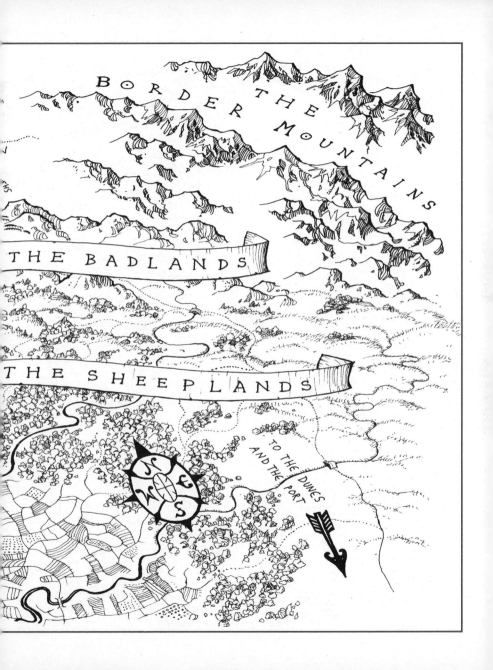

THE YEAR BEFORE:
ON THE NIGHT OF THE
APPRENTICE SUPPER

It *is night on the Marram Marshes*; a full moon shines down
on the black waters and illuminates the night-time Things
who are going about their business. Silence hangs in the air,
broken occasionally by the glugs and gurgles of the Quake
Ooze as the creatures that live beneath it make their way to a
feast. A huge ship with a full complement of sailors has sunk
into the Ooze and the Things are hungry—but they will have
to fight the Quake Ooze Brownies for the leftovers. Every
now and then a bubble of gas throws something from the ship
up to the surface, and great planks and spars covered in a thick

black tar float across the top of the Ooze.

Night-time on the Marram Marshes is no time for a human being to be abroad, but in the distance, paddling steadily towards the ship, is a figure in a small canoe. His fair curly hair hangs limp in the damp marsh air, and his piercing green eyes stare angrily into the night as he mutters furiously to himself, replaying over and over a fierce argument he has had that very evening. But what does *he* care any more? he asks himself. He is on his way to a new life, one where his talents will be recognised and not passed over in favour of an upstart nobody.

As he nears all that can be seen of the ship—a single mast sticking out of the Ooze topped with a limp and ragged red flag with a line of three black stars—he steers the canoe into a narrow channel that will take him to the very foot of the mast. He shivers, not with the cold, but from the feeling of fear that hangs in the air, and the thought that beneath him lies the ship's carcass, picked clean by the Quake Ooze Brownies. Now the debris is slowing him down. He propels the canoe forward until he is suddenly forced to a halt—there is something under the water blocking his path. He peers into the brackish sludge and can see nothing at first, but then . . . then he sees something below him, ice-white in the moonlight. It is moving . . . moving up through the water, and suddenly a skeleton, picked clean and bright by the Brownies, breaks the surface, sending a plume of black slime over the occupant of the canoe.

Shaking with a mixture of fear and excitement, the canoeist allows the skeleton to climb aboard and settle itself behind him, sticking its sharp kneecaps into his back. For he knows by the rings still on the bony fingers, that this is what he has been hoping to find—the skeleton of DomDaniel himself, Necromancer, twice ExtraOrdinary Wizard and, in the canoeist's opinion, a far superior Wizard to any he has met so far. And particularly superior to the one he has just been forced to share an Apprentice Supper with.

The canoeist makes a deal with the skeleton. He will do all that he can to Restore him to life and to allow him to reclaim his rightful place in the Wizard Tower, if only the skeleton will accept him as his Apprentice.

With a nod of his bony skull, the skeleton agrees to the deal.

The canoe resumes its journey, directed by the somewhat impatient bony forefinger of the skeleton jabbing the canoeist in the back. At last they reach the edge of the Marsh, whereupon the skeleton climbs out of the canoe and leads the tall, fair-haired young man into the bleakest place he has ever been.

As the young man follows the shambling gait of the skeleton through a desolate landscape, the thought of what he has left behind briefly crosses his mind. But only briefly, for this is his new life now and he will show them all—and *then* they'll be sorry.

Especially when *he* becomes the ExtraOrdinary Wizard.

✛ I ✛
SPIDERS

Septimus Heap tipped *six spiders into a jar*, screwed the lid down tight and put them outside the door. Then he picked up his broom and continued sweeping out the Pyramid Library.

The Library was cramped and dark. It was lit by a few fat candles that spat and spluttered, and it smelled weird—a mixture of incense, musty paper and mouldy leather. Septimus loved it. It was a Magykal place, perched right at the top of the Wizard Tower and hidden away deep inside the golden Pyramid, which crowned the Tower. Outside, the hammered gold of the Pyramid shimmered brightly in the early-morning sun.

After Septimus had finished sweeping, he made his way slowly along the shelves, humming happily to himself while he sorted out the Magykal books, parchments and spells that the ExtraOrdinary Wizard, Marcia Overstrand, had, as usual, left in a mess. Most eleven-and-a-half-year-old boys would rather have been out in the bright summer morning, but Septimus was where he wanted to be. He had spent quite enough summer mornings outside—and winter ones, come to that—in the first ten years of his life as Young Army soldier, Boy 412.

It was Septimus's job, as Apprentice to the ExtraOrdinary Wizard, to tidy the Library every morning. And every morning Septimus found something new and exciting. Often it was something that Marcia had left out especially for him: maybe a Conjuration that she had come across late at night and thought might interest him or a dog-eared old spell book that she had taken from one of the Hidden shelves. But today, Septimus reckoned he had found something for himself: it was stuck underneath a heavy brass candlestick and looked slightly disgusting—not the kind of thing that Marcia Overstrand would want to get her hands messy with. Very carefully he

prised the sticky brown square off the bottom of the candlestick and put it in the palm of his hand. Septimus examined
his find and felt excited—he was sure it was a Taste Charm.
The thick, brown, square tablet *looked* like an old piece of
chocolate; it smelled like an old piece of chocolate; and he was
pretty sure it would taste like an old piece of chocolate too,
although he wasn't going to risk it. There was a chance it
might be a poison Charm that had dropped out of the large
box labelled: TOXINS, VENOMS AND BASYK BANES, which
teetered unsteadily on the shelf above.

Septimus pulled out a small Enhancing Glass from his
Apprentice belt and held it so that he could read the thin
white writing that looped across the square. The words said:

> Take me, shake me,
> and I will make thee:
> Quetzalcoatl's Tchocolatl.

Septimus grinned. He was right, but then he usually was
when it came to Magyk. It *was* a Taste Charm—even better,
it was a *chocolate* Taste Charm. Septimus knew just the person
he wanted to give it to. Smiling to himself, he slipped the
Charm into his pocket.

Septimus's work in the Library was nearly done. He climbed up the ladder to tidy the last shelf and suddenly found himself eye to eye with the biggest, hairiest spider he had ever seen. Septimus gulped; if it had not been for Marcia insisting on him removing every single spider that he found from the Library, he would happily have left this one alone. He was sure the spider's eight beady eyes were trying to stare him down, and he didn't like its long, hairy legs either. In fact all eight legs looked as though they were planning to run up his sleeve if he didn't grab the spider fast.

In a flash, Septimus had the spider in his hand. The creature scrabbled angrily against his dusty fingers, trying to prise them open with its surprisingly powerful legs, but Septimus held on tight. Quickly he made his way down the ladder, passing the small hatch that led out on to the golden roof of the Pyramid. Just as he reached the bottom of the ladder, the spider bit the inside of his thumb.

"Ouch!" Septimus yelped.

He grabbed the spider jar, unscrewed the lid one-handed and dropped the creature in, much to the dismay of the six other spiders already there. Then, with his thumb beginning to throb, Septimus screwed the lid back on as tightly as he could. Careful not to drop the jar, in which six small spiders were now being chased around and around by one large hairy one, Septimus made a quick exit down the winding, narrow, stone stairs which led from the Library into the apartment of the ExtraOrdinary Wizard, Madam Marcia Overstrand.

Septimus hurried by the closed purple and gold door to Marcia's bedroom, past his own room, and then ran down some more steps and headed for the small potion room beside Marcia's study. He put down the jar of spiders and looked at his thumb. It wasn't a pretty sight; it had become a deep red colour and some interesting blue blotches were beginning to appear on his hand. It also *hurt*. Septimus flipped open the Medicine Chest with his good hand and found a tube of Spider Balm, the entire contents of which he squeezed over his thumb. It didn't seem to do much good. In fact it seemed to make it worse. Septimus stared at his thumb, which was swelling up like a small balloon and felt as though it might be about to explode.

Marcia Overstrand, whom Septimus had now been Apprenticed to for almost a year and a half, had found the spiders waiting for her on her triumphant return to the Wizard Tower after ousting the Necromancer, DomDaniel, from his brief second time as ExtraOrdinary Wizard. Marcia had thoroughly Cleaned the Tower of Darke Magyk and restored the Magyk to the Wizard Tower, but she could not get rid of the spiders. This had upset Marcia, for she knew that the spiders were a sure sign that Darke Magyk still lingered in the Tower.

At first, when Marcia came back to the Tower, she was too busy to notice anything amiss—apart from the spiders. She had, for the first time, an Apprentice to think about; she had the Heaps—who were now living up at the Palace—to deal with and a bunch of Ordinary Wizards to sort out and settle back into the Tower. But as Septimus's first summer at the Wizard Tower had drawn on, Marcia had begun to notice, out of the corner of her eye, a Darkenesse following her. At first she had thought she was imagining it, for every time she glanced back over her shoulder and had a proper look, there was nothing to be seen. It wasn't until Alther Mella, the ghost of Marcia's old tutor and ExtraOrdinary Wizard, had told her that he could see something too that Marcia knew she was not imagining things—there *was* a Darke Shadow following her.

And so, for the last year, piece by piece, Marcia had been building a ShadowSafe, which was nearly finished. It stood in the corner of the room, a tangle of shiny black rods and bars made from Professor Weasal Van Klampff's special Amalgam. A strange black mist played around the bars of the

ShadowSafe, and occasionally flashes of orange light leaped between them. But at last the ShadowSafe was nearly finished, and soon Marcia would be able to walk inside it with the Shadow following her and walk out again, leaving the Shadow behind. And that, Marcia hoped, would be the end of the Darkenesse in the Tower.

As Septimus stared at his thumb, which was now twice its normal size and turning a nasty purple, he heard Marcia's study door open.

"I'm off, Septimus," said Marcia purposefully. "I've got to go and pick up another part of the ShadowSafe. I told old Weasal I'd be down this morning. It's almost the last piece. We've only got the Stopper to collect after this, Septimus, and that will be that. Goodbye Shadow."

"Aargh," Septimus groaned.

Marcia peered suspiciously around the door. "And *what* are you doing in the potions room?" she asked irritably, catching sight of Septimus's hand. "My goodness, what *have* you done? Have you burned yourself doing a Fire Spell again? I don't want any more singed parrots hanging around here, Septimus. They smell disgusting and it's not fair to the parrots either."

"Aargh. That was a mistake," muttered Septimus. "I meant to do a Firebird Spell. It could have happened to anyone.

Ouch—I've been bitten."

Marcia came in, and behind her Septimus could see a slight murkiness in the air as the Shadow followed her into the potion room. Marcia bent down and looked more closely at Septimus's thumb, almost enveloping him in her purple cloak as she did so. Marcia was a tall woman with long, dark, curly hair and the intense green eyes that always came to Magykal people, once they were exposed to Magyk. Septimus had the same green eyes too, although before he had met Marcia Overstrand they had been a dull grey. Like all ExtraOrdinary Wizards who had lived in the Wizard Tower before her, Marcia wore the lapis and gold Akhu Amulet around her neck, a deep purple silk tunic fastened with the ExtraOrdinary gold and platinum belt and a Magykal purple cloak. She also had on a pair of purple python shoes, carefully chosen that morning from a rack of about a hundred other almost identical purple python shoes that she had taken to stockpiling since her return to the Wizard Tower. Septimus wore, as usual, his only pair of brown leather boots. Septimus liked his boots, and although Marcia often offered to get some new ones made for him in a nice emerald python skin to match his green Apprentice robes, he always refused. Marcia just couldn't understand it.

"That's a *spider* bite," said Marcia, grabbing hold of his thumb.

"*Ouch!*" Septimus yelled.

"I don't like the look of that at all," Marcia muttered.

Neither did Septimus. His thumb was now dark purple. His fingers looked like five sausages stuck on a football, and he could feel sharp pains shooting up his arm towards his heart. Septimus swayed slightly.

"Sit down, sit down," said Marcia urgently, throwing some papers off a small chair and guiding Septimus down on to it. Quickly she took a small vial out of the Medicine Chest. It had the words SPIDER VENOM scrawled on it and contained a murky green liquid. Marcia took out a long, thin glass dropper from the scary-looking medical instruments that were lined up in the lid of the chest like bizarre cutlery in a picnic basket. Then she sucked up the green venom into the dropper, being extremely careful not to get any in her mouth.

Septimus pulled his thumb out of Marcia's grasp. "That's poison!" he protested.

"There's a Darkenesse in that bite," said Marcia, putting her thumb on top of the venom-filled dropper and carefully holding it away from her cloak, "and the Spider Balm is making it worse. Sometimes you have to fight like with like.

Venom with venom. Trust me."

Septimus did trust Marcia; in fact he trusted her more than anyone else. So he gave her back his thumb and closed his eyes while Marcia dropped Spider Venom on to the bite and muttered what sounded to Septimus like an Anti-Hex Incantation. As Marcia did so the shooting pains up his arm died away, his light-headedness left him and he began to think that maybe his thumb would not explode after all.

Calmly, Marcia replaced everything back in the Medicine Chest, and then she turned and considered her Apprentice. Not surprisingly, he looked pale. But she had, thought Marcia, been working him too hard. He could do with a day out in the summer sunshine. And, more to the point, she didn't want his mother, Sarah Heap, coming round again either.

Marcia had still not forgotten the visit Sarah had made not long after Septimus had become her Apprentice. One Sunday morning Marcia had answered a loud banging on the door, only to find Sarah Heap on the other side, accompanied by an audience of Wizards from the floor below, who had all come up to see what the noise was—for no one ever dared bang on the ExtraOrdinary Wizard's door like that.

To the amazement of the assembled audience, Sarah had then proceeded to tell Marcia off.

"My Septimus and I were apart for the first ten years of his life," Sarah had said heatedly, "and, Madam Marcia, I do not intend to spend the next ten years seeing as little of him as I did for the first ten. So I will thank you to let the boy come home for his father's birthday today."

Much to Marcia's annoyance, this had been greeted with a small round of applause from the assembled Wizards. Both Marcia and Septimus had been amazed at Sarah's speech. Marcia was amazed because no one ever spoke to her like that. *No one.* And Septimus was amazed because he didn't realise that that was what mothers did, although he rather liked it.

The last thing Marcia wanted was a repeat visit from Sarah. "Off you go then," she said, half expecting Sarah Heap to appear and demand to know why Septimus looked so pale. "It's time you spent a day with your family. And while you're there, you can remind your mother to make sure that Jenna gets off to Zelda's tomorrow for her MidSummer Visit to the Dragon Boat. If I had my way she would have left days ago, but Sarah will insist on leaving everything to the last minute. I'll see you tonight, Septimus—midnight at the latest. And the chocolate Charm is yours, by the way."

"Oh, thanks." Septimus smiled. "But I'm fine now, really. I don't need a day off."

"Yes, you do," Marcia told him. "Go on, off you go."

Despite himself, Septimus smiled. Maybe a day off would not be so bad. He could see Jenna before she went and give her the chocolate Charm.

"All right then," he said. "I'll be back by midnight."

Septimus headed for the heavy purple front door, which recognised Marcia's Apprentice and flung itself open as he approached.

"Hey!" Marcia shouted after him. "You've forgotten the spiders!"

"Bother," muttered Septimus.

WIZARD WAY

S eptimus *stepped on to* the silver spiral stairs at the top of the Tower. "Hall, please," he said.

As the stairs began to move smoothly down, turning like a giant corkscrew, Septimus held up the spider jar. He squinted at the occupants, which now numbered only five, and wondered if he had seen the hairy spider before.

The hairy spider looked back at Septimus with a baleful stare. It had certainly seen *him* before. Four times to be precise, the spider thought crossly; four times it had been picked up, stuffed into a jar and dumped outside. The boy was lucky it hadn't bitten him before. Still, at least there was some decent food in the jar this time. The two soft young spiders had gone down very nicely, even though it had had to chase them around the jar for a while. The hairy spider settled down and resigned itself to the journey. Again.

The silver spiral stairs turned slowly, and, as they took Septimus and his catch down through the Wizard Tower, he got some cheery waves from the Ordinary Wizards who lived on the floors below and were beginning to go about their business for the day.

There had been much excitement when Septimus had first arrived at the Wizard Tower. Not only was Marcia Overstrand returning in triumph after ridding the Wizard Tower, not to mention the entire Castle, of a Darke Necromancer, but she was also bringing with her an Apprentice. Marcia had spent ten years as ExtraOrdinary Wizard without taking on an Apprentice. After a while some of the Ordinary Wizards had been known to mutter that she was too fussy for her own good. "What did Madam Marcia expect to find, for goodness' sake—the seventh son of a seventh son? Ha!" But that was exactly what Madam Marcia Overstrand *had* found. She had found Septimus Heap, seventh son of Silas Heap, who was a poor and untalented Ordinary

Wizard and himself the seventh son of Benjamin Heap, an equally poor, but considerably more talented, Shape-Shifter.

As the silver spiral stairs slowed to a smooth halt on the ground floor of the Wizard Tower, Septimus jumped off and made his way across the Great Hall, hopping from side to side to try to catch the fleeting colours that played across the soft sandlike floor. The floor had seen him coming and the words GOOD MORNING, APPRENTICE ran across the shifting patterns and flitted in front of him as he made his way over to the massive solid-silver doors that guarded the entrance to the Tower. Septimus murmured the password, and, noiselessly, the doors swung open before him, sending a brilliant shaft of sunlight into the Hall, which drowned out all the Magykal colours.

Septimus stepped out into the warm midsummer morning. Someone was waiting for him.

"Marcia's let you out early today," said Jenna Heap. She was sitting on the lowest of the huge marble steps that led up into the Wizard Tower, carelessly swinging her feet against the warm stone. She wore a simple red tunic edged with gold and tied with a gold sash, and a sturdy pair of sandals on her dusty feet. Her long dark hair was held in place by a slim gold circlet that she wore around her head like a crown. Her dark eyes had a teasing glint in them as she regarded her adoptive brother. He looked as scruffy as usual. His curly straw-coloured hair was uncombed, and his green Apprentice robes were covered in dust from the Library—but on his right index finger, his gold Dragon Ring shone as brightly as ever.

Jenna was pleased to see him.

"Hello, Jen." Septimus smiled, his brilliant green eyes blinking in the bright sunlight. He waved his jar of spiders at her.

Jenna leaped up from the step, her eyes fixed on the jar. "Just don't let those spiders out anywhere near me," she warned him.

Septimus jumped down the steps, shaking the jar at her as he went past. He went over to the Well on the edge of the courtyard, and very carefully, he tipped the spiders out of the jar. They all landed in the bucket. The hairy spider had another quick snack and started climbing back up the rope. The three remaining spiders watched the hairy one leave and decided to stay in the bucket.

"Sometimes, Jen," said Septimus as he joined Jenna by the steps, "I think those spiders just go straight back up to the Library again. I recognised one of them today."

"Don't be silly, Sep. How can you recognise a spider?"

"Well, I was pretty sure it recognised *me*," said Septimus.

"I think that's why it bit me."

"It bit you? That's horrible. Where?"

"In the Library."

"No, where did it bite you?"

"Oh. Look, here." Septimus waved his thumb at Jenna.

"Can't see anything," she said dismissively.

"That's because Marcia put some venom on it."

"*Venom?*"

"Oh, that's just something we Wizards do," said Septimus airily.

"Oh—you *Wizards*," scoffed Jenna, getting up and pulling at Septimus's green tunic. "You Wizards are all crazy. And, speaking of crazy, how *is* Marcia?"

Septimus kicked at a pebble and sent it skittering over to Jenna.

"She's not crazy, Jen," he said loyally, "but that Shadow follows her everywhere. And it's getting worse, because I'm beginning to see it now."

"Eurgh, creepy." Jenna kicked the pebble back to Septimus, and the pair played pebble football across the courtyard and into the cool shade of a tall silver archway lined with deep-blue lapis lazuli. This was the Great Arch that led out of the Wizard Tower courtyard and into the broad avenue known as

Wizard Way, which ran straight to the Palace.

Septimus shook off all thoughts of Shadows and ran into the Great Arch ahead of Jenna. Then he spun around and said, "Anyway, Marcia says I can have the day off today."

"A whole *day*?" asked Jenna, amazed.

"A whole day. Till midnight. So I can come back with you and see Mum."

"And me. You're going to have to see me all day too; I haven't seen you for ages. And I'm going off to Aunt Zelda's tomorrow to see the Dragon Boat. It's MidSummer Day in a few days' time, in case you'd forgotten."

"Of course I haven't forgotten. Marcia keeps going on about how important it is. Here, I've got a present for you." Septimus fished the chocolate Charm out of his tunic pocket and gave it to Jenna.

"Oh, Sep, that's lovely. Er, what is it exactly?"

"It's a Taste Charm. It'll turn anything you want into chocolate. I thought it might be useful over at Aunt Zelda's."

"Hey—I could turn all that cabbage and pilchard stew into chocolate."

"Cabbage and pilchard stew . . ." said Septimus wistfully. "You know, I really miss Aunt Zelda's cooking."

"No one else does." Jenna laughed.

"I know," said Septimus. "That's why I thought you'd like the Charm. Wish I could come and see Aunt Zelda too."

"Well you can't—because I'm the Queen."

"Since when, Jen?"

"Well, I *will* be. And *you're* just a lowly Apprentice." Jenna stuck her tongue out at Septimus, who chased her out of the Great Arch and into the heat of Wizard Way.

As they came out from the shadows of the Arch, Jenna and Septimus Heap saw Wizard Way spread out before them, bright and empty in the early morning sun. The huge white limestone slabs formed a broad avenue all the way to the Palace Gate, which glinted gold in the distance. Tall silver torch posts lined Wizard Way, holding the torches that were used to light the Way at night. That morning each one carried a blackened torch, which had burned out the previous night, and would be replaced and lit that evening by Maizie Smalls, the TorchLighter. Septimus loved the sight of the torches being lit; from his room at the top of the Wizard Tower he could see right down Wizard Way, and Marcia often found him gazing dreamily out of his window at lighting-up time when he should have been doing his incantation preparation.

Jenna and Septimus moved out of the sun's glare and into the cooler shadows of the squat buildings that were set back and lined the Way. The buildings were among the oldest of the Castle and were built of a pale weatherworn stone, pitted and marked by thousands of years of rain, hail, frost and the occasional battle. They were home to the numerous manuscript makers and printing houses that produced all the books, pamphlets, tracts and treatises that were used by the Castle inhabitants.

Beetle, who was General Dogsbody and Inspection Clerk at Number Thirteen, was lounging outside sunning himself and he gave Septimus a friendly nod. Number Thirteen stood out from all the other shops. Not only was it the only one to have all its windows stacked so high with papers that it was impossible to see inside, but it had also recently been painted purple, much to the distaste of the Wizard Way Conservation Society. Number Thirteen housed the Magykal Manuscriptorium and Spell Checkers Incorporated, which Marcia and most of the Wizards used regularly.

As they neared the end of Wizard Way, Jenna and Septimus heard the clatter of horse's hooves echoing on the empty road behind them. They turned around to see in the distance a dark, dusty figure on a huge black horse gallop up to the Manuscriptorium. The figure dismounted in a hurry, quickly tied his horse up and disappeared inside, closely followed by Beetle, who looked surprised to have a customer so early in the morning.

"I wonder who that is," said Septimus. "I haven't seen him around here before, have you?"

"I'm not sure," said Jenna, thinking. "He looks sort of familiar, but I don't know why."

Septimus did not reply. His spider bite had suddenly sent a stabbing pain up his arm, and he shivered as he remembered the Shadow he had seen that morning.

✢ 3 ✢
A DARK HORSE

*G*udrun the Great was guarding the
Palace Gate. She was floating
a few feet off the ground and dozing
peacefully in the sunshine. Gudrun, an
Ancient ghost who was one of the
very early ExtraOrdinary Wizards,
was dreaming of the old
days when the Wizard
Tower was new. She was
almost invisible in the
bright sun, and Jenna
and Septimus were
so busy discussing
the mysterious
horseman that

they walked straight through her. Gudrun the Great nodded dreamily to them, mistaking them for a pair of her own Apprentices from long ago, who had been twins.

The year before, Alther Mella had taken over the task of running the Palace and the Castle until the Time was Right for Jenna to be Queen. He had decided that, after ten years of the hated Custodian Guards stomping up and down in front of the Palace and terrorising the population, he never wanted to see soldiers guarding the Palace again. So Alther, a ghost himself, had asked the Ancients to act as guards. The Ancients were elderly ghosts; many of them were at least five hundred years old, and some of them, like Gudrun, were even older than that. As ghosts become more transparent with age, most of the Ancients were quite hard to see. Jenna was still not used to walking through a doorway and discovering that she had also walked through the dozing Second Keeper of the Queen's Bedpost or some such ancient dignitary. She would only realise her mistake when she heard a quavery voice wishing her, "Good morn to thee, fair maiden," as the trodden-upon Ancient suddenly woke up and tried to remember where he or she was. Luckily the Palace had not changed much since it had been built, so most of the Ancients could still find their way around. Many of them were old ExtraOrdinary Wizards,

and the sight of a faded purple cloak flitting through the maze
of endless corridors and rooms at the Palace was not unusual.

"I think I just walked through Gudrun again," said Jenna.
"I hope she didn't mind."

"Well, I still think it's odd having ghosts guarding the
gates," Septimus replied, looking at his thumb, which seemed
all right again, much to his relief. "I mean anyone could just
walk in, couldn't they?"

"That's the idea," said Jenna. "Anyone *can* walk in. The
Palace is here for everyone in the Castle. It doesn't need
guards to keep people out any more."

"Hmm," said Septimus. "But there might be some people
you still need to keep out."

"Sometimes, Sep," said Jenna, "you get too serious for your
own good. You spend far too much time cooped up in that
smelly old Tower, if you ask me. Race you!"

Jenna ran off. Septimus watched her as she raced across the
lawns that spread in front of the Palace, dusty and brown in
the midsummer heat. The lawns were long and wide and were
cut in two by the broad drive, which swept up to the entrance
of the Palace itself. The Palace was one of the oldest buildings
in the Castle; it was built in the ancient style, with small, for-
tified windows and battlements running along the top of the

walls. In front of it was a shallow ornamental moat that was home to some fearsome snapping turtles left by the previous occupant, the Supreme Custodian, which were almost impossible to get rid of. A broad, low bridge spanned the moat and led to a pair of heavy oak doors, which were thrown open in the early-morning heat.

Septimus liked the Palace now. It was a welcoming building with its yellow stone glowing warmly in the sun. As a boy soldier he had often stood guard outside the gate, but then it had seemed a dark, gloomy place, occupied by the dreaded Supreme Custodian. Even so, Septimus had never minded standing guard, for although it was often boring and cold, at least it was not frightening like most of the things he had had to do in the Young Army.

In the summer Septimus would watch Billy Pot, the Lawn Cutter, who had invented a Contraption. The Contraption was meant to cut the grass. Sometimes it did and sometimes it didn't, depending on how hungry the occupants of the Contraption—the lawn lizards—were. The lawn lizards were Billy's secret—or at least he thought they were—although most people had figured out how the Contraption worked. And when it worked it was simple: Billy pushed the Contraption along and the lizards ate the grass. When it didn't work, Billy lay down on the grass and yelled at them.

Billy Pot kept hundreds of lawn lizards in lizard lodges down by the river, and every morning he would select the twenty hungriest lizards, put them into the cutting box at the front of the Contraption and wheel them off to the Palace lawns. Billy hoped that one day he would actually finish cutting the lawns before it was time to start all over again; he would have liked to have a day off now and then. But this never happened. By the time he had pushed the Contraption across the huge expanse of grass and the lawn lizards had done their job, it was time to start all over again.

As Septimus set off across the grass, trying to catch up with Jenna, who was far ahead of him, he heard the familiar clanking sound. A moment later Billy Pot appeared in the distance, pushing his Contraption across the broad path that ran in front of the Palace moat, slowly heading for the new day's patch of grass. Septimus speeded up, determined not to let Jenna get too far ahead. But she was bigger and faster than he was, even though they were exactly the same age. She had soon reached the bridge.

Jenna stopped and waited for Septimus to catch up. "Come on, Sep," she said. "Let's go and find Mum."

They walked over the bridge and arrived at the Palace doorway. The Ancient at the doors was awake; he was sitting on a small gold chair, placed carefully to catch the sun, and had been watching Jenna and Septimus's approach with a fond smile. He smoothed down his purple cloak, for he too had been a much-respected ExtraOrdinary Wizard in his time, and smiled at Jenna.

"Good morning, Princess," said the ghost, his thin voice sounding as though it came from a great distance. "How nice to see you. And good morning, Apprentice. How is the Transforming going? Have you managed the Transubstantiate Triple yet?"

"Almost." Septimus grinned.

"Good lad," said the Ancient approvingly.

"Hello, Godric," said Jenna. "Do you know where Mum is?"

"As it happens, Princess, I do. Madam Sarah told me that she was going to the kitchen garden to pick some herbs. I told her that the Kitchen Maid would do that for her, but she insisted on going herself. Wonderful woman, your mother," said the Ancient wistfully.

"Thank you, Godric," said Jenna. "We'll go and find her— hey, *what*?" Septimus had grabbed her arm.

"Jen—look," he said, pointing to a dust cloud approaching the Palace Gate.

The Ancient, still in a sitting position, floated up from his chair and hovered in the doorway, peering out into the sunlight.

"A Darke horse. And a Darke rider," his voice echoed thinly.

Septimus pulled Jenna into the shadows behind the ghost.

"What are you doing?" Jenna protested. "It's only that horse we saw before. Let's see who the rider is."

As she stepped out into the light of the doorway, Jenna saw the horse approaching. The rider rode the horse hard, sitting forward on the animal and urging it on, his dark cloak streaming out behind him. The horse did not stop at the gate, but carried straight on through Gudrun the Great and thundered up the driveway. Unfortunately Billy Pot was still on his way to his patch of grass. He had just started to push the Contraption across the drive when he and the Contraption were forced to make a swift change of direction to avoid the oncoming horse. Billy made it but the Contraption was not so lucky. Unused to doing anything quickly, it fell to pieces where it stood. The lawn lizards ran off in all directions, and Billy Pot found himself gazing at a pile of metal in the middle of the Palace drive.

The horseman thundered on, oblivious to Billy Pot's loss

and the lizards' newfound freedom. The horse's hooves kicked up the midsummer dust and beat with rhythmic hollow thuds against the dry ground as it rapidly approached the Palace.

Jenna and Septimus waited for the horseman to take the usual path around to the stables at the back of the Palace, but to their surprise the rider ignored it and spurred the horse on over the bridge. Expertly, without breaking the horse's stride, the horseman galloped over the threshold of the door and rode straight through Godric. Jenna felt the damp heat of the horse as it passed close, letting go a long fleck of horse spittle, which landed on her tunic. She turned to protest to the horseman, but he was gone—cantering across the hall at full speed. With his horse's hooves skidding on the stone flags and sending up sparks, he executed a sharp left turn into the gloom of the Long Walk, the mile-long corridor that ran down the middle of the Palace like a backbone.

Godric picked himself up from the floor and muttered, "A coldness . . . a coldness went through me." He subsided shakily back into his chair and closed his transparent eyes.

"Are you all right, Godric?" Jenna asked, concerned.

"Yes, indeed," murmured the old ghost faintly. "Thank you, your honour. I mean, thank you, your Princess."

"Are you sure you're all right?" Jenna peered at the ghost

but he had fallen asleep.

"Come on, Sep," whispered Jenna. "Let's see what's happening."

The inside of the Palace was dark after the brilliant sunshine. Jenna and Septimus ran across the central hallway to the Long Walk. They stared down the seemingly endless, dimly lit expanse, but there was no sight or sound of the horseman.

"He vanished," whispered Jenna. "Maybe he was a ghost."

"Funny sort of ghost," said Septimus, pointing to some dusty hoofprints on the faded red carpet that was laid on the huge old flagstones. Jenna and Septimus turned down the east wing of the Walk and followed the hoofprints. Once, before the Supreme Custodian had taken over the Palace, the Long Walk had been full of wonderful treasures—priceless statues, rich hangings and colourful tapestries—but now it was a dusty shadow of its former self. During his ten years of occupation, the Supreme Custodian had stripped all the most valuable possessions from the Palace and sold them to fund his lavish banquets. Now, Jenna and Septimus walked past a few old paintings of previous Queens and Princesses, which had been rescued from the basement, and some empty wooden chests with broken locks and wrenched hinges. After three

Queens, all of whom looked somewhat bad-tempered, and a cross-eyed Princess, the hoofprints made a sharp right turn and disappeared through the wide double doors of the Ballroom. The doors were already thrown open, and Jenna and Septimus followed the hoofprints in. There was no sign of the horseman.

Septimus let out a low whistle. "This place is *big*," he said.

The Ballroom was indeed huge. When the Palace had been built it was said that the entire population of the Castle could have fit inside the Ballroom. Although this was no longer true, it was still the biggest room that anyone in the Castle had ever seen. The ceiling was higher than a house and the massive windows, which were full of small panes of stained glass, stretched from floor to ceiling and threw an array of rainbow colours across the polished wooden floor. The lower panes of the windows were thrown open in the heat of the summer morning. They led out on to the lawns at the back of the Palace, which swept down to the river.

"He's gone," said Jenna.

"Or Disappeared," muttered Septimus. "Like the Ancient said, 'a Darke horse and a Darke rider.'"

"Don't be silly, Sep. He didn't mean it like *that*," said Jenna. "You've spent too long at the top of that Tower with a spooked

Wizard and her Shadow. Anyway, he's only just gone out through that window—look."

"You don't know that for sure," Septimus objected, stung at being called silly by Jenna.

"Yes, I do," said Jenna, pointing to the pile of horse dung steaming on the step. Septimus made a face. Carefully they stepped out on to the terrace.

It was then that they heard Sarah Heap scream.

⊬ 4 ⊦
SIMON SAYS

J ust one *little message rat*," Sarah
Heap was saying tearfully to the
dismounted dark horseman, as
Jenna and Septimus reached the
door to the walled kitchen
garden. The man had his
back to them. He stood
awkwardly, holding on to his
horse with one hand and
patting Sarah, who had
thrown her arms around
his neck, with the
other.

Sarah Heap
looked small and

almost frail beside the man. Her wispy fair hair straggled down
to her shoulders, and her long blue cotton tunic with the
Palace gold edging on the sleeves and hem could not hide how
thin Sarah had become since her return to the Castle. But her
green eyes were bright with relief as she looked up at the dark
horseman.

"Just one message to let me know you were safe," chided
Sarah. "That's all I needed. All *we* needed. Your father has
been worried sick too. We thought we would never see you
again . . . gone for more than a year and not a *word*. You really are a bad boy, Simon."

"I am not a *boy*, Mother. I am a man now. I am twenty years
old, in case you had forgotten." Simon Heap detached Sarah's
arms from his neck and stepped back, suddenly aware that he
was being watched. He swung around and did not look particularly pleased to see his youngest brother and adoptive
sister hanging back uncertainly by the kitchen garden door.
Simon turned back to his mother.

"Anyway, you don't need *me*," he said sulkily. "Not now
you have your precious long-lost seventh son back.
Particularly as he has done so well for himself—taking *my*
Apprenticeship."

"Simon, *don't*," Sarah protested. "Please don't let's argue over that again. Septimus took nothing from you. You were never *offered* the Apprenticeship."

"Ah, but I would have been. If that brat hadn't turned up."

"Simon! I will not have you talk about Septimus like that. He is your brother."

"If you believe what the old witch Zelda saw in a pool of dirty water was true. Which I don't, personally."

"And don't talk about your great-aunt like that either, Simon," Sarah said in a low voice, becoming angry. "Anyway, I know that what I saw—what we all saw—is true. Septimus is my son. And he is your brother. It is time you got used to it, Simon."

Septimus retreated into the shadows of the doorway; he was upset by what he had heard, but not surprised. He remembered only too well what Simon had said on the night of his Apprentice Supper at Aunt Zelda's cottage in the Marram Marshes. That night had been the most amazing night of Septimus's life, for not only had he just become Marcia's Apprentice, he had also found out who he really was—the seventh son of Sarah and Silas Heap. But, in the early hours of the morning, after the celebrations, Simon Heap had had a terrible argument with his parents. He had stormed off into the darkness, taking a canoe across the

Marram Marshes, much to Sarah's horror (and his brother Nicko's, who had only just acquired the canoe). After that Simon had vanished—until now.

"Shall we go and say hello, Sep?" whispered Jenna.

Septimus shook his head and hung back.

"You go," he told Jenna. "I don't think he wants to see me."

Septimus stood in the shadows and watched Jenna as she walked into the kitchen garden and threaded her way through the lettuces that Simon's horse had trampled flat.

"Hello, Simon." Jenna smiled shyly.

"Aha—I hoped I might find you here, in your *Palace*. Good morning, Your Majesty," said Simon in a slightly mocking tone as Jenna approached.

"I'm not called that yet, Si," said Jenna, a little uncertainly. "Not until I'm Queen."

"Queen, eh—and won't we be grand then? You won't be speaking to the likes of us when you're *Queen*, will you?"

Sarah sighed. "Do stop it, Simon," she said.

Simon looked at his mother, then at Jenna. His irritable expression changed to something darker as he gazed at the view through the open door of the garden. His greenish-black eyes took in the mellow stonework of the ancient Palace and the tranquillity of the lawns. How different it was from the chaotic room he had grown up in surrounded by his five younger brothers and his little adoptive sister, Jenna. In fact, it was so very different that he no longer felt his family had anything to do with him. Particularly Jenna, who, after all, was no blood relation anyway. She was nothing more than a cuckoo in the nest, and, like all cuckoos, she had taken over the nest and destroyed it.

"Very well, Mother," said Simon harshly. "I *will* stop it."

Sarah smiled hesitantly. She hardly recognised her eldest son any more. The man in the black cloak who stood before her felt like someone else. And not someone that Sarah liked very much.

"So," said Simon, slightly too jovially, "how would my little sister like a ride on Thunder here?" He patted his horse proudly.

"I'm not sure about that, Simon," Sarah said.

"Why ever not, Mother? Don't you trust me?"

Sarah was silent for just a second too long. "Of course I do," she said.

"I'm a good rider you know. Spent the last year riding through the mountains and valleys up in Border Country."

"What—the *Badlands*? What were you doing out there?" asked Sarah with a note of suspicion in her voice.

"Oh, this and that, Mother," said Simon vaguely. Suddenly he took a step towards Jenna. Sarah moved forward as if to stop him, but Simon reached Jenna first, and in one easy movement he lifted her up and put her on the horse.

"How do you like that?" he asked Jenna. "Thunder's a lovely animal, isn't he?"

"Yes. . ." Jenna said uneasily, while the horse shifted about beneath her, as if impatient to be gone.

"We'll just go for a ride down the Way, shall we?" said Simon, sounding almost like his old self, as he put his foot into the stirrup and swung into the saddle behind Jenna. Suddenly Sarah found her eldest son looking down at her from what seemed to be a great height, and about to do something she was unable to stop him from doing.

"No, Simon, I don't think Jenna should—"

But Simon kicked his horse and pulled on the reins. The beast wheeled around, trampling the thyme that Sarah had been about to pick, and galloped off, through the kitchen gar-den door and around the side of the Palace. Sarah ran out behind him shouting, "Simon—Simon, come back . . ."

But he was gone, leaving nothing but small lingering clouds of dust where the horse's hooves had struck the dusty path.

Sarah didn't know why she felt frightened; after all, it was only her son taking his sister for a ride on his horse. What was wrong with that? Sarah looked around for Septimus; she was sure she had seen him arrive with Jenna, but Septimus was not there. Sarah sighed. It had been wishful thinking, that was all; she had been imagining things again. But she decided that when Simon and Jenna came back from their ride she would go straight down to the Wizard Tower and get Septimus back for the day. After all, Jenna had to leave for her midsummer visit to the Dragon Boat the next day, and it would be nice for Septimus to see her before she went. She wouldn't stand for any argument from that Marcia Overstrand either. Septimus needed to spend more time with his sister, and with her, too. And maybe if Simon got to know Septimus a little better it would put an end to all this unpleasantness.

And so, preoccupied with her thoughts and watched by three escaped lawn lizards, Sarah knelt down to try and rescue the crushed thyme, while she waited for Jenna and Simon to return.

✤ 5 ✤
THUNDER

Jenna *clung to the horse's* wiry mane as Simon cantered across the Palace lawns, scattering all the lawn lizards that Billy Pot had only just rounded up.

Jenna loved horses; she had her own horse, which she kept in the stables and rode every day. She was a good horsewoman and a brave one, too. So why did she feel so scared? Was it, she wondered, as Thunder hurtled through the Palace Gate at breakneck speed, because Simon rode the horse so angrily, and roughly, too? Simon wore a pair of sharp spurs on his black boots and they were not just for show. Jenna had already seen him touch the horse's flanks with them twice, and she didn't like the way he pulled so sharply on the reins either.

Simon galloped down the middle of Wizard Way. He looked neither right nor left and paid no attention to anyone who might be crossing the road—as Professor Weasal Van Klampff happened to be doing just at that moment. The Professor, unaware of the fact that Marcia was on her way to see *him*, had something to tell Marcia, something that needed to be said well away from the remarkably acute hearing of his housekeeper, Una Brakket.

As Professor Van Klampff wandered absentmindedly across Wizard Way, rehearsing in his mind how he was going to explain his suspicions that Una Brakket was up to something—although he was not sure what—the last thing he expected was to be knocked down by a huge black horse thundering by. But, unfortunately for the Professor, that is exactly what did happen. And when he picked himself up, bruised and shaken but otherwise unharmed, Professor Van Klampff could not remember why he was there at all. Did he perhaps need some more parchment . . . a new pen . . . a pound of carrots . . .

two pounds of carrots? The tubby little man with the half-moon glasses and straggly grey beard stood for a while in the middle of Wizard Way, being fussed over by the concerned Beetle and other assistants from neighbouring shops and offices, shaking his head and trying to remember why he was there. Some niggling feeling at the back of his brain told him it was important, but it was gone. Weasal Van Klampff shook his head and turned back for home, stopping to buy three pounds of carrots on the way.

Thunder, meanwhile, was cantering headlong down Wizard Way, past the shops, printers and private libraries, where the proud owners were pottering about, setting out the special-offer manuscripts and end-of-line parchments. At the sight of the black horse charging by they stopped and stared for a moment, wondering what the Princess was doing with the dark horseman. What was the hurry?

In no time at all, Thunder reached the Great Arch. Jenna expected Simon to slow down and turn the horse around to go back to the Palace, but instead he yanked hard on the reins, and the horse veered abruptly off to the left and hurtled down Cutpurse Cut. The narrow street was dark and chill after the bright sun of Wizard Way, and it smelled rank. An open drain ran down the middle of the cobbles, and a thick brown sludge was flowing slowly along it.

"Where are we going?" Jenna yelled, scarcely able to hear herself above the clattering of the horse's hooves, which echoed off the ramshackle houses on either side of the alley-way and filled her head with noise. Simon made no reply, so Jenna yelled again, louder this time.

"Where are we going?"

Still Simon said nothing. Suddenly the horse took a left turn, narrowly avoiding an oncoming meat pie and sausage cart, and skidded on the slime that ran beneath its hooves.

"Simon!" protested Jenna. "Where are we going?"

"Shut up!" Jenna thought she heard him say.

"*What?*"

"You heard. *Shut up*. You're going where I take you."

Jenna twisted around to look at Simon, shocked at the sud-den sound of hatred in his voice. She hoped she had misun-derstood what he said, but, when she saw the coldness in his eyes, Jenna knew she had heard right. A sharp chill of fore-boding jumped through her.

Suddenly the horse changed direction again. It was almost as though Simon was trying to shake off anyone who might be following them. He yanked on the reins, pulling the horse violently to the right, and Thunder plunged into Squeeze

Guts Slip, a dark passage that ran between two high walls. Simon's eyes were two slits of concentration as the horse tore down the narrow passageway, its hooves sending up sparks from the flints beneath them. At the end of the dark passage Jenna could see open daylight, and as they hurtled towards it, Jenna made a decision. She was going to jump.

As Thunder burst into the sunlight, Jenna took a deep breath, and suddenly, unbidden by Simon, the horse skidded to a halt. A small figure in green Apprentice robes had stepped out in front of them and was fixing the horse with a piercing stare. Thunder was being Transfixed.

"Septimus!" gasped Jenna, more pleased to see him than she had thought possible. "How did you get here?"

Septimus did not answer. He was too busy concentrating on Thunder. He had never Transfixed anything as big as a horse, and he wasn't sure if he could talk and Transfix at the same time.

"Get out of my way, brat!" Simon shouted. "Unless you want to get trampled." Angrily Simon spurred the horse on but Thunder refused to budge. Jenna knew this was her chance. Taking Simon unawares, she made a dive for the ground, but Simon's reaction was quick. He grabbed Jenna's hair and yanked her back into the saddle.

"Ow—let go!" yelled Jenna, hitting at Simon.

"Oh, no, you don't!" Simon hissed in her ear, twisting her hair painfully.

Septimus did not react. He hardly dared move.

"Let . . . Jenna . . . go," he said slowly and carefully, his intense green eyes still fixed steadily on Thunder's eyes, which were wide open and showing a large expanse of white.

"What's it to you, brat?" snarled Simon. "It's none of your business. She's nothing to do with you."

Septimus stood his ground and kept staring at Thunder. "She's my sister," he said quietly. "Let her go."

Thunder shifted uneasily. The horse was caught between two masters and he didn't like it. His old master was still there in the saddle, almost part of Thunder himself, and, as ever, his master's wish was also Thunder's wish: his master wished to go forward, therefore Thunder wished to go forward too. But standing in front of him was a new master. And the new master would not allow Thunder to pass, however much his old master jabbed him in the side with his sharp spurs. The horse tried to roll his dark brown eyes away from Septimus's stare, but he could not move them. Thunder pulled his head back, whinnying haplessly, Transfixed by Septimus.

"Let Jenna go. *Now*," Septimus repeated.

"Or what?" asked Simon with a sneer. "Or you'll put one of your pathetic little spells on me, will you? Let me tell you this, brat, I have more power in my little finger here than you will ever have in your whole miserable life. And if you don't get out of my way *now*, I will use it. Got that?" Simon pointed the little finger of his left hand at Septimus and Jenna gasped—on his finger was a large ring with a Reverse symbol on it. It looked horribly familiar.

Jenna tugged her head away from Simon's grasp. "What's wrong with you, Simon?" she yelled. "You're my brother. Why are you being so horrible?"

In reply, Simon grabbed hold of Jenna's gold sash and twisted it hard in his left hand, while he tightened his grip on Thunder's reins with his right. "Let's just get this straight, *Princess*," he snarled. "I am *not* your brother. You are just some unwanted kid my gullible father brought home one night. That's all. You have caused nothing but trouble for us and you have ruined our family. *Understand?*"

Jenna went white. She felt as though someone had hit her in the stomach. She looked down at Septimus for help, and for a brief moment Septimus glanced up at her, as bewildered as she was. But in that very moment when Septimus met Jenna's gaze, Thunder knew he was free. The horse's nostrils flared with excitement, his muscles tensed and suddenly he was away, cantering at full speed into the sunlight and on to the cobbled road that led to the North Gate.

Stunned, Septimus watched the horse disappear. His head spun with the effort of Transfixing the horse, which had fought him all the while and had been nothing like the practice rabbit which Septimus was used to Transfixing. Septimus knew he had one last chance to get to Jenna, and he shook his head to try and clear the muzziness that the enchantment had left. Then, shakily, he Transported himself to the North Gate.

Down at the *North Gate,* Silas Heap was playing a game of Counter-Feet with Gringe the Gatekeeper. Silas and Gringe had recently made up a long-standing feud. When Simon Heap, Silas's eldest son, had tried to run off with and marry Gringe's only daughter, Lucy, both Silas and Gringe had been horrified. Gringe had shut Lucy up in the gatehouse attic to stop her from running away again. It was not until Silas came to see him some time later with the news that Simon had gone off into the Marram Marshes in the middle of the night—and had not been seen since—that Gringe had at last let Lucy out of the attic. For Gringe knew as well as anyone that the chances of surviving in the Marram Marshes at night were slim.

Silas and Gringe found they had a lot in common. There was Lucy and Simon for a start—and then there was Counter-Feet. Both Silas and Gringe had fond memories of playing Counter-Feet as boys. Counter-Feet was now a very rare board game, although it had once been commonplace in the Castle, and the Premier Counter-Feet league final used to be the highlight of the year.

At first sight the game appeared to be a simple board game played with Counters. The Counter-Feet board consisted of two castles divided by a river down the centre. Each player had a set of Counters of various shapes and sizes in their own team strip, and the aim of the game was to get as many of your own Counters over the river and into the opposing player's castle. But there was a twist in the game: the Counters had minds of their own—and, more importantly, feet of their own.

This was why the game was so popular, but unfortunately this was also the reason for the game's rarity. The Charms that created the Counters had been lost in The Great Fire three hundred years ago. And since then, most sets of Counter-Feet had gradually become incomplete as over the years their Counters had up and left in search of adventure or just in search of a more interesting box of Counter-Feet. And while no one ever objected to opening his or her box and finding that a whole new colony of Counters had taken up residence, it was a different matter when you discovered that all your Counters had got bored with you and left. So three hundred years later, most Counters had disappeared: flushed down drains, trodden into the ground or simply having a good time in small, undiscovered Counter colonies under the floorboards.

Most Wizards, including Silas, played the Magyk version of Counter-Feet, where the castles and the river on the board were real—although smaller, of course. Ever since he was a boy, Gringe had always wanted to play with a Magyk set of Counter-Feet. When Silas had mentioned to Gringe that he actually had a complete and sealed Magyk Counter-Feet set somewhere in the attic with all his books, Gringe had miraculously overcome his long-standing dislike of the Heap family and suggested that they might, perhaps, have a game or two together sometime. It had soon become a regular occurrence which both looked forward to.

Earlier that morning, Silas had left the Palace and taken the short cut to the North Gate, carrying with him his precious box of Counter-Feet. Silas had walked slowly, for beside him loped a large, unkempt wolfhound with creaky joints. Maxie was no longer the young dog he had been, but he still went everywhere with his master. As an Ordinary Wizard, Silas Heap wore a deep-blue tunic fastened with a silver belt. Like all the Heaps he had fair, curly hair, although his was now beginning to acquire a dusting of grey, but his green eyes were still bright. As he walked through the sunny, early-morning streets, he hummed a contented tune to himself, for unlike Sarah Heap, Silas did not worry about anything for very long and reckoned that things eventually turned out for the best.

Silas and Gringe had sat down companionably outside the gatehouse and set up the Counter-Feet board, while casting expert eyes over the Counters and trying to work out what their characters might be that day. Counters were fickle, and you never knew how they might turn out from one game to the next. Some Counters were easily persuaded to go where you wanted them to; others were not. Some would appear to do as you asked and then betray you at the last minute. Some would fall asleep just when you needed them to do something important, and others would run madly around the board creating havoc. The trick was to quickly understand both your Counters and your opponent's Counters, then use your knowledge to get across the board and into the opposing cas-tle. Every game was different: some contests were chaos, some were aggressive and the best were hilariously funny. Which is why, as Septimus Appeared at the North Gate, the first thing he heard was Gringe's loud guffaw.

"Ha, you didn't expect 'im to do a *double duck*, Silas, did you now? He's a right one that little fat one is. I thought 'e'd do summat like that. I think that puts my Spare back on the board, don't you?" Gringe, a stocky, somewhat argumentative man in a leather jerkin, leaned over and took a large round Counter out of a tub by the side of the board. The Counter kicked its short, fat legs with excitement and ran on to the board.

"Hey," protested Gringe, dismayed, as the Counter jumped straight into the river and disappeared into the depths of the water, "yer not supposed to go in there you little b— well, well, ain't this your little lad, Silas? Where did 'e come from then? I dunno, you 'Eaps get just about everywhere, you do."

"I'm not falling for that one, Gringe." Silas chuckled, intent on trying to persuade one of his Counters, the Tunneller, to squeeze into the tunnel that led under Gringe's castle. "I know what you're up to, Gringe. As soon as I take my eyes off the board, your Kicker will have kicked my Tunneller into the river. I wasn't born yesterday, you know."

"But it's your little Apprentice lad, Silas. I think 'e's up to some Magyk."

Septimus's Transport was taking some time to wear off. He still looked a bit misty. Underneath the table, Maxie whined and the hairs on the back of his neck rose.

"Good try, Gringe," said Silas, trying to get his Pusher to shove the Tunneller under the castle without much success.

"No, 'e *is* 'ere. Hello, lad. Come to see your dad, have you?"

At last Silas took his eyes off the game and looked up.

"Oh, hello, Septimus," he said, surprised. "Well, well, are you doing Transports already? He's a clever one, my youngest. Apprentice to the *ExtraOrdinary Wizard*, you know," Silas told Gringe, not for the first time.

"Really? You don't say?" muttered Gringe, who had his arm up to his elbow trying to retrieve his Counter from the river. He had forgotten that Silas's game was the deluxe version that came with mini crocodiles.

"Ouch!" yelped Gringe.

"Dad, Dad!" yelled Septimus. "It's Jenna! Simon took Jenna. They're coming this way. Get Gringe to raise the draw-bridge. Quick!"

"What?"

Silas could see Septimus's lips moving but he could hear nothing. Septimus was not quite there yet.

"Raise the drawbridge, Dad!" Septimus's voice came back on the last word.

"Yes, what is it? No need to shout, Septimus."

The clatter of horse's hooves sounded behind them and Septimus knew it was too late. He jumped out in front of the horse in a last, desperate attempt to stop them, but Silas grabbed hold of him and pulled him back.

"Careful! You'll get yourself trampled."

Simon's horse thundered by. Jenna shouted something to Septimus and Silas, but her words were lost in the thudding of the horse's hooves and the rush of the wind as the huge black horse sped past.

Septimus, Silas and Gringe watched the horse with its two riders go pounding over the drawbridge. When they reached the dirt track on the other side, Simon pulled the horse sharply to the right, and, with its hooves slipping on the dry dirt as it turned, the horse sped off towards the North Road. The North Road, as Septimus knew from his map studies in the Young Army, led along the river, over the One Way Bridge and after a day's fast riding would take them into the Border Country, or Badlands, as it was often called in the Castle.

"Disgusting!" exclaimed Silas, staring after the horse. "That was a case of reckless riding if ever I saw one. Showing off to his girlfriend, that's all it was. Young men should not be allowed fast horses if you ask me. With them it's always speed, speed, speed, with no thought of anyone else—"

"*Dad!*" shouted Septimus, desperately trying to get a word in. "Dad—that was *Simon!*"

"Simon?" Silas looked confused. "What do you mean? *Our* Simon?"

"It's Simon and he's taken Jenna!"

"Taken her where? Why? What is going on? Why doesn't anybody ever tell me anything?" Silas sat down again, aware that the day was beginning to go wrong and not sure exactly why.

"I'm trying to tell you," said Septimus, exasperated. "That was Simon and he's—" But Septimus was interrupted again. Lucy Gringe, a pretty girl with deep-brown eyes and light brown hair tied into two long plaits that hung to her waist, had appeared at the gatehouse door. She wore a simple, long, white summer tunic, which she had embroidered herself with an odd assortment of flowers, and on her feet was a pair of heavy brown boots laced-up with pink ribbon. Lucy was well known for her unusual approach to clothes.

"Simon?" asked Lucy, looking pale under her freckles. "Did you say that was *Simon?*"

"Lucy, I will *not* have you mention that name here," growled Gringe, staring at the Counter-Feet board and wondering how such an enjoyable morning could suddenly turn into such a nightmare. But, he told himself sternly, he should have known better. Wasn't that always the way with the Heaps? They were nothing but trouble.

"Yes, it was Simon, and he has taken Jenna away," said Septimus flatly, the urgency gone from his voice as he realised that it was too late now to do anything about it.

"But," murmured Silas, "I don't understand . . ."

Lucy Gringe understood. She understood only too well.

"*Why?*" she screamed. "Why didn't he take *me?*"

✠ 7 ✠
THE GREENHOUSE

He *was riding like a* madman, Sarah," puffed Silas, who had found Sarah with her friend, Sally Mullin, potting herbs in the Palace greenhouse at the bottom of the kitchen garden. "He would have trampled Septimus into the ground if I hadn't pulled the lad clear—and Jenna was screaming her head off. It was awful."

"No!" Sarah gasped. "I don't believe it."

"Jenna wasn't screaming, Dad," said Septimus, trying not to upset Sarah any more than she was already. "Jenna wouldn't scream. She just shouted something, that's all."

"What?" asked Sarah. "What did she shout?"

"I don't know," said Septimus glumly. "I couldn't hear. The horse was making so much noise."

"Maybe she was saying she'd be back soon. Maybe Simon just took her out for a jaunt along the river," said Sarah, trying hard to convince herself and not doing a very good job of it.

Sally, who was living at the Palace while her Tea and Ale House was being rebuilt, put a consoling hand on Sarah's arm. "You mustn't worry yourself, Sarah," she said. "He's just a headstrong young man showing off his fast horse to his sister. They all do it. He'll be back soon."

Sarah gave Sally a grateful glance, but, deep down, Sarah had a very bad feeling about Simon. Something had happened to him; something had changed him from *her* Simon into—what?

Silas was still trying to catch his breath. He and Septimus had run all the way from the North Gate, leaving Maxie asleep under the Counter-Feet table and Gringe dragging Lucy up to the gatehouse tower to stop her from running off in pursuit of Simon.

Alther Mella floated anxiously above the potting bench. He had spent the previous night down at the Hole in the Wall Tavern, a favourite haunt for ghosts, and had not left as early that morning as he should have. Alther was annoyed with himself. If he'd been there, maybe he could have stopped Simon, although Alther wasn't quite sure how. But at least he could have tried.

Sarah pushed a stray wisp of straw-coloured hair back behind her ear as she fiddled distractedly with some parsley seedlings. "I'm sure Simon wouldn't take Jenna away against her will," she insisted, stabbing at the soil with her trowel.

"Of course he wouldn't," said Sally soothingly.

"But that's just what he *has* done," Septimus insisted. "Jenna didn't want to go with him. I Transfixed the horse and he wouldn't let her get off. He got really angry."

"Well, he did seem very proud of his horse," said Sarah. "Maybe he was just upset about you Transfixing it. I'm sure he will be back soon with Jenna."

"He's *kidnapped* her, Mum," said Septimus, almost angry now. He could not understand why Sarah kept making excuses for Simon. But Septimus was still not entirely used to how mothers behaved.

Alther Mella floated dismally through a discarded pile of flowerpots.

"It's my fault, Sarah," said Alther. "I blame myself. If I had allowed proper guards at the Palace Gate instead of those useless Ancients, this would never have happened."

"You mustn't blame yourself," said Sarah, giving the old ghost a wan smile. "Even a guard would have let Simon in. He is a Heap after all."

"But they wouldn't have let him *out*, would they?" said Septimus pointedly. "Not if Jenna had told them she didn't want to go."

"Septimus, you shouldn't speak to Alther like that," scolded Sarah. "You should be more respectful to an ExtraOrdinary Wizard, especially the one whom your tutor was Apprenticed to."

"Ah, Sarah." Alther sighed. "The boy is right."

Alther floated off the potting bench and hovered beside Septimus. Compared with the Ancients in the Palace, Alther looked positively substantial. His purple ExtraOrdinary robes, although a little faded, looked almost real, even down to the bullet hole and dark brown bloodstains just below his heart. The ghost's long white hair was scraped back into its usual ponytail, and his green eyes had a bright glint in them as he regarded Marcia's Apprentice.

"So," said Alther to Septimus, "what do you propose we do now?"

"*Me?* What do *I* think we should do?"

"Yes. As the Apprentice of the ExtraOrdinary Wizard, I

thought you might like to stand in for Marcia."

"We go after Jenna. And get her back. That's what we *have* to do."

Sarah dropped the trowel she had been poking the seedlings with. It landed with a clang in the middle of Alther's foot. The ghost stepped back hastily.

"Septimus," declared Sarah, "you are *not* going anywhere. It's bad enough with Jo-Jo, Sam, Edd and Erik all running wild in the Forest, getting up to goodness knows what and refusing to even come and see their mother. Then there's Nicko, who's gone off with that Rupert Gringe boy testing some boat or other, and not come back yet, even though he promised he'd be home last week to take Jenna down to Aunt Zelda's— *anything* could have happened to him, I'm just so worried— and now Simon and Jenna are gone . . ." At this Sarah suddenly broke into loud sobs.

Silas put his arms around Sarah. "There, there, love, you mustn't worry. Everything will be all right," he murmured soothingly.

"I'll go and bring you a nice cup of tea and a big slab of barley cake," said Sally, "and everything will feel much better, just you see." And she bustled off to the Palace kitchens.

But Sarah would not be comforted. "Simon and Jenna,

gone," she wailed. "Why? Why would Simon do such a thing? Why would he take Jenna away?"

Alther put a ghostly arm around Septimus's shoulders.

"Come on, lad," he said. "Let's leave your parents alone for a while. You can take me to see Marcia."

Septimus and Alther made their way out of the Palace and took the Snake Slipway, which led down to the Castle Moat.

The Castle was surrounded by water. Most of the water consisted of the river, as the Castle was built on the inside of a wide river bend, but some of the water was in the form of a moat, which had been dug when the Castle walls were built. The Moat was wide and deep and was full of river water, for both ends of the Moat ran into the river itself. It was a popular place for fishing and, in the summer, for swimming. A large wooden pier had recently been built out into the middle of the Moat for the Castle children to swim from, and the enterprising Rupert Gringe had just started renting out his new invention, the small Rupert paddleboats, to those who fancied messing about on the water for an hour or two. This had been extremely popular with everyone in the Castle, except for two people: Weasal Van Klampff and his housekeeper, Una Brakket, who had the misfortune to live beside the new pier and above the boathouse where the Ruperts were stored.

Septimus knew the way to Professor Van Klampff's house far too well for his liking. Almost since his first days as Apprentice, Marcia had sent him over every Saturday morning to knock on the Professor's door and collect one of the many and complex pieces of the ShadowSafe. But even if the Professor had a piece ready—which was a rare event—and actually gave it to Septimus, Una Brakket would waylay him at the door and demand it back. She did not, she would tell Septimus, trust a *boy* with such a valuable object. Marcia herself must come and collect it. A long-distance battle had ensued between Marcia and Una, with Septimus batted to and fro like a shuttlecock. Every Saturday morning, Septimus would wait outside Professor Van Klampff's house for as long as he could stand being laughed at and shouted at by a group of boys from the Young Army Resettlement Home, who always hung around the pier, daring each other to jump into the water.

Eventually, to Septimus's relief, Alther had advised Marcia to give in and collect the components herself. Una Brakket may have a point, Alther advised; the ShadowSafe was indeed a complex and highly Magykal device, and it was not fair to make Septimus responsible for it. Just to irritate Una, Marcia had taken to occasionally arriving unannounced in the early hours of the morning.

Half an hour ago, the boys on the pier had watched the ExtraOrdinary Wizard stride down the Snake Slipway and give a vicious tug on the bellpull that hung beside Weasal Van Klampff's thick wooden door. Marcia had waited impatiently on the Slipway. She tapped her purple python shoes irritably on the stone cobbles while she heard mutterings and scufflings inside the house, until Una Brakket—who knew by the long, insistent ringing of the bell that it was Marcia—opened the door. Eventually.

And now Septimus was back at the dreaded front door once again. Alther was no protection, as the ghost could choose to whom he would Appear, and quite understandably he chose not to Appear to a bunch of mocking boys. But Septimus, in his bright green tunic and shiny silver Apprentice belt, had no such choice. Sure enough the chorus of catcalls soon started:

"Too stuck-up to talk to us then, are ya?"

"Greeny-guts, greeny-guts!"

"Hey, caterpillar-boy! Whatcha doin' back here again?"

And so on. Septimus longed to turn the lot of them into caterpillars, but it was against the Magyk code—and the boys knew that.

"Here we are," Septimus told Alther, as he reached up and gave the bellpull a hefty tug. Far, far away, unheard by either Alther or Septimus, a small bell rang—much to the annoyance of the housekeeper. Septimus knew they were in for a wait; he turned to the ghost who was hovering behind him, staring up at the house.

"Do you think you'll be able to come inside?" Septimus asked Alther, hoping that he would be able to.

"Hmm . . . I'm not sure," replied Alther. "It looks familiar. I remember going to a party down by the Moat. It was quite a party too—we all ended up in the water. I *think* it was in this house, but . . . well, I'll soon find out when we go inside."

Septimus nodded. He knew that, as a ghost, Alther could only go to places that he had been during his life. Alther had pretty much travelled all the roads and alleyways in the Castle, and, as ExtraOrdinary Wizard, he had been in most of the official buildings. But people's houses were another matter— Alther had been a popular young man in his day but even *he* had not managed to be invited to every single house in the Castle.

The door was suddenly thrown open.

"Oh, it's you again," said Una Brakket, who was a tall, spiky-looking woman with extremely short black hair.

"I need to see the ExtraOrdinary Wizard," said Septimus. "Please."

"She's busy," snapped Una.

"It's very urgent," Septimus insisted. "It's a matter of life or death."

The housekeeper shot Septimus a suspicious look. She stood at the door for a moment, weighing the two almost equally unpleasant prospects of having Septimus in the house or having the ExtraOrdinary Wizard angry with her for not letting Septimus in.

"All right then. Come in." The housekeeper held the door open and Septimus entered, closely followed by Alther. But, as Alther crossed the threshold of the house, there was a sudden violent rush of air, and the ghost was hurled straight out the door and Returned to the street.

"Bother," muttered Alther as he picked himself up off the cobbles. "I remember now. The party was at the house next door."

"It's very windy out there all of a sudden," said Una, puzzled. She slammed the door crossly, leaving Alther floating outside; then she turned to Septimus, who was standing in the gloomy hallway, wishing he was still outside in the sun with Alther.

"You had better come down to the Laboratory," she said.

✢ 8 ✢
THE LABORATORY

*S*eptimus stepped over a large paper
bag full of carrots and followed
Una Brakket down the dark hallway. Previously he had only been
allowed into the narrow front
room that overlooked the street,
but, as he followed the housekeeper deep into the gloomy
recesses of the hall,
Septimus was surprised
to find that the house
seemed to go on for ever.

Una Brakket
stopped by a low
door and lit a candle.

Soon Septimus was following her down some steep wooden steps into a damp and musty-smelling cellar. The cellar was long and narrow with a low vaulted roof, and the sounds of the paddleboats being dragged out of the boathouse echoed eerily through the walls. It was stuffed full of what looked like years of accumulated junk: there were heaps of rusty tripods and Bunsen burners, stacks of wooden boxes stuffed full of ancient yellowing papers, piles of broken scientific instruments and even an old pair of ice skates hanging on the wall.

With Septimus trotting behind, Una strode to the back of the cellar and went through a small archway. The light of her candle quickly faded as she disappeared around a corner, and Septimus found himself in pitch-blackness, unsure of which way to go—but that didn't worry Septimus, for the Dragon Ring that he wore on his right index finger began to glow, as it always did in the dark, and soon he had enough light to see where he was again.

"Where are you? I haven't got all day," Una Brakket's sharp voice cut through the gloom as she came back to see where Septimus had gone. "I don't allow boys with candles down here," she snapped, noticing the light glowing from his hand.

"But—" Septimus protested.

"In fact I don't allow boys down here at all. And if it were up to me I wouldn't even let them in the house. Nothing but trouble, boys."

"But—"

"Now just put that candle out and follow me."

Septimus stuffed his right hand into his tunic pocket and followed Una Brakket into a narrow brick-lined tunnel. The tunnel wound its way deep beneath the streets of the Castle, taking them underneath the neighbouring houses and gardens. The candle flame flickered and guttered in the cold gusts of air that eddied through the tunnel, bringing with them damp smells of earth and mould. As they progressed onward, an icy chill settled in the air; Septimus shivered and began to wonder where exactly Una was taking him.

Suddenly she stopped—a thick wooden door barred the way. From a bundle of keys that hung from her belt, the house-keeper selected the largest one and pushed it into the keyhole, which was oddly placed in the middle of the door. Septimus was just peering around her to see what she was doing when a loud whirring noise started up from behind the door.

Una Brakket jumped back suddenly, landing heavily on Septimus's foot.

"Ouch!"

"Get back!" She gave Septimus a hefty shove and sent him flying back into the tunnel a split second before the wooden door came crashing down in front of them like a small draw-bridge.

"Wait there," snapped Una. "You are not to come any far-ther. *I* will tell Madam Marcia that she is required." With that Una Brakket strode across the door as if it really was a draw-bridge.

Septimus followed her into the Laboratory.

Professor Weasal Van Klampff's Laboratory was the strangest place that Septimus had ever seen, and he had seen some very odd places since he had become Marcia's Apprentice.

The Laboratory was bathed in a low blue light. It was a long, thin, vaulted underground room and contained a forest of murmuring, bubbling vials and flasks, flagons and funnels, all connected by a large glass tube which looped and soared down the entire length of the Laboratory. From the end of this apparatus a blue gas, which Professor Van Klampff believed kept Shadows at bay, bubbled into the air, giving the whole place a distinctive smell that reminded Septimus of burned pumpkin.

Septimus peered through the blue haze, trying to see where

Marcia was. At the far end of the Laboratory he could just about make out the tall figure of Marcia and the stumpy shape of the Professor. Marcia was holding a tall glass tube full of a shiny black liquid; she had been startled by the bang of the door falling open and was staring into the blue vapor to see what was going on.

"What are *you* doing here?" she called out, surprised at Septimus's sudden appearance behind Una. "It's meant to be your day off, Septimus. I don't want your mother complaining again."

"It's Jenna!" yelled Septimus, expertly dodging Una Brakket as she reached out to grab him and setting off through the haze towards Marcia.

"What? What's Jenna?" asked Marcia, confused, her head still spinning from the endless mathematical formulae that Professor Van Klampff had been explaining in an effort to show Marcia why the ShadowSafe was taking so long to make. He had been busy showing Marcia the amazingly complex moulds that were used to construct each interconnecting part of the ShadowSafe when Septimus had rung the doorbell and Una Brakket had very reluctantly gone to answer it. Marcia had been glad to see the housekeeper go, for Una was hanging around like an irritating bluebottle, which Marcia had had great trouble resisting the urge to swat.

"She's gone!" yelled Septimus, reaching the ExtraOrdinary Wizard just before Una Brakket could grab him. He ducked behind Marcia, leaving her standing between him and the irate housekeeper.

"Well, I'm glad to hear it," said Marcia, confused at the dance Septimus and Una appeared to be doing around her. "I thought Sarah was leaving it a bit late to get her off to the Dragon Boat. It's only two days to MidSummer Day."

"No!" said Septimus. "She's not gone to Aunt Zelda's. She's been *kidnapped*."

"*What?*" Marcia dropped the glass tube she was holding. The Professor and Una Brakket both gasped in dismay—for the tube contained the Amalgam for the ShadowSafe.

"Is this some kind of joke?" Marcia asked, staring at the glistening black sludge that now covered her purple snakeskin shoes—and at Professor Van Klampff, who had fallen to his knees and was desperately trying to scrape up his precious Amalgam.

"No," said Septimus bleakly. "I wish it was."

"Oh, it's bound to be a joke. Or more likely a fib," Una Brakket said bitterly as she joined the Professor on the floor and took a large metal scraper to Marcia's shoes.

"Get off my shoes, will you?" said Marcia icily. "I don't want this stuff rubbed into them." Marcia fixed Una with a glare. "Anyway," she declared, "Septimus always tells the truth."

"Huh," said Una Brakket, angrily scraping. "Just look what's happened. You let a boy into the Laboratory and something gets broken. I knew it would."

"Jenna—*kidnapped*?" said Marcia, trying to move away and finding that her feet were stuck to the floor. "How . . . *who*?"

"Simon," said Septimus, anxious to be gone. "Simon took her away on his horse. We have to go after her, we should send some Trackers out and—"

"Don't *do* that, Una. Simon who?" asked Marcia.

"Simon. My brother. Come on, Marcia, please hurry."

"Simon *Heap*?"

"Yes. I tried to stop him. I Transfixed his horse but—"

"Did you? A whole horse," said Marcia, pleased with her Apprentice. "Well done. If you can Transfix a horse you can Transfix anything. But he Overcame you?"

"No—well, yes, I suppose so, sort of—but that's not the point." Septimus's voice was rising to a despairing shout. "The point is that Jenna has been kidnapped and we're not *doing* anything!"

Marcia put her arm around Septimus's shoulders. "It's all

right, Septimus. Simon is Jenna's brother; she's quite safe with him. You really mustn't worry so much. I'm afraid that spider bite has put you a little on edge. It's one of the side effects of Darke Spider Venom, you know. But I can see it's time we went."

Marcia addressed Weasal Van Klampff, who was staring woefully at the black sludge that Una Brakket was painstakingly scooping up and putting into a jar. "I am going now, Weasal. I shall expect the piece tonight."

"Tonight?" gasped the Professor. "But, Marcia, I thought you understood how complicated it is. How difficult the mould is to configure and—"

"You've already done the mould, Weasal. You've just showed it to me. All you have to do is make some more of that stuff and pour it in. I don't see what the fuss is about."

The Professor looked anxious. "But Una is going out tonight," he said. "Country dancing."

"Well, jolly good for Una," snapped Marcia. "Just stop dithering, Weasal, and get a move on."

Weasal Van Klampff cast a worried glance at Una Brakket, who was wearing an extremely disgruntled expression. "B-but," he stuttered, "if we—I mean I, er—make the Amalgam too quickly, it's possible that a Shadow might

Appear here. In the Laboratory . . ." whispered the Professor.

"Well, I'm sure Una will take care of it," said Marcia crisply. "I will be down to collect the piece tonight."

"And what time tonight would that be, Madam Marcia?" Una inquired frostily. "Approximately."

"*Approximately* when I get around to it," Marcia replied in glacial tones that would have sent anyone other than Una Brakket into a complete panic. "And now, Mrs Brakket, if you would care to show my Apprentice and myself out?"

Una Brakket smiled for the first time, or rather, the corners of her mouth moved upwards and showed her teeth, which glowed blue in the Laboratory lights.

"With *great* pleasure," she said.

✛ 9 ✛
NUMBER THIRTEEN

*S*eptimus *trailed along behind* Marcia and Alther as they walked and floated down Wizard Way back to the Tower. He was listening intently to their conversation.

"If I were you, Marcia," Alther was saying, "I'd do a quick Search of the Farmlands north of the Castle. Simon can't have got that far yet. He'll still be riding through them on his way to the Border Country, and I'd bet my life—well, I'd bet my, er, ponytail—that's where he's heading. You could Travel across the Farmlands in no time. I'd go myself but I wouldn't be much use. Never did like farms much when I was alive. Too many smells and unpredictable animals with pointy horns for my liking. If I went out there I'd just spend all my time being Returned. And frankly, Marcia, being Returned takes the stuffing out of me. I still feel quite winded."

To Septimus's dismay, Marcia was not convinced.

"Look, Alther," she said, as she kept up a fast pace along Wizard Way, leaving Septimus breathless, "I have no intention of leaving the Castle if the Princess is no longer within the walls. You know what happened last time we were both gone—DomDaniel just walked in. Who is to say it may not happen again? But no one needs to go after Jenna; she'll be back soon. I really don't think there's anything to worry about; all we know for sure is that Jenna has gone off riding with her brother—"

"Adoptive brother," interrupted Alther.

"All right, if you want to be picky about it, her adoptive brother, although Jenna is as much a Heap as any of the boys, Alther. She sees them as her brothers and they see her as their sister."

"Except for Simon," said Alther.

"You don't know that," objected Marcia.

"I do."

"Oh, don't be so awkward, Alther. How can you possibly know that? Anyway, as I was saying, Jenna has gone off riding with her *adoptive* brother, and all we know is that he didn't want her to get off the horse when Septimus asked her to. If you ask me it's just Simon not doing what his little brother tells him to. It's hardly surprising, really. He's jealous of Septimus being my Apprentice. He's hardly going to do what Septimus tells him to, now is he?"

"Marcia, Septimus believes that Jenna has been kidnapped," said Alther solemnly.

"Look, Alther, Septimus is not quite himself today. He was bitten by one of those Darke spiders this morning and you know how paranoid that can make you. Remember when you got bitten by one when you were Fumigating that old Capnomancer who was causing a health hazard above the pie shop in The Ramblings?"

"You mean the mad mouse-woman?"

"Yes, her. Well, you spent the rest of the day thinking that I was trying to push you out of the window."

"Did I really?"

"Yes, you did. You Locked yourself in your study and Barred the windows. It wore off by the evening, and I'm sure that by this evening Septimus will be fine, Jenna will be back from a nice ride with her brother and we'll all wonder what the fuss was about."

Septimus had heard enough and, angrily, he slipped away. He realised that he was going to have to do something himself, without Marcia's help. There was someone he wanted to see.

Marcia and Alther continued on their way, unaware that Septimus had gone.

". . . and Simon Heap is not to be trusted," Alther was saying.

"So you tell me, Alther. But there's no proof of that, is there? He is a Heap after all. I know they're a strange lot, and some of them are definitely two sandwiches short of a picnic, but they are an honest family. After all, they are an ancient Wizard tribe."

"Not all Wizards are good Wizards, Marcia, as you know to your cost," said Alther. "I'd very much like to know what Simon has been doing for the last year or so, and why he's turned up here all of a sudden, just before MidSummer Day. I still think it was Simon who betrayed you in the Marram Marshes."

"Nonsense. Why would he do that? It was that irritating

Message Rat. You can never trust a rat, Alther, especially one that likes the sound of his own voice. And while we are on the subject of irritating, I really don't think much of your recommendation. Old Weasal Van Klampff is an old fusspot and his housekeeper gives me the creeps, always hanging around and watching everything. The ShadowSafe is taking *ages* and every time I get a piece home it's an absolute nightmare trying to put it together. I still haven't managed to get the last bit to fit properly."

"Those Safes are complicated things, Marcia. Anyway, there's no alternative. Weasal's family has been making them for generations. They invented the Amalgam and no one else knows the formula. His father, Otto, rid me of a particularly nasty Spectre and it took him two years to sort it out. It takes time, Marcia—you have to be patient."

"Perhaps," snapped Marcia. "Or perhaps I should just get something simple from the Manuscriptorium."

"No," said Alther, very definitely. "A ShadowSafe is the only thing that will get rid of a Shadow permanently, and that is *not* suitable work for the Manuscriptorium. Anyway, there is something about that Chief Hermetic Scribe that bothers me."

"Really, Alther, you are in a suspicious frame of mind

today. Anyone would think that the spider had bitten *you* as well."

Alther could see he was going to get nowhere with Marcia; he knew very well how stubborn she could be at times. They had had many battles in the past, when he was the ExtraOrdinary Wizard and she was his Apprentice, and even then he had not always won. Now that he was a ghost he had no chance at all. It was Marcia who was now the ExtraOrdinary Wizard, and if she thought she knew best, which of course she always did, then Alther was going to have to put up with it.

"I'll be off then, Marcia," said Alther a little sulkily, and then, noticing that Septimus was no longer following, he asked, "Where's the lad gone?"

"I told you, Alther, it's his day off. I imagine he's gone to see his mother," said Marcia briskly. "Now, if you'll excuse me, I have work to do. I'll see you later, Alther."

"Possibly," Alther replied grumpily. He watched Marcia stride off into the Great Arch with her purple robes flowing behind her and, just visible as she entered the shade of the Arch, a dimness following her. Alther sighed—the Shadow was getting stronger. If he squinted and looked sideways he could almost see an outline of a large shambling figure matching Marcia step for step as she strode through the Arch. The sooner the ShadowSafe was finished, the better.

Alther rose up into the air and flew as fast as he could down Wizard Way to try and shake off the feeling of foreboding that had taken hold of him. As he shot past the front of the Magykal Manuscriptorium and Spell Checkers Incorporated he was too preoccupied to notice Septimus Heap's green-robed figure disappearing through the door.

Inside the Manuscriptorium, Septimus stood still for a moment to allow his eyes to adjust to the gloom. He was in the small front office where customers came and placed their orders for new spells, brought old, unstable spells to be checked out and ordered copies of formulae, conjurations, incantations and even the odd poem.

To Septimus's surprise the office was empty, so he walked through to the small door at the back and peered around. The Manuscriptorium was quietly busy. All Septimus could hear was the scratching of nibs on paper and a few muffled coughs and sneezes as the summer cold that always spread through the Manuscriptorium lingered on. Hard at work in the gloom were twenty-one scribes, each seated at a high desk lit by its own lamp, which hung from the ceiling and illuminated the scribe's painstaking work.

"Beetle?" said Septimus in a loud whisper. "Beetle, are you there?"

The nearest scribe looked up and gestured with his pen to the far end of the room.

"He's out back. They've got an Unstable just come in. He's trying to Bin it. Go through if you like, but don't get too close to the Bin."

"Thanks," said Septimus. He tiptoed through the ranks of desks, attracting a few glances from the bored scribes, and slipped out the door into the yard. A scene of utter chaos met him.

"Grab it!" Beetle was yelling. "It's getting away!"

Beetle, a stocky boy with a shock of black hair who was about three years older than Septimus, was struggling violently with something invisible and trying to shove it into a large red bin that stood in the middle of the yard, and had DANGEROUS BIN—DO NOT OPEN written on it. Beetle was yelling at two pale and lanky scribes who looked as though the slightest breeze would knock them to the ground.

"Want a hand, Beetle?" asked Septimus.

Beetle glanced up and looked at Septimus gratefully.

"Would ya, Sep? It's a wild one, mind. An invisible bog-ridder we think. Some idiot dug it out yesterday and Revived it. Been sleeping quietly in a cupboard for dunno how long before then. Why people can't leave well enough alone I don't—hey, get off you little—"

The bog-ridder had picked up the Bin and upended it over Beetle's head. Septimus sprang forward and grabbed the Bin off Beetle. Beetle stood bemused for a moment, staring around the small yard that was surrounded on all sides by a high brick wall, trying to work out where the bog-ridder might have gone. The two scribes looked terrified and had squashed themselves into the corner farthest away from the Bin.

"We gotta get it into the Bin, Sep," said Beetle breathlessly. "More than my job's worth to let it escape."

Septimus stood quietly for a moment, watching for any disturbance the bog-ridder would surely make as soon as it moved. Suddenly he saw a ripple pass across the brickwork of the wall. Septimus sprang forward, picked up the Bin and ran to the corner where the two scribes were cowering.

Bang! Septimus slammed the Bin down.

"Ouch!" yelled the taller of the scribes as Septimus caught his toes with the edge of the Bin.

"Got it!" Septimus shouted triumphantly.

"Ouch, ouch, *ouch!*" yelled the scribe hopping around in

circles, holding on to his bruised foot.

"Sorry, Foxy," said Septimus, leaning heavily on the Bin to make sure the bog-ridder stayed safely where it was, while Foxy hobbled away on the arm of the other scribe. Septimus helped Beetle slide the lid under the upended Bin, and then they carefully set the Bin the right way up. Quickly, Beetle wrapped the Bin in a stabiliser net, tied it securely and put it outside the back gate, ready for collection by the Bin Disposal Squad.

"Thanks, Sep, I owe you one," said a grateful Beetle. "Anything I can do for you, anytime, just let me know."

"Well, as it happens," said Septimus, "there is."

"Ask away then," said Beetle cheerily, linking his arm through Septimus's and steering him into the small kitchen at the side of the yard where Beetle always had a kettle on the hob.

"My brother Simon came in earlier," said Septimus. "I wonder if you could tell me what he wanted?"

Beetle took two mugs off the shelf and dropped a FizzBom cube into each one to make up some FizzFroot. FizzFroot was a favourite drink of both himself and Septimus; it was made from an everlasting FizzBom spell that the Manuscriptorium had refurbished for someone who had never collected it. The drink was actually ice-cold but needed boiling water to activate it.

"Here y'are," said Beetle, giving Septimus his mug and sitting down on the stool next to him.

"Thanks, Beetle." Septimus took a big mouthful of Fizz-Froot and smiled. He had forgotten how good it tasted. Marcia disapproved of fizzy drinks, particularly those created by spells, and Septimus was not allowed any, which made the occasional forbidden FizzFroot with Beetle taste even better.

"I've not seen any of your brothers in here, Sep," said Beetle, puzzled. "I mean, most of them are out in the Forest now, aren't they? I heard they'd gone a bit wild. Gone off with the Wendron Witches and turned into wolverines or something."

"It's not that bad, Beetle," Septimus told him. "They just love the Forest, that's all. My grandfather is a tree out there somewhere. It's in the family."

"Excuse me? Your granddad's a *tree?*" Beetle spluttered and inhaled some FizzFroot up his nose.

"Eurgh. Not all over me, Beetle. Keep your snot to yourself," said Septimus with a laugh. "My grandfather was a Shape-Shifter. He became a tree," he explained, wiping the sleeve of his tunic.

Beetle let out a low whistle, impressed.

"Not many Shape-Shifters about any more, Sep. Do you know where he is then?"

"No. Dad goes out and looks for him sometimes. Hasn't found him yet though."

"How does he know?"

"Know what?"

"That he hasn't found him? I mean, how do you tell which tree is your father and which tree isn't?"

"Dunno," said Septimus, who had often wondered the same thing. "Look, Beetle," he said, steering Beetle back to the question he had asked him before, "you *must* have seen Simon. He came in first thing this morning. Jenna and I saw him. Jenna would tell you—" Septimus stopped as he suddenly saw a vivid picture of the terrified Jenna thundering by on Simon's horse, on her way to . . . where?

"The only person who came in this morning was the Traveller," said Beetle.

"Who?"

"The Traveller. That's what he calls himself. Everyone thinks he's a loony, but I think he's scary, Sep. And I reckon that Old Foxy does too, although he'd never let on. The Traveller often comes in with a package for Old Foxy—you know, Foxy's dad—he's the Chief Hermetic Scribe. They spend ages in the Hermetic Chamber and then the Traveller goes off again. Never says a word to anyone. Weird. Old Foxy looks white as a sheet after he's gone."

"Does the Traveller have green eyes and hair a bit like mine?" asked Septimus. "Was he dressed in a long black cloak? And have a big black horse tied up by the door?"

"Yep. That's him. Horse ate my bag of apples what I brought for my lunch, though I didn't dare mention it. But he don't look much like your brother, Sep. He's not like a *Heap* if you know what I mean. Heaps ain't scary. They may be mad, but they ain't *scary*."

"But Simon *is* scary," said Septimus. "Really scary. And he's taken Jenna. He's kidnapped her."

Beetle looked shocked. "The Princess?" he gasped. "The Traveller's kidnapped the Princess? I don't believe it."

"That's the trouble," said Septimus. "No one will believe it. Not even Marcia."

⊹ I O ⊹
LEAVING

S eptimus was in his room, packing his bag.

His small, round room at the top of the Wizard Tower was neat and orderly, a result of its occupant's ten years of training in the Young Army. Dreadful and dangerous as those years had been for Septimus, now that the Young Army was disbanded and he was reunited with his family, he had begun to stop despising everything that he had learned as a boy soldier. He was no longer wildly untidy just because he could be; after a brief period when it had resembled the Municipal Rubbish Dump, his room was now neat and ordered. The room bore other traces of his previous life too: its dark-blue curving walls and ceiling were covered with the constellations, accurately painted by Septimus, who had had to memorise them for his Young Army night exercises. And in his cupboard he always kept an emergency back-pack, packed strictly in accordance with the Young Army regulations.

Septimus's emergency backpack contained:

> *compass (1)*
> *eyeglass (1)*
> *water bottle (1)*
> *bedroll (1)*
> *socks (3)*
> *mess tin (1)*
> *tinderbox (1)*
> *spare flints (2)*
> *kindling (moss, dried, bunch of)*
> *ex Young Army regulation pen knife (1)*
> *catapult (1)*
> *wire, length of (1)*
> *rope, length of (1)*

To this Septimus was now busy adding a few things that reflected his new life as Apprentice to the ExtraOrdinary Wizard. They were:

> Unseen Charm *(1)*
> Seeker's Charm *(1)*
> Fast Freeze Charm *(1)*
> Double Action Escape Pack *(1)*

Plus a few bits and pieces that he thought may come in useful:

> *The Little Book of Survival and Bushcraft*
> by Ram Seary *(1)*
> Wiz Bix, *everlasting, packet of (1)*
> Mint Blasts, *tubes of (3)*

There wasn't room for much else, but there was one last thing that Septimus wanted to take. It broke all the rules because it was both unnecessary and heavy, but Septimus didn't care. Down the side of the backpack Septimus stuffed the smooth iridescent green rock that Jenna had given him when he had first known her. With some difficulty, Septimus buckled up the backpack and put it on. It was heavier than he had expected.

"Is that you, Septimus?" Marcia called out as he came down the stairs and headed for the front door. He jumped in surprise.

"Yes," he replied warily.

Marcia was kneeling on the floor beside the ShadowSafe. In front of her was a huge piece of paper with an extremely complicated diagram on it, which she was examining closely. For a brief, horrible moment, Septimus caught a glimpse of a large murky figure leaning over her, also peering at the paper—but when Septimus looked more closely the Shadow faded from view. But he knew it was still there, hovering behind Marcia, silently staring at the plans for its own demise. Septimus put down his heavy backpack; he felt bad about leaving Marcia alone with her dark companion.

"What's a flange?" asked Marcia.

"A what?"

"A *flange*. It says here attach piece Y to the long, upright D, taking care to align holes P and Q with the corresponding holes N and O in the left-hand *flange*. I can't see a wretched flange anywhere." Marcia rifled irritably through a large box of fixings that Professor Van Klampff had given her for the construction of the ShadowSafe.

"It's not in the box," said Septimus. "It's that bit that sticks out. Look, there—" He ran his finger down a curved projecting rim that ran the length of the edge of the ShadowSafe. The Amalgam felt like glass to the touch—silky smooth and cold.

"Well, why didn't it say so," said Marcia grumpily as she slotted piece Y—a long, curved triangular section—on to the ShadowSafe, carefully aligning holes P and Q with holes N and O. Marcia dusted down her tunic with an air of satisfaction. "Thank you, Septimus, it's looking good, isn't it? Only one more piece to go down the side here, then the final Stopper and"—Marcia twisted around, trying to catch sight of her Shadow—"*you* will be gone, you pathetic creature."

Septimus looked at the ShadowSafe. Good was not the word he would have used to describe it—weird, maybe, or just plain ugly was more like it. It rose from the floor, dominating the room with its shiny blackness and bizarre shape, which reminded Septimus of a gnarled hollow tree. The odd assortment of moulded panels, which Professor Van Klampff had so carefully constructed, had come together to form a roughly conical enclosed space, open at the top, with a long narrow gap running from top to bottom through which Marcia and her Shadow—for a Shadow must Follow whether it wants to or not—would eventually squeeze. Then someone, probably one of the more senior Wizards (as Marcia felt it was a lot of responsibility for her young Apprentice), would place the last piece, the Stopper, in the hole in the top, and Marcia would walk out, free at last, leaving the Shadow trapped inside, like a lobster in a lobster pot. After that it was a simple job for the Bin Disposal Squad.

"Hang on, Septimus," said Marcia, suddenly remembering what she had said to him earlier, "what are you doing back here? I gave you the day off. You should be up at the Palace with your mother."

"I'm going to find Jenna," Septimus said, picking up his backpack and heaving it on to his shoulders. "Seeing as no one else will."

Marcia sighed. "Look, Septimus," she said patiently, "Jenna will be back soon, mark my words. You're just a little upset after your spider bite. It's perfectly normal."

"I am *not* upset," he said indignantly.

"Septimus," said Marcia, "I know you think I don't believe you—"

"I know you don't believe me," said Septimus.

"—but, just to put your mind at rest, I have done a Remote Search of the Farmlands across the river and there is a horse

with two riders on its way to the North Gate. It is bound to
be Jenna and Simon after their morning out. And I have sent
Boris—"

"Boris?" asked Septimus.

"Boris Catchpole. Moved in yesterday, he's a new sub-
Wizard—a bit old really to get started as a Wizard but he's
very keen. He's part of our Second-Chance Scheme. He
trained as a Tracker in the Army. Got as far as Deputy
Hunter, believe it or not."

"Old *Catchpole?*"

"Yes, do you know him?"

"He's horrible!"

"He's not so bad. Well, apart from his breath, that is.
That's pretty bad. I must have a word with him about it sometime. Anyway the past is the past. We should welcome him
in. Well, we *will* be welcoming him next week with the tradi-
tional Wizard Warming Supper, and as Apprentice you will of
course be there."

Septimus looked gloomy.

"All part of the job, Septimus," said Marcia briskly. She
looked at her glum Apprentice standing by the door weighed
down by his heavy backpack. His green eyes looked sad. His
sister had chosen to go away on one of his few days off, and it

was hard on the boy. Marcia knew that Septimus was very close to Jenna after their experiences together in the Marram Marshes.

"Look, Septimus, if you want to take your adventure bag or whatever it is you've got there and go outside the Castle to wait for Jenna to come back, that's fine. Off you go. It's a lovely day and you could walk up to the One Way Bridge and watch out for her."

"All right," he said doubtfully.

"I'll see you later then," said Marcia with a fond smile. "And don't forget to take Jenna straight back to the Palace. Why don't you stay the night? Then you can spend some time with Jenna and your parents—and come to think of it, you can make sure Jenna gets off to the Marram Marshes tomorrow. The boat has been ready for her at the Palace Quay for a week now, and I am really worried that she won't leave in time. Your mother does tend to leave everything to the last minute." Marcia sighed. "You know, I am sure when the Queen used to go for her MidSummer Visit she *must* have left earlier than this, although the funny thing is I can't ever remember her going. I mean, she must have gone on the royal barge, but I don't remember it and neither does Alther. And how did she get across the Marsh? Sometimes, Septimus, I worry about Jenna. There are so many things her mother would have told her about, and who can do that now? How will she ever know how to be Queen?"

"I suppose we all have to help her," said Septimus. "Which is what I'm trying to do."

"Yes, of course you are," said Marcia soothingly. "Now you go and have a nice day. Give Jenna my love when you see her, and tell her I hope she has a good MidSummer Visit."

Marcia made everything sound so normal that Septimus started to allow himself to believe that Jenna really was coming back.

"Yes," he said, a little more brightly. "All right then. I'll do that. I'll see you tomorrow."

"Off you go," said Marcia as the huge purple door to the ExtraOrdinary Wizard's rooms threw itself open for the Apprentice.

"Bye," replied Septimus. He stepped on to the silver spiral stairs and they began to move, quickly taking him out of sight. The purple door closed itself quietly, and Marcia did something she had never done before: she wandered upstairs and went, uninvited, into Septimus's room. She walked over to his window and waited for him to emerge from the Tower. Then she watched his progress across the Wizard Tower courtyard, a small figure in green carrying his heavy backpack, his unruly, pale, straw-coloured hair making it easy to see him even from twenty-one floors up. As Septimus disappeared into the shadows of the Great Arch, Marcia walked away from the window and out of the room, gently closing the door behind her.

Septimus took the short cut to the North Gate. The short cut was a high path set into the Wall that surrounded the Castle. It was narrow and unfenced, and was somewhat alarming if you did not have a head for heights, which Septimus did not. On the right-hand side of the path was a sheer drop of about twenty feet on to roofs, into backyards or, in one terrifying stretch, a drop of fifty feet straight on to the Ramblings Road, which led to The Ramblings. The Ramblings was a huge warren of a building that formed the east wall of the Castle and sprawled for three miles along the river. It was a noisy, busy place filled with a maze of passages and rooms where many of the Castle inhabitants lived and worked, and it was where the Heaps had lived before their sudden move into the Palace.

On the left-hand side of the path were the thick stone battlements of the Wall. As he walked along the path, Septimus stared fixedly at the worn yellow stones of the ancient Walls and told himself not to look down.

Once Septimus had made the mistake of glancing to his right just as he was walking above the Ramblings Road. A feeling like an electric shock had run through him, starting at his feet and ending in his head, making him sway dangerously. He had had to sit down, then close his eyes and crawl to the nearest exit steps. But Septimus believed in conquering his fears—which was what always took him up to the Wall, rather than through the longer, but much less scary, alleyways and sideslips to the North Gate.

Today, as Septimus hurried along the path, he paid little attention to the height—he was too busy thinking about Jenna and planning what to do. Although he had begun to wonder whether Marcia was indeed right and Jenna was on her way back, something deep down told Septimus that Jenna was in trouble.

And if Jenna was in trouble, he was going to help her—whatever it took.

✢ I I ✢
JENNA'S JOURNEY

Septimus was right. The horse and riders that Marcia had found in her Remote Search were in fact Jake and Betty Jago, who ran a small market garden in the Farmlands and were on their way to visit Betty's mother in The Ramblings. But far away, trotting through the apple orchards of the lowland hills, was another black horse with two riders: one small and dark-haired, with a gold circlet around her head, the other tall and wild-eyed, with his long straw-coloured hair streaming back from his face as he pushed his tiring horse onward.

As he rode, Simon was occupied with his thoughts. He was amazed that it had all been so easy. When he had ridden into the Palace, Simon had expected, at the very least, to be stopped and questioned. But there had been no one there, and so, he thought with a grim smile, the Heaps only had themselves to blame. Because Simon had not really expected to snatch Jenna so easily, he felt a little scared of his own success. He was afraid she might be troublesome; he knew she had a mind of her own and remembered her throwing some serious tantrums when she was little, although he had always been able to make her laugh and forget about whatever was troubling her.

Simon shook his head crossly to rid himself of any fond memories he might have of his little adoptive sister whom he had lived with and loved for the first ten years of her life. That, he told himself sternly, was the past. Marcia Overstrand had marched into their lives on Jenna's tenth birthday and ruined everything, and that had been the end of his family as he knew it. The last straw was when his parents were duped by that boy from the Young Army into thinking he was their precious seventh son and, to top it all, the upstart got the only thing that Simon had ever wanted—the ExtraOrdinary Apprenticeship. Now he cared for no one—except for Lucy Gringe.

If Simon had not been able to snatch Jenna, he had planned to take Lucy away with him that day. But work had to come first. Simon was a conscientious Apprentice, who had been busy doing his Master's bidding for the past year. He had not been looking forward to snatching Jenna, but orders were orders. It had to be done. Lucy would have to wait a little longer—although just at that moment, Simon would have much preferred it be Lucy sitting on his horse, laughing as they cantered through the apple orchards, rather than Princess stony-faced Jenna, who sat like a rock in front of him.

Apart from her few months spent in the Marram Marshes, Jenna had never been out of the Castle before, and she was struck by how green and varied the Farmlands were. If she had been with anyone but Simon it would have been a wonderful journey. The sun was hot but not oppressively so; since the bright blue skies of the early morning, a few clouds had drifted in from the west and taken the edge off the heat. Simon had allowed Thunder to slow down to a brisk trot and occasionally the horse fell into a leisurely walk as they reached a small incline. Jenna could not stop herself from gazing around and being amazed at how beautiful the countryside was.

Jenna was not going to give Simon the satisfaction of seeing how scared she was. She sat stiff and upright, using her riding skills to go with the horse as he made his way along the endless dusty tracks weaving through the Farmlands, which stretched for miles on the other side of the river.

They had stopped once by a stream on the edge of a hay meadow to give the horse a drink and to allow him to graze for a while. Simon had offered Jenna some food, but she had refused; she was not hungry. Like the horse, Jenna drank from the stream, and when Simon had said it was time to move on she had made a run for it, dashing across the shallow stream and down a narrow track. At the end of the track Jenna could see a small house with an old woman sitting outside, dozing in the shade. But as she hurtled along the dusty path, she heard the sound of Thunder galloping up behind her, and in a moment Simon had grabbed her and lifted her roughly back into the saddle. They did not stop again.

As the day wore on, the lush meadows of the river flood-plain gave way to the gently sloping hills of the Lowlands. The soft fruit crops and orchards of the small farms and market gardens changed to hillsides of vines, and still Thunder carried on, climbing upwards as the hills became more pro-nounced and the misty blues and purples of the Border Mountains began to rise before them.

Now Jenna began to realise that Simon was not going to let her go. For much of the morning she had hoped that whatever strange joke he was playing on her would soon come to an end, that he would suddenly turn Thunder around and canter back to the Castle. Jenna had even decid-ed exactly what she was going to say to him when they got back, and once or twice she thought he was about to do just that. But Thunder carried on, now walking more often than trotting, as the hills became steeper and the air clearer and more chill.

It was late afternoon, and they had reached the grim slate quarries in the sheep-filled foothills of the Bad-lands when Jenna at last broke the heavy silence between them.

"Why are you taking me away, Simon?" Jenna asked. "Where are we going?"

Simon did not reply. But, as Jenna looked ahead to the looming mass of the Border Mountains, she already knew the answer to her second question. And she wasn't sure she really wanted to hear the answer to her first.

✢ I 2 ✢
JANNIT MAARTEN'S BOATYARD

As *Septimus neared the North* Gate he heard the sound of raised voices.

"You can't stop me, Father!" Lucy Gringe was yelling. "You can't keep me locked up any more. I am not a child. If I want to go after Simon, then I will. So there!"

"Over my dead body!" came Gringe's low growl.

"With pleasure!"

"Stop it both of you. *Please!*" shouted Mrs Gringe. "I'm sure Lucy isn't really going to run, are you, dear?"

"Of course I am, Mother. Right now!"

"Oh, no, you're not!" yelled Gringe.

"Oh, yes, I am!"

"Oh, no, you're *not.*"

Septimus arrived at the North Gate just in time to see

Gringe dart inside the gatehouse. A moment later there was a loud clanking noise as the massive chains of the drawbridge started to move slowly around the huge cogs on the ground floor. Gringe was winding up the drawbridge.

Lucy Gringe knew the sound well; she had heard it every sunset and sunrise of her life. Septimus watched Lucy sidestep Mrs Gringe—a short but athletic-looking woman who looked remarkably similar to her husband—and make a run for the bridge.

"Stop!" yelled Mrs Gringe, running after her daughter. "Stop—you'll get yourself killed."

"Fat lot you care," screamed Lucy, her long plaits streaming out behind her, as she went tearing up the slowly increasing incline of the drawbridge, intending to throw herself across the widening gap between the bridge and the opposite bank. Mrs Gringe raced after her daughter. Suddenly she launched herself into an expert flying tackle and brought Lucy crashing down on to the thick wooden planks of the bridge.

In the gatehouse the deafening clanking of the chains drowned out all the sounds of the drama outside. With a determined grimace, Gringe carried on winding up the bridge, unaware that Lucy and Mrs Gringe were now fiercely fighting each other as Lucy struggled to reach the end of the bridge.

But with every second, the incline was becoming steeper, and soon it was far too steep for Lucy to make any headway at all. It was all she could do to stay where she was, with her fingers clutched around an iron ring embedded in the wood while Mrs Gringe clung like a limpet to Lucy's left boot.

Inside the gatehouse the heavily sweating Gringe gave another turn to the chains and the drawbridge reared up yet again. It was now beginning to point towards the sky. Suddenly Lucy could hold on no longer. Her fingers let go of the ring, and she and her mother were sent slithering down the nearly vertical slope. And as they landed in a bruised and squabbling heap on the cobbles of the gate, the drawbridge closed with a loud clang and an earthshaking thump. Gringe, exhausted by his effort, collapsed on the floor and resolved to be nicer to the Bridge Boy, who usually wound up the bridge. He wouldn't like to have to do *that* again in a hurry.

Septimus slipped away. He didn't have time to wait around for the Gringes to patch up their quarrel and let the bridge down again. He decided to go down to Jannit Maarten's boatyard, where Jannit ran a ferry service across the Moat, if she happened to be there. Septimus decided to take a chance that she would be.

Half an hour later Septimus had reached the tunnel under

the Castle wall that led to Jannit Maarten's boatyard. The yard
was on a quay beside the Moat, just outside the Wall.
Septimus walked through the damp, dripping tunnel and soon
emerged into the sunlight and a chaotic jumble of boats. As he
started picking his way carefully through assorted sails, ropes,
anchors and endless contraptions that were essential for
building boats, Septimus at first thought that the boatyard was
deserted, until the sound of voices drifted to him from the
edge of the Moat. Septimus made his way over to them.

"Sep! Hey, Sep! What are *you* doing here?" It was a voice
that Septimus knew well. Nicko Heap had noticed the unmistakable green tunic among the boatyard clutter. Nicko was
standing in the prow of a long, narrow boat; he was a little
taller than his brother Septimus and much more solidly built.
And unlike his brother's pale complexion—a result of weeks
on end spent inside the Wizard Tower—Nicko's smiling face
was a deep wind-burned brown. His long fair hair was caked
with salt from the sea; the curls were tangled from the wind
and had a number of brightly coloured braids woven through
them. The braids were a summer craze among the young
boatmen at the Port, and Nicko had taken to the braids with
enthusiasm along with a collection of wristbands to match.
Like Septimus and all the Heaps, Nicko had the deep green

eyes that Wizard children get when they come into contact
with Magyk. Nicko was not interested in being a Wizard, but
he could turn his hand to a few spells if he had to, and, like all
the Heap children (except Septimus), he had been taught
Magyk as a child by his parents.

Next to Nicko was a tall young man with bright, spiky, red
hair, wearing a grumpy expression, who Septimus knew to be
Rupert Gringe, Lucy's brother. Jannit Maarten, the boatbuilder, was on the boatyard pontoon securing the boat with
a rope.

"Nicko—you're back!" yelled Septimus happily, leaping
over a pile of planks and some old buckets and running
towards his brother. He was surprised at how pleased and
relieved he felt to see him. Nicko would understand about
Jenna; Septimus was sure of that. Jannit Maarten smiled at
Septimus—she was fond of all the Heaps. Nicko had recently
started helping her and Rupert at the boatyard and she was
impressed with him.

Jannit was a small, strong-looking woman in a grubby blue
smock. She had a pleasant nut-brown, deeply lined face, and
her hair was plaited into a long, thin, grey ponytail which
hung sailor-style down her back. Jannit lived and breathed
boats; she slept in the small tumbledown hut at the entrance

of the boatyard and rarely ventured out of the yard.

Although there were other boatyards at the Castle, Jannit Maarten's was the best. She had taken on Rupert Gringe as her apprentice when he had just turned eleven and it was— she was fond of telling anyone who would listen—the best thing she had ever done. Rupert was a gifted boatbuilder. He had an eye for the line of the boat and an instinctive sense of how each boat he built was going to sit in the water, and of how she would respond to the wind.

Jannit was almost as pleased with Nicko. Nicko's first project was helping Rupert build a new *Muriel* for Sally Mullin, who had given her much-loved boat to the Heaps for their escape the previous year, and Jannit could see that he had a good eye and was skilful with his hands.

Nicko was also a natural sailor, better, in fact, than Rupert Gringe; and so it was to Nicko, much to Rupert's irritation, that Jannit addressed her question, "How did she sail then?"

"Like a dog in a bucket," growled Rupert, determined not to let Nicko get a word in.

Jannit's face fell. The boat had been her pet project but nothing had gone right with it from the start. She looked at Nicko for his opinion.

"It wasn't good, Jannit," he admitted. "We capsized twice.

Then the mast broke. Had to get repairs down at the Port."

"It was *that* bad?" said Jannit. "I must be losing my touch."

"Nah. Of course you're not," said Rupert. "Just teething troubles. We'll sort it out."

"Oh, well." Jannit sighed. "You boys will be wanting to get back and see your families. Off you go—I'll sort things out here."

"All right, Jannit," said Rupert, "I'll be off then. I'm looking forward to a bit of peace and quiet after that creaking, moaning boat we've been stuck on."

"Er, Rupert," Septimus said, feeling that he ought to say something. "It's, um, not exactly . . . *quiet* at the gatehouse. There's been a bit of trouble."

Rupert looked at Septimus suspiciously. He had inherited his father's mistrust of the Heaps, and although he had to admit that Nicko Heap wasn't too bad, he was none too sure about the fancy Wizard's Apprentice all dressed up in his swanky bright green tunic and dinky Apprentice belt.

"Yeah?" he said warily. "What trouble?"

"Well, Simon—"

"I knew it!" exploded Rupert. "I knew it would be your blasted brother! I'll get him this time. I *will!*"

"He's not—"

Rupert Gringe hurtled off across the boatyard.

"—there now," Septimus finished lamely as Rupert tripped over a bucket and disappeared into the tunnel more quickly than he had expected to.

"What's up, Sep?" asked Nicko, who could see his younger brother was upset.

"Simon kidnapped Jenna and no one will believe me, not even Marcia," Septimus gabbled in a rush.

"*What?*"

"Simon's kidnapped Jenna and—"

"'S all right, Sep, I heard what you said. Come and sit down and tell me about it." Nicko climbed ashore and put his arm around Septimus's shoulder. They sat together with their feet dangling in the Moat while Septimus told Nicko the whole story. As the story progressed Nicko's expression became increasingly worried.

Finally Septimus came to the end and said, ". . . but I bet *you* don't believe me either."

"'Course I believe you."

"Do you?" Septimus looked at Nicko questioningly.

"Yeah. I know people are after Jenna. I was going to tell Mum to be more careful. Seems like I'm too late . . ."

"What do you mean—*people?*" asked Septimus. "You

mean, not just Simon?"

"Well, maybe Simon has something to do with them. I wouldn't be surprised. But when me an' Rupert were down at the Port getting a new mast—which reminds me I must tell Jannit that the new one is rubbish and won't last five minutes—well, we spent a lot of time in the Blue Anchor Tavern by the docks. You get all sorts in there. We met Alther's old girlfriend Alice Nettles. She works for the Customs House now—"

"Yes—and?" said Septimus impatiently, wondering where Nicko's ramblings were leading him.

"And Alice told us that there was someone in Port looking for Jenna."

"*Who?*"

"Dunno who. A dark stranger, Alice called him. Just come in from the Far Countries. His ship was still anchored offshore, waiting for a berth on Customs Quay, but he'd got himself rowed in and he'd been asking all sorts of questions about the Princess."

"What kind of questions?" asked Septimus.

"Oh, you know the kind of thing. Was she really alive? Where could he find her? Stuff like that. Alice just stonewalled him. She's good at that, is Alice."

Septimus stared at the murky water of the Moat. "That's it then. I bet Simon is taking Jenna to the dark stranger," he said gloomily.

"He probably paid Simon well enough," said Nicko, who did not have a good opinion of his eldest brother.

"And I can guess who the dark stranger is . . ."

"Can you?" asked Nicko, surprised.

"DomDaniel," whispered Septimus.

"But he's dead."

"He *disappeared*. Sucked down into the Marsh. But that doesn't mean he's dead, does it? From what I know of him, he *likes* being under the ground."

"I don't know, Sep," said Nicko. "Even Simon wouldn't do a thing like that—would he?"

Septimus looked Nicko in the eye. "Look, Nik, no one else believes me about Jen being in danger so I don't expect you to either. But I don't care what anyone says. I'm going to go and get her back." Septimus stood and heaved his backpack over his shoulders.

"I'll be off then," he said. "Tell Marcia where I've gone. And Mum and Dad. See you." Septimus turned to go.

"Hang on, you dillop," protested Nicko. "I *do* believe you. And you are *not* going off on your own either, Sep. How are you going to find her?"

"I'll find her somehow," said Septimus.

"Yeah, one day maybe. If you're lucky. Now I know someone who is the best tracker I have ever met. He'll lead us
straight to her. I'll get a boat from Jannit and we'll go and find
him. You sit right down there again and take that bag of
boulders off."

Septimus didn't move.

"Go on, Sep. Do as you're told. I'm your big brother and
I'm telling you. Right?"

"You're not *that* much bigger," muttered Septimus, but he
sat down all the same.

⊹→ I 3 ⊹→
THE FOREST

Nicko and Septimus pulled their boat up on to a shingle beach in a small inlet on the edge of the Forest. Nicko knew it well; this was where he always moored his boat when he came to visit his brothers.

They had sailed about five miles down river from the Castle on the outgoing tide. Jannit had insisted on Nicko taking a small lugger—a good riverboat which had a cabin in case they had to spend the night in it, but Nicko had hopes of getting straight into the Forest and finding the boys' camp before the sun set. He had no intention of walking through the Forest at night, for it was a dangerous place after dark. Wild packs of wolverines roamed through the trees and many unquiet spirits and malevolent beings hovered in the air. Some trees were carnivorous and would turn into traps at night: they would swoop their branches down and enfold their victims, taking the life blood from them, so that by morning there would be nothing left but a dried-out skeleton hanging among the leaves.

It was late afternoon when they arrived at the beach, and Nicko knew they had five hours of daylight left which was, he reckoned, easily long enough to reach the boys' camp safely.

Septimus had not been in the Forest since he was a Young Army Expendable. He had spent many terrifying nights there as part of the Do-or-Die night exercises that the boy soldiers had to endure. They would be woken in the middle of the night and taken off to somewhere dangerous—very often it was the Forest.

There were two nights in the Forest that Septimus would never forget. One was the time that his very best friend, Boy 409, had rescued him. A pack of wolverines had trapped him and were about to pounce. Boy 409 had rushed to his side, yelling so loudly that the lead wolverine had, for a brief moment, become confused, and in that moment Boy 409 had hauled Septimus to safety. The other terrible night had been when Septimus wouldn't have cared very much if a pack of wolverines *had* pounced on him. That was when Boy 409 had fallen overboard on their way down the river to the Forest. The river was rough and flowing fast and a freak wave had hit the Young Army boat. The boat was overloaded and Boy 409 had lost his footing and fallen overboard. He was never seen again. Septimus had begged the Leader Cadet to go back for Boy 409 but he had refused. Boy 409 was just another Expendable, and the whole point of a Do-or-Die exercise had been to weed out "the weak, the scared and the stupid," as the Leader Cadet had put it. But usually the Do-or-Dies, as they were known, simply weeded out the unlucky.

When Nicko was satisfied that the boat was properly tied up to allow for the rise and fall of the tides, and everything onboard was neatly stowed away, he pulled a tattered piece of paper from his pocket.

"Here's the map," he said, showing it to Septimus. "Sam drew it."

Septimus looked at the wiggling lines that wandered across the scrap of paper like slug trails over a pane of glass. "Oh," he said. He didn't think much of the map, but Nicko seemed confident.

"'S all right," said Nicko reassuringly. "I know the way. Follow me."

Septimus had no trouble following Nicko as they started their journey into the Forest. The outskirts of the Forest were fairly easy to walk through; the trees were widely spaced, and dappled sunlight shone through the branches high above their heads. Nicko confidently took a narrow track and walked briskly along, weaving in and out of the trees along the winding, snakelike track.

As Nicko led them steadily deeper into the Forest, the trees became larger and grew closer together, the sunlight faded into dark green shadows and a heavy silence began to enclose them. Septimus kept close behind Nicko as the track grew narrower and more overgrown. Neither of them spoke; Nicko was trying to remember the way, and Septimus was occupied with his own thoughts. He was wondering what he was doing, walking deep into the Forest when he had set off to go to the Farmlands. Jenna must be miles away by now, on the other side of the river—and here he was going in the opposite direction, just because Nicko had persuaded him to. After a while Septimus broke the silence and said, "Are you sure they'll want to help?"

"Of course they will," replied Nicko. "They're our

brothers, aren't they? Brothers stick together. Except for Simon, of course."

Septimus was anxious about meeting his brothers. He had been reunited with most of his family for a year and a half, but in all that time Sam, Edd, Erik and Jo-Jo had been living wild in the Forest. Silas had promised to take Septimus to visit them but somehow it had never happened. Marcia was either too busy to let him go or Silas got the date confused and turned up on the wrong day.

"What are they like?" Septimus asked Nicko.

"Well, Sam is an amazing fisherman. Can catch anything he wants. I did wonder if we might see him on the beach, as it's one of his fishing places. Edd and Erik are just a laugh. Always playing jokes on everyone and switching places. They still look so alike that I can't always tell the difference. And Jo-Jo is quiet but really clever. He likes herbs an' stuff—a bit like Mum, I suppose."

"Oh," said Septimus, trying to picture them but without much success. He still could not get used to being part of such a large family, after spending the first ten years of his life with no family at all.

"But," said Nicko, "like I said, the one we've really come to see is the tracker, Wolf Boy."

"The one they found in the Forest?"

"Yeah. He lives with them now. They think he'd been living with the wolverines for a while, but the wolverines probably chucked him out when he got too big and stopped smelling like a cub. He was wild when the boys first came across him. He bit Sam on the leg and scratched Erik quite badly. His fingernails were horrible—all yellow and long and they were curved like claws. But he got tamer in the last Big Freeze when Edd and Erik gave him food and now he's not too bad. Still a bit smelly though, but then they all are. You get used to it after a bit. But Wolf Boy is the best tracker ever. He'll lead us straight to Jenna, that's for sure."

"Does he have big teeth and fur?" asked Septimus warily.

"Yeah, huge yellow fangs and hairy hands."

"Really?"

Nicko turned around and gave Septimus a big grin. "Gotcha!"

After a while they reached a small clearing in the Forest, and Nicko suggested they stop for a few minutes to look at the map. Septimus took off his backpack and immediately felt so light that he thought he might float up through the trees.

"Want a mint?" he asked, offering the purple tube of Mint Blasts to Nicko.

Nicko looked at the tube suspiciously.

"What do they do?" he asked warily. Nicko knew all about Septimus's weird taste in sweets and had never quite got over eating a self-renewing banana chew that had kept Reappearing in his mouth no matter how many times he had spat it out.

"Nothing," said Septimus. "They're just mints."

"All right then."

"Hold out your hand." Septimus put a few tiny green balls into Nicko's hand. Nicko tipped his head back and shoved the Mint Blasts into his mouth as if he were taking a gulp of medicine.

"Not—" warned Septimus.

"*Mm-rrrr-aah!*"

"—all at once."

"Aargh. They went up my nose." Nicko spluttered. Three small Mint Blasts shot out of his nose.

"Oh, they sometimes do that. The trick is to just hold them in your mouth and let them explode. They really wake you up, don't they?"

"I think my eyes are going to pop out."

"Well *I* like them." Septimus took a few for himself and put the tube in his backpack. "Want some Wiz Bix then?" he asked.

"You must be joking," said Nicko, his eyes streaming.

Nicko wiped his eyes, unfolded Sam's map and peered at it. Then he looked around the clearing.

"Can you see a standing stone anywhere?" he asked Septimus. "There should be one over there." Nicko pointed vaguely to a cluster of trees. "It looks a bit like a bird."

"No," said Septimus, who had had his doubts about Sam's map since he'd seen it. "Nicko, are we lost?"

"No, 'course not," said Nicko.

"Well, where are we then?"

"Not quite sure," mumbled Nicko. "Better go on until we find somewhere I recognise."

As Septimus followed Nicko deeper into the Forest he felt more and more uneasy. The trees were getting even closer together; some of them had huge trunks and felt very ancient. Septimus sensed the atmosphere around them change—the trees became strange. Each one seemed different to him; some were benevolent presences and others were not. Once or twice Septimus thought he felt a tree shift slightly as they passed by, and he imagined it turning and staring at them as they walked on. The sunlight had completely disappeared and had been replaced by a dim green light, which filtered through the tightly knit branches above their heads. It was easier to walk now that the undergrowth had grown less tangled and wild in the dimmer light, and for much of the time they were walking over a thick bed of fallen leaves. Every now and then Septimus heard a scuffling or rustling sound as a small creature ran away. Septimus didn't mind those sounds; he knew they were just tree rats or Forest weasels, but once or twice he heard the snapping of branches as something quite large crashed away from them—or was it towards them?

Septimus began to feel very uneasy. They had been in the Forest for what seemed like hours, and he was sure that the daylight—such as it was—was fading into twilight. As he followed Nicko he could see no sign of a track, and he began to wonder if they were lost. But still Nicko doggedly pushed on through the ferns and bracken and Septimus dutifully followed him, until they reached a small clearing.

Septimus stopped—now he *knew* they were lost. "Nicko," he said, "we've been here before. An hour ago. Look, I recognise that hollow tree with the puffballs all around it."

Nicko stopped and looked at Sam's map. "We can't be lost," he said. "Look, here we are." Septimus looked where Nicko's stubby finger was pointing.

"On that squashed ant, you mean?"

"What squashed ant?" Nicko squinted at the map, which was hard to see now in the fading light. After a few seconds of staring at the scruffy piece of paper, Nicko said, "Oh, *that* squashed ant."

"We're lost, aren't we?" said Septimus.

"Oh, no, I don't think so. Look, I agree that may be an ant but we're still on that track here. And if we follow it along . . . there . . . see, we come to the camp. Honestly, Sep, we're almost there."

They set off again with Septimus reluctantly following. After a while he said, "We've been here before too, Nik. We're just going around in circles."

Nicko stopped and leaned wearily against a tree. "I know, Sep. I'm sorry. We're lost."

↤ 14 ↦
LOST

Night fell fast in the Forest once the sun had set.

Septimus and Nicko were sitting gloomily on a fallen tree. Septimus was holding his compass in the palm of his hand, trying to see which way the quivering needle was pointing. The light was nearly gone, and the Dragon ring was beginning to glow, but it didn't help that Septimus's hand was shaking. A familiar sense of dread was stealing over him, which always came with the approach of night in the Forest.

"It's the Forest twilight now, Nik," whispered Septimus.

"We ought to keep still for a while. It's not a good time to be moving—not while things are shifting."

Far away in the Castle, Silas and Sarah watched the sun set from the Palace roof and realised at last that Simon was not going to bring Jenna home. In a state of panic, they set off for the Wizard Tower to see Marcia. They met her on Wizard Way as she was heading to see Weasal Van Klampff.

Deep in the Forest, at its very centre, Septimus and Nicko sat silently together. Septimus felt the sun drop behind the hills, the air grow chill and the shift between day and night begin. The Forest was changing into a night-time creature as the darkness closed in, and, with a sense of foreboding, Septimus recognised the strange feeling of thickness in the atmosphere that the Forest night brought with it.

"I'm really sorry, Sep," Nicko mumbled desolately.

"Shh," Septimus whispered. "Don't speak unless you have to."

Nicko sat quietly, trying to keep calm. He didn't like the Forest much even in the daylight. He hated the feeling it gave him of not being able to escape quickly, of being trapped in the middle of the endless tangle of tree trunks and branches—

although as long as he kept moving and could see where he was going, Nicko could just about stand it. But not now. Now that a thick blanket of blackness was beginning to surround them, he felt a panic rising inside him, which made him want to scream out loud. Nicko had only felt like that once before in his life, when he had been trapped in the Castle rubbish chute, but that time he had been with Marcia and she had quickly freed them. This time he was on his own.

"When you were here on a night exercise, what did they teach you? I mean, what did you have to do?" whispered Nicko.

"Well, er, once in the unarmed animal-combat exercise we had to dig a wolverine pit and spend the night waiting for a wolverine to drop in. It didn't though—not into our pit any-way. But we lost three boys in the pit near us. They put up a good fight but the wolverine won. It was an awful noise. Then sometimes on compass-reading exercises they tied a boy to a tree and we had to try and find him before he got eaten. Didn't always get there in time—"

"Ah," said Nicko with a shudder. "Shouldn't have asked. Thought they might have taught you some survival skills."

"They did," said Septimus. "Keep out of the way of any-thing that runs faster than you and has more teeth than you.

Watch out for the carnivorous trees 'cause you can never tell which ones they are until it's too late. Oh, yes—and the most important thing of all—"

"Yes?"

"Don't stay out in the Forest after dark."

"Very funny," mumbled Nicko.

"I think," Septimus whispered, "that we should try and find somewhere safe to spend the night. Up a tree would be best—"

"Up a carnivorous tree, you mean?"

"Nicko, just be quiet, will you?"

"Sorry, Sep."

"Like I said, we should climb up a tree—and it's just luck whether it's carnivorous or not."

"What, you can't tell?"

"Not at night. You just take your chance. That's what the Night Forest is all about, Nik. Anyway, like I said, if we can get up a tree we should be safe from wolverines, though of course we'll have to keep watch for bloodsucking tree rats."

"Great."

"And some of the older trees are infested with leaf leeches. I spent a night in a tree once with the Leader Cadet, and when I woke up in the morning I thought he'd hidden himself with camouflage. But he was covered from head to foot with leaf leeches." Septimus gave a chuckle. "Served him right."

"Stop!" hissed Nicko. "Just *stop*. I don't want to hear any more—OK? Let's just find a tree and cross our fingers."

Septimus hauled his heavy bag on to his shoulders and they set off; this time Nicko followed Septimus. Septimus's Dragon Ring was shining brightly in the dark, and he pushed his hand into his pocket to douse the glow. He knew that a light would draw every creature to them for miles around and would particularly attract Forest Wraiths. Septimus trod slowly and silently through the trees, and Nicko followed him as carefully and quietly as he could. But Nicko was less agile than Septimus, and, try as he might, every now and then his foot snapped a twig or rustled a leaf. Septimus knew that sooner or later a creature or a Thing would hear them. They needed to get up into the safety of a tree fast. Desperately he scanned every tree they passed to see if there were any low branches that might give them a handhold. But there were none. They were in the middle of the ancient part of the Forest, where all the trees grew tall and kept their branches high above the ground.

Suddenly Septimus felt a pincerlike grip on his arm.

"Ouch!"

"Shh!"

Septimus spun around to see Nicko still clutching his arm and staring wide-eyed into the darkness.

"Sep, what's that—over there—I saw something yellow and shining."

Septimus scanned the darkness using the Army trick of glancing sideways to see in the dark. It was the sight he had been dreading—they were surrounded by a sea of yellow eyes.

"Rats," muttered Septimus.

"Rats?" whispered Nicko. "Oh, that's a relief. For a moment I thought it was wolverines."

"It *is* wolverines. Loads of them."

"But you said it was *rats*." Nicko sounded aggrieved.

"Shut up, Nicko. I'm trying to think. Can you get my Fast Freeze Charm out of my bag?" Septimus gulped. "Quickly . . ."

"Can't you do a Fast Freeze without a Charm yet?"

"No. Hurry up!"

Nicko tried to open Septimus's backpack but his hands were shaking so much he couldn't even find the buckle in the dark. Septimus was annoyed with himself. He knew he should have taken the Charm out of the bag so it would be ready when he needed it. But he hated the Night Forest as much as Nicko did, and somehow his brain seemed to have stopped working.

"I can't undo your stupid bag," hissed Nicko with panic rising in his voice. "Can't you Transfix them like you did that horse?"

"What—get them to form an orderly line so that I can do them one at a time you mean?"

"Can't you do 'em all at once?"

"No."

Septimus scanned the waiting pairs of yellow eyes. They were getting nearer and spreading out. He knew the wolverines were beginning their practised routine of encircling their prey. If he and Nicko waited any longer they would be trapped in the middle of the circle.

"Run!" hissed Septimus. "*Now!*"

Nicko did not need telling twice. Septimus took off through the trees and Nicko was right behind him, ducking and diving around the massive tree trunks, leaping over fallen branches and skidding on the slippery leaves whenever Septimus took a tight zigzag turn. But every time Nicko glanced back he saw the yellow eyes easily keeping pace, as the wolverine pack got into its nightly routine of chasing its prey and working up a good appetite for supper.

Suddenly Septimus caught his foot in a rat hole and crashed to the ground.

"Get up, Sep," gasped Nicko, dragging him to his feet.

"Aah! My ankle . . ." Septimus moaned.

Nicko was unsympathetic. "Come *on*, Sep. Get going. There's a pack of wolverines behind us in case you'd forgotten."

Septimus hobbled on but, try as he might, he could no longer run; his ankle kept giving way beneath him. He stopped beside a tree and took off his backpack.

"What are you doing?" gasped Nicko, horrified.

"It's no good, Nik," said Septimus. "I can't run. You make a break for it. I'll try and find the Fast Freeze Charm before they close in on me."

"Don't be stupid," snapped Nicko. "I'm not leaving you here."

"Yes, you are. I'll see you later."

"No, you won't. They'll eat you, you idiot."

"Just *go*, Nicko."

"*No!*"

As Nicko spoke, the last wolverine in the pack closed the circle. They were surrounded. Trapped. Nicko and Septimus backed up against the thick rough trunk of a tree as, slowly and stealthily, the ghastly ring of yellow lights tightened around them. They stared at the sight, unable to believe that it was really happening. Like everyone else in the Castle, they had had nightmares about this very moment, but the reality was much stranger than it ever had been in their dreams. It was almost beautiful, in a hypnotising kind of way. An expectant silence fell as though all the night creatures had stopped what they were doing and were watching the performance, which tonight, for one night only, had come to their part of the Forest.

Nicko broke the spell. He kicked the backpack over. The buckle came undone and the contents tumbled out on to the Forest floor. Both he and Septimus fell to the ground, scrabbling through the contents, frantically looking for the Fast Freeze Charm.

"There's so much rubbish in here!" hissed Nicko. "What's it look like?"

"Not rubbish. Glass icicle."

"But where? Where, where, *where*?"

"Uh-oh. I can smell them."

The foul smell of wolverine breath—a mixture of rotting meat and gum disease, for the Forest wolverines had chronic teeth problems—filled the air. With a feeling of dread, Nicko and Septimus slowly looked up and found themselves staring straight into the eyes of the lead wolverine. The lead wolverine who would give the signal for the pack to pounce.

A long, low snarl began somewhere deep in the stomach of the lead wolverine. The signal had begun. The surrounding yellow eyes brightened, muscles tensed and saliva began to flow. Toothaches forgotten for the moment, the wolverine pack flicked their tongues over their muzzles and bared their long yellow and black teeth.

The snarl grew louder and louder until suddenly, the lead wolverine threw his head back and gave a bone-chilling howl.

The pack pounced.

The tree pounced.

The tree got there first.

✢ 15 ✢
The Tree

Septimus and Nicko shot into the air. Two long, sinuous branches, which had been hovering above their heads waiting for the right moment, had seized them. At the end of each branch were five smaller, more dextrous branches, like the fingers on a hand. Each hand was wrapped tightly around the boys like a well-fitting wooden cage and held them in what felt like a grip of iron. After grabbing Septimus and Nicko with surprising speed, the tree slowed down as it took them higher and higher, pulling them up through its leaves and branches, taking them into the very centre of the tree.

Septimus closed his eyes tightly as they were lifted through the cold night air, but Nicko kept his eyes wide-open in shock as they travelled up, up through the massive tree, until they were high above the baying pack of wolverines. Nicko glanced below to the ring of yellow eyes that surrounded the tree and were staring, unblinking, at the sight of the night's supper— and a good supper too—whisked from their jaws.

The tree, like all trees, moved slowly and deliberately. Why rush when you had hundreds of years in which to live your life? Why rush when you were more than three hundred feet tall and a king of the Forest? After what felt like a lifetime, Septimus and Nicko were set down in a fork near the top of the tree. The branches that had been caging them slowly unwound from their captives and hovered above them, as though planning their next move.

"Is it going to eat us now, Sep?" whispered Nicko, his voice shaking.

"Dunno," mumbled Septimus, who still had his eyes closed tightly. He could feel how high they were above the ground, but he did not dare look.

"But it's let go of us, Sep. Maybe we could escape while we've got the chance . . ."

Septimus shook his head miserably. He was paralysed by

the height; he could no more move than fly to the moon. Nicko stole another glance downwards. Through a gap in the leaves he could see the circle of wolverines, eyes glittering hungrily, waiting in the hope that their prey might still turn up—or drop down—for supper. Suddenly it crossed Nicko's mind that this must have happened to the wolverine pack before. Sometime in the past, some poor victim must have been swept from the pack by a carnivorous tree, and then escaped the clutches of the strangling branches, only to find himself back in the middle of the wolverine ring. Nicko imagined what a terrible fate that was for someone—until it suddenly struck him that that was happening to *them*. Nicko let out a loud groan.

"What's the matter, Nik?" mumbled Septimus.

"Oh, nothing. We're about to be eaten either by a carnivorous tree or a pack of wolverines, and I can't quite make up my mind just now which one I fancy most."

Septimus forced himself to open his eyes. It wasn't quite as bad as he had feared. He couldn't see much at all—the moonless night was dark and the tree's dense summer foliage obscured any view of the long drop to the ground. "Well, no one's eaten us yet," he said.

"*Yet*," muttered Nicko.

But as Nicko spoke, the two branches that hovered above began to move down towards them again. Nicko grabbed hold of Septimus's sleeve. "C'mon, Sep," he whispered urgently. "It's now or never. We've got to get out of here. I reckon we can make a break for it—this tree is *slow*. It only got us because we were too busy with the wolverines to notice it coming for us. If we climb down fast, it won't be able to catch us."

"But then the wolverines will get us," whispered Septimus, who was convinced the tree could hear what they were saying.

"They might give up. You never know. Come on, it's our only chance." Nicko began to crawl along the branch.

The last thing Septimus wanted to do was to move any-where—he was, after all, at least three hundred feet above the ground. But, knowing he had no real choice, Septimus half-closed his eyes so that there was no chance of catching sight of the huge drop to the ground and slowly began to inch his way along the branch behind Nicko. Nicko had already reached the fork in the branch where he was planning to start his climb down. He turned and held out his hand to Septimus.

"Come on, Sep. You're even slower than this tree. Come on, it's easy."

Septimus did not reply. His hands were clammy with fear and he felt sick.

"Don't look down," Nicko encouraged. "Just look at me. Come on, you're nearly there . . ."

Septimus looked up at Nicko and suddenly his head swam, a strange faraway buzzing started inside his ears, and his clammy hands lost their grip on the smooth branch.

Septimus fell.

He fell too fast for Nicko to do anything. One moment Nicko was sitting on the branch watching his brother crawl towards him, the next moment he was sitting watching an empty space. And all he could hear was the sound of Septimus crashing through the tree far below him, followed by a howl from one of the waiting wolverines.

And then silence. Nicko heard nothing more, except the rustling of leaves and branches and the stillness of the Forest. Nicko sat numbly on the branch, unable to move. He should start his climb down; he should try and get to Septimus but he dreaded what he was going to find. And so, slowly, reluctantly, Nicko began the long climb to the Forest floor, but, as he clambered down through the tree, a long thin branch suddenly looped itself around his waist and held him fast. Nicko struggled and tried to unwind the branch, but it was as tight as a band of iron. Angrily Nicko kicked out at the tree.

"Let me go!" he shouted. "I've got to get my brother!" In a

fury Nicko tore the leaves around him to pieces, snapping as many twigs as he could find.

"Ouch," said a low, slow voice, but Nicko heard nothing.

"I hate you, you *pig* tree!" he yelled, punching and flailing at it. "You're *not* going to eat me. Or Sep. Just you try." Nicko gave way to a frenzy of kicking, shouting and insulting the tree, remembering all the bad language that he had recently picked up at the Port and from Rupert Gringe. In fact Nicko was surprised at how much he knew. So was the tree, who had never heard anything like it before.

The tree impassively ignored Nicko's outburst. It just held him tight while far below it carried on doing what it had been doing ever since Septimus had fallen. Nicko was still shouting at the tree when the branches beside him parted and Septimus appeared back at his side, wrapped up tightly in a cocoon of leaves and twigs. Nicko fell silent. He went white. This, he thought, is what spiders do to their prey. Only the week before he had sat on the boat and watched a spider wrap a struggling fly into a cocoon of silk, and then suck it dry while the fly still lived.

"Sep!" Nicko gasped. "Are you all right?" Septimus did not answer. His eyes were closed and he looked deathly white. A terrible thought crossed Nicko's mind. "Sep," he whispered.

"Sep, has it started to eat you?" He struggled to reach Septimus but the branch held him tight.

"Nicko," came a low voice.

"Sep?" asked Nicko, wondering why his brother sounded so strange.

"Nicko, please stop struggling. You might fall. It is a long way down and the wolverines are still waiting for you. Please keep still."

Nicko stared at Septimus, wondering how he was managing to talk without moving his lips.

"Sep, stop being silly, will you?"

"Nicko, listen to me, this is not Septimus speaking. Septimus has hit his head. He needs to rest."

A chill ran through Nicko, and for the first time in the Forest he felt really scared. He had known where he was with the wolverines and he had known where he was with the carnivorous tree—they had wanted to eat him. It wasn't nice and it wasn't friendly but at least it was understandable. But this low, ghostly voice was different. He had no idea what it was; it seemed to be all around him, and the spookiest thing of all was that it knew his name.

"Who are you?" whispered Nicko.

"Do you not know? I thought you had come to see me

specially." The voice sounded disappointed. "I never see any-one any more. No one ever comes to see me. I would have thought my son might have made the effort, but oh, no, can't be bothered as usual I suppose. So when I saw my two youngest grandsons I naturally thought . . ."

"*Grandsons?*" asked Nicko, taken aback.

"Yes, you and Septimus," said the voice. "I would have known you anywhere, you look so much like Silas did when he was a lad."

Suddenly a huge feeling of relief flooded through Nicko. He hardly dared believe their luck.

"You're not—you're not Grandpa Benji, are you?" he asked the tree.

"Of course I am. Who did you think I was?" said the voice.

"A carnivorous tree," said Nicko.

"*Me?* A carnivorous tree? Do I look like a carnivorous tree?"

"I don't know. I've never seen one."

"Well, let me tell you, they don't look anything like me. Mangy things they are, don't even bother to keep themselves clean. Smell of rotting meat. Nasty black leaves and covered in fungus. Give the Forest a bad name."

"Oh . . . oh, fantastic! I don't believe it. Grandpa Benji . . ."

Nicko sank back in relief and his grandfather unwound the branch that had been stopping his grandson from moving.

"You're not going to start climbing down now, are you?" asked the tree. "Those wolverines will wait a while yet. Just stay still a moment and I'll make you up a bed. Don't move."

"No. All right, Grandpa. I won't," said Nicko rather faintly. He sat on the branch feeling like a small lump of jelly. And, for the first time since he had set foot in the Forest, he began to relax.

The tree busied itself weaving its branches into a platform and covering them with a soft bed of leaves.

"There," the tree said proudly when it had finished, "you see, it's no trouble at all to make up a bed. Any of you boys can always come and stay. Your father too. And your dear mother. Any time."

The tree carefully lifted Septimus on to the platform and laid him down, still wrapped in the cocoon that held him safely.

"I only just caught him in time, you know," the tree told Nicko. "A second later and the wolverines would have had him. As it was one of them jumped up and snapped at the lad. It was close."

Nicko crawled on to the platform beside Septimus and

started to unwind the cocoon. As he did so, Nicko saw that a large bruise was appearing on Septimus's head where he had hit a branch on his way down.

"Ouch . . ." mumbled Septimus. "Gerroff, Nik."

Nicko was so happy to hear Septimus's voice. "Hey, Sep—you're all right. What a relief."

Blearily, Septimus sat up and looked at Nicko. The bruise above his eye throbbed, but he didn't care; he knew they were safe. As he had fallen through the tree Septimus had hit his head and been briefly knocked out, but, while he was being gently lifted back up through the leaves, the sound of the tree's deep voice all around him had pulled him back to consciousness, and Septimus had heard his grandfather's conversation with Nicko. At first he had thought he was dreaming, but when he opened his eyes and saw Nicko's relieved expression, he knew it must be true.

"Mrrer . . ." Septimus mumbled, grinning faintly.

"It's Grandpa Benji, Sep. We're safe!" Nicko told him excitedly. "But you gotta go to sleep now," he said, noticing how pale his brother looked. "You'll be fine in the morning." Nicko lay down on the platform beside Septimus and held on to him tightly, just to make sure he didn't fall off again.

The moonlight shone down through the leaves, and

Grandpa Benji swayed to and fro in the night-time breeze, lulling the boys into a peaceful doze. They had just dropped off to sleep when a terrible howling echoed through the tree.

"Aroooooooooooh!"

This was followed by an awful coughing, spluttering noise.

"Ach ach ach!"

Nicko knew it was the wolverines. "They can't climb trees, can they Sep?" he asked.

Septimus shook his head and wished he hadn't.

With some trepidation, Nicko and Septimus looked down through the platform to the wolverines. The whole pack seemed to have gone mad. They were running around and around the tree, yelping and yowling and desperately pawing at their noses.

"What are they doing?" muttered Nicko.

Suddenly Septimus snorted with laughter. "Look," he said, "they've eaten my backpack—"

"Well, I wouldn't have thought it tasted *that* bad," said Nicko.

"—and they've found the Mint Blasts!" Septimus laughed.

✛ 16 ✛
THE BADLANDS

While *Septimus and Nicko were* getting lost far away in the Forest, Simon Heap was taking Jenna deep into the Badlands.

Thunder stumbled slowly up a narrow track, which wound through endless slate quarries, some old and abandoned, others with signs of recent work, although eerily deserted. The disturbed earth and the shattered rocks gave off a malevolent atmosphere, and Jenna felt her spirits sink. Far above her, a mournful moan drifted from the desolate tops of the hills— the east wind was blowing in and thick grey clouds were piling up in the sky. The sunlight grew dim and the air became chill. Simon wrapped his long black cloak around him, but Jenna was shivering; all she had to keep her warm was her light summer tunic.

"Stop shivering, will you?" growled Simon.

"I don't have a cloak like you do," snapped Jenna.

"You wouldn't want a cloak like mine." Simon sneered. "Too much Darke Magyk for Little Miss Perfect here."

"You shouldn't joke about that stuff, Simon," protested Jenna.

"Who said I was joking?" asked Simon.

Jenna fell silent, still shivering.

"Oh, have this then and stop fussing," said Simon, exasperated. He fished out a cloak from his saddlebag and grumpily handed it to Jenna. Jenna took the cloak, expecting to find a rough horse blanket, and was amazed at what Simon had given her. It was the most beautiful cloak that she had ever seen—a rich, deep blue, finely woven from the softest wool combed from the belly of a mountain goat, and lined in golden silk. Simon had intended it as a present for Lucy Gringe. He had planned to leave it outside the gatehouse, with a note tucked inside the lining that only Lucy would find. But when Simon had arrived at the North Gate early that morning, with his dark cloak pulled high around his face to avoid Gringe recognising him, he had seen Silas jauntily walking down the street carrying the box of Counter-Feet. The last person Simon wanted to see was his father, and he had quickly changed direction and taken a short cut to Wizard Way. Silas had not even noticed him—he had been too busy going over his strategy for that morning's game. So now, to Simon's irritation, the beautiful and extremely expensive cloak he had chosen for Lucy was wrapped around Little Miss Princess Perfect.

Jenna pulled Lucy's cloak tightly around herself. She was warm now, but very tired, in front of Simon on the weary horse. The dark slate quarries went endlessly on, and Thunder was plodding up a steady incline. The track had narrowed; it was bound on one side by steep slate cliffs that rose into the overcast sky, and on the other side by a deep ravine, at the bottom of which was a dark swirling river full of jagged rocks and treacherous whirlpools. Jenna wondered if Simon was ever going to stop; he seemed to have no concern for her or his horse. Thunder was tiring fast, and once or twice the

horse had lost his footing on the loose scree, which covered
the sides of the grey slate hills, and had nearly sent them all
plunging into the river below.

Suddenly Simon spoke. "Whoa, Thunder, whoa there,
boy." Thunder slowed to a halt and shook his head, snorting
wearily. Jenna glanced about, suddenly anxious now that they
had stopped.

Quickly, Simon dismounted from Thunder and took the
reins. "You can get off," he told Jenna. "We're here."

With a sinking feeling, Jenna slipped off the horse and
stood, undecided whether to make a run for it or not. The
trouble was, there didn't seem to be anywhere to run to.
Simon read her thoughts.

"Don't be stupid and run off," he told her sharply. "There's
nowhere for you to go, unless you want to find yourself in a
Land Wurm's Burrow."

"Don't try and frighten me, Simon," said Jenna. "You know
as well as I do they only come out at night."

"Oh, do they now? Of course I forgot—Little Miss *Princess*
knows everything there is to know, doesn't she? Well, I can
leave you out here tonight, if you like. There's a nice selection
of Wurm Burrows up there if you want to go and have a
look."

Jenna was not tempted to take up Simon's challenge. She had been told too many stories about the huge grey Land Wurms that lived in the slate hills and preyed on passing travellers at night. Some Castle people thought they were nothing more than old miners' tales, told in order to keep people out of the slate workings, where the purest gold was sometimes found, but Jenna knew better. So she stood beside Thunder in Lucy's cloak and stared fixedly at the ground, determined not to give Simon the pleasure of seeing her look frightened.

Simon took hold of Thunder's bridle.

"Follow me," he told Jenna, and he led the horse up a steep winding path while Jenna followed, glancing behind to check that she was not being trailed by a Land Wurm. She had a feeling that Simon would not rush to her rescue if she was.

Suddenly the path came to an unexpected end at a sheer rock face.

"Home sweet home," said Simon with a wry grimace. Jenna stared at him, wondering if Simon had perhaps lost his mind. It would explain a lot.

"*Open to you commands, Master your, Nomis,*" muttered Simon. Jenna listened carefully to what he said and shivered— it was, she knew with a feeling of horror, a Reverse

Incantation. She took a step back, unwilling to be close to any Darke Magyk.

Silently, part of the rock face Transformed into a massive round iron plug, which swung outwards and upwards to open for its Master. Jenna glanced behind her; it briefly crossed her mind to turn and run, but the sight of the dark and lonely valley and the sound of the wind whining across the hilltops was not appealing. Then, as she glanced up, Jenna saw something that made her heart jump into her mouth—from a dark, perfectly round hole halfway up a nearby overhang, she thought she caught sight of a pair of pale red Land Wurm eyes staring out at her.

"Well, are you coming in or not?" asked Simon, jangling Thunder's bridle impatiently.

It was a choice between the Land Wurm and Simon—Simon won, but only just. Jenna took a deep breath and followed him and Thunder into the rock face.

✢ 17 ✢
THE BURROW

The iron door clanged shut behind them and they were plunged into total darkness. Jenna tried to keep calm and told herself what Silas had always said to her when she was afraid of the dark—*remember, though you can see nothing, no* Thing *can see you.*

As Jenna was reciting this to herself under her breath, Simon drew something from his pocket and cupped it in his hands. Then he breathed on it, muttering a few words that Jenna could not make out, and his hands began to glow with an eerie green light.

"Home, Sleuth," said Simon, throwing the object to the ground. A glowing ball of green light bounced away in front of them, illuminating the smooth round tunnel just enough for them to find their way.

"Follow me," Simon said sharply to Jenna, his voice echoing in the dark. "Don't bother to waste your time looking for a way out. There isn't one. And in case you're wondering where we are, we're in an old Burrow." Simon chuckled to himself. "But don't worry, little sister dear, the Land Wurm that lived here has gone."

"Land Wurm?" gasped Jenna.

"Yes. If you don't believe me just reach out and touch the sides of the Burrow. Silky smooth from all that lovely Wurm acid, and still beautifully slimy too. Nice, huh?"

Jenna could not help herself—she had to know if Simon was telling the truth—so she gingerly ran a finger along the rock. It was disgusting—icy smooth and covered with a glutinous slime that stuck to her finger. She fought down the urge to be sick and wiped her slime-covered finger on Lucy's cloak. It was almost impossible to get the slime off; it seemed to have an affinity with human skin.

Holding her finger away from her, Jenna followed Thunder's clattering, slipping hooves as Simon led him through the dark tube of the Land Wurm's Burrow. The Burrow felt, thought Jenna as she followed the serpentine bends, horribly like walking through the inside of the Wurm itself.

The Wurm had been a long one, but eventually they reached the end of the slime-lined tube, and Thunder stumbled into a huge round cavern.

"This is the Wurm Chamber, where the Wurm slept in the day and hibernated in the winter," said Simon, catching sight of Jenna's horrified look in the green light of the ball. He continued, enjoying Jenna's expression too much to stop. "If you look at the walls you can see the different-sized coils of the Wurm etched into them. All perfectly smooth from the acid of course." Simon lovingly stroked the side of the cavern, and Jenna noticed that he didn't seem to mind the Wurm slime at all.

"You see, the Wurm needs somewhere to turn around so that she can go out of the Burrow facing the right way. Just so that she doesn't miss a tasty morsel like you walking past. She sleeps here until nightfall and then goes out hunting. Just think of all those lovely Wurms who were curled up in their Burrows while we were riding through the quarries this afternoon."

Jenna shuddered, despite trying not to.

"And over here we have Thunder's stable, don't we, boy?" Simon patted his horse affectionately and led him across the Wurm Chamber to an area covered in straw, with a manger attached to the wall and a drinking trough hewn from the rock, which was fed by a dripping spring just above it.

Simon picked up the green ball and placed it on a ledge in the wall so that the light shone down on the horse and turned him an eerie greenish-black. "Make yourself at home, Sis," he said, "while I settle Thunder down for the night." He threw Jenna a small rug from one of the saddlebags.

"Is—is this where you *live*?" asked Jenna. She put the rug down on the cavern floor as far away from Simon as she could get and sat down, trying her best to avoid touching any Wurm slime.

"You think I live *here*, in this dump? What do you take me for—some kind of loser, living like a tramp?" snapped Simon, his suddenly angry voice echoing through the Wurm Chamber.

"N-no," stammered Jenna.

Simon glared at her coldly and then, to Jenna's relief, went back to tending his horse, which seemed to calm him down. Jenna watched him take the bridle and the heavy saddle off Thunder and hang them up, and then he rubbed the horse down and covered him with a blanket. Once Thunder was settled, Simon turned his attention back to Jenna and strode over to her.

"This, let me tell you," he said, staring down at her, "is just the *beginning* of my domain. You have no idea just how much I control. *No idea at all.*" Jenna stared at Simon and saw the same mad glint in his eye that he had had when she had turned to look at him in Cutpurse Cut.

"Get up," Simon said roughly. "It's time you saw just how powerful your dear brother really is."

Jenna hung back. "No. No, thank you, Simon. I'm really tired."

"You don't think I would let my honoured guest sleep in the stable, do you?" Simon grabbed her arm and pulled her up from the rug.

"Come!" he yelled to the green ball. Sleuth jumped off its ledge and bounced around Simon's feet like an eager puppy. Simon kicked it and sent it flying down the narrow passage that led out of the Wurm Chamber. Then Simon propelled

Jenna along in front of him, pushing her roughly down the tunnel.

Jenna stumbled along, slipping on the loose shale that covered the ground, until they reached the foot of some steep steps cut into the slate.

"Up!" Simon snapped. Sleuth bounced on to the first step and started its climb. Simon gave Jenna a shove. "You too. Go on."

Jenna started up the steps. A thick rope was fixed to the wall and she clung to it as she wearily climbed up, and up, and up, following the never-tiring ball. Simon was close behind her and she could hear his breath coming faster as they climbed higher. Soon the air became fresher and Jenna's spirits lifted a little as she realised that they were going up towards the outside world again. At last Sleuth reached the top step. Simon grabbed Jenna's shoulder.

"Wait here," he told her. He kicked the ball away and strode through a tall archway, disappearing into the darkness. Jenna stood at the top of the steps, trembling with cold and tiredness, and drew the cloak around her. She stared into the gloom but could make out nothing at all, though she could feel a few stray raindrops hitting her face. Jenna stuck out her tongue to catch them and taste the fresh air.

Simon was back a few minutes later with a Glo Lamp—a long glass tube stuffed full of writhing Glo Grubs that he had hastily scooped out of the grub barrel and poured into the tube. Fresh out of the barrel, the Glo Grubs glowed brightly.

Simon beckoned Jenna through the archway but she hung back. "You can stay out there all night if you want," he told her, "but I wouldn't advise it. There's a Magog Chamber at the bottom of the steps. Didn't you notice?"

Jenna remembered Magogs from the time she had met them on board DomDaniel's ship. Reluctantly she decided that, yet again, Simon was the better of two evils.

Jenna followed Simon through the archway.

✢✢ 18 ✢✢
THE CAMERA OBSCURA

W elcome to the
Observatory—
my place," Simon said, for
a moment letting himself
slip into the role of the
older brother showing
off to his sister. "Come
inside and take a look."

Jenna stepped through
the archway and a
terrible feeling of
dread came
over her.
She stared into the
gloom; the place

felt chill and eerie. Jenna knew that there was something
Darke in the air. Despite the best efforts of the Glo Grubs,
Jenna could make out very little apart from a huge white circle, which glowed like the moon and seemed to float above the
floor. Simon pushed her towards the circle, but Jenna resisted.

"Oh, come on," said Simon, propelling Jenna forward and
confusing her by sounding like his old self for a moment.
"You'll like this, all kids do."

"I'm not a kid," said Jenna. "I'm—"

"Yeah, yeah, I know. You're Miss Princess high and mighty.
Well, you'll like it anyway. Whatever you are. I'll uncover the
lens and then you'll see it—my Camera Obscura."

A chill shot through Jenna. Where had she heard those
words before? Surely that horrible boy—DomDaniel's
Apprentice—had boasted about having a Camera Obscura? A
strange noise came from far above Jenna's head; she glanced
up and could just about make out a tall domed roof with a long
wooden pole hanging down from something in the middle.
What *was* it?

Suddenly Simon snapped, "Stop daydreaming and look at
the dish."

Jenna looked down at the huge white circle before her, and
to her amazement she could see a finely detailed picture of the

ravine she had just travelled through.

"Good, huh?" Simon smirked. "Better than all that witchy rubbish old Zelda did. This, little sister, is the *real* world."

Jenna knew he was talking about the night the Heaps had all stood on a rickety bridge and seen themselves reflected in the light of a full moon, while Aunt Zelda, a White Witch, had asked the moon to show them the family of a small boy soldier, Boy 412. Jenna decided it was wiser to say nothing.

Simon took hold of the pole, and he began to walk slowly around the white dish. The pole moved with him, and far above their heads a thin creaking noise began as the lens that focused the scene on to the white dish of the Camera Obscura began to turn through a full circle. As it turned, the scene before them changed, and despite herself, Jenna was entranced. She had never seen anything like it before; the picture was bright and intricately detailed—but strangely silent.

"So you see," Simon said, moving very slowly to allow Jenna to take in the changing scene before her, "you can have no secrets from me. I can see *everything*. I can see the Castle, I can see your precious Palace and I can even see mad Marcia in the Wizard Tower with that upstart Apprentice who thinks he's my brother. I see it all."

Jenna stared at the scene. It was beautiful, but everything

was very small and far away. She didn't really understand how Simon *could* see everything.

In the distance, beyond the Badlands and the Farmlands, she saw the Castle outlined against the setting sun. As she stared at the image, she saw seagulls flying silently across the sky and boats moving slowly up the river. Jenna could just about pick out the Palace by its wide green lawns stretching to the river—and all at once she felt a terrible longing to be home.

"Want to have a closer look?" asked Simon with a sneer. "Want to see how much they're missing you?"

Jenna did not answer, but Simon opened a drawer in the platform under the dish and took out a large brass magnifying glass. He held it above the dish, clicked his fingers and muttered, *"Magnify do descry we that all . . ."*

Suddenly everything on the white dish jumped in size.

"You see," said Simon, "I see everything clearly now. The Chief Hermetic Scribe at the Manuscriptorium had it. He collects Reverse memorabilia. Reckons that this Enlarging Glass was owned by the first Darke Wizard. D'you know who that was, little sister? Have they taught you that in your Princess history lessons yet?"

Jenna did not respond. She had recently developed Septimus's dislike of even hearing the Reverse side mentioned.

Septimus had a theory that even by talking about it you could invite it in.

"Well, I'll tell you anyway," said Simon. "It was none other than Hotep-Ra. The very first ExtraOrdinary Wizard. The one who brought your precious Dragon Boat here. Don't look so surprised. So you see, we—the Reverse side—are the true inheritors of the Castle. And don't go thinking you'll be seeing your precious Dragon Boat again, either. Because you *won't*."

Simon chuckled, pleased with the effect he was having on Jenna, who looked white. She refused to meet Simon's eyes and was resolutely staring at the scene on the dish.

Simon followed her gaze and turned his attention back to the Camera Obscura. Then, as though he had thrown a switch, he suddenly became the older brother again.

"Good, isn't it?" he said, waving the Enlarging Glass over the dish, seeking out scenes and making them leap in fine detail. "Now, here we have the Forest . . . ah, there's a boat tied up on the beach where Sam fishes. I miss Sam . . . not much else to see in the Forest. Too dense. Although at night I can sometimes see the wolverines' eyes . . . Now let's go up the river to the Castle . . . here's old Jannit's boatyard . . . now where's my little brother Nicko? He came back today with Rupert. Did you know that, Jenna? No, I didn't think so. But

I did. I saw them coming up the river before I left. And . . . ah, yes, there's the North Gate and that idiot Gringe arguing with that imbecile son of his . . . now where's my Lucy? There she is, sitting by the Moat. Waiting. But she'll wait for me a little longer. Now there's the Wizard Tower. Look at that window there—there's Marcia in her study and her Shadow keeping her company as all good Shadows should. See how he watches her every move? Now let's go somewhere you know well, shall we? Here we are . . . the Palace. Home sweet home, eh? If I am not mistaken, there are my dear misguided parents up on the roof. Are they looking at the sunset do you suppose, or are they wondering when their son and heir is going to bring back their little cuckoo?"

"Shut up, Simon!" yelled Jenna. "I hate you, I *hate* you!"

She hurled herself away from the images of Silas and Sarah and raced towards the steps. But Simon was faster. In a moment he had grabbed her and held her prisoner again. But not before Jenna had seen something hidden in the shadows that she really wished she hadn't—a bleached white skull grinning at her from the seat of an ornate wooden throne.

"I think you have met before," Simon said with a smile. "Let me introduce you to the head of my Master, DomDaniel."

✛ 19 ✛
CHOCOLATE

Jenna couldn't sleep. Not because of the icy chill of the cell air, or because of the hard little bed, the thin scratchy blanket or because her clothes felt cold and damp. She could not sleep because of the thought of the skull staring empty-eyed at her door. Whenever she closed her eyes an image of the grinning white skull drifted by and woke her with a start.

Jenna gave up trying to sleep. She wrapped herself in Lucy's cloak, her mind racing as she went over the events of the day. Until she had seen the skull, Jenna had found it hard to believe that Simon meant her any harm. In her mind he was still her eldest brother, the reliable one who always helped her out when she was in trouble and showed her how to do her homework. But that was before Simon had picked up the skull, cradled it in his arms and told her how he had rescued DomDaniel's skeleton from the Marram Marshes on the night of the Apprentice Supper and that he was now DomDaniel's Apprentice. "How about *that*, little Miss Princess? And unlike his last useless Apprentice, I am carrying out his every wish to the letter. And his very particular wish was to have the Castle free of any interfering royalty, such as yourself. He considers the power of the Queen an intolerable imposition on any ExtraOrdinary Wizard. As do I. So, if we want some proper Magyk back in the Castle—not just Marcia's dinky little spells—then *someone* has to go." Simon had looked at her with a horrible coldness in his eyes, which stayed with her still.

Jenna sat on the edge of the bed, thinking. She wondered why Simon hadn't already got rid of her. He could have easily pushed her off the ravine into the river or just left her out for the Land Wurms. But Jenna already knew the answer. Whatever Simon might have said, he had still wanted to show off to his little sister. But he had done that now, and tomorrow it would be a different story. Maybe tomorrow he *would* leave her out for the Land Wurms—or the Magogs.

Jenna shivered. She heard a low noise drifting through the wall and her heart leaped into her mouth. It was a strange, regular, snorting noise, and she knew what it was—it was the *skull*. The noise got louder and louder; Jenna pressed her hands over her ears to blot out the awful sound, and then suddenly she realised what it really was: Simon was snoring. Which meant that Simon was asleep and she was awake. She could try and escape—she *must* try and escape.

Jenna tried the iron door. It was bolted but there was a small gap between the door and the wall, and Jenna wondered if she could push something through the gap and somehow undo the bolts. She looked around the cell but Simon had not been so considerate as to leave her a hacksaw. Jenna put her hands in her pockets, wondering if she had anything on her that could help. Septimus would have the very thing, she thought. He always carried his Young Army knife, which had about a hundred and one different uses, mostly involving horses' hooves. She missed him.

The thought of Septimus made Jenna remember the chocolate Charm he had given her that morning. Where had she put it? There it was, damp and sticky, stuck at the bottom of her tunic pocket. She pulled out the Charm, held it in her palm and squinted at the inscription:

Take me, shake me,
and I will make thee:
Quetzalcoatl's Tchocolatl.

Well, she thought, it was worth a try.

Jenna tried to remember what Septimus had said when he had told her how to use the Charm. She cupped both of her hands together and shook the Charm up and down as hard as she could to Activate it. As she did so, she whispered the words written in the small brown square and concentrated all her thoughts on what she wanted. Sure enough, the Charm began to work. It grew warm and smooth in her cupped hands, as though it were a real piece of chocolate. Then, just as Septimus had said it would, it began to buzz like a small fly trapped in her grasp. Jenna waited until the Charm was almost too hot to hold, and then quickly placed it on the object she wanted to turn into chocolate—the door of the cell.

Jenna did not really believe that Septimus's Charm could turn a thick iron door into chocolate. But, as she pushed the Charm against the door, to her amazement she felt the hard pitted metal change into a smooth surface that was cool, rather than icy cold, to the touch. Something else had changed too. Jenna sniffed the air—the cell was filled with the faint smell of cocoa. Hesitantly, Jenna took the Charm off the cell door. The Charm was cool now; she slipped it back into her pocket and gazed at the door. At first Jenna thought it seemed much the same as it had before, except now, as she looked more closely, she could see that the rusty hinges and even the flap over the keyhole were beautifully moulded in chocolate. Never in her life had Jenna seen so much chocolate and, unfortunately, never had she felt less like eating it.

Jenna soon discovered that a massive slab of three-inch-thick chocolate, chilled hard on a cold night, is not easy to shift. She pushed as hard as she could against it but the slab stayed as firm as if it were still iron. She decided to start scraping some shavings off the door to make it thinner, but it was hard work and she thought it would take all night.

Jenna sat down disconsolately on the edge of the bed and ate some of the shavings—it was extremely good chocolate, even better than the Choc Chunks from the sweetshop at the end of Wizard Way—while she wondered what to do. After a few minutes the chocolate began to help her think more clearly, and Jenna realised that she needed to find something

sharp to help cut a hole in the door. Simon had made sure that
there was nothing sharp in the cell, but, as Jenna hunted
around, she soon discovered that even Simon did not think of
everything. He had forgotten about the bedsprings.

Jenna threw the thin mattress off the bed and quickly
unwound one of the looser bedsprings until she held a sharp,
pointed piece of metal in her hand. Then she set to work,
scraping away a hole in the door big enough to squeeze
through, while, to her relief, Simon's snores carried on reverberating through the walls.

An hour later, Jenna's bedspring had cut a large rectangle at
the bottom of the door. All she had to do was give it a push
and hope that it did not fall over with too loud a thud.
Carefully, Jenna pushed against one edge of the rectangle and
to her delight, it moved easily. Very quietly, Jenna laid the
thick slab of chocolate on the floor, and, in case she got hungry later, she broke off the keyhole cover and stuffed it into
her pocket. Then she squeezed through the opening, stood up
and wiped her chocolatey palms on her tunic.

Simon was still snoring loudly; the snores echoed around
the circular chamber and were strangely comforting, for at
least they were human. Jenna tiptoed past the huge white dish

of the Camera Obscura, glancing down for a last look at the strangely compelling scene outside, and noticed that Simon had left the Enlarging Glass lying on the dish. Jenna picked up the Glass and stuffed it into her tunic pocket. Now Simon would not find it so easy to see where she had gone.

Next, Jenna found the Glo Grub Tub. Simon had not replaced the barrel lid properly and a bright yellow light shone from the gap. The Glo Grub Tub was a large wooden barrel, full almost to the brim with hundreds of thousands of tiny Glo Grubs wriggling around. Jenna took a Glo Lamp from a neat line of empty lamps placed next to the barrel, picked up the scoop and filled the glass tube with squirming Glo Grubs. Jenna did not like using Glo Lamps, but she had no choice. Sarah Heap refused to use them because once the grubs were put in a lamp they did not live longer than a few hours. It was, Sarah said, a terrible thing to kill so many creatures just for a person's own convenience. Sarah used good old-fashioned candles.

"I'm sorry, grubs," Jenna whispered as she scooped them up.

Jenna filled the lamp and left the lid of the Glo Grub Tub open to give the grubs a chance to escape. She raised the lamp and, for the first time, she really saw the place that Simon Heap had made his own.

The Observatory was a huge round chamber. The walls, roughly hewn out of the solid slate mountain, sloped upwards and inwards until they met at the lens for the Camera Obscura. A thick milky slab of glass set into the roof let in the moonlight, and Jenna realised that most of the Observatory was below ground. Silently, she crept past the metal Thunderflash Chamber and past neatly ordered shelves containing piles of Darke books, Reverse Conjurations, Hexes and Curses. She averted her eyes from a sinister-looking collection of flasks in which she could see misshapen creatures dimly floating in a yellow liquid. Every so often a bubble of gas rose from the bottles and filled the air with a foul smell. In a distant corner a small glass-fronted cupboard glowed with a dull blue light. It was fastened with an impressive array of bolts. Inside, coiled up, lay a small black snake.

Simon Heap's snores reverberated through a large wooden door, which he had painted purple and covered with Darke symbols. Jenna passed the door and as she did so she trod on Sleuth. Somehow Jenna managed to change her scream into a strangled squeak, but Simon's snores stopped. Jenna froze, holding her breath. Was he awake? Should she run while she had the chance? Would he hear her footsteps? What should she do? And then, to her horror, Sleuth began bouncing on the spot. With each bounce a soft thud echoed around the Observatory. In a flash, Jenna scooped up the ball and a few seconds later Sleuth had been pushed deep into the contents of the Glo Grub Tub. Jenna closed the lid, snapped the lock shut and apologised to the grubs for the second time that night.

Muttering the Protection Spell that Marcia had taught her some time ago, Jenna crept past the ever-watchful skull, wondering what Simon had done with the other bones. As she went by she was sure that deep inside the skull a pair of eyes was watching her. She dared not look.

Once past the skull, Jenna ran. She tore through the archway and raced down the steep steps as fast as she could, as though DomDaniel himself were chasing her. Every now and then she glanced behind just to make sure that he wasn't.

When she reached the foot of the steps, Jenna stopped and listened for footsteps. There were none. Her spirits lifting a little, she took a step forward. Her feet shot out from underneath her and she came crashing to the ground. The Glo Lamp leaped out of her hand, scattering Glo Grubs across the ground. Jenna scrambled back to her feet and brushed off her tunic. Magog slime. A shudder of nausea passed through her, followed by a feeling of panic. Quickly she gathered up as many Glo Grubs as she could find, and, holding them in her cupped hand, she moved fast and silently along the tunnel towards Thunder's stable.

Jenna reached the Wurm Chamber safely, with no telltale swish of a Magog behind her. Thunder was standing quietly at his manger, chewing on the hay that Simon had left for him. He looked up as Jenna emerged from the tunnel.

"Hello, Thunder," she whispered. Thunder glanced at Jenna for a moment and then turned his attention back to the hay.

Good, thought Jenna, he remembers me. She walked slowly to the horse and patted his mane. It seemed cruel to take him out again into the cold night air, but she had no choice. She took the bridle off its hook and very gently approached Thunder. The horse didn't seem keen; he shook his head and snorted noisily.

"Shh," whispered Jenna. "Shh, Thunder. It's all right. It is." She patted his nose gently and then reached into her tunic pocket for the chocolate keyhole cover and offered it to him in her outstretched palm. Thunder nibbled at it delicately and looked at Jenna with a faintly surprised air. Jenna was quite sure that Simon never gave his horse chocolate. And quite right too; she never gave her horse chocolate either, but sometimes bribery was the only option.

With the hope of more chocolate, Thunder allowed Jenna to put his bridle on and saddle him up again. Jenna was just about to lead the horse out when she thought of something. She scooped up a handful of pebbles from the ground and, using the Charm again, she turned them into chocolate. Then Jenna stuffed most of the chocolate pebbles into her pocket, keeping one to wave under Thunder's twitching nose.

"Come on, Thunder," she coaxed softly, "come on, boy, let's go."

✢ 20 ✢
LAND WURM

Open to you commands, *Master your, Nomis.*" Jenna forced the words from her mouth. She had never uttered a Reverse Incantation before and hoped she never would have to again, but now she had no choice. The Wurm Burrow was sealed with a massive plug of immovable iron, and Jenna knew that if she turned *that* into chocolate there was no way she would be free by morning. She held her breath, hoping that she had remembered the Incantation correctly.

She had. To her relief, the thick iron plug swung silently outwards, and the dim moonlight of an old moon filtered into the Wurm Burrow, along with a gust of wind and a few drops of rain.

"Come on, Thunder, come on, boy," whispered Jenna, encouraging the reluctant horse out into the night with a chocolate pebble. The dark quarry was not a pleasant prospect; a mournful wind was howling and sweeping down the ravine, bringing with it the beginnings of a cold rain. Jenna pulled Lucy's cloak around her, shivering as the chill night air hit them. Then she led Thunder down the steep path from the Burrow on to the track that ran along the side of the ravine.

"Hold still, hold still, Thunder," she whispered, as the horse looked about nervously and flicked his ears, listening to the night sounds. Jenna swung herself up into the saddle, wondering how Thunder would take to a new rider. The horse did not object, maybe because he had already become used to Jenna during the long day's ride. When Jenna said, "Walk on, Thunder, walk on," and gently pressed her heels against the horse's flanks, Thunder moved off at a leisurely pace, heading back down the track that he had struggled up only a few hours before.

Jenna felt quite at ease with the huge horse. Although he belonged to Simon, Thunder seemed a good-natured animal, and he walked surefooted along the track while Jenna sat bolt upright, scanning the sheer rock face for any signs of movement. The sooner they were through the ravine, she thought—encouraging Thunder into a brisk trot—the better.

As they rounded the first bend, Thunder came to a sudden halt. A landslide blocked their path. "Oh, no," gasped Jenna.

There was no way through. A huge pile of jagged boulders and massive slabs of slate had fallen across their path. To their right was a sheer rock face and to their left, at the bottom of the ravine, was the river—flowing fast and dangerous.

They would have to go back.

Jenna tried to coax Thunder to turn around but the horse refused to move. He shook his head and his bridle jingled noisily.

"Shh, Thunder," soothed Jenna. "Come on, around you go." But Thunder would not budge. Heart in her mouth, Jenna slipped off the horse and led him round with the help of another chocolate pebble. Then she was straight back in the saddle again and, with a heavy heart, retracing their steps back up the track, back towards the Burrow.

It was tough going. Thunder was now walking into the

teeth of the wind, but he was happy that he was heading for home. When they reached the small path that led to the Burrow, Thunder stopped, expecting Jenna to get off and lead him back to his warm stable.

"No, Thunder, you're *not* going home. Walk on." Thunder shook his head, jingling his bridle again.

"Shh. *Please*, Thunder. Walk *on*," Jenna whispered as loudly as she dared, terrified that somehow Simon would hear her. She gave the horse a determined kick and Thunder very reluctantly moved off. Jenna glanced behind them, half expecting to see Simon emerge from the Burrow, but the iron plug still gaped open and showed nothing but a dark, empty space.

After they had passed the Burrow the track levelled out, which made the going easier for Thunder, but the wind began to strengthen and, with it, the rain became heavier. Dark clouds blew in and a sheet of lightning silently lit the jagged tops of the ravine. A few moments later the rumble of thunder reached them.

Jenna and Thunder pressed on. The moonlight dimmed and the quarry became dark, lit only by the lightning playing across the sky. The wind howled down the ravine, blowing stinging rain into their faces. Both Jenna and Thunder half closed their eyes and kept their gaze fixed firmly on the track—until a movement high in the rocks ahead caught Jenna's eye. She looked up, hoping that it was just a scudding cloud that had caught her attention. But it was something much more substantial than a cloud.

It was the blunt grey head of a Land Wurm.

A Land Wurm takes a long time to come out of its Burrow, and Jenna had caught sight of the Wurm as it first poked its head into the night air. She knew, from travellers' tales that Silas used to tell, that it was not the Wurm's head that was the dangerous part; it was its tail. The tail of a Land Wurm was fast and deadly; when a Land Wurm had you in its sights it would flick its tail like a lasso and drop it over your head. Then it would coil the tail around and crush you. Very, very slowly. Although sometimes, Silas had told her, if the Land Wurm was not particularly hungry, it would carry you back into the Wurm Chamber and store you for a while, still alive, in order to keep you fresh. A Land Wurm preferred fresh meat, still warm.

Jenna remembered an occasional visitor to the Heap rooms who, among the younger Heaps, was known as Dribbly Dan. Dribbly Dan had a wild look in his eyes and had scared the younger ones, but Silas had told them to be nice to him. Dan had, according to Silas, been a completely dribble-free quarry worker until he was taken by a Land Wurm and kept in the Wurm Chamber for three weeks. He had survived by licking Wurm slime and eating rats. He had finally managed to escape one night when the Wurm had been tempted out by a large flock of sheep—and an inexperienced shepherd—that had wandered into the quarry. But Dan had never been the same after his three weeks in the Wurm Chamber.

There was no way that Jenna wanted to end up like Dribbly Dan—or worse. She looked up at the Wurm, trying to judge whether to speed up and go past it or whether to stop and turn back yet again. But Jenna knew that if she turned back she would be caught between the Land Wurm and the landslide, and between *them* would be Simon's Burrow with Simon quite probably awake by now and searching for her. She had no choice—she had to get past the Wurm before its tail was free of the Burrow.

"Gee up, Thunder," Jenna said in a low, urgent voice, giving the horse a nudge with her heels, but Thunder just kept up his slow trudge through the wind and the rain. Jenna glanced at the Wurm again. Its Burrow was high above them, and still quite distant, almost at the top of the old quarry workings that rose from the track. The Wurm's head was now well out of the Burrow, and Jenna saw that its dim red eyes had locked on to her and Thunder.

"Get *on*, Thunder," Jenna yelled in the horse's ear, giving him a hard kick at the same time. "Or do you want to be eaten by a Land Wurm?" She flicked Thunder with the reins, and suddenly Thunder put his ears back and took off like a rocket, galloping along the track as if to show Jenna that if she wanted fast, then *fast* was exactly what she was going to get.

As they galloped towards the Land Wurm, Jenna could tell that the creature had seen them coming; it was pouring out of its Burrow at full speed, like a thick, never-ending stream of grey sludge.

"Go, Thunder, *go!*" Jenna screamed urgently above the howl of the wind and the rain as the horse pounded along the track, taking them ever closer to the Wurm. Still the Wurm came streaming out, slipping down the rock face so fast that Jenna suddenly realised she could not be sure that Thunder would get past the Wurm before it reached the track. She crouched down on the horse like a jockey, keeping the wind resistance low and talking in his ear, encouraging him on. "*Go, Thunder, go, boy . . . go!*"

And Thunder went, galloping at full tilt now, as if he too knew that both their lives depended on him. As the Wurm reached the bottom of the cliff, and Thunder was closing the gap, Jenna looked up to see if the tail was free of the Burrow. There was no sign of it yet, but she knew that any moment it could come shooting out. She turned her attention to the path just in time to see the Wurm's head reach the track.

"Go, Thunder," she yelled, and then, as the Wurm slipped across the track and barred their way, Jenna screamed, "*Jump, Thunder!*"

Thunder jumped. The powerful horse sailed into the air and took them high above the great grey monstrosity that slithered below them. And as Thunder landed on the other side of the Wurm and galloped onwards, the Wurm's tail whipped out of the Burrow and shot through the air with a *crack*.

Jenna felt the wind whistle and heard a bang as the tip of the tail sliced the top off the rock behind them. She could not stop herself from looking back—the tail had missed them by no more than a few feet.

The weak red eyes of the Land Wurm followed its prey along the track and the tail gathered for another strike, whirling itself high into the air like a huge lasso. But, as it smashed down on to the track for the second time, Thunder cantered around a tall rocky outcrop, and the Wurm lost sight of them.

Thump! Something landed behind Jenna.

Jenna wheeled around in the saddle, ready to fight the tail with all the strength she possessed—but there was nothing there. All she could see was the steep slate outcrop rapidly disappearing into the night as Thunder galloped on.

"Phew," said a small, slightly querulous voice behind her. "You cut that . . . a bit fine. Nearly gave me . . . a heart attack . . . that did."

"Wh-who's that?" asked Jenna, almost more scared of the strange little voice than she had been of the Land Wurm.

"It's me—*Stanley*. Don't you remember me?" The voice sounded somewhat aggrieved. Jenna peered into the darkness again—there *was* something there. It was a rat. A small brown rat lay sprawled across the horse's back, desperately clinging to the saddle.

"Could you just . . . stop for a mo while I . . . sort myself out?" the rat asked, bouncing around on Thunder's back as the horse galloped into the night. "I think I've . . . landed on my sandwiches."

Jenna stared at the rat.

"Just slow . . . down . . . a bit," he pleaded.

"Whoa, Thunder," said Jenna, reining the horse in. "Slow down, boy." Thunder slowed to a trot.

"Ta. That's better." Still clinging tightly to the saddle, the rat hauled himself to a sitting position. "I'm not a natural horse rat," he said, "though I suppose they're better than donkeys. Don't like donkeys. Or their owners. Mad as snakes the lot of them. Don't get me wrong—I don't mean that about horses. Or their owners. Perfectly sane. Most of 'em at any rate, although I must say I have known some that—"

Suddenly Jenna remembered who the rat was. "Message Rat!" she gasped. "You're the Message Rat. The one we rescued from Mad Jack and his donkey."

"Got it in one," grinned the rat. "Spot on. But yours truly is no longer a Message Rat—had a bit of an argy-bargy with the Rat Office in the bad old days. Ended up in a cage under the floor for weeks. Not nice. Not fun. Got rescued and retrained with the"—the rat stopped and looked around as if to check whether anyone else might be listening—"Secret Rat Service," he whispered.

"The what?" asked Jenna.

The rat tapped the side of his nose knowingly. "Very hush-hush—know what I mean? Least said, soonest mended and all that."

"Oh," said Jenna, who did not have the faintest idea what the rat meant but did not want to get into a conversation about it just then. "Yes, of course."

"Best thing I ever did," said the rat. "Just finished my training last week in fact. And then, blow me down, my first mission is for the ExtraOrdinary. Quite a coup, I can tell you. It impressed the lads on the course."

"Oh, that's nice," said Jenna. "So what's this mission, then?"

"Find and return. Priority number one."

"Ah. So who do you have to find and return?"

"You," said Stanley with a grin.

⊹ 21 ⊹
THE SHEEPLANDS

D*awn was breaking when Thunder's* hooves slipped and slid around the last bend of a shale-covered footpath, and Jenna saw to her delight that at long last they had reached the end of the Badlands. Stanley saw nothing. The rat was clinging to the edge of the saddle with his eyes tightly closed, convinced that any minute now all three of them would be plunging over the edge of the path to the rocks below.

Jenna stopped for a moment and gazed out across the wide flat fields of the Sheeplands, which were spread out before them. It was beautiful, and it reminded her of the first morning she had woken up at Aunt Zelda's and sat on the doorstep watching and listening to the Marsh. Far away on the horizon a brilliant band of pink clouds showed where the sun was rising, while the fields themselves were still shrouded with the soft grey light of early dawn. Pockets of mist lay over the water channels and the marshy parts of the fields, and a peaceful silence filled the air.

"We've done it, Thunder," Jenna said with a laugh, patting the horse's neck. "We've done it, boy."

The horse shook his head and snorted as he breathed in the salty air that was blowing in from the sea on the other side of the Sheeplands. Jenna led Thunder down on to a wide grassy track and then let the horse loose to graze on the springy grass, while Stanley lay sprawled across the saddle, snoring loudly, having at last fallen into an exhausted sleep.

Jenna sat on the edge of the track and leaned back against the foot of the slate cliff. She felt ravenous. She rummaged through Simon's saddlebag and found a stale loaf, a small box of dried fruits and a rather battered and bruised apple. Jenna ate the lot and washed it down with a drink from an ice-cold spring that bubbled at the base of the cliff. Then she sat and gazed at the mist, which was slowly disappearing to reveal the round woolly shapes of grazing sheep dotted across the pastures.

The peaceful silence, broken only by the steady munching of the horse and the occasional cry of a lone marsh bird, made Jenna feel very drowsy. She tried to fight the urge to fall asleep, but it was impossible. A few moments later, she was curled up in Lucy's cloak, deep in a dreamless sleep.

At the very moment Jenna fell asleep, Simon awoke. He sat up in his bed, aching all over and feeling irritable. He was not sure why. And then he remembered. Jenna. He had snatched Jenna. He had *done* it—done what had been asked of him. His Master, Simon thought as he got out of bed, would be pleased. But Simon had an uneasy feeling in the pit of his stomach that would not go away. For now he had the second part of his task to fulfill. He had to take Jenna down to the Magog lair. He wandered into the Observatory and noticed that Sleuth was not at its post guarding his bedroom door.

"Sleuth!" Simon yelled angrily, expecting the ball to come

bouncing over to him. *"Sleuth!"* There was no response. Feeling even more irritable, Simon padded across the cold and clammy slate in his bare feet to fix a glass of Nekawa to settle his nerves. Carefully, he poured a muddy brown liquid with tendrils of floating mould into a tall glass, cracked a raw egg into it and gulped it down. It tasted foul.

Feeling more awake, Simon looked around the slate chamber to see where Sleuth had gone. Sleuth would regret leaving its post when Simon found it, he'd make sure of that—

"What the—*what's going on?*" Simon raced over to the cell door. The Jenna-sized slab of chocolate lay flat on the floor, and Simon did not need to open the cell to know that he would not find Jenna inside. But he opened it anyway, angrily throwing the door back so that it hit the wall with a violent bang and promptly shattered into thousands of pieces of the very best chocolate.

Simon swore. All his hopes vanished at the sight of the empty cell. He threw himself to the floor and had a few minutes of what Sarah Heap used to call "tantrum time" before he finally got up from the floor and began to think again. Jenna couldn't have got far. He would send Sleuth after her with a Tag.

"Sleuth!" Simon yelled furiously at the top of his voice.

"Sleuth! If you don't come out right now you will be sorry. *Extremely* sorry!"

There was no response. Simon stood in the silent Observatory and smiled to himself. Now he knew what had happened: Jenna had taken Sleuth with her. The silly kid had thought that Sleuth was just a handy light. He'd find them both down in the Burrow. Simon's musings were interrupted by a strange sound coming from the Glo Grub Tub. He went over and found the lid was locked. That was odd—he could-n't remember locking the Tub; in fact he never bothered to lock the Glo Grubs—they were all too scared to even try to escape. So what had he done with the key? And what was that noise? Simon put his ear to the Tub and heard the unmistak-able sound of bouncing. *Bouncing?* Sleuth!

After giving up the search for the key, Simon took a crow-bar to the lid and levered it off. Sleuth shot out like a cork from a bottle, showering Simon with hundreds of sticky Glo Grubs.

"Right!" yelled Simon. "That's it! She's in for it now. Tag on Jenna, Sleuth. Go!" Simon hurled the sticky green ball across the Observatory and followed it as it bounced past the skull, through the archway and shot off on the long descent down the steps. Sleuth and Simon reached the bottom of the steps, skidded on the Magog slime and raced along the passage that led to the old Wurm Chamber.

"She'll be down here, Sleuth," Simon puffed as they neared the Wurm Chamber. "Down here, scared out of her wits. Or maybe she's done me a favour and found herself a nice Magog. Save me a lot of trouble that would, Sleuth. Hey—*careful*, you stupid ball." Simon ducked to avoid Sleuth as the ball suddenly bounced back at him. "Just get in there, will you?" he shouted. "This is no time to be playing games." The ball tried again but bounced back and hit Simon on the nose. Furious, Simon snatched up the ball and strode into the Wurm Chamber— straight into the thick slimy hide of a Land Wurm.

Simon recoiled in shock. What had happened? How on earth had the Land Wurm got in? And then a terrible thought struck Simon.

"My horse!" he screamed. "It's eaten my horse!"

Jenna woke with a start from a bad dream. She sat up awkwardly, feeling cold and damp, to find she was surrounded by a circle of curious sheep, lazily chewing the grass around her. Jenna stood and stretched. She had wasted enough time asleep; she and Thunder had to get moving and somehow Jenna had to get to Aunt Zelda's. She climbed into the saddle while Stanley snored on.

"Stanley," said Jenna, shaking the rat awake.

"Wherrr . . . ?" mumbled the rat, half opening his eyes and gazing blearily at Jenna.

"Stanley, I want you to take a message to Aunt Zelda. You know where she lives and—"

Stanley raised a paw in protest. "Let me stop you right there," he said. "Just so that we understand each other, I do not take messages any more. Absolutely, no way, do I perform the duties of a Message Rat. My license was revoked after that nasty business with the ExtraOrdinary, and I have positively no wish to venture into the Message Rat area of operations again. Ever. No, *sir*. I mean Madam."

"But it's MidSummer Day tomorrow, Stanley, and I—" protested Jenna.

"And, if you think I am going out on to those wretched Marshes again you are sadly mistaken. It was a miracle I survived the last journey what with the Marsh Python eyeing me up for supper and those vicious Brownies with their little teeth snap, snap, snapping at my feet, not to mention that moaning-minnie of a Marsh Moaner following me, wailing in my ear and driving me *crazy*. Ghastly place. Why a cultured young person like yourself wants to set foot in that pestilential pit again is beyond me. If you take my advice I'd—"

"So that's a 'no' then, is it?" Jenna sighed.

"Yes. I mean no. I mean *yes* it's a '*no*.'" The rat sat up in the saddle and looked around him. "It's nice here, isn't it?" he said. "Came here on holiday with my ma when I was a little lad. We had some relations who lived in the ditches that run out of the Marshes to the sea. Lovely sand dunes down on the beach and convenient for the Port if you hitched a ride on a donkey cart"—Stanley shivered—"or preferably a fast horse. We had some good times hanging out down at the Port when I was a teenager. Lots of rats there. You wouldn't believe the things that went on. I remember—"

"Stanley," said Jenna, an idea forming in her mind. "Does that mean you know the way to the Port?"

"Of course," said Stanley indignantly. "As a member of the Secret Rat Service, you can rely on me to get you anywhere. I am as good as a map. Better than a map, in fact. I have it all in my head, see"—the rat tapped the side of his head—"I can go anywhere, I can."

"Apart from the Marram Marshes," observed Jenna.

"Yes. Well. The Special Marsh Rats do that. More fool, them. Like I said, I am not setting foot in that noxious swamp ever again."

"Ah, well. Walk on," said Jenna, giving Thunder a gentle

nudge with her heels.

"Very well then," said Stanley, "if you feel like that about it." The rat jumped from the saddle and landed a little awkwardly on the grass.

Jenna stopped the horse.

"Stanley, what *are* you doing?" she asked.

"What you told me to do," said Stanley grumpily. "I'm walking."

Jenna laughed. "I was talking to the *horse*, silly. Get back up here."

"Oh. Thought you were cross I wouldn't take you through the Marshes."

"Don't be daft, Stanley. Just get back on the horse and show me the way to the Port. I can remember the way to Aunt Zelda's from there."

"You sure?"

"Yes. *Please*, Stanley."

Stanley took a running jump, leaped into the air and landed lightly behind Jenna.

It was a beautiful summer's morning. The Sheeplands stretched before them, and on the horizon in the far distance Jenna could see the thin, brilliant white line of the sea glinting as the early-morning sunlight glanced off the water.

A firm, gravelly track took Thunder, Jenna and Stanley across the pastures, leading them along invisible boundaries, past lambing pens and the occasional reed bed and over wide plank bridges that crossed the water channels running from the Marshes on their way to the sea. Jenna let the horse amble slowly along and stop whenever he wanted to snatch at a tasty-looking tuft of grass and munch on it as he went. As the heat of the sun began to burn off the last of the mist, which still hung over the water channels, Jenna felt the dampness in her clothes evaporate, and at last she began to feel warm.

But as the chill from the Badlands left her, Jenna started to think more clearly. And the first thing she thought about was Simon. What was he doing now? Anxiously, Jenna glanced behind her. The steep black rock of the slate quarries rose from the flat Sheeplands like a cliff from the sea; above it lay the low grey cloud, casting a deep shadow. The Badlands were still too close for Jenna's liking; she needed to put some distance between them.

"Gee up, Thunder," said Jenna, urging the horse into a brisk walk and resisting taking him into a trot. She knew Thunder must be tired and they still had a long day's ride to the Port ahead of them. Behind her the rat sat up perkily on the horse's back, hanging on to the saddle with one paw with the air of a seasoned rider. Jenna turned around again and checked the Badlands. Suddenly she had an uncomfortable feeling that her escape had been discovered.

✢ 2 2 ✢
CAMP HEAP

The next morning in the Forest found Nicko and Septimus standing at Grandpa Benji's feet. Or foot. The bright summer sun shone through their grandfather's leaves and cast a pale green light on the Forest floor. And on the chewed remains of Septimus's backpack.

"My whole kit—gone," Septimus complained. "They've eaten everything."

"Everything except for us," Nicko pointed out, "which is probably the most important thing."

Septimus was not listening. He was on his hands and knees examining the ground at the foot of the tree.

"I wouldn't run my hands through those leaves like that," said Nicko with a grimace.

"Why not? I'm looking for something."

"Use your head, Sep. Loads of wolverines. Hanging around waiting for supper. Getting excited. Eating Mint Blasts. So what do you *think* they do?"

"It must be here. They can't have eaten *that* . . . I dunno, Nik, what do they do?"

"Poo."

"Eurgh!" Septimus jumped to his feet.

"And then they hide it under the leaves."

"Eurgh, no!" Septimus wiped his hands on his tunic, stepped back and trod on what he was looking for. "Found it! It's here. Oh, *fantastic*."

"What?" asked Nicko, curious. "What's so important?"

Septimus held up the iridescent green rock that he had so carefully packed in his backpack.

"Oh," said Nicko, suddenly reminded of why they were in the middle of the Forest. "I see."

"Jenna gave it to me."

"I know. I remember."

They were both silent for a moment and Septimus stared intently at the rock. Then suddenly he burst out, "Oh, I hate wolverines! Look what they've done. They cracked it." Septimus cradled the rock in his hands and showed it to

Nicko. "Look," he said, "there." A small jagged crack ran across the widest part of the rock.

"Well, it could be worse, Sep," said Nicko. "It's not broken. I suppose one of the wolverines must have crunched it or something. I bet it didn't do its teeth much good."

"I hope not. I hope they all fell out," said Septimus as he put the rock into the pouch that hung from his Apprentice belt.

It took Septimus and Nicko a while to say goodbye to their grandfather, and many promises to bring the rest of the family to visit him, but at last they set off through the Forest in search of the boys' camp.

Sometime later, just as Septimus's ankle was beginning to throb painfully and he was wondering if they were lost again, they came across a wide path.

"I know where we are!" said Nicko triumphantly.

"Really?" There was some doubt in Septimus's tone.

"Really. Just follow me, Sep."

"Now when did I hear that before?" said Septimus.

"Don't be mean," said Nicko sheepishly. "Look—down there—can you see the camp?"

Nicko and Septimus were standing at the top of a small

incline. The path dropped away in front of them, winding between the trees and leading to a small clearing. A thin line of smoke rose slowly into the still, early-morning air, and, as Septimus watched, the gangly figure of one of his brothers stepped out from what looked like a large pile of leaves and stretched and yawned in the warm sun.

"Erik!" yelled Nicko. "Hey, Erik!"

The figure looked up, bleary eyed.

"C'mon, Sep," said Nicko, "time to meet the rest of us."

Ten minutes later, Septimus found himself sitting alone by the campfire pit. Almost as soon as Nicko had introduced him to Sam, Jo-Jo, Edd and Erik with the air of a magician pulling a rabbit from a hat, they had all disappeared, taking Nicko with them. They had told Septimus they were going to inspect the nets that Sam had laid out in the river to catch the fish coming in on the morning tide. And Septimus may as well make himself useful and stay and keep watch over the fire, which was kept burning night and day.

Septimus stared at the fire and wondered if all family reunions were like this. Although he had been very nervous about meeting the rest of his brothers, he had thought that they might have been pleased to see him; but the boys had just stared at him as though he were a frog in a jar. And then he had realised that they were not even staring at him but at his smart green cloak and tunic, and at his silver ExtraOrdinary Apprentice belt, which had glinted embarrassingly in the sun and made him feel as though he was showing off. He had quickly pulled his cloak around him to hide it, but then, Septimus thought glumly, that had made him look stupid—like he was bothered about how he looked. Or else it had made him look like a wimp who felt cold . . . or scared, or. . . . And then, as he had stood there wrapped in his cloak his brothers had, one by one, managed a grunt that Septimus had taken as a "hello," although it could just as easily have been "dillop." In fact, the more he thought about it, the more he was sure that was what they had said. Septimus put his head in his hands, thinking what a complete idiot his brothers must have thought he was.

As Septimus sat staring into the fire, wondering why he had let Nicko bring him here when he should be looking for Jenna, he was aware of someone joining him. He turned to see one of his brothers—but which one? Septimus had been too busy feeling embarrassed to be sure who was who.

"Hi," said the boy, poking at the fire with a stick.

"Hi," said Septimus, wishing he had a stick too.

"You the one that was dead then?" asked the brother.

"What?"

"Yeah. Dead. I remember Mum talking about you sometimes to Dad when she thought we weren't listening. You
were dead. But you weren't. Weird." The brother poked the
fire some more.

"Weird," agreed Septimus. He stole a sideways glance at
the boy. It wasn't Sam, that was for sure. Sam, who was not
much younger than Simon, was a man now, with a pale fuzz
on his face and a deep voice. And Edd and Erik, he remembered noticing, both wore their hair in long matted strands,
twisted like rope. Septimus reckoned it had to be Jo-Jo. A little older than Nicko and a little taller too, but much thinner,
with matted wild Heap hair, all straw-coloured curls, which
was kept in place by an intricately plaited band of different-
coloured strips of leather worn around his head. The boy
caught Septimus's glance.

"Jo-Jo," he said with a grin. "That's me."

"Hello," said Septimus, picking up a nearby stick and
poking it at the fire.

Jo-Jo stood and stretched. "You watch the fire and I'll go
and sort the fish. Sam got a good catch last night. And Marissa
brought some bread over this morning."

"Marissa?" asked Septimus.

"Oh, she's one of the Wendrons. You know, Wendron Witches. She made me this." Jo-Jo proudly touched the leather band that he wore around his head.

Sometime later Septimus was sitting by the fire holding a fish on a stick over the low flames. The flames spit and crackled as the fish cooked. Each cooked fish was divided into six pieces by Sam, then put on a chunk of Marissa's bread and passed around the boys. It was the best thing that Septimus had ever tasted. As they sat eating in companionable silence, Septimus at last began to relax and enjoy being with his brothers. No one except for Jo-Jo had said anything to him, but they had given him a job to do—he was, it seemed, the cook for the day. As each fish was eaten, Sam passed him the next one to hold over the fire, and soon Septimus felt as though he had spent all his life cooking fish around a campfire with his brothers. In fact, if it hadn't been for the nagging worry about Jenna in the back of his mind, everything would have been perfect.

It was after they had finished the fish that Nicko at last told his brothers about Jenna and Simon.

"Si—kidnap Jenna?" Sam had said. "I don't think so. I mean, just because he and Dad had a disagreement at Aunt

Zelda's about not being the Apprentice . . . well, I don't see why you think he's suddenly gone bad."

"Yeah," agreed Edd and Erik.

"Though he did really want to be a proper Apprentice, didn't he?" said Edd after a few minutes' thought.

"Yeah," said Erik. "He used to go on about it all the time. It got really boring."

"He told me once that the reason Marcia Overstrand didn't have an Apprentice was because she was waiting for him," Jo-Jo said. "I told him he was crazy. Then he kicked me."

"But he used to help Jenna with her homework an' everything," said Sam. "He was much nicer to her than he was to any of us. So why would he suddenly kidnap her? Doesn't make sense."

Nicko felt as frustrated as Septimus had that no one would believe that Simon had snatched Jenna.

There was a grumpy silence around the fire as all six brothers stared at the flames and the remains of fish bones scattered in the ashes. Soon Septimus could stand it no longer. "Where's Wolf Boy?" he asked.

"Asleep," said Jo-Jo. "Doesn't wake up till it's nearly dark. Like the wolverines."

"I need to talk to him," Septimus persisted.

Jo-Jo snorted. "Well, he won't talk back. Doesn't say anything. What do you want to talk to him for?"

"We need his help," said Nicko. "I told Sep he would be able to track down Jenna."

"Well, that's his bender over there." Jo-Jo pointed to what looked like a large pile of leaves.

"C'mon, Sep. Let's go and wake him up," said Nicko, getting up from the fire. "The thing is, Sep," said Nicko in a low voice, as they walked over to Wolf Boy's bender, "Sam and the lads have kind of slowed down since they've been living here. They don't say much, which is the Forest way, and they don't do anything in a hurry. They don't really bother about the outside world; they're almost like Forest creatures now. So if you want anything done—like getting hold of Wolf Boy— you have to do it yourself."

Septimus nodded. Like Nicko he was used to Castle living, used to having a job to do and people around him who expected him to do it. Forest living, he thought, would drive him crazy.

Septimus and Nicko made their way across the camp while their brothers lay around the fire, idly throwing sticks and leaves into it and watching the flames flare briefly. Camp Heap was not very big; it consisted of four rough shelters in a small clearing, set around the central fire pit. The shelters, which the boys called benders, were made from long thin branches of willow cut down by the river and then bent to form hoops and stuck into the ground. Once they were in the ground, the willow hoops continued growing, and, as it was summer, they had a full crop of leaves of their own. The boys had also woven in more branches, long grasses and anything else they could find. Inside the benders they slept on thick piles of leaves, which were covered with rough woven blankets that Galen, the Physik Woman and Sarah Heap's old teacher who lived in a nearby tree house, had given them when they first set up the camp. These had now been supplemented with furs and brightly coloured soft blankets made for them by the local young Wendron Witches.

Sam's bender was the biggest and the most solidly built. Edd and Erik shared a large, ramshackle heap and Jo-Jo had a neat tepeelike structure covered with beautifully plaited grasses that Marissa had helped him build.

Wolf Boy's bender looked like a pile of leaves; it was right on the edge of the camp, facing into the Forest. Nicko and Septimus had already walked around it twice, looking for an entrance, when suddenly Septimus noticed a bright pair of brown eyes staring at him from the leaves.

"Oh!" he gasped, and an odd shiver ran through him.

"Hey, Sep, you look like you've seen a ghost." Nicko laughed. "It's only Wolf Boy. He does that all the time. Never lets you see him first. Probably been watching us ever since we arrived."

Septimus looked pale. His heart was pounding; Wolf Boy's eyes staring at him had spooked him almost as much as the wolverines had the night before.

"Yeah," he mumbled, lapsing into Forest talk.

Suddenly the pile of leaves gave a lurch and a small wiry figure emerged, covered in dirt and bits of twig. Wolf Boy stood tensed like a runner waiting to start a race, glancing about. Nicko and Septimus instinctively stepped out of his territory.

"Don't look straight at him. Not to begin with. He gets scared," Nicko muttered under his breath.

Septimus could not help but steal a brief glance, and to his relief, Wolf Boy looked much more like a boy than a wolf. And he didn't even smell too bad either, more like damp earth than a wolverine. Wolf Boy was definitely human. He wore a short tunic of indeterminate colour, which was tied around his waist with an old leather belt, and he had long, brown, matted hair, Forest style. His bright brown eyes, once they had finished checking out his surroundings, turned their attention to Nicko and Septimus—particularly to Septimus, who he looked up and down with a faintly puzzled air. Septimus felt the old embarrassment about his fancy clothes returning and, not for the first time, wished he had taken the time to roll in mud before coming to Camp Heap.

"Hi," said Nicko after a while. "You OK?"

Wolf Boy nodded, still staring at Septimus.

"We've come to ask you to help us," said Nicko in a slow, calm voice.

Wolf Boy at last took his gaze off Septimus and regarded Nicko with a solemn stare.

"We need you to help us find someone. Someone who has been taken away."

Wolf Boy showed no reaction.

"You understand?" asked Nicko. "It's really important. She's our sister. She's been kidnapped."

Wolf Boy's eyes widened briefly in surprise. Now it was Nicko and Septimus who were doing the staring, waiting for a response.

At last it came. Slowly, very slowly, Wolf Boy nodded.

✛ 23 ✛
WOLF BOY

Y ou ought
to talk to
Morwenna before you go,"
Jo-Jo told Septimus and Nicko.
They were back at the campfire
saying goodbye to Sam, Jo-Jo, Edd
and Erik. Wolf Boy stood behind them, staring at Septimus, who shifted uncomfortably.

He always knew when someone was watching him.

"Morwenna's scary," said Nicko. "What do we want to talk to her for, anyway?"

Jo-Jo heaved himself to his feet while the others lay on their backs, idly staring up at the small patch of brilliant blue sky, which shone through the leaves.

"She's the Witch Mother," said Jo-Jo. "She knows everything. I'll bet you she'll know where Jenna has gone."

"Perhaps we ought to see her," said Septimus. "Dad says that Morwenna has the gift of second sight."

"She's still scary," said Nicko, "and she always hugs you like she's going to squash you flat."

"C'mon," said Jo-Jo, "I'll take you there. It's on your way anyway."

A mocking chorus started up from the three boys lying around the fire.

"He's going to see Mar-iiii-ssa, he's going to see Mar-iiii-ssa, he's going to see—"

"Oh, shut up," growled Jo-Jo. He stormed out of the clearing and headed into the trees.

"Bye then," said Nicko to the remaining Heaps.

"Bye."

"Yeah."

"See ya."

"Um. Bye," said Septimus.

"Yeah."

"Bye."

"See ya."

Nicko and Septimus caught up with Jo-Jo, who was waiting for them behind a tree, out of sight of his brothers. They set off together, with Wolf Boy following noiselessly as they made their way through the trees. Jo-Jo knew the way well; he took them along a narrow but well-worn path that, after about half an hour's walking, brought them to the Wendron Witches' Summer Circle.

The Summer Circle consisted of a circle of tepees, constructed just like Jo-Jo's. They were perched on the top of the only hill in the entire Forest. It was a small hill and did not even reach above the canopy of the Forest itself, but it was light and airy and gave the witches a good view of all that went on around them.

As the four boys followed the footpath that spiralled around the hill, taking them up towards the tepees, a steady hum of purposeful chatter drifted down to them. Suddenly a voice called out, "Joby-Jo! Hello!"

"Marissa!" Jo-Jo called back, smiling broadly.

"*Joby-Jo*—is that what she calls you?" snorted Nicko, as a tall girl with long brown hair appeared at the top of the hill, waving and laughing.

"So?" asked Jo-Jo. "So what if she does?"

"So *nothing*. Just asked." Nicko smirked.

Marissa came running down the hill to meet them.

"Marissa," said Jo-Jo, "these are my brothers Nicko and Septimus."

"What—*more* brothers, Joby?" Marissa laughed. "How many brothers do you need?"

"Don't need any more, that's for sure. I've brought them to see Morwenna."

"Good. She's expecting you. I'll take you to her. She's up in the Circle."

Morwenna Mould, Witch Mother of the Wendron Witch Forest Coven, was sitting on a rug at the entrance of the smartest tepee in the Circle. She was a large, impressive woman and she wore a capacious green summer tunic, which was tied around the middle with a white sash. Her long greying hair was held back with a green leather headband, and her piercing witch-blue eyes watched Wolf Boy, Jo-Jo, Nicko and Septimus—particularly Septimus—make their way across the Circle to her tepee.

"Thank you, Marissa dear," said Morwenna, then turned

and smiled at the boys. "Welcome to the Forest, Septimus, Nicko. I have heard so much about you both from your father, my dear Silas. And you both look so much like him. In fact wherever I go in the Forest now I seem to bump into small— and indeed, some not so small any more—versions of Silas. And all with the same wonderful green eyes too. Now, boys, sit down beside me for a few minutes. I won't keep you long, for you have a hazardous journey before you."

Nicko shot Septimus a glance, which said, *What does she mean, hazardous?*

Septimus raised his eyebrows at Nicko but kept his gaze fixed on Morwenna. Septimus liked the Witch Mother, but he knew that underneath Morwenna's motherly appearance something unpredictable and powerful lurked. Until Morwenna had taken over the Forest Coven, the Wendron Witches had been greatly feared by the inhabitants of the Castle. But since Morwenna had become Witch Mother, the Wendron Witches had changed, although no one knew why—except for Silas Heap. Silas Heap knew it because one night many years ago, when he was a young man with only one baby son, and Morwenna was a beautiful young witch, Silas had rescued Morwenna from a pack of wolverines. In return Morwenna had offered him anything he wanted and, to her disappointment, he had asked that the Wendron Witches stop preying on the inhabitants of the Castle. A few years later, when Morwenna Mould became Witch Mother, she had kept her promise—but no one was sure how long the apparent truce would last, and it was still considered wise not to offend the Forest Coven.

Morwenna began to speak in a low, musical voice, and everyone paid attention. "You are going on a long journey and I foresee some troubles ahead," she said. "There are three things you must know. The first is that you will search for, and indeed find, your sister in the Port. The second is that a tall dark man, a stranger to some but not to all, will also search for your sister in the Port." Morwenna paused. The boys waited politely for her to tell them the third thing they must know, but Morwenna stayed silent, lost in thought and gazing at the changing patterns of the leaves against the sky.

Eventually Septimus said, "Excuse me, Witch Mother, but what is the third thing we must know?"

"What?" Morwenna snapped herself out of her reverie. "The third thing? Oh, yes—don't go to the circus."

Nicko burst out laughing. Septimus nudged him urgently and said, "Nik—don't be rude. It's not funny. "

"Yes . . . it is," spluttered Nicko under his breath, his shoulders shaking. He rolled on to the grass and lay on his stomach with his hands over his head, emitting loud snorting noises.

"I'm sorry about my brother, Witch Mother," said Septimus, worried. "He nearly got eaten by a wolverine last night and it has affected his mind." Septimus aimed a kick in Nicko's direction. It had no effect. Nicko was beside himself, snorting like a pig in a trough.

Morwenna smiled. "Do not worry, Septimus, I am used to the antics of young Heaps now. Maybe before your brothers had come to live in our Forest I would not have understood, but now, believe me, nothing surprises me where a Heap is concerned. They are their father's sons. And Nicko is only laughing. There is no harm in laughter."

Morwenna stood up. Septimus, Jo-Jo, Marissa and Wolf Boy respectfully leaped to their feet. Nicko still lay on the grass, shoulders shaking.

"Well, boys," Morwenna said, "we will meet again." She reached into her pocket and brought out a small bundle of soft leaves, which she pressed into Septimus's hand. "These will take away your bruise from the fall you had last night," she said to him, "and the swelling from your ankle."

"Thank you, Witch Mother," Septimus said. He hauled Nicko to his feet. Nicko's eyes were streaming, and he was weak with laughter. "I will take my brother away now, Witch Mother.

I am sorry for his rudeness. Thank you for your advice."

"Heed it well, Septimus, and you will find what you are looking for." Morwenna smiled. "Farewell, boys. I wish you good speed on your journey." She turned and disappeared into the tepee.

Nicko made a beeline for the edge of the Circle and threw himself to the ground. Then he rolled over and over, hurtling down the grassy slope, still shaking with laughter. A moment later Septimus joined him.

"Nicko," he chided, "you just do *not* laugh at a Wendron Witch Mother. Ever."

"I—I'm sorry, Sep," spluttered Nicko. It was just . . . it was all so serious . . . and *witchy* . . . and we all sat *waiting* and . . . and I thought the third thing would be something . . . *really* important . . . and then she said . . . she said—"

"*Don't go to the circus!*" Septimus gave in and, yelling with laughter, he rolled down to the bottom of the hill with Nicko.

"You were really disrespectful to the Witch Mother," said Jo-Jo grumpily when he and Wolf Boy joined them at the bottom of the hill. "Marissa is cross. She says I shouldn't have brought you."

"Oh, don't—*hic!*—be silly, Jo-Jo," said Nicko, who had stopped laughing but now had the hiccups.

"Are you going now?" Jo-Jo asked in a tone of voice that meant he hoped they were. "I'll take you to the boat."

Nicko and Septimus nodded. They both wanted to be out of the Forest and on their way to find Jenna before the day drew on.

Jo-Jo glanced in Wolf Boy's direction. "You still taking him with you—or is he staying here?"

Septimus looked at Wolf Boy only to meet his deep brown eyes staring at him again. He wished he would stop staring like that. Surely even Wolf Boy should have got used to the Apprentice robes by now. They weren't *that* weird, were they?

"He's staying here," said Septimus.

"But, Sep, we need him. He's the reason we came here," said Nicko. "We'll never find Jenna without him now. The trail is over a day old. Only Wolf Boy can pick up a trail that cold."

"But we know where Jenna is now," said Septimus. "She's in the Port."

Nicko was silent for a moment.

"You didn't believe that mad witch, did you?" he asked, amazed.

"Nicko! She's not mad."

"She's a witch though. And worse than that, she's a Wendron Witch. They used to kidnap babies. And if the baby was a boy they'd leave him out for the wolverines. And if you got lost in the Forest and asked them the way, you'd end up in a Witch Pit. Bo Tenderfoot's aunt spent two weeks in a Witch Pit and she—"

"Bo *who*?"

"Jenna's best friend. You remember. Nice kid with carroty hair."

"Look, Nik, concentrate. We want to find Jenna. Remember? That's why we're here. And I believe Morwenna. Even Marcia says Morwenna has second sight, and Marcia thinks witches are a waste of space. I think Jenna is in the Port."

"Don't know why she'd go there," grumbled Nicko. "It's a dump."

"Simon must have taken her there—to hand her over to that stranger you said was asking about her and that Morwenna said was looking for her. We've got to get there as soon as we can."

"OK." Nicko sighed. "We'll go to the Port."

Jo-Jo led the way down the beach where the boat was moored, and, despite what Septimus had said, Wolf Boy still followed them. Then, when Nicko had untied the boat and Jo-Jo was pushing them off the shingle into the deeper water, Wolf Boy suddenly took a flying leap and landed in the boat, just as the current was taking it out into the middle of the river.

"Hey!" yelled Nicko as the boat rocked precariously. "What d'you think you're doing?" Wolf Boy crouched on the deck like a wild animal and stared at Septimus until Septimus could stand it no longer.

"Stop staring at me!" he yelled.

Wolf Boy's brown eyes did not flicker. They looked at Septimus closely until Septimus felt a strange shiver of recognition pass through him. He had been here before. On a boat. On the river. By the Forest. With Wolf Boy.

Suddenly he felt cold. He squatted down in the boat next to Wolf Boy, staring at him in return. "Four-oh-nine?" Septimus whispered.

Wolf Boy nodded and spoke for the first time in four years.

"You." He grinned. "Four-one-two."

They sailed down the river on the outgoing tide. Wolf Boy and Septimus sat on the deck of the boat with their arms around each other's shoulders smiling broadly.

"He reminds me of you when we found you," mused Nicko. "I remember you never said a word. Just stared at us as if we were all mad. It gave me the creeps."

"Oh," said Septimus. "Sorry."

"We didn't mind. Not really. We liked you. Just couldn't

understand why you didn't speak. But it must be something to do with the Army. Must have been *horrible.*"

"It was," said Wolf Boy very slowly, getting used to the sound of his own voice. "You couldn't trust anyone. But I trusted 412."

A silence fell in the boat. Nicko busied himself adjusting the sails and Septimus stared at the river. After a while Septimus said to Wolf Boy, "I tried to get them to go back for you. I really did. But they wouldn't. They *wouldn't.* The Leader Cadet laughed and said—what did we expect? It was a Do-or-Die. And you were the first Die. He was really excited about that. I tried to jump in after you but the Leader Cadet knocked me out. I came to when the boat landed and they threw me in the water. I'm sorry. I should have saved you."

Wolf Boy said nothing for a while. And then he said, "No, I should have saved *you.* I escaped the Army and you didn't. I swam ashore and hid. The next morning I saw you in the Forest. But I was afraid of being seen, so I stayed hidden. I should have saved you and we could have both been free. Not just me."

"It doesn't matter," said Septimus. "I would never have found out who I was if you had. And we're both free now."

"Free . . ." murmured Wolf Boy, gazing dreamily over the side of the boat as it cut through the calm green water, heading for the Port.

⊹⊹ 24 ⊹⊹
THE PORT

I t had been a long, hot day.
Jenna, Stanley and
Thunder were making
their way along the
beach. The sea was
calm and sparkled a bril-
liant blue in the sunlight,
and the sand dunes
stretched for mile after
mile. Jenna had just
given Thunder the last of
the water from the bottles
she had filled from the spring that morning. She tipped the
bottle to give herself and Stanley a drink and discovered that
there was nothing left but a hot trickle of rusty water that

tasted of metal. Irritably she shoved the bottle back into the saddlebag and wondered, not for the first time, if Stanley's idea of reaching the Port by riding along the beach had been such a good one.

Jenna had soon discovered that it was very tiring for the horse to walk along soft sand. She had taken Thunder down to the tide line where he could walk on the firm sand left by the receding tide, but as the afternoon wore on the tide came in. Now the sea was high on the beach and Thunder was ploughing laboriously through the soft dry sand that spilled from the sand dunes.

The sun was low on the horizon when at last Thunder wearily plodded around the foot of the final sand dune, and to her delight, Jenna could see the Port in the distance, silhouetted against the reddening sky. Jenna felt tired and sunburned, but she kept up a stream of encouraging words to Thunder, urging the heavy-footed horse on to their destination.

Stanley, however, was wide awake. "I always get excited when I first see the Port," he declared, sitting up in the saddle behind Jenna and looking around brightly. "So many things to do, so many rats to see. Not this time, of course. Got a job to do this time. Who'd have thought it, eh? Secret Rat on a Find and Return mission for *royalty*. What a start to my new career.

That'll show Dawnie. And her stupid sister. Huh!"

"Dawnie?" asked Jenna, leaning forward and patting Thunder's neck.

"My missus. As was. She's living with her sister, Mabel, now. And between you and me she's beginning to regret it. Ha! Mabel is not the easiest rat to live with. In fact she's a downright impossible rat to live with, if you ask me." Stanley shot a glance at Jenna, wondering whether a few stories about Mabel's shortcomings would go down well and decided against it. Jenna looked tired and preoccupied. "Not long to the Port now," he said assuringly.

"Good," Jenna answered, sounding more confident than she felt. The rapidly lengthening shadows of the sand dunes and the chill breeze coming off the sea had made her realise that she had no chance of reaching Aunt Zelda's cottage before dark. She was going to have to spend the night in the Port, but where? Jenna had heard many stories from Nicko about the Port lowlife—the smugglers and muggers, the pickpockets and cutpurses, the blaggers and baggers, all waiting to pounce on an unwary stranger as soon as night fell. What was she going to do?

"Come on, Thunder," she said. "Let's get there before dark."

"No chance of that," Stanley told her, chirpily. "Got another hour to go at least. If not more."

"Thanks, Stanley," muttered Jenna, glancing anxiously behind her, for she suddenly had the strangest feeling that she was being followed.

Night had fallen by the time Thunder walked along the gravelly town beach and headed up the south slipway on the outer edge of the Port. Thunder's hooves jarred on the stone cobbles after the soft sand, and the noise made Jenna uneasy. The outskirts of the Port were dark and eerily quiet. Tall, dilapidated warehouses lined the narrow streets and towered into the night sky, making the streets feel like deep ravines and reminding Jenna uncomfortably of the Badlands. Most of the buildings were deserted, but, as the sound of Thunder's hooves bounced off their brick walls and echoed in the streets, Jenna caught a glimpse every now and then of a figure, silhouetted in an opening high above the street, looking down at them and watching their noisy progress.

Stanley poked Jenna in the back.

"Aargh!" she screamed.

"Hey, take it easy. It's only me."

"Sorry, Stanley. I'm tired. This place is creepy. And I don't know where to stay tonight. I've never stayed here on my own before." It crossed Jenna's mind that she had never stayed *anywhere* on her own before. Ever.

"Well, why didn't you say? I thought we'd be stopping with the Chief Reeve or some such high and mightiness." Stanley sounded disappointed.

"No," mumbled Jenna.

"I'm sure he'd be only too pleased if he knew a personage of your importance was on his patch, so to speak. I'm sure he'd be honoured to—"

"No, Stanley," Jenna said firmly. "I don't want *anyone* to know I'm here. I don't know who I can trust."

"Fair enough," said Stanley. "I can see that Mr Heap has got you a bit rattled. Don't blame you. He's a nasty character. Well, in that case I suggest Florrie Bundy's place. She runs a very secluded outfit down by the docks, and there are some stables around the back for the horse. I'll take you there, if you like."

"Oh, thank you, Stanley." Jenna felt as though a weight had been lifted from her. She hadn't realised just how much she had been worrying about where to stay. Now all she wanted to do was to find a room and go to sleep.

"It's not what I'd call smart, mind," Stanley warned her.

"You'll have to put up with a bit of honest dirt. Well, quite a lot of dirt, actually. And it's probably not particularly honest, if I know Florrie. But she's a good enough soul."

Jenna was too tired to care any more. "Just take me there, Stanley," she said.

Stanley guided Jenna through the warren of old warehouses until they reached the bustling dockside in the commercial part of the town. It was here that the tall ships came in after months at sea, laden with exotic herbs and spices, silks and fine woven cloths, gold and silver bullion, emeralds and rubies, and South Sea Island pearls. As Thunder approached the dockside, Jenna could see that a huge ship, with a beautifully carved prow carrying a figurehead of a striking dark-haired woman, was being unloaded. The dockside was lit with burning torches that cast long flickering shadows over the throng of sailors, porters and dockhands who were scurrying like ants going back and forth from their nest, up and down the gangplank, busy unloading the wares from the ship.

Thunder came to a halt at the edge of the busy crowd, unable to push any farther through the throng, and Jenna was forced to wait for the crowd to clear before she could go on. Fascinated by the scene before her, she sat on the horse and watched four sailors as they struggled down the gangplank with a massive golden chest. Close behind them staggered a dockhand carrying an ornate vase almost twice his height, from which Jenna could see a few gold coins spilling each time he took a step. Behind him ran a small boy, picking up the coins and gleefully stuffing them into his pockets.

When the treasures reached dry land, they were carried across the dockside, where they disappeared through the massive open doors of a cavernous, candlelit warehouse. Jenna watched the stream of riches pour into the building, and she noticed an imposing woman in a long blue tunic with the yellow braid of a Chief Customs Officer on her sleeves, standing at the door. The woman was flanked by two clerks sitting at high desks, each with an identical, rapidly lengthening, list in front of them. As every precious object came through, the bearers paused for a moment while the Customs Officer told the clerks what to note down. Occasionally a tall dark man, richly dressed in foreign-looking robes of a heavy deep red silk, interrupted her. The Customs Officer seemed somewhat impatient with the man's interruptions and did not let him stop her flow of instructions to the clerks. Jenna guessed that the man was the ship's owner, disputing the Officer's assessment of his cargo.

Jenna had guessed rightly. At the Port, when a ship was

finally unloaded and all was safely stored in the bonded warehouse, one list would be given to the owner of the ship, and
Alice Nettles, Chief Customs Officer to the Port, would keep
the other—and the key to the warehouse—until all the duty
payable had been agreed between her and the owner. And
paid. This could take anywhere from a few minutes to never,
depending on how desperate the owner was to get hold of his
cargo. And how stubborn he was. There were half a dozen
abandoned and rotting bonded warehouses, some of which
Jenna had passed that evening, which still contained the
disputed cargos of ships that had entered the Port many
hundreds of years ago.

The flow of goods from the ship began to slow, and a
steward on the dockside started paying off some of the
workers. Jenna was beginning to attract a few stares now
that the pace had slackened and the workers had time to
look about them. From inside the warehouse the tall for-
eigner standing beside Alice Nettles had, to Alice's relief,
taken his eyes off his incoming cargo. He had turned his
attention to the small yet striking figure outside: the gold
circlet around her dark hair glinting in the torchlight, her
bright red tunic with its gold hem shimmering as she sat
upright on a black horse, with a rich, dark blue cloak falling

from her shoulders. The man muttered something to Alice Nettles. She looked surprised and nodded, not for one minute taking her attention from a large golden elephant that was being carried past her. The man left her side and moved towards the door.

Jenna, meanwhile, had become aware of the attention she was attracting from the dockhands. She quickly slipped down from Thunder and began to lead the horse through the swarm of workers, guided by Stanley, who was sitting on Thunder's head, searching for gaps in the crowd. "Left a bit. No, no, right a bit. I meant *right*. Oh, look, there's a gap there. *There*. You missed it. You'll have to go around now."

"Oh, do be quiet, Stanley," Jenna snapped. She felt suddenly uneasy—she *knew* she was being followed. All she wanted to do was get through the crush, jump back on to Thunder and ride away.

"I was only trying to help," Stanley muttered.

Jenna ignored Stanley and pushed forward with the horse. "Excuse me . . . sorry, can I just get through . . . thank you . . . excuse me . . ." She was nearly there; she could see clear space in front of her now. All she had to do was get through this group of sailors who were busy untangling a rope, and then she'd be off—so why was Thunder insisting on hanging back now, just when she needed him to go forward? "Come on, Thunder," Jenna said, irritably. "Come *on*." She felt a sudden tug on the reins and swung around to see what Thunder had caught himself on.

Jenna gasped; a large hand had grabbed hold of the reins. She looked up, expecting to see one of the sailors angry because Thunder had stepped on his rope, but instead she found herself staring at the dark-haired stranger she had seen standing beside the Customs Officer.

"Let go," Jenna told the man, angrily. "Let go of my horse."

The stranger kept his grip on the reins and stared intently at Jenna. "Who *are* you?" he asked in a low voice.

"None of your business," said Jenna briskly, determined not to show how scared she was. "Let go of my horse."

The man dropped his grip from the reins but he did not drop his gaze from Jenna's face. He stared at her with an intense expression that Jenna found unsettling. Flustered, she looked away and quickly swung herself back into the saddle, kicking Thunder into a fast trot and leaving the stranger staring after her on the dockside.

"Left here. I said *left!*" shouted Stanley, hanging on tight to Thunder's ears.

Thunder shot off to the right.

"Don't know why I bother," Stanley muttered. But Jenna didn't care which way they were going. Any direction was fine, as long as it was as far away from the tall stranger as possible.

⊹ 2 5 ⊹
THE DOLL HOUSE

I am *not lost*," said Stanley indignantly. "A member of the Secret Rat Service is *never* lost. I am merely reassessing the direction."

"Well, get a move on and reassess a bit faster," said Jenna, glancing along the street, "before that man from the docks catches up with us. I'm sure he followed me."

Stanley and Jenna were in the middle of The Rope Walk, a street just off Tavern Row, in the seedier part of the Port.

Jenna had dismounted from Thunder when the rat insisted that the extremely ramshackle house in front of them was Florrie Bundy's lodging house. Unfortunately, it was not. It actually belonged to the notorious Port Witch Coven, who were most definitely not White Witches and did not take kindly to a rat banging on their door late at night. Stanley had narrowly avoided becoming a toad. It was only Jenna's speedy intervention with a silver half-crown—which she gave the witch to buy back the toad spell—that had saved him.

"I don't understand it," Stanley muttered a little shakily, running his paws over his face just to make sure he still had rat fur and not toad warts. "I was *sure* that was Florrie's place."

"Maybe it was," said Jenna disconsolately. "Maybe the witches changed her into a toad too."

The street was busy with people coming and going. A late-night circus performance was taking place on a field just out-side the Port, and noisily chattering circus-goers were pushing past Jenna, Thunder and Stanley.

Out of the chat, two familiar voices reached Jenna's ears.

"But she said, *Don't go to the circus.*"

"Oh, come on. It'll be fun. You're not going to take any notice of all that rubbish she told us, are you?"

Jenna knew those voices. She scanned the crowd but could

see nothing. "Septimus? Nicko?" she shouted.

"That's funny, Sep," said a voice behind a very large woman who was walking towards Jenna, carrying two huge picnic hampers, "I thought I heard someone yell our names."

"Probably some other people called the same."

"No one's got weird names like us, Sep. Especially like *you*."

"Well, Nicko is pretty peculiar if you ask me. At least mine means something."

Now Jenna was sure—and suddenly, there was Septimus's straw-coloured hair bobbing around behind one of the picnic hampers. She darted forward and grabbed him.

"Septimus!" she yelled. "It's *you*—Oh, Sep!"

Septimus stared at Jenna. He could not believe his eyes.

"Jen?" he gasped. "But . . . hey, *Jen*. Oh, you're all right. You're *safe*. And you really are here. I don't believe it!"

Jenna swung Septimus around in a bear hug; then Nicko pounced on them both and nearly squashed them.

"Hey, hey! We found you, *we found you*. Are you OK, Jen? What happened?"

"Tell you later. Hey, is he with you?" Jenna had noticed Wolf Boy. He had hung back from the reunion and looked a little lost.

"Yep. Tell you later," Nicko said with a grin.

"Look, would you mind getting off my tail?" Stanley asked Nicko, who in his excitement had stepped on the rat. Nicko glanced down; Stanley glared up at him. "It hurts," he said. "You've got very heavy feet."

"Sorry," said Nicko. He moved his boot. "Hey, look, Jen. It's the Message Rat."

"*Secret* Rat," Stanley corrected. "Go anywhere. Do anything."

"Except find Florrie Bundy's lodging house," said Jenna.

"Found it," declared Stanley, pointing to a garish building with all the bricks painted in different colours, next to the Witches' house. On the door was a big hand-drawn, painted sign that read

THE DOLL HOUSE

BOARD AND LODGING FOR DISCERNING CUSTOMERS

NO CREDIT

"She's decorated it since I was last here. And changed the name. Follow me."

Ten minutes later, the horse boy had taken Thunder to the stable at the back of the house and Nurse Meredith—a large, dishevelled woman with mad, staring eyes—had told them that she had taken over from Florrie not long ago. Nurse Meredith had carefully counted out Jenna's money three times and thrust it into a deep pocket in her none-too-clean apron.

Now Jenna, Nicko, Septimus, Wolf Boy and Stanley were following the bulky figure of the Nurse up a dusty flight of stairs.

"You'll have to go in the annexe," she told them, as she squeezed around a particularly tight corner. "It's my last room. You're lucky. I'm very busy tonight, what with the circus being in town. Very popular with the circus crowd, I am."

"Really?" said Jenna politely, carefully stepping over a large doll that was sprawled across a step. The lodging house was stuffed full of dolls of all shapes and sizes. They were imprisoned in glass cases, piled high on overcrowded hammocks slung from the ceiling and nailed to the walls. An endless array of dolls was lined up on the stairs and Nicko had already managed to tread on at least two. Septimus was doing his best to avoid even looking at them. The dolls made him shiver; there was something dead about their gaze, and as he passed each one he could not shake off the feeling of something watching him.

"Mind my babies!" said Nurse Meredith sharply, as Nicko

stepped on yet another doll. "You do that again and you'll be out of here, young man."

"Sorry," Nicko mumbled, wondering why Jenna wanted to stay in such a strange place.

At last they reached the top of the house, but as they did so, a loud banging on the front door reverberated up the stairs. Nurse Meredith leaned over the banister and yelled down to the skivvy who lived in the cupboard under the stairs.

"We're full, Maureen. Tell 'em to buzz off."

Maureen scuttled off to open the door. Jenna looked down, curious to see who on earth would want to stay in the Doll House. As the thin, timid skivvy pulled the door open, Jenna gasped and jumped back into the shadows. Standing on the doorstep was the figure she had dreaded seeing—the stranger from the docks.

"What's wrong, Jen?" Nicko whispered.

"Th-that man at the door. He followed me from the docks. He's after me . . ."

"Who is he, Jen?"

"I- I don't know. But I think he must have something to do with Simon."

"Well, I don't care *who* he is to do with, missy," snapped Nurse Meredith. "He's not staying here tonight."

Far below them Maureen's reedy voice could be heard. "I'm sorry, sir. We are full tonight."

The stranger's voice was breathless and a little agitated. "I do not wish to stay, miss. I was only enquiring. I was told that a young lady with a horse was staying—"

"*Tell him to buzz off, Maureen!*" the Nurse yelled down.

"Er, sorry, sir. Buzz off, please," said Maureen apologetically, and closed the door firmly.

To Jenna's dismay the stranger continued to bang on the door, but Nurse Meredith was having none of it.

"Go and chuck a bucket of dirty dishwater over him, Maureen!" she yelled crossly. Maureen went to do her bidding and Nurse Meredith turned her attention to her latest guests.

"Follow me, please," she said, and she climbed out of a tall window.

Jenna, Nicko and Septimus glanced at each other. Follow her out the window? *Why?*

Nurse Meredith's head appeared in the window. "For Heaven's sake, I haven't got all night," she chided. "Are you coming or not? Because if you're not I'll go and get the gentleman that just called and let him have the room. Ungrateful kids."

Jenna quickly climbed out the window. "No, no, don't give

it to him. We're coming."

The annexe was reached by a narrow wooden bridge, which spanned the gap between the Doll House and the house next door. Septimus only managed to get across by holding on to Wolf Boy and not looking down into the precipitous gap between the two houses. At the end of the bridge Nurse Meredith threw open another window.

"It's in there. Squeeze past and climb in on your own. I can't be doing with clambering in and out of windows all night."

Septimus thought that squeezing past Nurse Meredith on a narrow bridge that wobbled with every step was even more terrifying than being surrounded by wolverines. But Jenna pulled him and Nicko pushed him until, with trembling legs, he fell through the open annexe window and lay on the floor, shaking and staring up at the stained ceiling. That was it now, Septimus decided. He would have to stay in the annexe room for ever. There was no way he could ever walk back across that bridge.

Once they were all in the room, Nurse Meredith peered in.

"House rules are on the door," she told them. "Any infringements and you'll be out. Got that?"

They nodded.

Nurse Meredith continued in a businesslike tone. "Breakfast is served only between seven o'clock and ten minutes past. There is hot water between four and four thirty in the afternoon only. No fires allowed, no singing, no dancing. Residents in the annexe are reminded that, although they remain guests of the Doll House, they are actually staying in the property of the Port Witch Coven and do so at their own risk. The management of the Doll House cannot be held responsible for any consequences arising from this arrangement. Oh, yes, and do you want the rat for supper? I don't think he'd stretch any further than a bit of soup, but Maureen could rustle you up some if you like. We're partial to rat soup, are Maureen and I. I'll take him down, shall I?"

"No!" gasped Jenna, grabbing hold of Stanley. "I mean, thank you—it's very kind of you, but we're not very hungry."

"Shame. Well, maybe for breakfast then. Goodnight." Nurse Meredith slammed the window shut and wobbled back across the bridge to the Doll House.

"Mmm. Nice place, Jen." Nicko grinned.

⊹ 26 ⊹
SLEUTH

It *was very early the next* morning, just as the eastern sky above The Rope Walk was turning pink, when a small, luminous green ball rolled noiselessly along the middle of the street and stopped outside the Port Witch Coven's house.

Sleuth paused for a moment, bouncing on the spot while it took stock. Sleuth was content. It knew it had nearly reached its destination. Since its Master had thrown it out with its Tag, it had faithfully followed not only Jenna's exact footsteps, but also the rhythm of her journey, speeding up where she had done so and stopping where she had stopped. Which is

why the green ball was waiting a moment at the very spot
where, not so very many hours ago, Jenna had questioned
Stanley's sense of direction.

This was how the Tracker Ball operated, and it was
extremely effective, although not without the occasional problem. Such as when, late that afternoon, ten feet of choppy sea-
water had covered the route that Jenna took earlier in the day,
when the tide was out. That had slowed Sleuth down a bit,
and getting covered in sand afterwards had not helped its
progress either. Sleuth knew its Master would not be pleased
about the delay and it was anxious to get on with its task. The
ball bounced up to the door of the Port Witch Coven, only to
feel a sudden urge to leave again. Sleuth was about to bounce
away when the door was flung open and a hand shot out and
grabbed it.

"Got it!" a triumphant witch yelled. Sleuth was furious. It
struggled but the witch held it tight in her grasp.

"Got *what*, Linda?" Sleuth glimpsed another, older, witch's
shocked face as Linda showed off her catch. Her face was
white with fright. "Oh, Covens above—are you trying to get
us all killed?"

"What are you going on about?" snapped the younger
witch. "You're just cross because you missed that rat earlier.

Anyway—it's *my* ball now. So shove off."

"Linda—for Coven's sake, let it go. It belongs to the Master. It's a Tracker Ball on a mission. Drop it right now!"

The witch dropped Sleuth like a hot potato. The ball shook itself and bounced back into the street, then made its way to the door of the Doll House. The two witches watched, fascinated, as Sleuth briefly bounced on the spot and, on the third bounce, squeezed through the letterbox and disappeared inside.

"Shame it's not come for anyone here," said the older witch. "We could have Kept them for the Master. That would have put us in his good books."

"We're never in the right place at the right time, are we?" Linda sighed gloomily as she slammed the door with a loud bang.

"Nicko?" whispered Jenna. "*Nicko?*"

"Werr?"

"Nicko, there's someone tapping on the window."

"'S only mad Nurse, Jen. Ger bakoo sleep," Nicko mumbled drowsily from his lumpy bed in the corner of the grubby room.

Jenna sat up in her equally lumpy bed and pulled Lucy's

cloak around her. She stared into the gloom, her heart pounding, and listened again. It sounded as though the Nurse was
bouncing a ball outside their window. Why? She hadn't
looked the sporty type. And then, as the fog of sleep finally left
Jenna's brain, she remembered. *Sleuth.*

Jenna leaped out of bed and immediately fell over the sleeping form of Septimus, who was wrapped up in a blanket on the
floor. He did not stir. Slowly, she crawled over to the window,
keeping low in the hope that Sleuth would not see her—
although Jenna suspected that it did not matter one bit
whether or not the Tracker Ball saw her. It *knew* she was here.

And then Jenna trod on something soft—and alive. She
opened her mouth to scream but before she could, a hand had
snaked over her face and covered the scream. A smell of damp
earth filled Jenna's nostrils and two big eyes stared at her.

"Shh," whispered Wolf Boy, who had been lying under the
window listening to Sleuth for the last five minutes. "There's
a Thing outside. I saw one just like it in the Forest once."

"I know," whispered Jenna. "It's come to find me."

"Do you want me to catch it for you?" asked Wolf Boy, his
eyes glittering in the green glow that was shining through the
grime on the window. Outside, Sleuth was growing brighter
by the second. It had found the quarry; now it was gathering

the energy to Tag the quarry. Once Sleuth had done that, it would return to its Master, mission accomplished. From then on, the quarry was Tagged, and its Master would know where to find it.

"*Can* you catch it?" wondered Jenna, thinking that Sleuth would be far too fast for Wolf Boy.

"Easy." Wolf Boy grinned, his dirty teeth shining a nasty shade of green in the ever-brightening glow. "Watch."

Quicker than a witch, Wolf Boy threw open the window and had Sleuth clasped in his hand in a flash. He slammed the window shut with a bang.

"Get him!" yelled Septimus, sitting bolt upright, his eyes open wide, still in the middle of a dream.

"What?" mumbled Nicko. "Wha—what's going on? Jen? Why's he gone green?"

Wolf Boy looked very peculiar. The bright pulsing light from the trapped Sleuth shone through his hands in a reddish-green glow, outlining the bones as dark shapes beneath his skin. The rest of Wolf Boy was turning a horrible shade of green as Sleuth glowed ever brighter, trying to gather the energy to escape.

The Tracker Ball was furious. It was so near and yet so far, for unless it could Tag the quarry, what use was it to its

Master? No more use than a bald old tennis ball, that's what. Sleuth knew all about bald old tennis balls, for it had once been one itself. Sleuth owed everything to its Master, Simon, and it would never let him down. Nothing was going to stop it from Tagging the quarry. *Nothing.*

However, Wolf Boy was doing his best. His strong wiry hands held Sleuth in a grip of iron, while Sleuth gathered all its energy and slowly but surely began to heat up. It was a risky ploy, but the Tracker Ball was willing to risk the possibility of meltdown. It would rather liquefy into a pool of rubber than fail its Master.

"Why are your hands green, 409?" asked Septimus, still bleary-eyed and under the impression he was back in the Young Army dormitory with Boy 409.

"Dunno. It's some kind of Thing. Jenna asked me to catch it. So I did. Funny, it's getting quite hot."

"It's Sleuth," whispered Jenna. "Simon's Tracker Ball. He's sent it to find me. What are we going to do with it?"

Septimus was suddenly wide awake. "Don't let it touch you, Jen. He's put a Tag on it. It *mustn't* touch you—got that?"

"I don't want it to." Jenna shuddered. "Horrible thing."

"If it doesn't touch you, it won't be able to go back to Simon and tell him where you are. So you're still safe. OK?"

Jenna looked anything but OK. She was pale and trembling
and had a green tinge about her.

"Ouch . . ." Wolf Boy muttered. "Ooh—ah. *Ouch!*"

"You all right?" asked Nicko.

"Ah . . . It's getting hot . . . I can't—I can't hold it . . .
Aargh!" Wolf Boy dropped the Tracker Ball, the palms of his
hands burned raw.

Sleuth was glowing so bright it hurt to look at it—it was
red-hot. At lightning speed it shot over to Jenna, jumped up
and touched her arm. Jenna screamed with pain and shock.
The ball hurled itself through the window, smashing the glass,
and burned its way through the wooden bridge, landing far
below in the witches' rotting rubbish heap with a loud hiss. It
lay for a moment deep in the pile of tea leaves, rabbit bones
and frog heads, and waited until it had cooled down.

Then, triumphantly, it shot out of the rubbish heap, shook
off a thick coating of tea leaves and sped away, back to its
Master, Simon Heap.

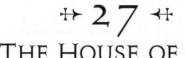

✢ 27 ✢
THE HOUSE OF THE
PORT WITCH COVEN

T here was
a stunned
silence in the annexe. It was
broken a few moments later
by Septimus, who gasped, "The
bridge—it's on fire!"

Nicko turned his attention from Jenna,
who was sitting with her hand clasped

over the small circular burn that Sleuth had left on her arm, and followed Septimus's gaze. Flames were flickering from the charred hole that Sleuth had made in the bridge, and as they watched, the dry, old, wooden bridge suddenly erupted in a ball of fire and fell six floors down to the ground with a crash.

"Uh-oh . . ." said Septimus.

"Rats," muttered Nicko.

"It's nothing to do with *rats*," Stanley protested. "It's all because of that Mr Heap, if you ask me. And I don't know what old Nursie's going to say about her bridge going up in flames either."

"Bother what old Nursie has to say about it," Nicko retorted. "That's the least of our worries. Have you forgotten where we are?"

"Stuck at the top of the headquarters of the Port Witch Coven," said Septimus glumly.

"Exactly," muttered Nicko.

Another silence fell. Wolf Boy shoved his burned hands under his arms and looked preoccupied. He was doing a slow dance from foot to foot, trying to take his mind off how much they were hurting. Jenna shook herself out of her own worries and went over to him.

"Are they bad?" she asked. Wolf Boy nodded, gritting his teeth.

"We ought to bandage you up," Jenna said. "Protect your hands. Here." She unwound the gold silk sash she wore around her waist and, using her teeth to start it off, she tore the sash in half.

Septimus and Nicko watched Jenna carefully wrap the gold silk around Wolf Boy's burned hands. But their minds were elsewhere, trying to think of a way to get out of the witches' house.

"Listen," said Septimus in a low voice.

"What?" whispered Nicko. Jenna and Wolf Boy looked up anxiously. What had Septimus heard?

"Can you hear anything?" muttered Septimus.

There was a tense silence while everyone listened for—what? Footsteps outside the door? Simon Heap at the window? Nurse Meredith discovering her bridge had been burned to cinders? After a few minutes, Nicko whispered, "I can't hear anything, Sep."

"Exactly. Nothing."

"Oh, Sep," protested Nicko. "We thought you'd heard something. Don't do that again, OK?"

"But that's it, don't you see? The bridge fell down with a

great crash into their backyard and the witches haven't stirred. Not a peep. *Nothing.* It's dawn and now they must have gone to bed. Marcia says that Darke Witches usually sleep all day and do their stuff at night. So we can just walk out. Easy."

"Oh, yeah, *easy* to walk all the way through a creaky old house stuffed full of traps and witches waiting to grab you and change you into a toad and then even *easier* to get out their front door which, I'll bet, is Barred with something nasty. Easy-peasy."

Jenna looked up from finishing off Wolf Boy's hands. "There's no need to be so grumpy, Nik. We don't have any choice anyway. We have to get out through the witches' house. Unless you want to jump the twenty-foot gap back to that creepy house full of dolls."

A few minutes later they were standing in the dingy, cobweb-strewn passageway outside the annexe. Nicko was invisible. He was using his Silent Unseen Spell that, with Septimus's help, he had eventually managed to get right, after much prompting—"No, Nik, it's *Not seen, not heard, not a whisper, not a word.* And you have to imagine it too. It's no good just rattling it off like a demented parrot." So far the spell seemed to have worked—at least they had managed to get out of the room without activating the Creak on the door. Jenna and Septimus both had an Unseen Spell, which was not silent, but they had decided not to use it. It did not seem fair to leave only Wolf Boy visible to the witches.

They stood uncertainly outside the annexe door, wondering which way to go; it was difficult to work out which way led up and which went down. The Port Witches were great home-improvement enthusiasts—although improvement was not the word most people would have used to describe the results of their efforts. Over the years the Coven had turned the house into a warren of dead-end corridors and twisted staircases that usually ended in midair or dropped you out of a window. There were doors that opened into rooms where the witches had taken the floors out and not got around to putting them back; there were dripping pipes sticking out of the walls and at every step a rotten floorboard threatened to snap and send you plunging to the floor below. Added to the home improvements were the Blights, Banes and Bothers that infested the house and were designed to trip up any unwary intruder.

A small blue Bother was hanging from the ceiling by a string just outside their door. The Bother was an unpleasant, one-eyed, spiky creature covered in fish scales whose sole purpose in life was to stop anyone from doing what he or she wanted to do—but first, before it could do anything, it had to catch the person's eye. Jenna had not noticed the Bother and had walked straight into it. She had stepped back at once, but it was too late—she had glanced up and met its beady blue eye staring at her. Now the Bother set about its task with glee. It bounced around in front of Jenna, chattering in its babyish way. "Hello, ickle girly. Hellooo, there. Are 'ooo losty-wost? Me wanoo help 'ooo. Ooh me *dooo*."

"Oh, shut up," Jenna muttered as loud as she dared, trying to edge away from the creature.

"*Oooh*. That's *rudy-wude*. Me only wanoo help 'ooo . . ."

"Sep, can you stop this Bother Bothering me before I throttle it?"

"I'm trying to think of something. You've got to calm down, Jen. Try to ignore the stupid thing."

"Oooh. *Nasty* boy. Nasteeee . . ."

"Sep," said Jenna irritably. "What are you waiting for? Just get rid of it, will you? Now!"

"Not rid of meeee. I *help* 'ooo."

"Oh, shut up!"

"Jen, Jen, don't let it get to you, that's how it works—it irritates you so much that you can't do anything. Just give me a moment. I've got an idea."

"Oooh. Nasty boy's got an *idea*. Oooh."

"I'm going to kill it, Sep. I *am*."

"Oooh, *bad* girly. Not nice saying things like that. Oooh."

Septimus was busy rummaging in his Apprentice belt. "Hang on, Jen. I'll just find my Reverse. Ah, here it is." He took out a small triangular Charm and laid it in the palm of his hand with the sharp end pointing towards the Bother.

The Bother looked at it suspiciously. "What 'ooo got there, nasteee boy?" it asked querulously.

Septimus did not reply. He took a deep breath and chanted very slowly and quietly so as not to wake the witches,

"Bothersome Bother, Bother no more,
Forget what you're created for."

"Oh, dear," said the Bother faintly. "I feel all peculiar."

"Good," muttered Septimus. "Sounds like it's working. Now, I suppose I had better test it."

"Be careful, Sep," said Jenna, who suddenly felt much less hot and Bothered.

Muttering a simple SafeShield Spell to himself, Septimus forced himself to look at the Bother.

"Good morning," said the Bother brightly. "How may I help you?"

"You're getting good at this Magyk stuff," Jenna whispered to Septimus.

Septimus grinned. He loved the feeling of a spell working right. The Bother hung from the ceiling patiently awaiting an answer. "Could you please show us the way out?" Septimus asked it politely.

"With pleasure," replied the Bother. "Follow me, please." The creature detached itself from its piece of string and landed lightly in front of them on all four of its spindly legs. Then it scuttled off and, to everyone's surprise, leaped into an open trapdoor.

"Quick," said Septimus, "we'd better follow it. You go first, Nik, so that we're still Silent."

They followed the Bother down a long and very precarious ladder, which took them all the way through the house. The ladder bounced and flexed with the unaccustomed weight— for none of the witches ever dared use it—and by the time they reached the ground, Septimus was shaking.

As they stepped off the ladder into darkness they were greeted with a chorus of malevolent hissing. Wolf Boy hissed back.

"What's that?" Jenna whispered.

"Cats," muttered Septimus. "Loads of them. Shh, 409,

don't annoy them." But Wolf Boy's hissing had done the trick—the cats were quiet, terrified by the sound of the biggest, fiercest cat they had ever heard.

The Bother waited until they were all safely off the ladder. "As you see, ladies and gentlemen, we are now in the Coven kitchen, which is the hub of household activities. Follow me, please, and I will conduct you to the exit."

The Coven kitchen smelled of old fried fat and cat food. It was too dark to make out much except for the dull glow of the stove and the green glittering of a forest of cats' eyes, which followed their Silent progress across the room.

They were soon out of the kitchen and keeping close behind the Bother as it scuttled along a narrow passage. It was hard to see where they were going, for the house was very dark and gloomy; black cloths were pinned up at the windows and the walls were covered with a dirty brown paint and a few cracked paintings of witches, toads and bats. But as they squeezed around a narrow corner, a dusty shaft of light suddenly fell across the passageway—a door creaked open and a witch wandered out.

Nicko stopped dead and Septimus, unable to see him, crashed into him, followed closely by Jenna and Wolf Boy.

Stanley, who was running in front of Nicko, was caught in the shaft of light.

The witch stared at Stanley with wide eyes, and, aghast, Stanley stared at the witch.

"Hello. You're my rat, aren't you, boy?" the witch said in a strange singsong voice. "Let me turn you into a nice fat toad."

Stanley's mouth opened and closed again, but no sound came out. The witch blinked slowly; then she turned and peered at Septimus, Jenna and Wolf Boy, who had all shrunk back into the shadows.

"You've brought your friends with you too . . . mmm yum. Children. We like children, we do . . . and here's my own special Bother, which I hung up last night . . ."

"Hello, Veronica," said the Bother, somewhat disapprovingly. "Are you sleepwalking again?"

"Mmm," murmured the witch. "Sleepwalking . . . lovely."

"Go back to bed now," the Bother said crossly. "Before you fall down that trapdoor again and wake them all up."

"Yes. Back to bed now . . . nighty-nighty, Bother," murmured the witch, and she shuffled off down the passageway, eyes wide-open and staring into space. Jenna and Wolf Boy squeezed against the wall to let the sleepwalking witch go by.

"Oh, *phew*," breathed Septimus.

"This way now, if you don't mind please, ladies and gentle-men," said the Bother briskly, and it scuttled off under a thick black curtain that was draped across the passageway. Septimus, Jenna, Wolf Boy, Stanley and the Silent Unseen Nicko pushed their way around the dusty curtain and sighed with relief—on the other side was the front door.

The Bother ran up the door like a lizard on a hot wall and busily set about opening an array of bolts, locks and chains. Jenna smiled at Septimus—they were nearly out.

And then it started.

"Ow! Help. *Help!* Someone's attacking me. Help. Get off. Get off me!" screamed a piercingly high metallic voice. One of the locks was Alarmed.

"Shh, Donald," the Bother told the lock crossly. "Stop fuss-ing, it's only me." But the lock would not be shushed. It set itself into a loud, repetitive wail. "Ooh-ooh-ooh *help* . . . Ooh-ooh-ooh *help* . . . Ooh-ooh-ooh *help* . . ."

Suddenly above their heads came the sound of running footsteps and then agitated voices. The Port Witch Coven was awake. A few moments later came sounds of heavy footsteps on the stairs, followed by a loud crack of splintering wood and a scream.

"You idiot, Daphne!" yelled a voice. "I'd only just fixed that step and now look at it. Ruined." An answering groan came from Daphne.

Another voice shouted, "I smell intruders. I smell a rat! Quick, quick! Go down the back way." What sounded like a herd of stampeding elephants thundered above. The house shook. The Port Witch Coven was on its way.

"Ooh-ooh-ooh *help* . . . Ooh-ooh-ooh *help* . . ." shrieked the lock.

"Sep?" Jenna turned to Septimus in a panic. "Sep—can you do anything?"

"Dunno. I'm thinking—hang on." Septimus fumbled in his Apprentice belt again and pulled out a small packet labelled Rush Dust. Quickly he poured it into his palm and threw it over the Bother. The Bother coughed and spluttered; then suddenly it speeded up until it was nothing more than a blue blur, scrambling up and down the door, shooting bolts, undoing locks and freeing chains, while all the time the lock continued its ear-splitting wail. "Ooh-ooh-ooh *help* . . . Ooh-ooh-ooh *help* . . . Ooh-ooh-ooh *help* . . ."

Suddenly Jenna heard the sounds of witches downstairs in the kitchen, but at that moment, the front door flew open, pinning the Bother flat against the wall. In a flash Jenna, Septimus, Nicko, Wolf Boy and Stanley were out of the house and tearing down The Rope Walk, hardly daring to glance behind to see if a stream of witches were after them.

Back in the house of the Port Witch Coven the hall floor finally surrendered to years of being eaten by Daphne's giant woodworm colony and plunged the entire Coven headlong into the basement—where their fall was broken by the accumulated contents of a leaking sewage pipe.

✢ 28 ✢
THE CAUSEWAY

Jenna, *Septimus, Nicko, Wolf Boy* and Stanley took the Causeway out of the Port towards the Marram Marshes. Jenna led the way and behind her trotted Thunder, shaking his head and snorting in the cool morning air, glad to be out of the smelly stable he had spent the night in at the rear of the Doll House.

Jenna had insisted on going back for Thunder. She was afraid that if they left the horse behind, Nurse Meredith might have been tempted to sell him to the meat pie shop down by

the harbour. So, when they had rounded the end of The Rope
Walk and still no witches had come out of the house, Jenna
had crept down the dirt track that ran behind the houses and
led Thunder away.

The Causeway ran along the high ridge that skirted the
fields at the edge of the Port. As they walked in the early-
morning haze, Jenna could see the faded circus tent and smell
the well-trodden grass from the crowds the night before. It
was a quiet and peaceful scene, but Jenna was on edge—the
burn on her arm from Sleuth stung and was a constant
reminder that Simon now had a Tag on her—and any sudden
movement or sound made her jump. So when, out of the corner of her eye, Jenna saw a small dark shape making a strange
clattering noise and heading towards her, she panicked and
grabbed hold of Septimus.

"Ouch!" gasped Septimus. "What's up, Jen—what is it?"
Jenna ducked behind him. Something was heading straight for
her.

"Eurgh—eurgh gettitoff! Gettitoffme!" Jenna yelled, frantically brushing a large spiky insect off her shoulder.

The boys knelt down and peered at the bug, which lay on
its back in the fine dust of the Causeway, legs slowly waving
in the air and making a faint buzzing noise.

"But I thought it was dead," said Septimus, poking at the bug with his finger.

"How did it get here?" asked Nicko, shaking his head.

Wolf Boy stared at the bug. It didn't look very edible to him. Far too crunchy, he reckoned, and spiky too. He would not be surprised if it had a nasty sting.

Jenna peered over their shoulders. "What is it?" she asked.

"It's your Shield Bug," Septimus said.

"No!" Jenna dropped to her knees and very gently picked up the bug and laid it in the palm of her hand. She brushed as much dust off it as she could, and after a few moments, watched by a fascinated audience, the bug stood up and shakily began cleaning its wings, buzzing and fussing as it tried to get everything back into working order. And then, suddenly, with a triumphant clatter of wings against its green armour-plated shell, the bug rose into the air and took its rightful place on Jenna's shoulder—just as it had done more than a year ago when it had first been created at Aunt Zelda's cottage. Jenna's spirits lifted; now she had something to defend herself with if—or was it when?—Simon came looking for her.

The large horse with a rat perched upon his saddle and four figures walking beside him made slow but steady progress

along the Causeway. They had passed the fields that surrounded the Port and had now reached the reed beds, which
provided thatch, baskets, flooring and all manner of bits and
pieces for the inhabitants of the Port. As the morning sun rose
higher it burned off the few remaining tendrils of mist that
hung over the reed beds, which stretched almost as far as the
eye could see. Beyond the reed beds lay the Marram Marshes,
still shrouded in thick marsh mist.

Stanley was keeping what he called a low profile. He was
not a happy rat that morning, for he had just recognised the
turn-off to Mad Jack's hovel where, the previous year, he had
spent the six most miserable weeks of his life being imprisoned in a rat cage; he had only managed to escape after starv-
ing himself until he was thin enough to squeeze through the
bars.

It was midmorning by the time Stanley saw that the reed
beds were growing sparser and he smelled the dank smell of
the Marram Marshes drifting in, and he at last relaxed—now
that they were well away from Mad Jack. Soon the Causeway
petered out into a boggy track and the group came to a halt.

Jenna shielded her eyes against the glare of the sun and
squinted into the Marsh. Her heart sank—she had no idea
where the track to Aunt Zelda's cottage was. The last time

she had been here with Nicko it had been covered in ice and snow during the Big Freeze and had looked nothing like it did now.

Septimus stood next to her. "I thought the Boggart would be waiting for us," he said, puzzled. "I'm sure Aunt Zelda must know we're here."

"Um, no, I don't think she does, Sep," said Jenna. "Her hearing's not so good now and she finds it hard to Listen. I'm going to send Stanley out to tell her where we are."

"Excuse me? Did I hear you correctly?" the rat asked incredulously.

"Yes, Stanley, you did hear me correctly," replied Jenna. "I want you to go to Keeper's Cottage and tell Aunt Zelda we're here."

"Sorry, Your Maj, but as I said earlier, I don't do marshes—"

"If I ask you to do marshes, Stanley, you *do* them. Understand?"

"Er . . ." Stanley looked somewhat taken aback.

"And if you don't do what I ask, I'll have you dismissed from the Secret Rat Service."

"But—"

"Is that clear?"

Stanley could not believe his ears. Neither could Septimus or Nicko; they had never heard Jenna sound so determined.

"Is that clear, Stanley?"

"As crystal. Absolutely." Stanley looked miserably towards the Marram Marshes. Jenna was, he thought with grudging admiration, going to be a much tougher cookie as Queen than her mother had been.

"Well off you go then," said Jenna. "Make sure you tell Aunt Zelda to send the Boggart out to the Port side with the canoe. And be as quick as you can. Simon put a Tag on me, remember?"

They all watched the rat as he ran off along the boggy track, took a flying leap into the rough sedge grass that grew on the outer marshes and disappeared from view.

"I hope he'll be all right," said Jenna, shading her eyes and gazing in the direction Stanley had gone. She had not liked threatening Stanley but she had felt there was no other choice. Since Sleuth had Tagged her she knew it was only a matter of time before Simon found her—and she longed to get to the safety of Keeper's Cottage.

"He's a good rat," said Septimus. "He'll be back with the Boggart soon, just you see."

They sat down on the side of the Causeway. Thunder

nibbled contentedly at the grass and Jenna passed around the water bottle she had filled up at the Port spring on the way out. Nicko lay down and gazed at the sky, happy to spend a morning doing nothing much. Wolf Boy was restless; his hands hurt him and after a while he got to his feet and paced up and down the track to take his mind off the pain.

Jenna and Septimus were on edge and watchful, scanning the Marsh and the reed beds for any unusual movement. Every now and then an eddy of wind rustled across the reeds, a water vole dived into the water with a muffled splash or a bird suddenly called out to its mate with a mournful marsh cry—and Jenna and Septimus jumped. But as midday approached and the air became warm and sultry, the wind dropped and the sounds of the animals and birds quietened. Jenna and Septimus began to feel drowsy and their eyes slowly closed. Nicko fell asleep. Even Wolf Boy stopped his pacing, lay down and rested his burning hands on the cool grass.

Above them the hot sun glowed white in the cloudless sky—and far away, beyond the Marram Marshes, a dark speck appeared on the horizon.

✢ 29 ✢
FIGHT & FLYTE

Septimus *saw it first.*
Something Darke
crackled in the air and
made the hairs on the
back of his neck bristle.
He sat up with a
sudden jolt.

"What's the matter?"
asked Jenna, waking up
with a start. "Ouch,"
she grimaced, as the
Tag burn on her arm
began to throb.

"Look—over
there." Septimus

pointed to the sky. "I-I don't like the look of it. It's too big for a bird."

Jenna rubbed her arm and squinted up at the bright blue expanse, following the direction of Septimus's finger. In the distance, high above the Marram Marshes, she saw a large, black, birdlike shape. "It might be a Marsh Kite. . ." she said uncertainly.

Septimus shook his head and stood to get a better look, shielding his eyes against the glare of the bright light. He looked pale and serious.

"Wassup?" asked Nicko, blearily opening his eyes. Wordlessly, Jenna pointed towards the approaching shape. Wolf Boy stopped his pacing and looked.

"Weird . . ." he muttered under his breath.

"What can you see?" asked Nicko, worried. He knew that Wolf Boy's sight was as keen as a hawk's.

"Looks like a massive, great bat . . . but, no, hang on a minute . . . gosh, it's going fast . . . it's—*no*, that's not possible—"

"What?" asked Septimus edgily. "What's not possible?"

"Some idiot up in the air. Flying."

"You sure, 409?"

"Yep, 412."

"But that *is* impossible—no one can fly like that—I mean, properly, like a bird," said Jenna, with a feeling of dread.

"They did once. So it's been said." Septimus whistled under his breath.

The black speck was moving fast and soon there was no mistaking the shape of a flying man, his black cloak streaming out behind him, swooping over the Marshes, zigzagging back and forth somewhat erratically, and scanning the land below. He was honing in fast on the Tag that Sleuth had provided.

"It *is* Simon!" gasped Jenna, hardly able to believe what she was seeing.

"We need to hide," said Septimus. "Come on, Jen, the reed beds—quick!"

"Well, I don't see what you're all so bothered about," declared Nicko, staring up at the approaching figure. "There's four of us here and it's only Simon after all—just old smarty-pants big brother Simon. OK, so he's learned to fly, but so what? I bet Sep can do that too. Can't you, Sep?"

"No, Nik. Not like that. That's the real thing—that's Flyte."

"But you can go up and down, can't you, Sep? That's flight."

"Only a few feet off the ground, Nik. I couldn't fly like that in a million years. I didn't think *anyone* could."

Jenna had taken refuge next to Thunder and was holding on tightly to his reins. Somehow she felt safer beside the solid, unflustered animal as she watched the approaching figure in the sky. Septimus stood beside her, determined to protect Jenna this time. From a secret pocket in his Apprentice belt he took his most precious Charm. It was a tiny pair of silver wings that Marcia had given him when she had first asked him to become her Apprentice. The wings sat in Septimus's right palm and glittered in the sun. Across the shining silver, four words were written in letters of pure gold: Fly Free With Me.

Septimus tried to remember what it was he had done that morning with Marcia beside the Boggart patch—which seemed so long ago now—when he had first held the Charm and felt the tingle of Magyk shoot through him. He remembered that he had said the words to himself and imagined that he really was flying. That was all. Surely there was more to it than that?

"See—I knew you'd be able to do it, Sep," said Nicko admiringly as Septimus's feet lifted a few inches off the ground. Septimus looked down and landed with a thump.

Jenna, meanwhile, had not taken her eyes off the dark figure in the sky. He was close enough now for her to see his

long straw-coloured hair streaming behind him as he came
down low above the reed bed, honing in on the Tag. At the
last minute, when it looked as if he might hurtle headlong into
the Causeway, Simon swooped up and skidded to a halt with
a look of extreme concentration on his face. This was Simon's
first attempt at Flyte. He had crashed three times on takeoff
from the top of the Observatory roof and had narrowly
avoided smashing into one of the marsh islands which had
been overrun with chickens. It was nothing like as easy as
Hugh Fox had told him it would be.

Simon hovered now with some difficulty, as if buffeted by
the wind, and stared in surprise at the group below. He had
seen something he had not expected to ever see again—something he thought had been eaten by the massive Land Wurm
that now inhabited his Burrow (which was about to give birth
to ten little Land Wurms and was consequently extremely
bad-tempered and hungry).

"You've got my horse!" Simon yelled at Jenna. "You—you
horse thief!"

Everyone was transfixed by the sight of Simon in midair.
Forgetting the danger, they watched him, wondering what he
was going to do next.

"Go away and leave us alone, Simon!" said Jenna fiercely.

"Leave my horse alone then," Simon retorted, and suddenly he lost concentration—and height. Falling fast, he landed awkwardly beside Jenna, turning his ankle. Jenna leaped out of the way, pulling Thunder with her.

"Go away, Simon," Septimus told him angrily.

Simon laughed. "So you are going to *make* me go away, you Young Army brat? I don't think so."

With a surprising turn of speed, Simon grabbed the reins from Jenna and at the same time caught hold of her arm. He twisted it up behind her back until Jenna gasped with pain.

"Let her go, you *pig*," Nicko demanded. He hurled himself at Simon, but Simon was ready with a StunFlash, which he threw at Nicko's feet. The StunFlash knocked Nicko to the ground and caught Wolf Boy as it bounced away. Nicko tried to get up, but he couldn't; his head felt as though it was nailed to the ground. He closed his eyes—the light was hurting them, and the noise inside his head was making him feel horribly sick.

"Just be grateful that I know you're my brother," Simon told Nicko as he lay pale and sprawled on the dusty Causeway. "I don't Harm family. Well, not terminally anyway. But I don't see any more family around me—only a couple of kids who've stolen our name for themselves. Just like one of them stole my horse."

Simon tightened his grip on Jenna.

"Stop it, Simon," gasped Jenna. "You're hurting me."

"Am I? *Ouch!*" Simon's free hand flew up to his neck. "Blasted Marsh Flies," he complained, looking at the smear of blood on his hand as, unbeknownst to him, Jenna's Shield Bug stood on his shoulder, having just missed Simon's jugular vein with its razor-sharp sword, and lined up the sword for a second stab. The bug was out of practice—ever since it had been parted from Jenna in what was now known as The Great Storm, the bug had had no one to protect and had spent much of its time chasing an old enemy, the Hunter, who was now a buffoon at the circus. But the bug had never forgotten Jenna, and when it had seen her walk past the circus tent, it knew that once again it had a purpose in life—to protect her from her enemies.

The Shield Bug's sword flashed towards Simon's neck.

"Stop!" Jenna yelled out, unable to let the bug kill someone she still saw as her brother.

The bug paused, confused. Why was it not allowed to complete its job? The small, heavily armoured creature stood on Simon's shoulder, still eyeing up his neck, its arm itching to raise its sword and strike.

"Stop what, Princess? Surely I am not still hurting you. In fact, it appears to be me who's been hurt—as ever," said Simon, somewhat self-pityingly. He stared around him, suddenly gloomy. His neck stung badly from the Marsh Fly bite, his ankle stabbed with pain when he put any weight on it and somehow he had to get this awkward girl back to the Badlands. This time he would enjoy leaving her out for the Magogs. "Get on the horse," he said sharply to Jenna. "We're going."

"No, we're not, Simon," Jenna told him calmly.

"Don't tell me what we are or are not doing. Get on the horse." Simon yanked at Jenna's arm angrily.

"If you do that again, Simon, I will tell my Shield Bug to finish what it has started. I don't want to, but I will."

"What Shield Bug?" Simon glanced around him warily, and then it dawned on him just what had bitten him. His hand flew to his neck. He caught the bug, tapped it with a Reverse, and rolled it up into a tight ball. Simon hurled the bug into the reed beds. "Oh, *that* Shield Bug," he smirked triumphantly. "Now get on the horse."

"*You* get on the horse." Septimus's voice came out of nowhere. "Then get out of here and don't come back."

Simon and Jenna both looked up in surprise. Septimus was

hovering about ten feet above them.

In a moment, Simon had let go of Jenna and shot up off the ground to confront Septimus. Jenna watched the two brothers squaring off to one another ten feet above the ground. Septimus's lack of height compared to Simon was no longer a problem, and he stared Simon in the eye, daring him to make a move.

"Let Jenna be, Simon," Septimus told him, concentrating hard on trying to speak and hover at the same time, which was not as easy as he had hoped. As soon as he thought of what to say he found himself dipping towards the ground. "Go back . . . whoops . . . to wherever you came from and . . . ah . . . take your Darke Magyk with you."

Simon's eyes darkened with anger. Septimus noticed that they had become almost black, with disconcerting flashes of green playing across the irises like lightning in a thunderstorm.

"You don't fool me; you're a fake," Simon sneered. "You're a fake Heap and fake Apprentice. You've just got hold of one of those dinky little Wing Charms. Ten a penny, they are. No manoeuvrability, no speed and you'll get no higher than a hovel's chimney with those." As if to prove his point, Simon shot far above Septimus, then whizzed down again and buzzed around him in circles, like an angry bee.

"Flyte," Simon continued, circling Septimus and trapping him in midair. "Flyte, as you should know, being the ExtraOrdinary Wizard's little pet, is the last Lost Art, which *I* have rediscovered." Simon was gratified to see a look of amazement flash across Septimus's face. He had the kid rattled now; he knew it. This was turning out to be fun—at last. "And wouldn't you like to know where I discovered it, you little worm, hey?"

Septimus stared at Simon, determined not to give anything away and focusing all his concentration on staying in the air.

"Of course," Simon carried on, "I'd really like to say that you can go home to *dear* Marcia and her faithful Shadow and tell them all about how the next ExtraOrdinary Apprentice has discovered the Lost Art of Flyte, but unfortunately for you and the lovely Miss Overstrand, you will not be going back. You will be staying here in the reed beds along with the Shield Bug. *For ever.*"

Now Simon stopped his manic circling and came to a halt in front of Septimus. Almost lazily Simon reached into his pocket, while Septimus watched him, wondering what he was about to do. Then, with a sudden flick of his wrist, Simon hurled a Thunderflash at Septimus. Somehow Septimus threw himself to one side, and, with a deafening roar, the Thunderflash shot past his ear, singeing his hair and scorching the side of his face. Burning with a brilliant white light, it shot into the reed beds and exploded with a deafening clap of thunder, sending up a huge plume of muddy water, which landed on Nicko and Wolf Boy and woke them from the StunFlash.

The shock waves from the Thunderflash threw Septimus off-balance and, to his horror, he found himself falling against Simon. As Septimus crashed into him, Simon threw off his cloak and wrapped it tightly around his youngest brother, pinning Septimus's arms to his sides. Septimus struggled and fought but, at a muttered Command from Simon, the Darke cloak Transformed into a huge black serpent and curled around him, trapping him within its coils. With every breath that Septimus breathed out, the snake tightened its grip, so that each new breath was shallower and harder to take. Slowly, deliberately, Septimus was having the life crushed from him.

Simon hovered and watched the proceedings with a smirk—until a sharp stone caught his hand and sent him tumbling backwards with surprise.

"You got him!" came Jenna's voice from below. "Quick, quick, do another one!"

Wolf Boy did not need telling; he was already lining up his catapult for another shot. He drew back the sling and let loose a small round stone. It caught Simon's right eye and sent him plunging to earth, screaming in pain. He hit the ground with a dull thud. The serpent fell away from Septimus and followed its Master. It landed with a thump and slithered off into the reed beds. Septimus, dazed and light-headed from lack of oxygen, sank slowly down until Jenna, Nicko and Wolf Boy caught hold of him and laid him down on the bank. They were too concerned with Septimus, who was deathly white with a blue tinge to his lips, to notice that Simon had struggled to his feet. It was only when Jenna heard the sound of Thunder's hooves galloping along the Causeway that she looked up.

Simon Heap, one hand held to his blinded right eye, the other grasping Thunder's reins, was on his way back to the Badlands.

✢ 30 ✢
ON MARRAM MARSH

Now?" Stanley said incredulously. "You want me to go back *now*?"

"That *is* what I said," snapped Aunt Zelda, who had just unwrapped Jenna's sash from Wolf Boy's burned hands and did not like what she found.

Stanley stood on the doorstep of Keeper's Cottage, looking out into the brilliant sunshine where Jenna, Nicko and Septimus were sitting beside the Dragon Boat. Jenna had a clean white bandage around her arm and Septimus looked much less pale after one of Aunt Zelda's Anti-Snake cakes. Nicko was happily dabbling his feet in the warm marsh water.

Stanley gazed at the Dragon Boat. It was the most beautiful boat the rat had ever seen, and he had seen a lot of boats. Her prow was a tall arched dragon neck covered in iridescent green scales, her head was a shimmering gold and her eyes were a deep dragon-green. The hull of the boat was wide and smooth and shone a deep burnished gold in the sunlight, and folded alongside it were a pair of leathery, green dragon wings. At the stern, where the massive mahogany tiller rested, the dragon's tail rose into the air, its golden arrow point flashing in the sunlight. It was a peaceful, happy scene and Stanley felt safe on Aunt Zelda's island—he didn't want to leave. Aunt Zelda, however, had other ideas.

"There's no point hanging around," she told him. "If you go now you'll be off the Marsh by nightfall. It's the longest day of the year today and the best day to travel through the Marsh. It's far too hot for most of the creatures; they'll all be under the mud keeping cool."

"Except for the Bogle Bugs," Stanley said, gloomily scratching an ear. "Got followed by a cloud of Bogle Bugs all the way here. I'm still itching. Nasty things."

"Did they go up your nose?" asked Jenna, joining Stanley on the doorstep.

"What?" asked Stanley.

"The Bogle Bugs. Did they go up your nose? That's what they do. They go up your nose and then they clean out all the—"

"Jenna, Jenna, please. There is no need to go into details. We all know quite well what Bogle Bugs do." Aunt Zelda's voice came from the other side of a half-open door under the stairs with the sign UNSTABLE POTIONS AND PARTIKULAR POISONS on it. She was in her potion cupboard, searching for some Burn Balm.

"Stanley doesn't," Jenna pointed out.

"Stanley doesn't need to," said Aunt Zelda, emerging from the cupboard with a large glass jar of pink ointment. "Bogle Bugs don't do rats. Anyway, I'm trying to get him to go back to Marcia and tell the poor woman—and your mother and father too—that you are all safe. There's no need to worry him about Bogle Bugs as well as everything else."

"Won't he go?" asked Jenna.

The rat raised a paw in protest. "Excuse me," he said. "I'm still here. And I didn't exactly say I *wouldn't* go, Your Maj. Just that I would rather *not* go. If it's all the same to you."

"Well it's not all the same to me," said Jenna. "Or to Aunt Zelda."

"No. Didn't think it would be, somehow. I'll be off then. Do you have anything in particular you would like me to convey to the ExtraOrdinary?" Stanley asked glumly.

"Tell Marcia—and my parents at the Palace—that we are all safe at Aunt Zelda's cottage and I have arrived in time for the MidSummer Visit."

"Fine. Will do, Your Majesty."

"Good," said Jenna. "Thank you, Stanley. I won't forget this, I promise. I know you don't like the Marshes."

"No. I don't." Stanley jumped off the doorstep.

"Wait a minute," Aunt Zelda called out. Stanley looked back, hoping that she may have changed her mind. "Would you like to take a sandwich with you? I've got some left over from lunch."

"Um, what would be in the sandwich, exactly?" asked Stanley warily.

"Cabbage. I stewed it all morning, so it's lovely and soft."

"Very kind of you, but no thanks. I'll be off now." And with that, Stanley ran down the path. He scurried over the Mott bridge and out on to the Marram Marshes.

"Well," said Aunt Zelda, "I hope he'll be all right."

"So do I," said Jenna.

By late afternoon, Wolf Boy had developed a fever. He lay on Aunt Zelda's sofa, his hands covered with Burn Balm and clean white bandages, mumbling deliriously, lapsing in and out of consciousness. Septimus sat beside him, holding a cool damp cloth on Wolf Boy's forehead, while Aunt Zelda leafed through a large and well-thumbed book, the *Witch and Warlock Pharmacopoeia*.

"It's a Darke burn, that's for sure," muttered Aunt Zelda. "I dread to think what that Simon Heap is up to. If he's incubated a Tracker Ball—and a very effective one too—who knows what else he can do."

"Flyte," said Septimus glumly, wishing that 409 would cool down.

"Flyte?" Aunt Zelda looked up from the book, eyebrows raised, with shock in her bright blue witch's eyes. "*Real* Flyte? Are you sure, Septimus—sure it wasn't just hovering and a bit of illusion? They're good at illusion, are the Darke ones."

"I'm sure. I mean he couldn't have got to us any other way. Not with the Marram Marshes to get across."

Aunt Zelda looked pensive as she continued turning the

thick, crackly pages of the *Pharmacopoeia*, looking for the right potion. "Well, I just don't believe it," she said as she scanned each page of closely written vellum, trying to pick out the symbols she was looking for. "I mean, where has he got it from?"

"Marcia says the Flyte Charm doesn't exist," said Septimus. "She says it was thrown into a furnace by the Last Alchemist. He Sacrificed it in order to make the purest gold."

"Maybe," Aunt Zelda said. "Or maybe not."

"Oh?" asked Septimus, who was always interested to hear what Aunt Zelda had to say about Magyk. Her approach was refreshingly different from Marcia's—and sometimes Aunt Zelda knew surprising things that Marcia did not.

Aunt Zelda looked up from the *Pharmacopoeia* and regarded Septimus with a thoughtful expression. "This is between you and me," she said in a low voice.

Septimus nodded.

"There is a story," Aunt Zelda continued, "that the Last Alchemist did not Sacrifice the Flyte Charm. That he kept it for himself. You see, it was made from the most beautiful gold there is—from pure gold threads spun by the Spiders of Aurum. He fell in love with it and could not bear to let it go. So he Concealed it."

"Where?" asked Septimus.

Aunt Zelda shrugged. "Who knows? At the top of the tallest tree in the Forest? Under his mattress? In his socks?"

"Oh." Septimus was disappointed; he had expected more.

"But . . ." Aunt Zelda continued.

"Yes?"

"I have always believed that the Flyte Charm was here."

"Here?" Septimus gasped. "In Keepers Cottage?"

"Shh. Yes." Aunt Zelda turned another page and squinted at the formulae scrawled across it. "Naturally I have looked everywhere for it, but the problem with these ancient Charms is that they come from the Darke Age of Magyk, and they often only respond to a touch of Darkenesse—and that is one thing, Septimus, that I do not possess. Or have any wish to possess."

The cloth on Wolf Boy's forehead had become hot. Still thinking about the Flyte Charm, Septimus got up and took the cloth into Aunt Zelda's small kitchen. He dipped it in a bucket of cool spring water and wrung it out, then sat down again beside Wolf Boy and carefully laid it back in place. Wolf Boy did not stir.

"But . . ." said Septimus.

"I thought there'd be a 'but'," Aunt Zelda said with a smile in her voice.

"But why did you think the Flyte Charm was here? I know you must have had a reason."

"Well—you know, Septimus, that a Keeper may not marry?"

"Yes."

"And quite right too, for no wife should have to keep secrets from her husband, and a Keeper has many secrets to keep. But Broda Pye, one of the early Keepers, was secretly married—to the Last Alchemist. It's my belief that her husband Concealed the Flyte Charm here. I also believe that she may have kept some part of it for herself, if her Keeper's Diaries are to be believed—so the Flyte Charm may not be complete."

"But . . ."

"Yes? Oh, this looks promising." Aunt Zelda was peering through her spectacles at a blackened page in the *Witch and Warlock Pharmacopoeia*.

"I don't see why he didn't just Conceal it in the Castle," said Septimus. "It was a dangerous journey to make with a precious Charm. Weren't the Marshes much worse in the old days— stuffed full of carnivorous pikefish and all sorts of Darke Things? Well, you wouldn't think he'd risk losing the Flyte Charm in some horrible bit of Quake Ooze, would you?"

Aunt Zelda looked up and regarded Septimus over the top of her spectacles. "There is more than one way to kill a cat," she said cryptically. And before Septimus could ask her what she meant, Aunt Zelda dumped the heavy *Witch and Warlock Pharmacopoeia* in his lap. "Have a look at that one," she said, pointing to the scorched page. "I think it might do the trick. It's got a genuine Boris Boil Reverse, so there's a bit of Darkenesse in it. What do you think?"

"*Black Burn Brew—a Cat's Claw Concoction,*" Septimus read. "*For added efficacy in suspected Darke contamination we recommend forming an Admixture with Boris Boil's Reverse Remedy Number III. Caution: DO NOT BOIL. See page xxxv for Final Formula. Apply immediately. Stable for thirteen minutes precisely. Dispose of with extreme care.*" Septimus gave a low whistle. "That sounds really complicated."

"It *is* really complicated," replied Aunt Zelda. "It will take me an hour or so to Mix it. But I know I've got all the ingredients. I always keep a bottle of Boil's Bane in the safe, and I bought some Cat's Claw from the year-and-a-day market last year." She got up and disappeared back into her potions cupboard.

Septimus stayed beside Wolf Boy, who lay white and still like a rock in the sun, burning up inside with a Darke fever.

Anxiously, Septimus watched the firmly closed potion cupboard door. He remembered it well from his previous time with Aunt Zelda. Inside was a small, dark cupboard crammed full of all manner of Aunt Zelda's most precious and delicate potions—and a trapdoor to the tunnel that had once led to the old temple where the Dragon Boat had lain under the earth for hundreds of years. But since the walls of the temple had been washed away in The Great Storm, the tunnel now went to the cabbage patch and Aunt Zelda had got into the habit of using it as a short cut.

Jenna appeared, silhouetted in the bright light of the doorway. "How is he?" she asked in an anxious voice.

"I don't think he's very well," Septimus replied quietly. "Aunt Zelda's doing a really complicated potion for him."

Jenna sat down beside Septimus. "Do you think he'll be all right, Sep?" she asked.

"I don't know—oh, that was quick—"

Aunt Zelda had burst out of the cupboard looking flustered. "Marsh Bane. I need fresh Marsh Bane. Would you believe it—*fresh*. Wretched recipe. Go ask Boggart, would you? Now. Please."

Septimus jumped up.

"No, Sep. You stay with him. I'll go," Jenna said.

"Tell Boggart it's urgent," Aunt Zelda called out after Jenna's departing figure. "Just ignore it if he makes a fuss."

The Boggart did make a fuss. Jenna had to call him three times before the large brown marsh creature surfaced from his mud patch in a sea of muddy bubbles.

"Can't a Boggart get no sleep on the hottest day of the year?" he demanded, his black eyes blinking crossly in the bright sunlight. "Waddyou want *now*?"

"I'm really sorry, Boggart," Jenna apologised, "but Aunt Zelda urgently needs some fresh Marsh Bane and she—"

"Marsh Bane? I gotto go an' get *Marsh Bane*?"

"Please, Boggart," pleaded Jenna. "It's for the boy with the burned hands. He's very ill."

"Oh. Well, I is very sorry to 'ear that. But I is also sorry to be out again gettin' sunburned and havin' no sleep. Not ter mention havin' ter ferret around under all them *disgustin'* slugs." The Boggart shuddered and blew a large bubble out of his snub, seal-like nose. Jenna caught a whiff of the fabled Boggart Breath; she stepped back and swayed slightly. Boggart Breath was even stronger in the hot sun.

"Tell Zelda I'll bring the Marsh Bane around as soon as I

finds some," said the Boggart, and with that he sank back into the mud.

A few minutes later Jenna saw him surface in the Mott, a wide channel that ran all the way around the island. She watched the Boggart make speedy progress along the channels and ditches that led from the Mott out into the Marsh until, some distance away, he came to the Hundred-Foot Pit where the Marsh Bane grew. Jenna watched him raise his head from the water, take a deep breath and disappear from view.

The Boggart closed his ears and nostrils and sank like a stone into the Hundred-Foot Pit. He was an expert diver and could hold his breath for at least an hour, so he did not mind the diving part of his errand at all. What he did mind, however, were the things he knew he would find on the bottom of the pit. The Boggart was not a squeamish creature, but the Great White Marsh Slugs—which were for ever in a state of semidecomposition—made even him shudder. A pile of the giant slugs lived at the bottom of the pit, and it was underneath these that the Marsh Bane flourished, nourished by the rotting slug flesh. Marsh Bane was a powerful catalyst for any potion, but *fresh* Marsh Bane . . . the Boggart shook his head disapprovingly. He hoped Zelda knew what she was doing, messing around with the fresh stuff.

Jenna sat beside the Mott, waiting for the Boggart to resur-
face. To while away the time she picked up a few small grey
pebbles and stroked them, in the hope that one of them might
be her old pet rock, Petroc Trelawney. Silas had given her
Petroc for her tenth birthday, but he had wandered off during
Jenna's last MidSummer Visit. Jenna still hoped she might
find him, but none of the pebbles she stroked stuck their
stumpy little legs out as Petroc would have done. She sighed
and threw them one by one into the Mott and hoped that the
Boggart would not be too long.

Jenna was not the only person waiting for the Boggart.
Beside the Hundred-Foot Pit, lying on a patch of soft grass, lay
the long, thin figure of a boy. He was dressed in a pair of ill-
fitting patchwork trousers and a loose tunic made from some
rough woven cloth. Despite Aunt Zelda's best efforts to feed
him up, Merrin Meredith, ex-Apprentice to DomDaniel, was
still as thin as a stick. It was now well over a year since Aunt
Zelda had nursed him back to life after he had been
Consumed by his old Master, but echoes of the experience
still hovered in the haunted look in his deep grey eyes. On his
good days Merrin did not mind Aunt Zelda's company, but on
his bad days—and this was one of them—he could not bear
to be near her, or anyone else. On these days, Merrin still felt

as if he were Consumed and did not really exist.

Merrin was cross. He had felt cross ever since a talkative rat had arrived with an urgent request for the Boggart to go out to the Port side of the Marsh and take the canoe to collect the horrible Princess girl. Merrin had hung around by the channel that came in from the Port side, and when the canoe came into view he had felt even more cross.

Sure enough, there was the stuck-up Princess girl sitting in the front of the canoe, just as he had expected. But there were three others with her. *Three.* One of them didn't look too bad. He was a thin, grubby boy who reminded Merrin of the pet wolf his old Master had kept for a while. But the other two were the last people in the world that Merrin wanted to see. There was that nasty Nicko boy who had once fought him and called him a pig and twisted his arm so that it had really hurt. But worst of all there was that Septimus Heap kid—the one who had stolen his name. His *own name.* It was no good that Aunt Zelda kept telling him that his real name was Merrin Meredith—what did she know? He had been called Septimus Heap all his life. It may have been a stupid name, but it was all he had known.

In a bad temper, Merrin had gone off to his place by the Hundred-Foot Pit. He knew he would not be disturbed until

Aunt Zelda called him back at dusk, but now, to his irritation, he *had* been disturbed—by the smelly old Boggart.

Merrin lay angrily jabbing a pointed stick into the mud, waiting for the Boggart to go away and leave him alone. After what felt like an age, there was a spluttering gurgle beside him, and he saw the Boggart's head break the surface of the thick brown water. Merrin said nothing; he was wary of the Boggart, as he was of most creatures. The Boggart shook his head and spat out a spray of foul-smelling water, some of which landed on Merrin.

"Disgustin'," the Boggart told Merrin. "Filthy things. There's more of 'em down there than ever. Had to *shovel* 'em out of the way. I'll be pickin' bits a slug outta me nails fer days. Eurgh." The Boggart shuddered. "Still, I got Zelda's Bane." He held up a fistful of wriggling white streamers that immediately began to shrivel up in the sunlight. "Oops," said the Boggart, plunging them back under the water. "Mustn't let 'em dry out." With that he was off along the channels to the Mott where Jenna saw him and ran to the bridge to meet him.

Merrin watched her while he speared an unsuspecting Marsh beetle with a well-aimed stab.

✢ 3 I ✢
DRAGONS

There had been two small explosions in the potion cupboard—and a good deal of foul-smelling green smoke had poured out from under the door when Aunt Zelda added the fresh Marsh Bane—but now, at last, after she had dripped thirteen drops of Cat's Claw Concoction on to his tongue, Wolf Boy was sleeping peacefully.

The MidSummer sun had just set. Jenna, Nicko and Septimus were sitting on the doorstep watching the last streaks of red disappear and the pinpoint light of Venus become steadily brighter in the darkening sky. Merrin was keeping as far away from them as he could. He was busying himself at the far end of the cottage, feeding and counting his large collection of ants, which Aunt Zelda let him keep in an assortment of old potion jars.

As midnight approached, Aunt Zelda lit a lantern for Jenna's yearly meeting with the Dragon Boat. Merrin was already upstairs huddled underneath his quilt. But, despite telling himself that he did not care one bit what that stupid bunch were doing with that weird boat, Merrin found himself drawn to the small attic window that looked out on to the Mott where the Dragon Boat was moored.

What Merrin did not understand—because, knowing of Merrin's delight in hurting living creatures, Aunt Zelda had taken care not to tell him—was that the Dragon Boat was indeed partly a living, breathing dragon. Many, many hundreds of years ago, the Dragon Boat had once been a complete dragon. She had been a rare human hatching, hatched by Hotep-Ra, the first ExtraOrdinary Wizard, long before he had ever dreamed of travelling to the Castle and building the Wizard Tower. Many years later, on a terrifying night when Hotep-Ra fled his own country and began his journey north, the dragon had Transformed herself into a beautiful boat in order to save him from his pursuers. It was a generous gift, for a dragon can undergo only one such transformation in a lifetime; thus Hotep-Ra's dragon knew she would remain a boat until the end of her days.

At the prow of the boat was the living dragon's neck and head, at the stern was her barbed tail. The sails were her wings, folded neatly along the sides of the large wooden hull. When she had Transformed, the dragon's ribs had become the hull's ribs supporting the curved wooden planks, and her spine, running down the length of the hull, had become the keel. Deep in a locked hold, which no one had opened—not even Aunt Zelda—beat her heart, silent and slow.

In the light cast by the lantern, Merrin watched Aunt Zelda walk with Jenna down to the Dragon Boat. They stood for a moment in front of the prow, gazing up at the green and gold head of the dragon. Then, to his amazement, Merrin saw the dragon's head *move*. Jenna stood still in the yellow pool of lantern light, while the prow of the boat dipped down to meet her, until the dragon's head was level with Jenna's face. The dragon's emerald-green eyes looked directly into Jenna's and cast a rich green glow over her dark hair. It was as if they were talking to each other without words, thought Merrin. He watched Jenna reach out to stroke the dragon's nose and somehow he could tell that the nose was soft and warm to the touch. Merrin felt a longing to touch the dragon too, but he knew it was not for him. He noticed, with a feeling of satisfaction, that it was not for that Septimus Heap boy, or the pig boy either, as they were hanging back in the shadows watching, just as he was.

Merrin watched Jenna put her ear close to the dragon's head. He thought he saw Jenna's smile fade and turn to a frown, and he wondered what the dragon had said. Merrin loved knowing what people were talking about; he had got into the habit of listening to other people's plots and schemings when he was DomDaniel's Apprentice, mostly because no one would talk to him, and it was the only way he got to hear the sound of a human voice that wasn't shouting at him. Intrigued now by the scene by the Mott, he hopped about impatiently at the window, longing to hear what was being said.

What Merrin did not realise was *no one* could hear what was being said. His first impressions were right: Jenna and the dragon were communicating without words, as all the Queens throughout the ages had done with the Dragon Boat. Every MidSummer Day, when the power of the Dragon Boat was at its height, the Castle Queen would visit the boat. The first visit of a Castle Queen had been many, many hundreds of years ago, when the Dragon Boat was being repaired by Hotep-Ra's boat builders after she had been shipwrecked at the mouth of the river on the way to the Castle. Those were sunny visits, with the Dragon Boat regaining her strength in the bright Marsh air. But, as Hotep-Ra grew old and his powers began to wane and his plans go awry, he had become afraid for the safety of the Dragon Boat and had walled her up in an old underground temple on the island where Aunt Zelda now lived. By the instructions of Hotep-Ra, the Dragon Boat was watched over by a succession of Keepers and visited by a succession of Queens every MidSummer Day. No one knew why this had to be done, for Hotep-Ra's writings had been lost. All the Keepers and the Queens knew was that it was one of the two things that kept the Castle safe—the other was the presence of the Queen.

And now the visit was complete, Merrin watched Jenna put her arms around the dragon's neck as if to say goodbye, and then as she let go, he saw the dragon slowly raise her head to its usual position and become nothing more than a beautiful boat once more. Jenna looked at the Dragon Boat for a moment and then she and Aunt Zelda walked back up the path. As they came nearer the cottage, Merrin lost sight of them. Suddenly Merrin felt very sleepy; the slow, silent scene that had been played out in front of him had had a strangely soporific effect. For once, instead of listening at the top of the

stairs as he usually did, he went back to bed and fell asleep.
For the first time ever, that night Merrin did not have his
usual nightmares.

Downstairs, Aunt Zelda had lit a small fire of apple wood
and was pouring some celebratory parsnip and cabbage juice.
MidSummer Night was an important night for all White
Witches, but it was especially important for the White Witch
Keepers on Draggen Island. Aunt Zelda was the latest in a
long line of Keepers, but she was the very first to have the
Dragon Boat moored outside her cottage, just like any ordinary marsh boat. In the past, on MidSummer Night, all the
previous Keepers had taken the Queen down through the
trapdoor in the potion cupboard and along the tunnel to the
old temple, where the Dragon Boat had been left by its first
Dragon Master, Hotep-Ra.

The Dragon Boat's second Dragon Master now sat sipping
parsnip and cabbage juice beside the fire, fiddling with the
Dragon Ring he wore on his right index finger and saying to
Jenna, "What's the matter? What did she say? Tell us, Jen."

Jenna did not reply. She stared into the fire, thinking hard.

Aunt Zelda came and sat beside them. "You should never
ask the Queen—or, indeed, the Queen-to-be—what the
dragon said. Even in the old days when the ExtraOrdinary

Wizards still knew about the Dragon Boat, they would not have dared to ask *that*," she told Septimus sternly.

"Oh. But Jen doesn't mind telling us, do you, Jen? Anyway, if it's something bad she shouldn't have to think about it all on her own."

Jenna looked up from the fire. "I don't mind Septimus asking," she said.

"I'm sure you don't," said Aunt Zelda. "But you do need to know about how things are done—how they've always been done. And without your . . . oh, dear . . . without your mother here to tell you . . . well, I feel I should let you know all that I can."

"Oh," said Jenna, and then lapsed into silence. After a while she said, "I *do* want to tell you what the dragon told me. She told me that she knows a Darke One is coming. She says she is no longer safe here—"

"Of course she's safe here," Aunt Zelda spluttered indignantly. "She is with *me*—I am the Keeper. I Keep her safe."

Jenna carried on, speaking in a low, steady voice, all the while staring at the fire, unable to look at Aunt Zelda while she was telling her so many unwelcome things. "The dragon said that since the temple was washed away and she has been outside, she has been expecting a Darke One to find her."

"Well, why didn't she tell you that when you came last year?" asked Aunt Zelda somewhat peevishly.

"I don't know," said Jenna. "Maybe she didn't want us to put her back under the ground again. She's only human—I mean, dragon. She loves the sun and the smell of the marsh air."

"Exactly," said Aunt Zelda. "It would be a terrible thing to hide her away again. And she looks so beautiful. I talk to her all the time now that she's out there."

Jenna wondered how she was going to tell Aunt Zelda what the Dragon Boat had asked her to do. "She says she must leave," Jenna mumbled.

"She *what*?" gasped Aunt Zelda.

"She wants me to ask her new Dragon Master to take her away to safety—to keep her safe just as the last one did when he put her into the old temple. I'm really sorry, Aunt Zelda, but that's what she said. She said the Time has Come for her to complete her journey to the Castle."

"But I am the Keeper," Aunt Zelda protested. "There have always been Keepers here . . . I have made the Keeper's Promise—to Keep her safe at all times. And I *will*. I can't let her go. I *can't*." She heaved herself up from the stool she was sitting on. "I'm going to make a cabbage sandwich. Does anyone want one?"

Jenna and Nicko shook their heads but Septimus hesitated a moment. Since he had become an Apprentice he had missed Aunt Zelda's cabbage sandwiches, and even though Marcia had made him one as a treat on his last birthday, it had not tasted the same. But he too shook his head; he did not feel at all hungry just then.

As he sat on the floor beside the fire, worrying about what he was expected to do with the Dragon Boat—not to mention what Aunt Zelda was going to have to say about it if he did— Septimus became aware of something pecking at him. It must be Bert, he thought, reaching out to shoo her away. Bert was Aunt Zelda's cat who had taken the form of a duck and was in the habit of pecking anyone who sat in her place beside the fire. But there was no sign of Bert.

"What's up, Sep?" asked Nicko.

"I felt something peck me. But Bert's not here . . . Ow! There it is again." Septimus jumped up. "Ouch! There's something in my pocket. It's biting me!"

"Eurgh," gasped Jenna. "I bet it's one of those Mud Snappers. They were jumping all over the place while I was waiting for the Boggart. Get rid of it, Sep. Chuck it out the door—quick!"

Septimus headed to the door.

"What's going on?" asked Aunt Zelda, coming back with a great doorstop of a cabbage sandwich in her hand.

"Sep's got a Mud Snapper in his pocket," said Jenna. "It's biting him."

"Vicious little brutes," said Aunt Zelda. "Make sure you throw it over the other side of the Mott, Septimus. We don't want it coming back indoors."

Septimus opened the door and gingerly turned out his tunic pocket. To his surprise, there was nothing there. Then, as his hand hovered near his belt, something poked its head from a large hole that had appeared in the pouch he wore at his waist. It bit his finger—hard, and this time it hung on to it.

"Aargh!" yelled Septimus, dancing around, frantically shaking his hand to try to get rid of the small green thing with very sharp teeth, all of which were sunk into his right index finger, just above his Dragon Ring.

"Good heavens," gasped Aunt Zelda. "What have you got there?"

"Getitoffme!" Septimus shouted, not daring to look. And then, the small green thing (which had not yet worked out how to breathe and bite at the same time) took a breath. It let go of Septimus's finger and, as Septimus gave his hand yet another wild shake, it arched high into the air, narrowly missing Aunt Zelda's collection of brooms that hung from the rafters. Everyone watched as, at the height of its trajectory, the creature opened two small wings and flapped them ineffectively as it headed straight for Jenna—and landed in her lap.

Jenna sat, staring with amazement at a small baby dragon.

⊹ 32 ⊹
SPIT FYRE

Y ou're stuck with it now," Aunt Zelda told Septimus as she bandaged his bleeding finger. "It Imprinted you when it bit your finger. It's going to be a bit of a handful when it grows up, mind. You ought to get yourself a Dragon Training manual from somewhere. Though where you'd find one nowadays, I don't know."

Septimus sat looking at the cracked remains of the rock that Jenna had given him during their previous stay with Aunt Zelda. She had found it while Septimus was helping her escape from the Hunter—it had been lying in the tunnel that led to the temple where the Dragon Boat was hidden. Septimus had treasured the rock; it was the very first present that anyone had ever given him. As he stared at the thick green eggshell that lay in pieces in his cupped hands, Septimus could not believe that his beautiful rock had turned out to be a dragon egg—what were the chances of *that* happening? he wondered.

The chances were remote. Septimus did not know that there were only about five hundred dragon eggs scattered throughout the world, and it had been many, many years since a human had helped to hatch a dragon. Dragon eggs are usually found in old, long-forgotten dragon haunts, and many people who find them do pick them up and keep them on account of their beautiful sheen. Not all dragon eggs are green—many are blue and occasionally a rare red is found. But generally they spend their days in display cabinets or tucked away in old shoe boxes and never hatch, for a dragon egg needs to follow a complicated sequence of events, all in the right order, all within a certain amount of time, to allow it to become a baby dragon. The last time that had happened had been five hundred years ago on a small desert island, when a lone shipwrecked sailor had awoken one morning to find that his treasured blue rock had hatched into an unexpected, and extremely troublesome, companion.

Like the shipwrecked sailor, Septimus had unknowingly done all the right things that needed to be done in order to hatch a dormant dragon egg. Firstly, he had kick-started the incubation by leaving the egg close to the fire at Aunt Zelda's on his last visit. A dragon egg needs sustained heat of over eighty degrees for at least twenty-four hours in order to get the process going. It then needs a year and a day of constant warmth and movement.

After rescuing the dragon egg from beside the fire, Septimus had decided to keep it in his pocket, which provided not only the warmth that the dragon needed but also the sensation of movement. A dragon will not hatch just because it is warm; it needs to think that its mother is carrying it around with her and will be there to care for it when it hatches. To a dragon egg, no movement means no mother. Septimus unwittingly provided the egg with a year and a day of warmth and quite enough running and jumping to convince the tiny dragon that its mother was very lively indeed. After the year and a day had passed, the dragon would be almost ready, but even at this stage all could go wrong. It now needed a sharp tap to wake it up—if this did not happen within the following six months, the dragon would die and never have the chance of hatching. A dragon mother would normally use this time to find a safe place in which to hatch and bring up the baby dragon. When she had done so she would give the egg a very gentle bite. Luckily for Septimus's egg, the wolverines had thoughtfully stepped in for the dragon mother when they had broken their teeth crunching the outer shell. At that point the baby dragon was very nearly hatched—nearly, but not quite. There was one last thing it needed, and this was provided not by Septimus, but by his brother Simon. The dragon egg needed a touch of Darkenesse.

All dragon mothers had different ways of providing the last requirement. Some would kidnap a passing Thing and show it to the egg; some would leave the egg outside a Darke Witch's house overnight and hope that it would still be there in the morning. Some dragons had enough of their own Darkenesse and no need to go looking for more. So when Simon's cloak had become a snake and wrapped itself around Septimus and the egg, it had provided the final touch and started the clock ticking. The baby dragon was then set to hatch in twelve hours' time—which was exactly what it had done.

"I don't know much about dragons—well, not newborn ones anyway," said Aunt Zelda as she finished bandaging Septimus's finger and the last bite of her cabbage sandwich at the same time. "But I do know that the sooner you give them a name the better. If you leave it too long they will be Nameless and never come when you call. It's hard enough getting them to take any notice of you at the best of times, from what I understand. And for the first twenty-four hours it should not leave your side—so you'd better let Septimus have it back now, Jenna."

"Here you are then, Sep," said Jenna a little regretfully. She scooped the tiny winged lizard out of her lap and handed it to Septimus. "It's cute, isn't it?"

Septimus stared at the sleeping dragon, which lay curled up in the palm of his hand. It felt surprisingly heavy for its size, cool to the touch and as smooth as the egg from which it had hatched.

Nicko gave a loud yawn and stretched sleepily. "Gotta get some sleep," he said. The yawn was catching.

"Name first, then sleep," said Aunt Zelda. "What's it to be?"

Septimus had no idea. He stared at the dragon and caught Nicko's yawn. He was far too tired to go making up names for dragons. Suddenly the dragon sat up and coughed up some egg sac; two tiny bursts of flame spluttered from its nostrils and scorched Septimus's hand.

"Ouch!" he gasped. "It's spitting fire at me. That's it—Spit Fyre. That's its name. *Spit Fyre.*"

"Go on, then," said Aunt Zelda.

"Go on what?" asked Septimus, sucking his burned fingers.

"Dragons like everything to be done by the rules," Aunt Zelda told him. "You have to say . . . now let me think . . . ah, yes—*Oh, faithful companion and fearless friend, who will be with me until the end, I name thee Spit Fyre*—or Poodle-Face or Derek or . . . well, whatever you happen to have decided."

Septimus stared at the dragon in his hand and murmured wearily, "*Oh, faithful companion and fearless friend, who will be with me until the end, I name thee Spit Fyre.*" The dragon gazed at him with its unblinking green eyes and coughed up some more egg sac.

"Yuck," said Septimus.

Septimus did not get much sleep that night. Spit Fyre was fretful; whenever Septimus dozed off the dragon nipped his fingers or scrabbled at his clothes with its sharp claws. Eventually, in a bad temper, Septimus stuffed the dragon back into the pouch he had kept the egg in and at last it settled down to sleep.

They were all woken far too early the next morning by Spit

Fyre fluttering frantically at the window like a butterfly trying to get outside.

"Tell it to be quiet, Sep," Nicko said blearily, stuffing his pillow over his head and trying to get back to sleep. Septimus got up and snatched Spit Fyre off the windowpane. He was already beginning to see what Aunt Zelda meant about a baby dragon being trouble. The dragon scrabbled against his hand with its sharp little claws, and Septimus shoved it back into its pouch again.

The morning sun was already high in the sky and shining through the marsh mist. Septimus knew he was too wide-awake to go back to sleep again. He glanced at Jenna, Nicko and Wolf Boy who were all still bundled up in their quilts and had gone back to sleep. Not wanting Spit Fyre to disturb them, Septimus decided to take the dragon outside for its first breath of morning air.

Silently he closed the heavy door behind him and walked down the path towards the Dragon Boat. Someone was already there.

"It's a beautiful morning," said Aunt Zelda pensively.

Septimus sat beside her on the wooden bridge that spanned the Mott. "I thought maybe the Dragon Boat should meet her baby. I mean, I suppose Spit Fyre is the Dragon Boat's egg?"

"I imagine so," said Aunt Zelda. "Although one can never be sure with dragons. But Spit Fyre has Imprinted you, so I wouldn't complicate matters. Here, I found this for you. I knew I had one somewhere." Aunt Zelda handed Septimus a small green book bound in what looked suspiciously like dragon skin. It was called *How to Survive Dragon Fostering: A Practykal Guide.*

"Of course what you really need is the *Winged Lizard's Almanac of the Early Years*," Aunt Zelda told him. "But I doubt that even the Pyramid Library has one of those. Unfortunately they were written in rather flammable parchment and you just don't get them any more. Still, this might be some help."

Septimus took the musty-smelling book and idly stared at the endorsements on the back cover.

"This book saved my life. No dragon tooth can get through the cover. Wear this book at all times."

"I only lost one finger while I fostered Fang, thanks to the handy hints section in this invaluable guide."

"After I got Imprinted by Skippy all my friends deserted me and I was going crazy until I read this book. Now I am allowed out of the Asylum at weekends—and who needs friends anyway?"

"Oh, thanks, Aunt Zelda," Septimus said gloomily.

Septimus and Aunt Zelda sat in a companionable silence,

each with their own thoughts, listening to the marsh sounds as the heat of the summer day began to seep through the mist and wake up the more active marsh creatures. Like Jenna, Septimus had become adept at identifying the different sounds, and he was sure he heard the squelch of the suckers of a couple of Water Nixies, followed by the sharp snap of a Mud Snapper and the splish-splash of some baby eels. Soon the heat of the sun had burned off the last remnants of the mist, and the clear blue sky promised a swelteringly hot day.

Aunt Zelda gazed up at the bright blue. There was something tense about her that caught Septimus's attention. He looked at Aunt Zelda. Her lined round face, which was framed by her crinkly and somewhat dishevelled grey hair, had an anxious look to it, and her deep blue witch's eyes glittered as she focused on something high in the sky. Suddenly she heaved herself up from the bridge and grabbed Septimus by the hand.

"Don't look up," she said in a low voice. "Don't run. Just walk slowly back inside with me."

Inside the cottage, Aunt Zelda quietly closed the heavy front door and leaned against it. She was pale and her eyes had a desolate expression.

"Jenna's right," Aunt Zelda whispered, almost to herself.

"The Dragon Boat . . . she'll have to leave."

"Why? What—what did you see?" asked Septimus, although he had guessed the answer.

"Simon. He's up there. Like a vulture. Waiting."

Septimus took a deep breath to try and quell the knotted feeling that had suddenly appeared in his stomach. "Don't worry, Aunt Zelda," he told her. "The Dragon Boat will be safe at the Castle. I'll take her back there."

Although he had no idea how.

✛ 33 ✛
TAKEOFF

Merrin watched the Dragon Boat through his eyeglass. He had found the eyeglass half buried in a Brownie burrow during one of his many lone expeditions on the Marshes, and it was his little secret from Aunt Zelda.

Merrin liked having secrets from Aunt Zelda, although they did not usually last long, as she invariably found them out. But he was sure that this secret was one that he had managed to keep—by means of burying the eyeglass under a slab of rock on the grassy knoll beside the Hundred-Foot Pit. Merrin knew that as long as Aunt Zelda did not see him using the eyeglass he would be safe, for there was no way she could get across the sinking bog that surrounded the pit—only Merrin was light and agile enough to jump over the hidden stepping-stones that lay just beneath the surface of the bog.

Merrin had guessed, rightly, that the eyeglass had once belonged to his old Master, DomDaniel. There was a Darkenesse about it that made Merrin feel comfortable and reminded him of old times. They may not have been happy times, but at least they were interesting and he was not stuck out on a smelly old Marsh with only a load of cabbages and an inter-fering old witch for company. He raised the eyeglass to his eye, careful not to let the sun glint off it and give his position away, and he smiled to himself to think it was he who was still alive on the Marsh and DomDaniel who was now nothing more than a pile of bones, picked clean by the Marsh Brownies. Serves him right, thought Merrin gleefully. That old Necromancer shouldn't have been so nasty to his faithful Apprentice.

It was now late in the afternoon and the high spring tide—
for it had been a new moon the day before—was filling up the
channels of the Marsh. Merrin's grassy knoll was now completely surrounded by black, peaty marsh water. The Marsh
was quiet in the sleepy late afternoon heat and Merrin lay idly
on the knoll. He had been observing the comings and goings
between the cottage and the Dragon Boat all afternoon and
could not make any sense of it. Aunt Zelda, who was usually
so bossy, seemed to be at a loss, dolefully hanging around the
Dragon Boat, while the Princess girl and the pig boy had busied themselves raising the mast and talking to Aunt Zelda.
The Septimus Heap boy had been on the boat for ages, which
really irritated Merrin, as he was never allowed on. Merrin
tried to see what Septimus was doing, but as far as he could
tell he was just looking at the tiller while the pig boy was
standing beside the Mott, talking to him. Stupid boys, thought
Merrin.

"Come on, Sep," Nicko was saying. "You've flown her
before so you can do it again. Easy-peasy."

"But I don't know what I did, Nik. I mean, I didn't do anything. The boat did it." Septimus was still staring at the
tiller—he was afraid to put his hand on it, a massive, curved
piece of mahogany, as the last time he had done that, the

Dragon Boat had come alive and set off to sea.

"Well, you're wearing the Dragon Ring this time, and you weren't before, so it should be even easier," Nicko pointed out. "I don't see what you're bothered about, Sep. Boats are a piece of cake."

Septimus looked at his Dragon Ring. He loved the ring, but right now he wished he did not have it—why was it *him* who had ended up as Dragon Master? Why couldn't it have been Nicko, who knew all about boats?

"Come on, Septimus." Aunt Zelda's voice came over the side of the boat. "Sometimes there are things we just have to do. I don't want to let the Dragon Boat go, and you don't want to take her away from me. But *I* have to let her go and *you* have to take her—that's the way it is. She must be where she wants to be, and she must be safe. It's for the best."

Septimus looked up from the tiller. "But what will you do without her?"

"I will get Wolf Boy's hands better and keep an eye on that misguided lad who's lurking out by the Hundred-Foot Pit and thinks I can't see him and that wretched Darke eyeglass he's found."

"409's staying here? With that awful Apprentice boy?"

"Wolf Boy is too ill to travel, Septimus. But Merrin will not be here much longer—I intend to take him back to his mother soon."

"His mother? He's got a *mother?*" Septimus looked amazed.

Aunt Zelda smiled. "Yes, I think even Merrin has a mother. And I suspect she may be your ex-landlady."

"*What?*"

"Where you stayed in the Port."

"One of the witches? Oh, that makes sense. I bet it's that really nasty one, Veronica. Come to think of it, she looked a bit like him."

Aunt Zelda shook her head. "Believe it or not, I think it's Nurse Meredith."

"Oh, yuck. All those dead babies. She's *worse* than a witch. So when are you going to take him to the Doll House?"

"As soon as I can leave Wolf Boy for a day, when his fever has gone. The burns will take longer to heal, there's a lot of Darkenesse in them. They'll need quite a bit more fresh Marsh Bane."

Septimus looked worried. "He will be all right, won't he?"

"Yes. He will. I'll bring him back when he's better."

"You'll come to the Castle?" Septimus was surprised.

"Well, there's nothing to keep me here now," Aunt Zelda said briskly. "And Keepers have been known to pay the Castle the odd visit. I'm sure Marcia would like to have me to stay, after all the weeks she spent here."

Septimus grinned at the thought of Aunt Zelda in Marcia's rooms.

"That's better," said Aunt Zelda, noticing Septimus's smile.

Ten minutes later Septimus had said goodbye to Wolf Boy and promised that he would see him again soon. Wolf Boy had given him a weak smile. "Not if I see you first," he'd said, and then closed his eyes and fallen asleep. Septimus had tip-toed out of the cottage, buttoning Spit Fyre firmly into a drag-on-proof bag that Aunt Zelda had found for him. The small dragon had been fast asleep all day, but the last thing he want-ed was Spit Fyre waking up and making a nuisance of himself while he was trying to fly the Dragon Boat.

Now Spit Fyre was safely stowed in a locker beside the tiller, and Septimus, Jenna and Nicko were on the Dragon Boat, ready to leave. Aunt Zelda was anxiously eyeing a small grey cloud hovering high in the sky just above the cottage. She had seen the cloud drift towards them as they were preparing the Dragon Boat and had thought it strange at the time, as the cloud was coming from the northeast and Aunt Zelda was sure that the wind was a westerly. Now she was worried, for the cloud had not moved for the last half hour, which was not normal cloud behaviour.

But the Dragon Boat was ready. It was time to leave.

"Jenna," said Aunt Zelda. "I have something for you." She reached up on tiptoe and passed something to Jenna's outstretched hand. "It's the key to the Queen's Room. In the Palace. You—you may need it."

It was a heavy gold key with a round emerald set into the top that reminded Jenna of the dragon's eyes. Jenna was confused. She had explored every part of the Palace since she had moved there with Sarah and Silas, but she had never seen the Queen's Room.

"But—where is the Queen's Room?" she asked.

"Er, I can't say, Jenna. But you will find it when The Time Is Right. You can be certain of that."

"When . . . when will that be, Aunt Zelda?" asked Jenna.

"When you become the Young Queen," said Aunt Zelda, somewhat unhelpfully.

"Er . . . OK. Well, thank you. It's a beautiful key."

Aunt Zelda stepped back from the boat. "Off you go now," she said rather too brightly. "No more hanging around." She gave another glance at the cloud, which was casting a small shadow over the prow.

"Take her back along the Mott, as far from the bridge as you can," Aunt Zelda called out. "She'll need a run up to get into the air."

"OK, Aunt Zelda," yelled the Dragon Master.

"Remember to head north, away from the sun."

"Yes, Aunt Zelda."

"And don't go too fast, for goodness' sake—unless you have to."

"No, Aunt Zelda."

"Don't fly *all* the way to the Castle or you'll tire her. Make sure you land when you get to the river."

"Don't worry, we will, Aunt Zelda."

"And—"

"Aunt Zelda, we'll be *fine*. Really."

"Yes. Sorry. I know you will." Aunt Zelda stepped away from the boat and gazed at the brilliant gold hull and the iridescent green shimmer of the dragon's head and tail, drinking it all in so that she could remember exactly how the dragon looked in the empty days to come.

Septimus took a deep breath and looked at Nicko. "Ready?" he asked.

Nicko grinned at him. "Aye, aye, cap'n."

"Is the dragon ready, Jen?"

Jenna was up at the prow with her arms around the dragon's neck. She whispered something to the dragon and then gave Septimus a thumbs-up sign. Septimus's heart was pounding; there was no putting it off any more—it was time for takeoff. He nervously placed his right hand on the tiller.

The dragon turned her head and fastened her emerald-green eyes on the small figure holding the tiller. She recognised the one who had released her from her prison under the ground. He looked a little different now. He no longer wore his red hat, which she had rather liked, and he was bigger—more solid somehow—and had a stronger air of Magyk about him. But he was still the same boy, still a little scared and still wanting to do what was best. The dragon approved. She would take him where he wished to go.

Septimus looked into the dragon's eyes, unaware that he had passed her test. His hand felt clammy as he clutched the tiller, and he wondered what he should do.

"She wants to know where you are taking her," Jenna suddenly called out.

"Tell her, tell her I am taking her where she wishes to go. I am taking her to the Castle," Septimus replied.

The dragon nodded. Slowly her head turned until her shimmering green eyes were gazing at Aunt Zelda; then the powerful neck dipped, down and down until the dragon's head rested on the grass at Aunt Zelda's feet. Aunt Zelda knelt and put her arms around the great green and gold head.

"Goodbye, my lady," whispered Aunt Zelda with tears in her eyes. "We will meet again."

Aunt Zelda retreated to the cottage door and the Dragon Boat began to move. The tide was at its height and the Mott was full to the brim with dark brown brackish water. The Dragon Boat was floating free, and with much creaking and groaning the huge creature backed away from the bridge, squeezing between the grassy banks along the straight stretch of water that ran in front of the Keepers Cottage. At the first bend in the Mott, the Dragon Boat could go no farther and stopped. Before her was only a short run for takeoff. The dragon eyed it doubtfully—she had never flown from such a confined space before. When she had sailed the seven seas with Hotep-Ra, she had taken off in the middle of wide, empty oceans, usually because her Master had become bored with long days at sea and had wanted a change of pace. She had never done anything like this before.

With some difficulty the dragon squeezed her folded wings

out from the confines of the banks of the Mott and lifted them up until they were raised high above her mast. The great, green, leathery folds which had lain at her side through two hot summers and one freezing winter were stiff and dry, and as the dragon began to open them, a terrible creaking and groaning noise, followed by an ominous crackling, filled the air. Septimus, Nicko and Jenna clasped their hands to their ears and watched the leathery folds of the dragon's wings painfully open like two great hands stretching after a long and heavy sleep. All three held their breath, afraid that the dragon skin between the fingers of the wings might split, but as the folds became smooth and the sun shone on the shining green scales, they could see that all was well and that once again the Dragon Boat proudly held her wings aloft.

She was ready to go.

The dragon took a deep breath. Her crew felt her shudder and the great wings began to move, churning the hot air around them and blowing their hair into their eyes. The golden boat inched forward. The wings beat powerfully and slowly, dipping right down to the ground and swooping high up into the air, gathering strength, and then with a stomach-churning lurch the Dragon Boat suddenly shot forward.

"*Stop!*" yelled Aunt Zelda at the top of her voice. No one heard.

With wings beating furiously, head outstretched, muscles in the great green neck tensed, the golden boat shot down the Mott in a spume of water, and, at the very last moment possible—accompanied by a loud crack and the sound of splintering wood—she lifted up into the air, taking most of the Mott bridge with her.

Steep and fast, the Dragon Boat climbed into the summer sky. As the remains of the Mott bridge fell away and landed close to the Hundred-Foot Pit, much to Merrin's shock, she wheeled around and headed across the Marram Marshes towards the river.

The Dragon Boat was at long last completing her journey to the Castle.

✣ 34 ✣
AIRBORNE

Heart *in her mouth,* Aunt Zelda watched the Dragon Boat climbing into the sky—it was an incredible sight. Although Aunt Zelda had seen the boat fly once before, when the dragon had done battle with DomDaniel's ship, the *Vengeance,* she had only caught glimpses in flashes of lightning. Now the boat sailed into the bright summer evening sky, sunlight glinting on her golden hull, greens and blues shimmering from her massive wings. The sight of the Dragon Boat, which she had looked after for so very many years, now flying free high above her took Aunt Zelda's breath away and tied her stomach up in knots.

But there was another, nastier, reason why Aunt Zelda's stomach was carefully tying itself into a particularly complicated knot. For, as the Dragon Boat had begun her run along the Mott, the suspicious grey cloud had suddenly shot forward, and a blindingly bright ball of light had come roaring out of it, aimed at the boat. Aunt Zelda had screamed, "Stop!" but no one had heard her, and it was far too late for the Dragon Boat to stop anyway.

Aunt Zelda picked up the splintered remains of a plank from the bridge—the only piece to have fallen on her side of the Mott. Her worst fears were confirmed, the plank was charred and still hot to the touch—it had been hit by a Thunderflash.

Aunt Zelda stared into the sky, holding her breath with fear. The Dragon Boat was still easy to see, for she did not fly fast; she was built for long-haul flight, slow and steady, saving her energy. She sailed majestically above the Marram Marshes, wings beating rhythmically, head held high—and

behind her scuttled the small dark cloud. Aunt Zelda's knees
suddenly felt very strange. She sank to the ground and started
biting her nails, something she had not done since waiting for
her Witch Graduation results.

Onboard the Dragon Boat everyone had just about got their
breath back after the takeoff. In fact, in the terror of the takeoff none of them had noticed the Thunderflash, or had any
idea Simon Heap was now trailing them. Jenna was up in the
prow; Septimus held the tiller and Nicko, who was not comfortable with any kind of boat taking to the air, had only just
opened his eyes. He stared up at the dragon's wings, which
were beating steadily. They were blowing surprisingly strong
gusts of air through the boat which, combined with the up
and down motion, made him feel as though the boat was at
sea, rather than a thousand feet in the air. Nicko began to
relax and look about him—and something caught his eye.

"There's a weird cloud behind us, Sep," said Nicko.

Septimus, who hardly dared look anywhere except straight
ahead of him, caught the concern in Nicko's voice and made
himself turn around. A dark grey cloud was flying towards
them in a deliberate, distinctly uncloudlike fashion.

"Simon!" muttered Septimus.

"Oh, *pigs*," said Nicko, squinting back into the sun, which was low in the sky. "Do you really think so?"

"It's a Darke cloud. I thought I felt something just now, but I told myself it was just because I was feeling scared about flying. It's the same sort of feeling really."

"What's he going to do then, Sep?"

"I dunno," Septimus replied, glancing behind him again. "But I don't suppose he's come just to say 'hello, that's a nice boat you've got there.'"

"Hmm," muttered Nicko. "Perhaps we ought to go a bit faster."

"Not sure how to do that. I could ask Jenna . . ." But without Septimus uttering a word, the dragon began to beat her wings more rapidly, and the great gusts of wind passing their faces grew into a gale.

But the cloud easily kept up with them, following the Dragon Boat as surely as if someone had tied it on with a piece of string.

"There he is!" Nicko suddenly yelled above the noise of the wings.

Septimus spun around in time to see Simon fly out from the cloud, and in a moment he was hovering behind them, easily keeping pace. Septimus stared back at his brother; he looked different somehow—what was it? And then he realised. Over his right eye, the eye that 409 had hit with the stone from his catapult, Simon wore an eye patch. Good old 409, thought Septimus. He smiled.

"I'll take that smile off your stupid face if you don't land that—that ridiculous *mutant*," Simon yelled at Septimus.

"What'd he say, Nik?" yelled Septimus.

"Dunno. Can't hear. Load of rubbish, I expect," Nicko shouted back.

"Hand over the Queenling and I'll let you both go!" shouted Simon.

"He's still yelling," said Nicko.

"Yeah. Keep an eye on him, Nik. Watch out for him reaching for a Thunderflash."

"He wouldn't—not up here."

"He *would*."

"If you don't bring that contraption down to land right now you will leave me no choice!" Simon screamed.

Neither Septimus nor Nicko had noticed that Jenna had joined them in the stern of the Dragon Boat. She looked angry.

"I have had enough of him chasing me." She raised her voice above the whooshing noise of the wings as they swept down, the wind blowing her hair across her face and into her eyes. "I *really* have." From her tunic pocket Jenna drew out the Enlarging Glass that she had picked up from the Camera Obscura.

"What's that, Jen?" said Septimus and Nicko at once.

"I'll show you. Watch!" Jenna held out the Glass so that the sun's rays were focused into a bright spot of light; then Jenna slowly moved the spot until it rested on Simon's face. For a moment there was no reaction, then all at once Simon's hand flew up to his face. He yelled and shot away, looking around to see what had burned him. Jenna tried to follow him with the light, but Simon ducked and weaved this way and that, searching for the Darke forces that were chasing him—for Simon had felt the Darkenesse from the Glass.

He soon worked out where it was coming from. "You!" yelled Simon furiously as he saw Jenna holding the Enlarging Glass. Shaking with rage, Simon took a Thunderflash from his belt. "*That* will be the last thing you ever do," he screeched.

This time they heard him—and seconds later they also heard the Thunderflash. A loud rumble shook the air as a brilliant ball of white light flew from Simon's outstretched hand and roared towards the Dragon Boat. Instinctively Jenna, Nicko and Septimus threw themselves on to the deck, although they knew that when the Thunderflash struck it would make no difference where they were. As they hit the deck, a terrifying thud knocked the boat sideways—the dragon reared her head in shock and the boat slewed over, tilting the deck to a crazy angle and sending the crew rolling to the opposite side. A fearsome noise of ripping cloth and crunching bones echoed around them, and then the thing they had all been dreading happened—the Dragon Boat began to fall.

Jenna forced herself to look up. A plume of black smoke trailed from the dragon's right wing, which hung limp and broken at her side, and the smell of burned flesh filled the air. The remaining good wing flapped frantically, trying to right the boat and stop the freefall to the Marsh below. Jenna clung to the side of the boat, willing the dragon to stay aloft. She saw the dragon painfully spread the injured wing out until, although it hung limp and broken, it was now horizontal and could act like a stabiliser. Slowly the deck tilted back to a small incline rather than a steep mountainside, but they were still falling. Leaving the boys at the tiller, Jenna inched her way up the sloping deck until she was back at the dragon's neck.

Simon's laugh echoed eerily around the boat. Although he had not quite scored the direct hit he had hoped for—due to the irritating fact that he could see through only one eye—he had wounded the dragon, and his next shot would finish the job. Simon took his third and last Thunderflash from his belt.

"*Now!*" Jenna whispered to the dragon.

The dragon's tail twitched. As Simon flew in close, it suddenly flashed in the sunlight; the golden barb whipped through the air and hit him full on, hurling him into the sky. Like a cricket ball heading for the boundary on a lazy summer's evening, Simon arched up, up into the blue in a perfect curve, until, at the peak of his parabola, gravity reclaimed him, and he began his descent, describing an equally perfect curve all the way down to the Hundred-Foot Pit.

Merrin was in the middle of a shouting match with Aunt Zelda when Simon Heap shot past him and entered the pit with the most enormous splash. Being soaked in filthy bog water did not improve Merrin's mood one bit. He was fed up with Aunt Zelda telling him what to do—what business was it of hers if he had an eyeglass? Wasn't he allowed *anything* of his own? She was as bad as DomDaniel. No, she was *worse*. At least DomDaniel had let him keep things—well, things that no one else had wanted.

The argument had erupted in the middle of Simon throwing his last Thunderflash. As the tremendous roar shook the

cottage, Aunt Zelda had looked away in despair, and a glint of
sun by the Hundred-Foot Pit had caught her eye. She had
seen Merrin gleefully watching the battle through his
Eyeglass. The Darke Eyeglass was bad enough, but what had
really got to Aunt Zelda was the expression on Merrin's
face—he looked happier than she had ever seen him before.
Happy, thought Aunt Zelda, at the fact that the three people
she loved most in the world were quite possibly about to fall
to their deaths.

"Put that wretched Eyeglass away!" Aunt Zelda had yelled
angrily.

Merrin had jumped with surprise and then pointedly
ignored her. He was not going to miss the best thing he had
seen in years.

"I will not have that Darke thing here any longer!" Aunt
Zelda carried on. "You will throw it in the pit *right now!*"

Goaded, Merrin had yelled back, "No, I won't!" and missed
seeing the swipe of the dragon's tail. But neither Merrin nor
Aunt Zelda missed the gigantic splash Simon Heap made as
he fell to earth and disappeared into the black depths of the
Hundred-Foot Pit.

Simon Heap shot all the way down to the bottom of the pit,
where he desperately fought his way out of a forest of clinging

strands of Marsh Bane. Fifty-five seconds later he emerged, gasping for breath and covered in decayed slugs. Merrin was nearly sick with the stench of it, but something drew him towards Simon; the boy offered him a hand and pulled him from the pit. Simon lay in a spluttering, slimy heap on the bright green grass of the knoll and coughed up a few slugs. Merrin sat beside him, staring at this stranger who had arrived out of the blue. Maybe he was a Sign. A saviour. A way out of being told what to do by Aunt Zelda. A way out of eating cabbage every day. He glanced up guiltily at the thought of Aunt Zelda, but she had rushed into the cottage and was nowhere to be seen.

Suddenly Simon sat up, coughed up a bucketful of marsh water and noticed Merrin for the first time.

"Where'd you get that?" he demanded.

"What?" asked Merrin in injured tones. Why, Merrin wondered, did everyone always talk to him as though he had done something wrong?

"That Eyeglass."

"Nowhere. I—I mean I found it. It's mine."

Simon looked at the boy, sizing him up. An unusual lad, he thought. Could be useful. But what was he doing here, out on the Marsh in the middle of nowhere?

"You live with the old witch, then?" Simon asked.

"No," Merrin said sulkily, as though Simon had accused him of something really bad.

"'Course you do. Where else would you live in the middle of this dump?"

"Yeah . . ." Merrin allowed himself a smile. "It is a dump, isn't it? Stupid cottage full of poxy little potions. She's got no idea what the real stuff is like."

Simon looked at Merrin with narrowed eyes. "And you do?" he asked in a low voice.

"Yeah. I was Apprentice to the best Necromancer there has ever been. He trusted me with everything. *Everything*."

Simon looked surprised. So this must be DomDaniel's old Apprentice. Somehow he had survived being Consumed—there must be something more to the boy than met the eye. An idea began to form in Simon's mind. "You must miss him terribly," he said sympathetically.

"Yeah," muttered Merrin, persuading himself that he did indeed miss DomDaniel. "Yeah, I do."

Simon looked Merrin up and down. He wasn't ideal, but he was someone he could do business with. And he wanted to get his hands on that Eyeglass. "D'you want a job?" asked Simon.

"A job?" asked Merrin, taken aback.

"Yes. You know, similar to what you did before."

"How similar?" asked Merrin suspiciously.

"How do I know," said Simon, somewhat exasperated, "seeing as I don't know exactly what you did before? Are you going to take the job or not?"

"Merrin!" Aunt Zelda's angry shout suddenly pierced the air. "Merrin, get away from that *evil man*—come back here right now!" Then, with more pressing things to do, she rushed into the cottage.

Merrin watched Aunt Zelda's angry patchwork figure disappear. How dare that old witch yell at him like that? What made her think he was going to do what she told him?

"Well," said Simon impatiently, "are you going to take the job?"

"Yes," said Merrin, "I'll take it."

"Shake on it," said Simon. Merrin took Simon's outstretched hand and before he knew what was happening, his arm felt as if it was being pulled from its socket.

"Aah!" Merrin yelled in pain as his feet left the ground and Simon pulled him roughly aloft. With some difficulty Simon managed to gain just enough height to take him over the roof of Keeper's Cottage—although Merrin's dangling feet caught in the thatch and one of the boy's boots fell off. Merrin looked down at the roof in horror, already regretting his snap decision. "Help!" he yelled.

His voice drifted down the chimney and did no more than enter Wolf Boy's fevered dreams. Aunt Zelda heard nothing. She was too busy to notice that the boy she had saved from being Consumed, the boy she had carefully nursed back to health, had left her and gone back to where he had come from.

The *Dragon Boat was*
rapidly losing alti-
tude. Septimus had just
managed to avoid crashing
into a small island overrun
with chickens—and that
had taken the Dragon Boat's
last ounce of strength. Now her
head hung low, her eyes were dull and
her one good wing was trembling with exhaustion.

"Tell her it's not far now. I can see the river," Septimus
called to Jenna, who was murmuring a constant stream of
encouraging words to the dragon. "Tell her if she can just
keep going for a few more minutes . . ."

"We're awful close to the ground, Sep," muttered Nicko,

peering over the side of the boat. They were skimming over a large area of bright green—which was a sure sign of the sinking Quake Ooze. "P'raps we ought to look for somewhere to crash-land."

"Like where?" snapped Septimus.

"I dunno. A flat bit I s'pose."

"A nice flat bit of Quake Ooze, you mean? With a load of Brownies in it?"

"All right, Sep. No need to get snappy."

Septimus's eyes were fixed on the river. "I just—I just want to get her back safe. *Whoaaaaaa!*" The boat gave a terrifying lurch. "Come on. Come on," Septimus muttered under his breath. "You can do it. Yes . . . yes, you *can.*"

Nicko willed the dragon on. He felt helpless, and feeling helpless on a boat was the worst thing in the world for Nicko.

Suddenly the deck tilted down ominously. "We're not going to make it, Nik," Septimus said flatly.

"Yeah, maybe not. Can you crash-land her?"

"Can't say I've tried recently. This is *scary.*"

"I know."

The Dragon Boat dropped again and Septimus felt as though he had left his stomach behind.

"Going down, Sep," Nicko said grimly.

"Yep. Down we—hey, hang on . . . what's that—oh, that's all we need."

A small white cloud had appeared over the Marsh and was racing towards them.

"Simon doesn't give up, does he?" said Nicko. "And I don't suppose he's come to give us a hand. Oh, pigs—he's *fast*."

No more than a few moments later the cloud was upon them, and a thick white mist had enveloped the boat.

"Can you see him, Sep?" Nicko's voice came through the cloud.

"No—where is he?" Septimus hung on to the tiller and stared grimly ahead, seeing nothing but impenetrable white and bracing himself for the crack of a ThunderFlash or the splash of the Quake Ooze.

Suddenly Jenna's voice came excitedly through the mist. "The dragon says she's being lifted up. She's being carried by the cloud."

As Jenna spoke, Septimus felt the whole boat relax. The shuddering with every beat of the dragon's wing disappeared, and the terrifying creakings and groanings that had accompanied the dragon's frantic attempts to stay airborne quieted. The only sound they could hear was the faint whoosh of air as the Dragon Boat was carried along.

"It's not Simon, is it, Sep?" Nicko whispered, somewhat overawed by the cloud.

"No—it's . . . well, I don't know what it is. It's weird," Septimus replied.

"Um—wonder where we're going?" said Nicko, spooked by the strange atmosphere of the cloud. It reminded him of something or someone, but he could not think what—or who.

Septimus was a little apprehensive too. His feeling of relief had been replaced by a sense of unease. He did not like the control of the Dragon Boat being taken out of his hands. He moved the tiller from side to side—it swung loosely, uselessly, and had no effect on the boat now.

Again Jenna's voice drifted through the mist. "Stop messing about!" she yelled.

"*What?*" Septimus yelled back.

"The dragon says stop messing about with the tiller; we're going to land," came Jenna's answering shout.

"*Where?*" Septimus and Nicko both shouted.

"On the river, silly. Where else?" yelled Jenna.

Septimus felt the boat dip and tip forward. He held the tiller tightly, unsure of what else to do—and suddenly he could smell the river. They were coming in to land and he could see nothing. Suppose they hit a boat? Or came in too steeply and sank? If only the cloud would go away and let him see where they were going. As if reading his mind, the mist rolled up into a small white cloud and shot off, back across the Marshes where it had come from.

Septimus paid no attention to where the cloud had gone; his gaze was fixed on the dark green water of the river, which was rapidly coming up to meet them. They were going too fast. Far too fast.

"Slow down!" he yelled at the dragon.

At the last moment, just before they hit the water, the dragon stretched out her wings as best she could, reared her head up and dropped her tail. She hit the water with a crash, bounced up and down and aquaplaned at full speed past a group of elderly fishermen who were known for their tall fishing tales. That night at the Old Trout Tavern they were not completely surprised when no one believed their latest story. By the end of the evening even *they* did not believe it.

The Dragon Boat finally slowed about half a mile up the river, just before a bend. She settled into the water, raised her good wing and spread it to catch the wind, but her broken wing trailed uselessly alongside and began to turn her in a circle, until Nicko stuck an oar over the other side for balance.

Septimus sat down wearily by the tiller and Jenna came to join him.

"That was great, Sep."

"Thanks, Jen."

"That cloud . . ." said Jenna. "Did it stop us from crashing?"

Septimus nodded.

"It was weird," said Nicko. "It smelled funny. Reminded me of something."

"Aunt Zelda's cottage," said Jenna happily.

"What? Where?"

"No—the *cloud*. It smelled of boiled cabbage."

At Keeper's Cottage Wolf Boy had woken from a deep sleep, and for the first time since he had held Sleuth, his hands did not hurt. He struggled to sit up, trying to remember where he was. Slowly it all came back to him; he remembered 412 saying goodbye and he remembered the cottage, but he most definitely did not remember the enormous glass flask that was blocking the front doorway. Wolf Boy had never seen anything like it. Beside the flask was a huge cork stopper, and beside the cork stopper stood Aunt Zelda, anxiously peering around the flask out at the deepening evening sky. The flask was about the same size as Aunt Zelda and about the same shape too.

Aunt Zelda noticed that Wolf Boy had woken up; she went and sat down beside him with a sigh.

Wolf Boy gazed at her, bleary-eyed. "412 OK?" he mumbled.

"We can but hope," said Aunt Zelda, keeping an eye on the flask. "Ah . . . here it comes!" As she spoke, a few tendrils of white mist wafted through the open door and into the flask. Soon the tendrils had become a long stream, pouring through the door and tumbling into the flask. Aunt Zelda jumped up and ran over to the massive flask, watching the mist stream into it and whirl around at high speed.

For some minutes the mist flowed in, filling the flask to the top. When the last tendril of mist had returned to the flask, Aunt Zelda drew a small bottle from one of her many patch-work pockets. Standing on tiptoe, she reached up and dripped one drop of a brilliant white liquid into the mouth of the flask. The mist swirled into a frantic whirlpool and swirled itself into a small, white, marshmallow-like blob.

"Good." Aunt Zelda sighed. "It's Cloud Concentrate again." She picked up the huge cork stopper with both hands and shoved it into the mouth of the flask. Then, with the ball of Cloud Concentrate rolling around like a solitary marble, she pushed the giant flask across the floor, opened a large door concealed behind bookshelves at the end of the room and manoeuvred the flask into a cupboard.

Aunt Zelda closed the cupboard door with a quiet click and went outside. Slowly she walked to the end of the island and looked out across the expanse of the Marshes, searching for any trace of the Dragon Boat. She saw nothing—there was no clue, no sign of what had happened to her. Aunt Zelda shook her head and hoped for the best, for that was all she could do, and retraced her steps to the Cottage. Now she was ready to deal with Simon Heap. Ready to send him on his Darke way and get that wretched boy Merrin out of his clutches before it was too late.

But as Aunt Zelda stepped on to the path she tripped over a solitary brown boot. She picked up the boot, saw straw from the thatch stuck in its eyelets—and she knew that, for Merrin, it was already too late.

⊹⊱ 36 ⊰⊹
RETURN

In the early hours of the next morning, while the weary Dragon Master dozed at the tiller, the Dragon Boat sailed around Raven's Rock and negotiated the tight left turn where the Moat branched off from the river. The Dragon Boat progressed purposefully along the Moat, watched only by some incurious gulls and Una Brakket.

The housekeeper, who was not sleeping well these days, had just woken from a bad dream that, as usual, had had something to do with Marcia Overstrand—although she could not quite remember what. She was sitting at the window feeling relieved that she had woken up, but when Una saw the Dragon Boat sail by, her spirits sank. She must still be dreaming, she thought. She peered out to see if Marcia was on the boat and sure enough, there was that irritating boy who was her Apprentice, so Marcia could not be far away. The

housekeeper sighed and wished her dream would end, preferably with Marcia Overstrand disappearing for ever. She sat
and watched the Dragon Boat sail around the bend that led to
the boatyard and waited for Marcia to appear.

The boatyard was deserted as the Dragon Boat drew up to the
pontoon. Nicko jumped from the prow with a thick azure-
blue rope in his hand, planning to secure her to a large post as
she came to a halt. But the Dragon Boat appeared to have
other ideas.

"Whoa!" yelled Nicko, running to keep pace with the
boat's progress along the pontoon. "Stop her, Sep. She's over-
running!"

Septimus was wide awake now. "She won't stop, Nik! Jen,
tell her to stop."

There was a splash as Nicko was forced to let go of the rope
to avoid being dragged into the water. Septimus started to
panic. How did you stop a boat, especially one that appeared
to have a mind of her own?

Jenna called back to Septimus, "She says she's not there
yet, Sep."

"Not where?" Septimus yelled as the Dragon Boat carried
on towards a deserted cutting at the far end of the boatyard, a

dead end that was known as the Cut.

"Not where she will be safe!" Jenna replied. "Hang on, Sep. She's going in here!" The Dragon Boat made a wide arc out into the Moat and then turned so that she was facing straight into the Cut. Nicko caught up and ran alongside them. Now, ahead of the Dragon Boat was the dead end of the Cut—the unyielding Castle Wall—and Nicko knew that the Dragon Boat was travelling too fast to stop. They were going to hit the wall.

Helplessly he yelled, "Stop! Stop her, Sep!" But Septimus could do nothing; the Dragon Boat was ignoring the Dragon Master. At the prow, Jenna saw the great mass of wall rear up before them, threw herself on to the deck and waited for the inevitable crash.

"Wo ... *ho!*" Jenna heard Nicko's yell of astonishment and felt the air suddenly chill and darken. A smell of underground dampness hit her nostrils and, as she dared to look up, the Dragon Boat came to a halt—inside the Castle wall, in a vast, vaulted lapis lazuli cavern.

Jenna picked herself up from the deck and whistled under her breath. "You can open your eyes now, Sep," she said. "The Dragon Boat's come home."

＊　＊　＊

On the other side of the boatyard, a candle flared to life in the window of the small ramshackle hut. Jannit Maarten was suddenly awake. A moment later the door to Jannit's shack opened, and the flickering flame disappeared as her candle dropped from her hand.

"What the—what in the name of Neptune is *that*?" Jannit gasped. She set off across the yard like a fox after a rabbit, leaping over the boats and the boatyard clutter, and a few moments later she was standing next to Nicko. Lost for words, Jannit surveyed an incredible new dimension to her beloved boatyard. Granted, it was a little ostentatious for Jannit's simple tastes. She herself would never dream of lining such a gigantic boathouse in lapis lazuli of all things, and she most certainly would not have gone to the trouble of drawing all those funny little pictures over it; and as for the gold inlay around the door—well that was just plain silly. But Jannit could see that it was a truly astounding space—and within it lay an incredible boat. Jannit, who was not given to emotion, found herself a little overcome and had to sit down suddenly on an upturned dinghy.

"Nicko," Jannit said faintly. "Is—is this something to do with you? Did you find this?"

"No, the—the Dragon Boat found it. She *knew* . . . ."

Nicko ran out of words. He could not get the image out of his head: the Dragon Boat, head held high, heading fast—too fast—along the Cut. And then, as he stared in horror at the thick Castle Wall looming before her, Nicko had seen a brilliant flash from a gold disc set high up in the wall that he had never noticed before. The dragon had breathed a ribbon of fire from her nostrils, and as the flames touched the gold, the seemingly solid stones had melted before her and the stunning lapis lazuli cavern had been revealed. Nicko had watched the Dragon Boat glide serenely inside and come to a gentle halt. It was the most wonderful thing that he had ever seen. He only wished Jannit could have seen it too.

Septimus and Jenna clambered out of the Dragon Boat and walked carefully along the marble walkways on either side of the Dragon House. They joined Nicko and Jannit outside, and silently all four watched the Dragon Boat settle herself, like a swan on her nest, into the safety of the Dragon House.

"You know," said Jannit, after a while, "once, when I was a girl, I read about something like this. I was a bit of a tomboy and my aunt gave me a wonderful book. Now, what was it called? Oh, yes, I remember—*A Hundred Strange and Curious Tales for Bored Boys*. Got me interested in boats, that did. But of course, it can't be the boat I read about . . ."

"Well," Septimus said quickly, "that was just a story."

Jannit shot him a glance, remembering that he was Marcia's Apprentice. "Yes," she said quickly, "of course."

Jenna and Septimus left Nicko and Jannit sitting with the Dragon Boat and set off for the Wizard Tower. Septimus had checked inside the dragon-proof bag and saw to his relief that Spit Fyre was still fast asleep, and so, carefully carrying the sleeping dragon, they walked wearily through the deserted streets. The new moon had set and it was dark, but Jenna and Septimus felt safe at night in the streets of the Castle, unlike those of the Port; they knew the twists and turns, the alleys to avoid and the short cuts to take. As they neared Wizard Way, the glow from the torches lit up the night, and they slipped down a narrow path. Soon Septimus pushed open the old wooden side gate that led into the courtyard of the Tower.

They had decided that Jenna would spend the rest of the night at the Wizard Tower and go back to the Palace in the morning. Jenna followed Septimus up the steep marble steps; he muttered the password and the heavy silver doors swung silently open.

Noiselessly the pair crossed the Great Hall. Jenna glanced down to see the words WELCOME, PRINCESS AND APPRENTICE,

UPON YOUR SAFE RETURN, WELCOME, SPIT FYRE flickering in subdued night-time colours across the floor. The inside of the Tower felt as strange as always to Jenna; the strong smell of Magyk in the air made her feel slightly giddy, and although she was aware of being surrounded by Magykal sounds she could not hear them properly—it was as if they were just out of reach. Jenna picked her way across the floor, which felt as though she were walking across sand, and followed Septimus on to the silver spiral stairs. As the steps began to move upwards, both she and Septimus wearily sat down for the long journey to the top of the Tower.

The spiral stairs were in night-time mode, which meant they travelled slowly and silently. Jenna dozily rested her head against Septimus's shoulder and counted the floors as they went up. A dim bluish-purple haze lit each floor and the gentle sound of snoring drifted from one or two of the older Wizards' rooms. As they approached the twentieth floor Jenna and Septimus stood, ready to step off. Suddenly Jenna grabbed hold of his arm.

"Look . . ." she whispered.

"What's *he* doing here?" muttered Septimus. Silently, he and Jenna stepped on to the landing and tiptoed towards Marcia's massive purple front door. A thin figure wearing brown robes edged with the blue flashes of a sub-Wizard and an oddly shaped plaid hat with earflaps tied under his chin was sitting on a small wooden chair outside the door, his head drooping as he slept.

"Who is it?" whispered Jenna.

"Catchpole," hissed Septimus.

The figure suddenly snapped awake. "Yes? Yes?" he said, looking around, confused. He caught sight of Septimus. "What do you want, 412?" he barked. Septimus jumped to attention. He couldn't help it; it was, for an awful moment, as if he were back in the Young Army again being shouted at by the disgusting Catchpole.

Suddenly Catchpole remembered where he was and—with a feeling of horror—who Septimus now was. "Ah . . . er, excuse me, Apprentice. I wasn't thinking. Very sorry. No offence meant."

Septimus still looked shocked, so Jenna said politely, "We're staying here tonight, would you let us in, please?" Catchpole peered into the gloom. His eyesight was not good (which was one of the many reasons he had been no good as a Deputy Hunter) and he had not realised anyone was with Septimus. When he saw who she was he jumped up, sending the chair clattering to the ground.

"Oh, goodness. It's . . . so sorry, Princess, I didn't see you."

"Don't worry, Catchpole," Jenna said with a smile, pleased at the effect she was having. "Just let us past, will you?"

"No. Sorry. Under orders to let no one through the door. Security measures. Sorry. Really terribly, terribly sorry about that," Catchpole said anxiously.

"Why?" asked Jenna.

"I'm just following orders, Princess." Catchpole looked wretched.

Septimus had had enough. "Oh, buzz off, Catchpole," he said. "We're going in whether you like it or not." He stepped forward and the heavy purple door recognised the Apprentice. It swung open and Jenna followed Septimus into Marcia's rooms, leaving Catchpole wringing his hands in despair.

It was pitch-black inside. "Why wouldn't Catchpole let us in?" Jenna whispered. "You don't think something awful has happened, do you?" Septimus stood quietly for a moment while the glow from his Dragon Ring grew brighter. He was listening hard.

"No," he said. "I can't feel any Darke stuff. Well, no more than the usual Shadow. And I can hear . . . yes, I'm sure I can hear Marcia breathing. Listen."

"I can't hear a thing, Sep," Jenna whispered.

"No? Oh, well, I suppose not. I'm learning to Hear Human Breath from Beyond. It's how Dad found you, you know. And how Marcia found me under the snow. I'm not that good yet, but I can easily hear Marcia."

"Oh. But how—how do you know it's not the Shadow breathing?"

"Easy-peasy. The Shadow doesn't breathe, silly. It's not alive. And it's certainly not human."

Hearing that did not make Jenna feel any better. "It's a bit dark in here, Sep," she said.

Septimus touched a candle beside the great stone fireplace. It flared to life, casting dancing shadows across the wall and illuminating the ShadowSafe, which lurked in the corner like a gigantic spider awaiting its prey. Jenna shivered. The ShadowSafe was creepy; there was something about it that reminded her of the Observatory.

"You cold, Jen?" asked Septimus. He clicked his fingers and some small kindling sticks jumped into the fireplace and set fire to themselves. Then a couple of big logs heaved themselves out of the log basket, thumped down on top of the kindling and obligingly burst into flames. Soon the warm firelight filled the room and Jenna began to feel less spooked.

"Come on," said Septimus, "you can have the visiting

Wizards' room. It's really nice. I'll show you." But Jenna hung back. She thought of the Shadow upstairs waiting beside Marcia.

"Thanks, Sep," she said. "But I'd rather stay down here by the fire."

Septimus glanced at Jenna's pale face. Being with all that Darke stuff at Simon's place had not done her any good, he thought. "OK, Jen," he said. "I'll stay with you."

Sometime later, a tall figure stood in the doorway and saw two forms asleep under a pile of her best purple blankets. Marcia lingered for a moment and smiled. That irritating ex-Message Rat had been right. They were safe. Well, of course she had known it all along, but even so, it was good to see them back again.

Marcia tiptoed away. The Shadow lingered and cast a malevolent glance at the two sleeping figures, its eyes briefly flaring a dull yellow, and then it turned and followed Marcia back up the chilly stone stairs.

✢ 37 ✢
IN SEARCH OF DRAXX

"What on earth is that?" Marcia demanded crossly, quickly forgetting how relieved she had been the night before to see Septimus and Jenna back safely. But Marcia was not feeling her best. She had woken to see the Shadow lounging on her pillow. This was not unusual, for over the past few months the Shadow had been growing more visible, especially first thing in the morning. But it had always been silent—until that moment. What had actually woken Marcia was the sound of a low, sepulchral voice calling her name over and over. "Marcia . . . Marcia . . . Marcia . . ."

In a fit of anger, Marcia had thrown one of her best purple python shoes at the ghastly Thing, but the shoe had, of course, gone straight through it. The shoe had shot across the room and smashed a small glass pot that Alther had given Marcia when, as his Apprentice, she had finally mastered a particularly difficult Projection. The broken pot had upset Marcia more than she expected, and she had stormed downstairs in a bad temper. She had had quite enough of the Shadow, she decided as she threw open the kitchen door and yelled at the coffee pot to *get a move on will you*. After breakfast she decided she would go straight down to old Weasal and insist on getting the Stopper—the very last piece of the ShadowSafe—immediately.

"*Septimus*," said Marcia in a loud voice.

Septimus sat up with a start and for a moment could not remember where he was. Marcia soon reminded him. "The Wizard Tower," she said, folding her arms crossly, "is a place of Magyk. Not a menagerie."

"What?" asked Septimus.

"Look at my best blankets—*full* of holes. I don't know where you found that giant moth, but you can take it straight back."

"What giant moth?" asked Septimus, wondering if he'd

missed something.

"Huh?" mumbled Jenna, emerging from under the pile of blankets.

"Oh, hello, Jenna," said Marcia. "Nice to see you back. The rat said—well, that wretched rat said a lot of things, most of it rubbish as far as I could tell—but he did say that you made it to the MidSummer Visit. Well done."

"Thank you," said Jenna sleepily. She sat up and stuck her foot through a large hole in the blanket. She wiggled her toes as if surprised to see them and suddenly something green pounced. "Ouch!" she yelled.

"Spit Fyre!" gasped Septimus, taken aback. Aunt Zelda had told him that the dragon would grow in sudden spurts but he had not expected this. Spit Fyre had eaten his way out of the dragon-proof bag and was now the size of a small dog. Septimus grabbed hold of the dragon and pulled him off Jenna's foot. "You all right, Jen?" he asked.

"Yes. I think so—still got ten toes," Jenna rubbed her foot, which was a little scratched from the dragon's claws. "Sep," she said, looking at Spit Fyre, whose small green tongue was flicking over Septimus's hand, hoping for breakfast, "he wasn't as big as that last night, was he?"

"No," muttered Septimus. He could tell this was going to

be trouble and he hardly dared look at Marcia. He knew what she would say. And, sure enough, she said it.

"I told you, Septimus. *No pets.* No parrots, no iguanas, no tortoises, no—"

"But—but Spit Fyre is not a pet. He's a Magykal tool. Like the practice rabbit in the courtyard."

"Septimus, a dragon is nothing like a practice rabbit. You have no idea of the trouble—"

As if to prove Marcia right, Spit Fyre wriggled out of Septimus's grasp and made a beeline for Marcia's feet. He had spotted the purple python shoes. Something in Spit Fyre's ancient dragon memory had just told him that dragons and snakes were enemies—and a nice purple snake would make a good snack before breakfast too. It did not occur to the two-day-old dragon that Marcia's shoes were only the skin of a snake, or that the feet inside them belonged to an irritable and powerful Wizard who had a particular fondness for her shoes and no fondness whatsoever for baby dragons. A streak of glistening green shot across the floor, latched itself on to Marcia's right foot and started chewing.

"Ow!" yelled Marcia, frantically shaking her foot. But Spit Fyre had learned his lesson since Septimus had shaken him off his finger two days earlier. He hung on tight and sank his sharp little dragon teeth into the snakeskin.

"Teeth Releath!" Marcia spluttered with some difficulty. Spit Fyre dug his teeth in harder.

"Teese Release!" Marcia yelled. Spit Fyre hung on and gave the python skin a good shake.

"Teeth Release!" Marcia shouted, getting it right at last. Spit Fyre let go of the purple python shoe, and, as if purple snakeskin was now of no interest to him at all, the dragon sauntered back to Septimus's side, sat down and regarded Marcia with a baleful expression.

Marcia collapsed on to a chair nursing her foot and gazing at her ruined shoe. Septimus and Jenna held their breath. What would she say?

"I suppose, Septimus," said Marcia after a long pause, "I suppose that—that *pest* has Imprinted you?"

"Um. Yes," admitted Septimus.

"I thought so." She sighed heavily. "It's not as if I don't have enough to worry about, Septimus—do you know how big they get?"

"I'm sorry," muttered Septimus. "I promise I'll look after him. Really I will. I'll feed him and housebreak him and exercise him and—and everything." She looked unimpressed.

"I didn't mean to get one," said Septimus gloomily. "He

hatched from Jenna's rock."

"Did he?" Marcia calmed down a little. "Did he really? A Human Hatching . . . well, well, that's quite something. Anyway, he will have to stay in your room for the time being. I'm not having him messing up any more things." And— although Marcia did not want to tell Septimus—she did not want the impressionable dragon tainted by any contact with the Shadow. If this was to be Septimus's companion then it must be kept as free from Darke Magyk as possible.

Marcia insisted on hearing all the details of Jenna's escape from Simon, and when she was told about the flight of the Dragon Boat to the Castle, she looked just a little triumphant. "So I am now the Keeper," she muttered.

Septimus was surprised. "I don't think so," he said. "I'm sure Aunt Zelda is still the Keeper . . ."

"Nonsense," Marcia retorted. "How can she be? Stuck miles away out on those Marshes. The Dragon Boat is here at the Castle—and quite right, too. She's a sensible boat, that dragon. Well, this Keeper won't let her down. Catchpole!"

Catchpole pushed the door open nervously. "You called, Madam Marcia?" He gulped.

"Yes. Take thirteen Wizards down to the boatyard at once.

They are to guard the Dragon Boat with their lives. Got that?"

"Thirteen Wizards . . . Dragon Boat . . . um, guard with lives. Er, yes. Thank you Madam Marcia. Will that be all?"

"I should think that is quite enough for you to manage at one time, Catchpole."

"Oh. Yes. Thank you, Madam Marcia."

"Oh—and Catchpole!"

Catchpole stopped his anxious retreat. "Er . . . yes, Madam Marcia?"

"When you've done that you may join us for breakfast."

Catchpole's face fell. "Oh," he said. And then, remembering his manners, "Oh, thank you, Madam Marcia. Thanks so much."

Breakfast was something of an ordeal for Catchpole. He sat awkwardly at the table, unsure of how to behave with Jenna and Septimus, let alone Marcia, who terrified him.

"I said keep the *Wizards* out, Catchpole, not my Apprentice. Can't you tell the difference?" Marcia told him crossly, while the stove let the coffee boil over for the second time that week. The stove was never at its best in the morning, and it always felt tense and anxious at breakfast. It was not helped by the fact that the coffee pot was upset at being shouted at and was not concentrating on the job at hand. To top it all off, there was a dragon chewing one of its feet. There was a loud hiss as the coffee hit the stove's hot plate and spilled on to the floor.

"Clean," snapped Marcia. A cloth leaped off the sink and quickly mopped up the mess.

Catchpole ate very little breakfast. He sat twisting his plaid hat in his hands, looking anxiously at Spit Fyre, who was in the corner by the stove, loudly gulping down great mouthfuls of porridge.

After breakfast—which for Spit Fyre was two roast chickens, three loaves of bread, a bucket of porridge, a tablecloth, a gallon of water and Catchpole's hat—Septimus, Jenna and Catchpole sat at the table and listened to the sounds of Marcia taking the dragon upstairs, pushing it into Septimus's room and barricading the door. There was an awkward silence around the table. Catchpole sat holding a pair of damp, detachable earflaps from his hat, which Spit Fyre had coughed up shortly after he had snatched the hat from Catchpole's grasp and swallowed it.

Jenna stood up. "Excuse me," she said, "but I think I'd better get back to Mum and Dad now. You coming too, Sep?"

"Maybe later, Jen. I'll see what Marcia wants me to do first."

"I'll tell you want I want you to do," said Marcia, coming back into the kitchen, somewhat dishevelled. "You are to go straight down to the Manuscriptorium and get a copy of *The Draxx Dragon Training Manual*. You want the original Wizard Fireproof Edition—don't let them put you off with the cheap paper one, it won't last five minutes."

"It's all right," said Septimus airily. "I've got this." He waved his copy of *How to Survive Dragon Fostering: A Practykal Guide*.

"That rubbish!" Marcia snorted. "Where on earth did you get that?"

"Aunt Zelda gave it to me," muttered Septimus, "and she said I should get—"

"—*The Winged Lizard's Almanac of the Early Years*," Marcia finished his sentence for him. "That's a load of rubbish too. Anyway, you won't find any of those as they were printed on some very flammable paper. It has to be *Draxx*, Septimus, nothing else will do."

To the accompaniment of some ominous thumps coming from Septimus's bedroom, Jenna and Septimus made a hasty exit from the ExtraOrdinary Wizard's rooms and set off in search of *Draxx*.

✳   ✳   ✳

Jenna and Septimus walked along Wizard Way, half expecting
a black horse and rider to appear again, but all seemed perfectly normal. It was midmorning by now, the sun shone
down between a few drifting white clouds and the Way was
busy with clerks on important errands—or looking as if they
were—and shoppers browsing through the stacks of books
and parchments laid out on tables outside the shops.

"What's up with Marcia?" asked Jenna as they neared the
Manuscriptorium. "She's even more grumpy than usual."

"I know," said Septimus unhappily. "I think the Shadow is
beginning to take her over—I wish there was something I
could do."

"Look, Sep," said Jenna, concerned, "maybe you should
stay with us at the Palace for a while."

"Thanks, Jen," replied Septimus, "but I can't leave Marcia
alone with that awful Shadow following her around. She needs
me."

Jenna smiled—she knew Septimus would say that. "Well,
if it gets too horrible with Marcia, you must come straight to
the Palace and tell Mum, promise?"

"Promise." Septimus gave her a hug. "Bye, Jen. Say hello to
Mum and Dad from me. Tell them I'll come and see them

later." He watched Jenna carry on up the Way towards the Palace until she had safely reached the gate. Then he pushed open the Manuscriptorium door with its familiar *ping* and walked into the dingy front office.

"Wotcha, Sep!" a cheery voice came from under the desk.

"Hello, Beetle." Septimus grinned.

"What can I do you for, oh wise Apprentice?" Beetle's head appeared above the edge of the desk. "Hey—you couldn't do me a quick Find Spell, could you? I've lost Old Foxy's best pen. He's back there having a blue fit."

"Well, I shouldn't really—oh, here, use my Magnet." Septimus took a small red magnet out of his Apprentice belt and handed it to Beetle. "Hold that with the open end pointing to where you think the pen might be and then think hard about the pen. You need to be quite close, though—the Magnet's not very strong. I'll be getting a better one when I've finished my FindersSeekers Project."

"Thanks, Sep." Beetle took the Magnet and disappeared back under the desk. A few moments later he emerged triumphantly with a slim black pen stuck on the end of it. "Saved my bacon, Sep. Thanks." Beetle gave Septimus back his Magnet. "You come down for anything special? Can I get you anything?"

"Er, I need *The Draxx Dragon Training Manual*. If you've got one."

"Wizard Waterproof, Wizard Fireproof, Wizard Advanced? Talking print or moving pictures? Deluxe or Economy Edition? Green or red cover? New or used? Big or—"

"Wizard Fireproof," interrupted Septimus. "Please."

Beetle sucked his teeth. "Hmm. Tricky. Don't know if we've got that one."

"But you said—"

"Well, of course in theory we've got 'em. But in practice we haven't. The *Draxx* is very rare, Sep. Most of 'em got eaten pretty quick. Or burned. Except for the Wizard Fireproof, I s'pose." Then, seeing Septimus's look of disappointment, Beetle whispered, "Here, seeing as it's you, I'll let you into the Wild Book and Charm Store. That's where it will be if we have one. You can have a look for yourself. Follow me."

Septimus squeezed past the large desk, and, glancing around to check no one had seen them, Beetle unlocked a tall narrow door concealed in the wooden panelling that lined the outer office. Beetle pushed the door open—which Septimus noticed was lined with heavy planks—and put his finger to his lips. "Gotta keep the noise down, Sep. Not meant to be in here. Don't make any sudden movements, OK?"

Septimus nodded and followed Beetle into the Wild Book and Charm Store. Beetle closed the door behind them, and Septimus caught his breath—he felt as if he were back in the Forest, surrounded by wolverines all over again. The Wild Book and Charm Store was dimly lit and feral-smelling. It consisted of two long lines of towering parallel shelves fronted with iron bars, behind which the Wild Books were crowded together. As Septimus cautiously followed Beetle along the narrow aisle he was followed by a chorus of low growls, scratchings and rustlings, as the books jostled behind the rusty bars.

"Excuse the mess," whispered Beetle, scooping up an assorted pile of ripped and teeth-marked Charms which had lumps of fur stuck to them and were covered in what looked to Septimus like bloodstains. "Had a bit of a punch-up last night between the Charms from an Ahriman Aardvark Enchantment Guide and a Wolverine Hex Pamphlet. Some idiot who doesn't know their alphabet put them together. Not a pretty sight. Now let me see . . . Dinosaurs . . . Drosophila—no, that's too far. Aha, Dragons should be here if we've got any. You have a look and see what you can find. I'll just go and check no one's looking for me up front. Don't want anyone to get suspicious." With that, Beetle scuttled off, leaving Septimus surrounded by fur, feathers and scales.

Holding his nose tightly, partly to keep out the smell, but also because he felt a huge sneeze coming on, Septimus peered into the gloom hoping to see something with *Draxx* written on it. The books did not like being stared at. They shifted about and one or two of the larger, more hairy ones emitted low, threatening growls. But was no sign of the *Draxx*, or anything to do with dragons at all.

Septimus was looking through the bars at a scaly book with no name on it when Beetle tapped him on his shoulder.

"Arrgh!" yelped Septimus.

"Shhh," hissed Beetle. "Your brother's here."

"What's Nicko want? Did he say?"

"Not Nicko. Simon."

⚜ 38 ⚜
THE HERMETIC CHAMBER

S imon!" *breathed Septimus.* "What's *he* doing here—again?"
"He's seeing Foxy's dad. As usual." Beetle sniffed disapprovingly. "Thick as thieves, those two are. Here, come with me." Beetle grabbed hold of Septimus's sleeve and pulled him along to the very end of the caged rows. Beetle knelt down beside an air vent and immediately jumped back up again, unnerved by a loud hiss from the *Zombie Snake Anti-Venom Formulae.* "Eurgh, I hate snakes. Gave me a shock, that did. Here, Sep, you don't mind snakes—you go there. You'll hear what's going on better anyway."

"Hear what, Beetle?" asked Septimus, squeezing in between him and the *Zombie Snake Anti-Venom Formulae.*

Beetle pointed to an air vent in the wall. "The Hermetic Chamber is through there," he explained. "You know—Old Foxy's room where they do all the secret stuff. I'm meant to keep the air vent sealed up but, well it gets pretty whiffy in here sometimes and you need a bit of a breeze going through. Listen, Sep, you can hear *everything*."

Septimus knelt down beside Beetle and suddenly Simon's voice came through as clearly as if he were standing next to him. He sounded irritated. "Look, Hugh, I'm telling you, there's something wrong with this Flyte Charm. It's totally unpredictable; frankly, I'm lucky to be here in one piece. I nearly dropped my new assistant in the Quake Ooze—mind you, that would have served the ungrateful little tyke right. I offer him the chance of a lifetime and he changes his mind mid-Flyte."

"You're not meant to carry passengers." Septimus heard the Chief Hermetic Scribe's disapproving voice. "The Art of Flyte is not a taxi service."

"Oh, don't be so prissy, Hugh. Sort it out, will you? I'm sure you can do something. Just beef it up a bit."

"*Beef it up a bit?*" Hugh Fox's incredulous tones drifted through the air vent. "This is the Lost Art of Flyte—the most arcane Art of all—and you come in here and tell me to *beef it up*. This Charm is the oldest I have ever seen; look at the gold—taken from the golden threads spun by the Spiders of Aurum, no less—so pure and soft that you hardly dare touch it."

"Oh for goodness' sake, Hugh." Simon sounded exasperated. "However wonderful the wretched thing may be, it's no good if it nearly kills the person using it. Anyway, I'm not so sure that it really is the Flyte Charm—it doesn't do half of what you told me it would."

Hugh Fox spluttered his reply. "I can assure you, Simon, that this is the real thing. I have been researching this for years and it was exactly where I expected it to be—Concealed with a Darke Unseen within the cover of this book." Septimus heard Hugh Fox thump something emphatically. "You have to show the Charm some respect, Simon, not *beef it up*."

"Look, Fox." Simon's voice sounded threatening. "I'd advise you to show *me* some respect. This is the Big Day. Everything's very nearly in place. If all goes well you'll have a new ExtraOrdinary Wizard to deal with. A *proper* one. And, even if I do say so myself, a decent Apprentice—yours truly, no less—not some Young Army boy who can't tell a cracked spell from an old sock."

"I've told you before, Simon," Hugh Fox said dourly, "I

don't get involved in politics. If you ask me we've had enough ExtraOrdinary Wizard changes. There's nothing wrong with the one we've got. The lad's all right too."

Simon's voice became ice-cold. "I wouldn't say any more if I were you, Fox. Don't want to find yourself Consumed, do you?"

"What?" gasped Hugh Fox, sounding terrified.

"You heard. Just get that Charm sorted. This is serious. I'll be back in an hour and I expect it to be working."

"I'll see what I can do," said Hugh Fox sullenly.

"Just *do* it, Fox. Anyway, you'll be pleased to know it's my last trip. I have the final piece—see?"

There was a gasp from the Chief Hermetic Scribe as something hollow was tapped and Simon laughed.

"Don't do that," said Hugh Fox. "I don't care who that was, it's not respectful."

"Don't tell me what to do," Simon snarled. "Anyway, you'll find out who it was—*is*—soon enough. Now open the door, will you?"

There was a loud hiss and then silence.

"Jumped-up little—" The remainder of the Chief Hermetic Scribe's opinion of Septimus's eldest brother was drowned out by the loud thump of a large book being slammed shut.

"Did you hear that?" Septimus whispered to Beetle as they got up and picked their way back between the Wild Books and Charms stacks. "What does he mean, *new* ExtraOrdinary Wizard?"

"Look, Sep," said Beetle as they reached the door to the outer office. "Everyone here thinks he's a loony. We get lots of those. Think they're going to rule the world with a few Darke Spells."

"Maybe he is," said Septimus.

Beetle did not reply. Safely back in the front office, he turned to Septimus and said, "Tell you what, I'll go and get Old Foxy out of the way for a few minutes. Then you can nip in and get the Flyte Charm. That'll cramp his style a bit. How about that?"

Beetle disappeared into the gloom of the Manuscriptorium. In a moment he was back, frantically beckoning to Septimus. "C'mon, Sep. Quick, we're in luck. Old Foxy's having one of his turns—he's gone to lie down. Follow me."

Septimus was a familiar figure in the Manuscriptorium, and none of the scribes even looked up as he followed Beetle to the passage that led to the Chief Hermetic Scribe's Chamber. The passage was narrow and pitch-black, for it turned back on itself seven times to avoid any direct line of flight from the

Chamber. At the end of the passage Beetle and Septimus found themselves in a small plain-white room lit by a single candle. The room was circular in order to avoid any rogue spells or charms getting lodged in the corners and was sparsely furnished. A large round table took up most of the space, and an old-looking glass, taller than Septimus, was propped up against the wall. But Septimus noticed none of this when he walked in behind Beetle—his eyes were immediately fixed on what lay upon the table. Not on the Flyte Charm, which was still attached to Simon's belt and carelessly thrown down upon the table, but upon the thick book that lay beside it.

"That's Marcia's book!" Septimus gasped.

"Shh!" whispered Beetle.

"But it is," Septimus whispered excitedly. "She had it with her when DomDaniel tricked her into coming back to the Castle in the Big Freeze. DomDaniel took it and she hasn't seen it since. She's been looking for it everywhere." He picked up the book. "Look—this is it, *The Undoing of the Darkenesse*."

Beetle looked confused. "So how come Foxy's got it?" he asked.

"Well, he won't have it for much longer," declared Septimus. "Marcia will be straight down to get her book back when I tell her where it is."

Beetle made a mental note to make himself scarce the moment he saw Marcia anywhere near the Manuscriptorium.

"Just get the Charm Sep, and let's get out of here," said Beetle, worried that Hugh Fox might suddenly reappear.

The Flyte Charm was a simple gold arrow. It was smaller than Septimus had expected and more delicate, with intricate patterns wrought from the gold. Its flights were made of white gold—they were curiously bent and misshapen, and Septimus wondered if this was why Simon had been having trouble. He reached out to pick it up and there was a sudden movement below his outstretched hand. Simon's belt twisted away, Transformed into a small red snake with three black stars along the back of its head, and coiled itself tightly around the Flyte Charm. It hissed and reared up, preparing to strike.

"Aargh!" Beetle yelled in horror then immediately clapped his hand over his mouth to stifle the shout. But it was too late—someone in the Manuscriptorium had heard him.

"Hello-ooo . . ." A hesitant voice came from the seven-turn passage. "Is there anybody there?"

"Sep," said Beetle urgently. "Sep—we've got to get out of here. Come on."

"Coo-eee," came the voice again.

"It's all right, Partridge," Beetle called out. "The Extra-Ordinary's Apprentice took a wrong turn. I'm just bringing him out now."

"Oh. Good. Was a bit worried there, Beetle. Mr Fox told me to keep an eye on the Chamber."

"No problem, Partridge. Be out in a moment. No need to come in," Beetle called out cheerily, and then in a low voice, "*Sep, just get a move on, will you?*" Septimus was still eyeing the snake, unwilling to let the Flyte Charm go.

"Oh, hello, Mr Fox, sir." The high-pitched voice of Partridge suddenly echoed around the Chamber. Septimus and Beetle stared at each other in panic.

"What are you doing? Get out of my way, Partridge," came the irritated tones of the Chief Hermetic Scribe.

"Oops . . . er, sorry, sir," squeaked Partridge, "was that your foot?"

"Yes, it is my foot, Partridge. Just get off it, will you?"

"Yes. Yes, of course I will, Mr Fox, sir. Sorry. Sorry."

"For goodness' sake get back to your desk and stop saying sorry."

"Sorry. I mean, yes, Mr Fox. If I can just squeeze past please, if you don't mind, Mr Fox. Sorry."

"*Oh, give me patience . . .*"

In the time it took for Partridge to untangle himself from Hugh Fox, apologise yet again and flee to the safety of his desk, Beetle had pulled a large brass lever that was set into the wall. A low hiss filled the room and this time it wasn't the snake. Underneath the table a concealed round trapdoor rose slowly from the floor and a chill breath of air came into the room.

"Get down there, Sep, now!" Beetle said urgently. Septimus cast a regretful glance at the snake, which was still tightly coiled around the Flyte Charm and hissing even more angrily, having mistaken the sound of the trapdoor for a rival snake. But with the tread of Hugh Fox's brisk footsteps coming closer, Septimus picked up Marcia's book and slipped through the trapdoor, closely followed by Beetle.

✠ 39 ✠
IN THE ICE TUNNELS

The trapdoor closed above them with a quiet hiss and settled into its seal. Septimus shivered. It was icy cold underneath the Hermetic Chamber—and pitch-black. Septimus's Dragon Ring began to glow with its usual warm yellow light.

"You've got some pretty good stuff, haven't you, Sep?" Beetle said admiringly. "But this is a better light for down here."

Bettle snapped open a small tin. Inside was a flat stone that gave off a bright blue light, making the white walls surrounding them glisten and sparkle.

Septimus looked around, expecting to find that they were in some kind of cellar. He was surprised to see that they were actually standing in the middle of a long white tunnel, which stretched on either side of them for as far as he could see.

"This is the first place Old Foxy is going to look," Beetle whispered, glancing up at the trapdoor anxiously. "We better get going." Beetle took down from the wall a large board with two metal strips running down either side of it. Beetle put the board on the white floor of the tunnel, sat down on it and smiled. "Jump aboard, Sep." Septimus went to do just that—suddenly his feet shot out from under him and he landed with a thud.

"Ouch," he gasped. "It's as slippery as ice. What *is* this stuff, Beetle?"

"Ice," said Beetle. "C'mon, get up, Sep."

"Ice? But it's the middle of summer. Where are we, Beetle?"

"In the Ice Tunnels of course," Beetle told him. "Where did you think we were?"

"I dunno. In a secret room under the Chamber I s'pose. *Ice tunnels*—what are they?"

"I thought you knew about the Ice Tunnels. Being the Number One Apprentice and all that. C'mon, Sep, get on the sledge."

There was hardly any room left for Septimus. He squeezed in behind Beetle and then realised he had left *The Undoing of the Darkenesse* on the ice. "Hang on, Beetle, there's no room for Marcia's book."

"Well, sit on it then," Beetle told him, somewhat exasperated. "And hurry up. Old Foxy will be shoving his pointy nose down here any minute now."

Septimus got up, plonked the book down on the sledge and sat on it. Septimus felt uneasy; he didn't like the Ice Tunnels at all. A chill wind was blowing, and as it swept by, Septimus could hear the sound of wailing and crying. It made the hairs on the back of his neck stand up.

"Right," said Beetle cheerily. "Hold on tight, we're off." The sledge shot off like a rocket, nearly hurling Septimus to the ground, but they had not even reached the first bend when the unmistakable sound of a hiss filled the tunnel—the trapdoor was opening. Beetle swerved into the wall and snapped his light tin shut. Septimus shoved his hand in his pocket to douse the light from the Dragon Ring, and they sat stock-still in the icy darkness, holding their breath. Suddenly a beam of light cut through the dark, shining down from the open trap-door, and the Chief Hermetic Scribe hung his head from the opening looking like a bizarre novelty lampshade. His pointed features peered to the left and to the right, and then his voice reverberated along the tunnel, sounding deeper and more impressive than it really was.

"Don't be ridiculous, Partridge. I can't see Beetle anywhere. Why on earth would he want to go down there—it's not Inspection Day. And why would he take the book? It's no good you trying to shift the blame when it is entirely your responsibility . . ." The rest of Hugh Fox's tirade was cut off by the hiss of the trapdoor closing.

"Let's get out of here!" Septimus muttered under his breath.

Beetle snapped open his light tin and the sledge shot off along the tunnel.

They travelled fast and the little sledge took the wide bends with practised ease. After a few minutes Beetle slowed the sledge down; Septimus relaxed his white-knuckled grip on the sides and glanced behind him.

"No point in rushing, Sep," said Beetle. "No one will be after us—we've got the only Charmed sledge."

"You sure?" asked Septimus, still looking back.

"'Course I'm sure. It is my sledge after all. I'm the only one who does the inspections."

"But what do you inspect, Beetle?" Septimus asked, as the sledge trundled itself up a steady incline. "And why?"

"Dunno *why*, Sep. Nobody tells me *why*. Just come down every week and have a whiz around on the sledge and look out for any cracks in the ice, thawing, disturbance—you know, stuff like that—and check all the trapdoors are Sealed."

"What, there are *more* trapdoors?" asked Septimus.

"Yeah, loads. All the old houses have 'em down in the cellars. Head down, and don't breathe in whatever you do—here comes Hilda." Septimus ducked just as a thin white streak of wailing mist swept towards them, spiralling along the glistening walls. The Ice Wraith passed over the sledge, swirling around Beetle and Septimus as they hurtled along, chilling them to the bone. As Septimus hunched down, he felt his hair crackle with ice; the air in his nose and mouth froze solid, and for a terrible moment he thought he would suffocate. And then suddenly the Wraith was gone, wailing and curling along the walls on her endless tour of the Ice Tunnels.

"Phew," Beetle breathed out heavily as he accelerated the sledge up a steep incline. "OK, she's gone now. She won't be back for an hour or so. Usually takes her that long to do the rounds. We'll easily be at the Wizard Tower by then."

"This goes to the Wizard Tower?" gasped Septimus, struggling to get his breath back.

"The Ice Tunnels go everywhere, Sep. Well, they go under all the really old bits of the Castle. They join up the Wizard Tower, the Palace, lots of the shops down Wizard Way and the old houses down by the Moat. Oops, tight corner coming up."

"Aargh! Not so *fast*, Beetle. But how come they're still iced-up in the middle of summer? It doesn't make sense."

"Well, I think it happened ages ago after something went wrong with something or other," said Beetle vaguely. "No one wants to get rid of the ice now because they don't want what's underneath it getting out."

"What is underneath, Beetle?"

"I dunno. Hold tight." Beetle swerved to avoid two pale figures in ragged grey robes, and Septimus nearly fell off.

"Sorry, Sep," said Beetle, righting the sledge and carrying on. "I hate going through ghosts, especially those two. They keep asking me the way out. Drives me nuts."

The sledge trundled on, the runners travelling effortlessly over the smooth ice; it travelled as easily up the gentle inclines in the tunnel as it did down. Septimus had become used to the chill winds and the occasional lost ghost and was almost

enjoying the journey when Beetle slammed the sledge to a
sudden halt and snapped his light tin shut. Ahead of them, a
yellow beam of light shone down like a spotlight from the roof
of the tunnel.

"What's that?" whispered Septimus.

"Someone's UnSealed a trap," whispered Beetle.

"Who?" asked Septimus, his heart beating fast.

"It's the Van Klampff trap," said Beetle under his breath.

"Look—" gasped Septimus. "Someone's coming down."

A pair of feet wearing ice skates dangled through the trapdoor. Septimus thought it must be Una Brakket, for the
rotund Weasal Van Klampff never would have fitted through
the trapdoor. For a brief moment the skates dangled uncertainly in the spotlight; then a familiar figure dropped down
and landed on the ice like a cat. Crouched, as if waiting to
pounce, Simon Heap peered into the dark.

"Who's there?" Simon called out a little uncertainly, his
eyes not yet adjusted to the gloom.

"Simon!" Septimus gasped.

"Someone call my name?" Simon's voice echoed eerily in
the tunnel. "Who are you?"

"Beetle—get us out of here!" came Septimus's urgent
whisper.

There was nothing Beetle wanted to do more. He slewed the sledge around and skidded away in a spray of ice.

"Hey!" came Simon's shout as, with a feeling of incomprehension, he recognised the hated green tunic of Marcia's Apprentice. "What are *you* doing down here, brat?"

"He's after us, Beetle!" yelled Septimus, looking over his shoulder as Simon, an expert ice-skater, picked up speed and hurtled after them in pursuit.

"We'll outrun him, Sep," said Beetle confidently, steering the sledge around another corner and straight through the two ghosts he had avoided earlier.

"Excuse me . . . the way out, please . . . could you tell us . . . the way out the way out the way out . . . ?" echoed through the tunnel.

"We lose him yet?" Beetle yelled.

"No!" Septimus yelled back.

"Right then, here we go!" Beetle shot off down a smaller tunnel, slammed the sledge to a halt and jumped off. In a moment he had shoved Septimus and the sledge through an open door in the ice wall and pushed it shut. Breathing hard, Beetle slithered to the icy floor. "Service hatch." He grinned. "He won't have a clue."

Septimus rolled off the sledge and lay on the ground, staring up at the ceiling of what was a small space carved out of solid ice. The door was also a block of ice and now that it was closed Septimus could see no sign of it. He guessed that it was the same on the other side. "Beetle," he said, "you're amazing."

"Think nothing of it, Sep. Want a SizzleStik?"

"A what?"

"They're nice and hot. I keep some here just in case I get really cold." Beetle fished out a small box from behind a couple of shovels and a blanket. He opened it and looked in. "There's banana and haddock and . . . er . . . beetroot flavour. Sorry, Sep, I seem to have eaten all the good ones."

"Beetroot flavour *what*, Beetle?"

"Chewy thing. Which d'you want?"

"Banana, please."

"You mean the banana and haddock?"

"Oh, yes, please. Aunt Zelda used to do a great banana and haddock pie. Lovely."

"Really? You can have all of them if you like, Sep."

Ten minutes later, Beetle cautiously pulled open the ice door and peered out. The only sign of Simon was two sets of ice-skate tracks—one set going down the tunnel past the service hatch, the other returning, but to Beetle's relief there was no sign of Simon having stopped and investigated the hideaway. Soon Beetle and Septimus were on the sledge, retracing their tracks back to the main tunnel.

"Tell you what, Sep," said Beetle. "We'll take the quick way to the Wizard Tower. Wasn't going to go that way as it's a bit up and down, but I reckon the sooner we're out of here, the better. OK?"

"You bet, Beetle."

A few minutes and numerous turns later, Beetle stopped the sledge and pointed out a sign carved into the ice. Picked out in black ice were the words TO THE WIZARD TOWER, written in an old-fashioned script, and an ornate arrow pointing down a much smaller and narrower ice tunnel that disappeared into blackness.

"Right," said Beetle. "You're gonna have to hold on tight now, Sep. This is where it gets hairy."

The sledge took the tight turn into the Wizard Tower tunnel. It waited for a moment as though gathering its courage, and then, to Septimus's horror, the ice below seemed to fall away and they dropped like a stone.

"Woo-hooooo!" Beetle's excited shout streamed out behind him as the sledge plummeted down an almost vertical slope, hit the ice at the bottom, flew up an equally steep incline, then shot off the top and landed with a jarring bump as the slope levelled off. Septimus was just getting his breath back when Beetle took a tight corner to the left and immediately slammed the sledge through an even tighter bend to the right—at which point Septimus and the sledge parted company. Beetle skidded to a halt in a shower of ice, spun the sledge around in a 180-degree turn and came back slowly to find Septimus.

"Pretty good, huh?" Beetle grinned. "You should see my triple turns—they're the best."

"Not just now, thanks, Beetle," said Septimus, painfully hauling himself up off the ice.

"Yeah. OK. Well, we're here anyway. Taxi service to your door, Sep. Not bad, eh?" Beetle pointed to a tall arch, which was, of course, solid ice. Above the arch two ornate letters were carved into the ice—*W.T.*

"There y'are. That's it," said Beetle.

"Oh . . ." said Septimus, eyeing the arch doubtfully. He picked up *The Undoing of the Darkenesse.* "Come on then, Beetle."

"What—me?" Beetle sounded surprised.

"Well, you can't go back, can you? What are you going to tell Foxy?"

"Oh, bother. I hadn't thought of that." Beetle got off the sledge and tied it up to a silver ring set into the ice. "You have to tie 'em up, otherwise they wander off," Beetle explained, seeing Septimus's surprised glance at the ring. "Everyone had their own sledge in the old days, Sep—and the Wizard Tower sledge was something special, so they say. But seeing as this is the last Charmed sledge, I don't want it disappearing."

"No," agreed Septimus. "You coming then, Beetle?"

Reluctantly, Beetle followed Septimus through the ice arch. Sitting at the bottom of a flight of ice steps was an almost transparent figure wearing the purple robes of an ExtraOrdinary Wizard. He was fast asleep.

Septimus stopped short and Beetle slid into him, sending Septimus skidding into the ghost.

"Oo . . . aargh . . ." moaned the ghost, waking up with a start. "Who goes there?"

"It's—it's me," stuttered Septimus. "I'm the Apprentice."

"Apprentice? Which one?" asked the ghost suspiciously.

"Apprentice to the ExtraOrdinary Wizard," Septimus told him.

"No, you're not. You're nothing like my Apprentice."

Septimus wondered how to break the news to the old Wizard on the steps. "Look, I'm sorry to have to tell you this," he said gently, "but you're not the ExtraOrdinary Wizard any more. You're a ghost. You're—well, you're dead."

"Hee hee. Got you there, boy. Of *course* I'm dead. Wouldn't be sitting here bored out of my mind if I were alive. What's your name, sonny?"

"Septimus Heap."

"Really? Well, well, well. You'd better go on up."

"And my friend too?"

"May as well. Off you both go. Turn left at the top and say the password. You'll find yourself in the broom cupboard just off the Great Hall."

"Thank you very much." Septimus smiled.

The old ExtraOrdinary Wizard settled himself down and closed his eyes. "My pleasure," he said, "and good luck, son. You're going to need it."

✢ 40 ✢
BEETLE IN THE TOWER

Septimus *pushed open the broom cup-*
board door and warily peered out.
He waited until a small group of
Ordinary Wizards discussing
the weather had wandered
past, and then he and Beetle
crept out. As Marcia's Apprentice, Septimus knew that he had
every right to be in the Wizard Tower
broom cupboard if he wanted to be, but he didn't want a
gaggle of curious Wizards discussing endless reasons why the
ExtraOrdinary Wizard's Apprentice might choose to be
there.

"Come on, Beetle," said Septimus.

Beetle did not reply. He was rooted to the spot, staring at

the multicoloured floor. "It wrote my name!" His voice slid from its usual gruff tones into an excited high-pitched squeak. "The floor wrote my name—it said, WELCOME, BEETLE. That is so weird."

"Oh, it always does that," said Septimus airily, forgetting how amazed he had been when it had first happened to him.

"And now it says, WELCOME, PRINCESS. Is she coming here, Sep? Is she really?" Beetle had often seen Jenna walking along Wizard Way but he never dreamed of actually meeting her.

"Who, Jenna? I shouldn't think so, Beetle. She only just went home."

The Tower's silver doors had begun to swing open and to Beetle's astonishment there stood Jenna, silhouetted against the bright sunlight. For a moment Septimus was surprised too, not to see Jenna—who now had the password to the Tower and could come and go as she pleased—but at the hot summer day outside. He had forgotten that outside the Ice Tunnels, the sky was blue and the sun was shining.

"Hello, Sep," said Jenna. "Can you go and see Mum? I told her you were back safely but she says she wants to see you with her own eyes."

"'Course I will, Jen. But I've got some stuff to do first. Simon is here."

"Simon—is here?"

"Well, not *here*. He's—he's down there." Septimus pointed downwards.

Jenna looked puzzled. "What, under the floor?"

Septimus lowered his voice. "There are Ice Tunnels under the Castle, Jen. He's in them. *Skating*."

Jenna burst out laughing. "Don't be daft, Sep. It's summer. There's no ice in summer."

"Shh," hushed Septimus. "We don't want anyone else to hear." He smiled at the Wizards, who were retracing their footsteps. "Good morning, Pascalle. Good morning, Thomasinn. Good morning, good morning."

"Good morning, Apprentice," came the chorused reply.

Septimus waited until the Wizards had wandered out into the sunshine. "And that's not all, Jen," he said. "It's true, Simon has got the Flyte Charm—I've seen it. He left it in the Hermetic Chamber. I would have got it too, but his belt Transformed into a snake and—"

"Ice tunnels . . . the Hermetic Chamber . . . a *snake*?" Jenna said, her eyes widening in disbelief. "Sep, what on earth have you been doing? You only went to get a copy of *Draxx*."

"Yes, well I met Beetle and things just sort of . . . happened."

Beetle shifted about self-consciously. He felt like a fish out of water standing in the Wizard Tower next to the Princess. Not that she had noticed him of course. And his best friend, Sep, was suddenly a different person, no longer someone you could muck about with and squirt FizzFroot out of your nose at.

"Oh, hello, Beetle," said Jenna, much to Beetle's amazement.

"Wha—h-how d'you know my name?" stammered Beetle.

"I read it on the floor." Jenna grinned. "I guessed it was you. You look just like Sep said."

"S-Sep told you about me?" Beetle went red.

"'Course he did. You're his best friend."

"Oh . . ." Beetle couldn't think of anything to say. He followed Septimus and Jenna as they wandered to the stairs and nearly fell off in surprise when the silver spiral started turning. By the time they reached the top, Beetle felt extremely dizzy. Give me the Ice Tunnels any day, he thought, as he staggered off after Septimus and Jenna. And then Beetle had to swallow hard—he had just seen the massive purple door that led to Marcia's rooms and he couldn't believe it—here he was on the top landing of the Wizard Tower outside the ExtraOrdinary Wizard's Rooms. No one, not even Old Foxy, got to the *top landing*. If they needed to see the ExtraOrdinary Wizard, they were always met in the Great Hall. They never came upstairs.

Catchpole was dozing quietly on his chair. Septimus stepped past him and, as usual, the heavy purple door recognised the Apprentice. It swung open and Septimus gave Beetle a friendly push across the threshold. "Come on, Beetle." He grinned. "It's not *that* smart in here."

It certainly wasn't. Marcia's normally neatly tended room was in chaos. A swath of broken furniture was strewn across the floor, topped off with assorted smashed pots, plates and vases.

Beetle said nothing. For all he knew the ExtraOrdinary Wizard's place always looked like this, and he had heard a few stories about the way Wizards lived from his uncle who did house clearances over at the Ramblings.

"What has happened?" gasped Jenna.

Septimus gulped. Something was missing; something that had dominated the room for almost a year was gone. And then Septimus realised that it was still there—but in pieces. "The ShadowSafe," he gasped. "It's been ripped apart. And—and where's Marcia?"

"Maybe the Shadow got her, Sep . . ." Jenna whispered.

Suddenly she grabbed Septimus's arm. "Look—" she gasped, pointing to something moving under a pile of purple curtains that had been torn down from the window. "The—the Shadow. It's under there."

"Quick, let's get out of here," said Septimus. But as Septimus, Jenna and Beetle backed towards the door, the thing under the purple curtains rushed towards them, tripped over a pile of torn velvet cushions and crashed into an occasional table, sending it smashing to the floor. Then a long green tail swept out and upended the last unbroken vase.

"Oh, Spit Fyre, you *bad* dragon," Septimus gasped with a mixture of dismay and relief, "what have you done?"

On hearing his name, Spit Fyre emerged from under the curtains. The dragon, which was now the size of a small pony, galumphed across the room to greet Septimus, tail swishing from side to side with excitement at seeing his Imprintor.

"Sit, Spit Fyre. Sit!" said Septimus, with no effect whatsoever. Spit Fyre rubbed his head against Septimus's tunic and banged his tail on the floor with a reverberating *thump* that sent soot cascading down from the chimney.

"Is this your new pet, Septimus?" A familiar voice came from the pile of soot. Alther picked himself up from the grate and floated out of the fireplace. "I'm amazed you've managed to persuade Marcia to let you have a dragon here. I take my hat off to you—or I would if I had one. Ah, hello, Princess. And the lad from the Manuscriptorium too."

"Hello, Alther," said Jenna, thankful that Alther had, as he so often did, turned up just when they needed him. Beetle, lost for words, just managed a faint smile.

Septimus said nothing. He was busy tussling with Spit Fyre over a piece of the ShadowSafe, which the dragon was determined to chew. Septimus wrested a long black bar from Spit Fyre's grasp, but the dragon snatched it back and swept its tail right through Alther's knees.

Alther did not like being Passed Through. It always made him feel sick. "You really ought to get a copy of *Draxx*," he said, somewhat tetchily.

"I *know*," Septimus replied, distracted. He and Spit Fyre had reached a compromise. The dragon had one half of the bar, and Septimus had the other, which he was staring at with a shocked expression.

"Alther," said Septimus, "there's something in the middle of this—it looks like a bone."

THE PLACEMENT

S*pit Fyre was snoring loudly beside* the fireplace. Alther had tried to get the dragon back to Septimus's room, but Spit Fyre's last growth spurt meant that there was no way he could fit up the stairs. Luckily, Septimus had found the half-chewed remains of *How to Survive Dragon Fostering: A Practykal Guide* and had managed to decipher a soggy Sleep Suggestion, which to his amazement had worked.

Jenna, Septimus and Beetle were now in the middle of a grisly task. They were collecting the smashed ShadowSafe and removing from each piece an assortment of bones—human bones.

"I thought we did some weird stuff at Number Thirteen, Sep, but this is something else. D'you do stuff like this every day?" Beetle was painstakingly taking apart some curved pieces, which had been at the top of the ShadowSafe, and were turning out to contain a full set of rib bones.

"No, not *every* day," Septimus replied with a grimace as he extricated a long thin bone from a narrow section that had formed one of the corners. "But this *is* the last Thursday of the month, Beetle, so what do you expect?"

Beetle handed yet another rib to Jenna, who was laying out the bones on the floor. "You do this every last Thursday—" He caught Septimus's smile. "Oh, ha ha, Sep. Nearly got me there. I make that fourteen now, ma'am."

"Jenna," corrected Jenna. "Call me Jenna, Beetle."

"Oh. Sorry . . . Jenna. Well, that's fourteen ribs so far and there are still some more in here. Look how neatly they've been fixed inside. They're so well hidden that you'd never know. Not in a million years. Ah, here comes another one—fifteen."

"Mm, lovely. Thanks, Beetle."

"Anytime, ma'am—Jenna."

Jenna surveyed the gruesome collection, carefully laid out like a bizarre jigsaw puzzle. There, on Marcia's best Chinese rug, the shape of a human skeleton was slowly forming, as Septimus and Beetle handed her a succession of bones.

"How much have you got there now, Jen?" Septimus asked after a while.

"Well,"—Jenna tried to remember what she knew from her Human Anatomy lessons at school—"there's almost two arms, and, um, eight fingers, no thumbs yet—I don't think so anyway. There are lots of little bones but I don't know where they go, maybe in the wrist . . . there's one whole leg still missing and no skull yet, thank goodness."

"Aha," Septimus said grimly as he pulled out a long thin section from under the upturned sofa. "I think leg number two is in here."

"This is so weird," muttered Beetle, as he handed Jenna a succession of small bones. She placed them carefully where she thought they belonged, then she stood up and surveyed her creation. She now had what looked like a full skeleton minus the head. Alther floated next to her, shimmering slightly and looking more transparent than usual. Jenna knew that was a sure sign that Alther was worried.

"What is it, Uncle Alther?" Jenna asked.

"I think, Princess, that this is a Placement. It's obviously an incomplete Placement, but what I'd like to know is exactly how incomplete it is."

"I suppose we could count the bones," said Jenna. "And then, if we knew how many there are in a skeleton, we'd know."

"But we don't know how many there are in a skeleton," said Septimus. "Well, I don't know, that's for sure."

"Neither do I," said Jenna.

"Two hundred and six," said Beetle.

"Beetle—you're amazing. Are you sure?" asked Septimus.

"Yep. I counted them once. It was part of the test that I had to take to get the job at the Manuscriptorium. I had one minute to look at the skeleton in the cupboard. Then they muddled it up and I had to put it back together—and count the bones. I counted two hundred, and Old Foxy told me to add six to that because there are three tiny bones in each ear that you can't see. So it's two hundred and six."

"Well, *you* ought to be doing this then, Beetle," said Jenna. "You'd be much better at it than me."

"Eurgh, no thanks." Beetle shuddered. "Don't like bones. They set my teeth on edge."

Jenna looked so disappointed that Beetle immediately relented. "Well, all right then," he offered. "I'll count them if you really want me to." Beetle started his gruesome count. Five counts later he sat back on his heels and said with relief, "Finished. That comes out the same as the last one. All the bones are there. Except for the skull, of course."

"Which will complete the Placement," said Alther.

"But why a Placement with a human skeleton?" asked Septimus. "Aren't they usually done with rats' or snakes' skeletons?"

"Usually," agreed Alther. "But this looks horribly like a Personal Placement—and those are lethal."

"'Scuse me," mumbled Beetle. "But what *is* a Placement?"

"I'm glad you asked that, Beetle," said Jenna. "Because I have no idea either." Beetle blushed.

"It's a Darke device," muttered Alther, floating above the skeleton, examining it closely. "A Placement is a way of gaining access to somewhere that would be impossible to get into any other way. The Wizard—and it usually is a Wizard, as these things can be dangerous—will, by some devious means, get the bones of a creature taken over the threshold of the place he wishes to enter. The person who you wish to Affect must carry them in willingly—you can't just chuck them in through the window. They must be taken in piecemeal, and when the last bone, always the skull, crosses the threshold, the creature reassembles itself and then does whatever task it has been sent to do. It is virtually unstoppable. But a Personal Placement—which has to be human bones—is one of the nastiest Darke devices of all. One touch from the Placement and the Intended is dead—and worse than that, they then spend a year and a day in Turmoil. At least when I became a ghost all I had to do was sit in that ghastly Throne Room for a year and a day . . . but to be in Turmoil for so long . . . that's terrible . . . terrible." Alther shook his head.

Septimus felt sick. "The Intended is Marcia, isn't it, Alther?" he whispered.

"I would say so, Apprentice. You know, I just don't understand how Weasal could do this—"

"Do what, Alther?" The purple door suddenly swung open and to everyone's surprise, Marcia breezed in, her Shadow slipping in behind her. Marcia was carrying what looked like a large hatbox. "Aagh!" she yelled. "That wretched, *wretched* dragon. Oh, I don't believe it."

"Marcia," Alther said very calmly, "you have a Placement

in here. I need to know what is in that box."

"What are you going on about, Alther? Septimus, take that pest of a dragon down to the courtyard. He's not staying inside a moment longer!"

But Septimus did not reply. He ran at Marcia, pushing her back towards the door. "Get out, Marcia. You've got to get out of here."

"Septimus, what are you doing?" said Marcia, pushing Septimus away. Septimus gave Marcia a violent shove and the final piece of the ShadowSafe—the large round Stopper—fell to the floor and smashed. Everyone stared in horror as a white skull bounced from the shards and rolled towards the bones lying on the floor. It took no more than a few seconds for the head to be reunited with the body.

The Placement was Complete.

✢ 42 ✢
IDENTIFY

T*he skeleton stood up uncertainly*, swaying slightly as if it were trying to get its balance—then suddenly, like a ghastly puppet, it lurched forward and headed straight for Marcia.

Marcia was pale but composed. Slowly she backed away from the skeleton, thinking fast.

Alther watched the Shadow follow Marcia, and he didn't like what he saw one bit. The Shadow was no longer the hunched and formless creature that Alther had watched follow Marcia around her rooms for the past year. It was now an almost solid being—it stood up straight and tall, its dim yellow eyes shining with excitement as it hovered by Marcia's shoulder. Waiting.

"Ellis Crackle!" gasped Alther. The Shadow looked up at the mention of its name.

"Are you trying to be funny, Alther?" snapped Marcia.

"Your Shadow, Marcia. It's Ellis Crackle."

"Right now, Alther, I don't care who that Shadow is." Marcia stepped back over a shredded cushion; her movement was mirrored by the advancing skeleton, which made an unpleasant clicking noise with each step towards her. Marcia took another step back. The skeleton took another step forward.

"For heaven's sake, Alther, this is serious," said Marcia. There was an undercurrent of panic in her voice.

"I know," said Alther quietly. "There is only one way out of this."

Marcia stepped back again. The skeleton stepped forward.

"You have to Identify," said Alther, floating a few feet off the floor and keeping pace with Marcia.

"Alther, I can't. I don't know who it is."

But Jenna knew who it was. All the time she had been

piecing the skeleton together, she had been thinking things through. "It's DomDaniel," she said. "It has to be."

Marcia glanced at Jenna, taking her eyes off the advancing bones for a moment. "Jenna—what do you mean?" she asked.

Jenna looked steadfastly at Marcia and not at the bones— she could hardly bear to look at the same grinning skull and the empty eyes that had followed her around the Observatory. "I mean—I mean *it's DomDaniel*. Simon had his skull but not his bones. But he told me he had found all of the bones on the Marsh. I wondered where they were . . ."

"Are you sure, Princess?" asked Alther quietly.

"Yes," said Jenna. "Yes, yes. I'm sure."

Marcia was dithering, muttering to herself. "But then it might *not* be him . . . it might be a bluff . . . in fact I'll bet it *is* a bluff . . . that's the sort of thing he'd do, Place some poor sailor from that ghastly ship . . . but then maybe it's a double bluff and it really *is* him . . . it's the kind of thing he'd love to do himself . . . Oh, *Alther*."

"You must trust Jenna. Identify it, Marcia. *Now*," said Alther in a low, careful voice, instructing Marcia as though she were still his Apprentice.

The skeleton was almost within reach of Marcia, and it began to raise its right arm towards her. All colour drained from her face. Marcia whispered, "If the Identify is wrong, Alther, then—then I—I'm finished."

"Marcia, you have nothing to lose. If it *touches* you, you're finished."

The bones took a big step forward.

Marcia took a corresponding step back and could go no farther; she had reached the door. She snapped her fingers and there was a loud *clunk*—two silver bars slid out of the wall and Barred the door. A quiet whirring noise followed, as the thick purple door SafetyLocked itself. Marcia smiled grimly; at least the rest of the Wizard Tower was protected from the havoc a successful Placement would wreak. She leaned against the door for support and began what she had to do. A purple haze of powerful Magyk began to flicker around the ExtraOrdinary Wizard, lighting up her deep-green eyes and shimmering across her long purple cloak.

Suddenly the skeleton lunged towards her—Marcia raised her hand and shouted, "I Identify!"

The skeleton stopped in its tracks. It regarded Marcia with as much of a taunting stare as an empty skull could manage, folded its arms and stood tapping its foot impatiently. *Go on*, it seemed to be saying, *surprise me, why don't you?*

Marcia was nonplussed. "Alther, it knows what I'm going

to say and it's not even bothered," she said urgently. "Jenna must be wrong."

"It's bluffing," said Alther, sounding much more confident than he felt.

Unconvinced, Marcia flashed Alther a weak smile. "Look after Septimus, Alther," she said. "I'll be back in a year and a day to check up on you."

"Yes. I will. Now do it."

Marcia raised her arm and pointed at the skeleton. She took a deep breath and said in a low, singsong voice,

> "Hand on heart,
> Eye to eye,
> I you Identify
> As . . ."

Marcia's voice faltered. She looked fondly at Septimus, Jenna, Alther and even Beetle, for what was quite possibly the last time she would see them as a living being.

> ". . . DomDaniel!"

A terrible shriek filled the air.

Jenna gasped in horror, convinced that the shriek had come from Marcia. Like a wailing banshee, the shriek continued, howling and yowling around the room. Unable to bear it, Beetle threw himself to the floor and shoved a cushion over his head. Jenna stuffed her fingers in her ears, but Septimus listened. He listened and he watched, with open ears and eyes, for he wanted to hear the sound of the most powerful Magyk he had ever seen, he wanted to know what it felt like—but most of all, he wanted to be part of it.

Septimus took a step towards Marcia.

Wrapping her Magykal purple cloak tightly around her for protection, Marcia was pressed back against the unyielding door. In front of her was the skeleton, its arms outstretched, reaching to seize the Akhu Amulet from Marcia's neck. Septimus watched the purple haze around Marcia grow darker and deeper and the shapes of Marcia and the skeleton grow dim within it.

Alther shook his head, worried by the continuing shriek. Something was wrong. The Identify was not working as it should.

Septimus reached the edge of the purple haze.

"No!" shouted Alther, trying to make himself heard above the terrible shriek. "Keep back, Septimus. This is dangerous Magyk."

Septimus ignored him. The shriek rose to an unbearable pitch and Septimus walked into the Magyk. He entered a thick silence where everything was slow and still, and he knew that Marcia had seen him. Her lips moved but no sound came, and she raised her hand as if to stop him from coming any nearer.

Septimus stood inside the Magyk, trying to understand what was happening. Now he could see the unmistakable shape of DomDaniel appearing around the bones—he recognised the Necromancer's short cylindrical hat, his straggly hair and his long black cloak—and his fat hands still reaching for the Amulet. Marcia had got the Identify right, so why wasn't it working? And then he realised why—Marcia was outnumbered.

Septimus now saw what Alther had seen; the Shadow was no longer just an indistinct form, but a wild-looking young man with yellow eyes, his teeth bared in a rictus smile. Ellis Crackle, one-time Apprentice to DomDaniel, stood next to Marcia, countermanding the Identify.

Wading as if underwater, Septimus moved through the Magykal haze towards Marcia. He saw Ellis Crackle reach out to push him away, and he knew that it was Apprentice against Apprentice. Septimus raised his hand; they met palm to palm and Septimus felt the coldness of the Shadow's touch. He looked Ellis Crackle in the eye and Ellis Crackle returned his gaze, yellow to green. Septimus concentrated hard, and slowly but surely he Transfixed the hapless Ellis Crackle.

Suddenly Alther, Jenna and Beetle saw Ellis Crackle shoot out from the swirling purple mist; in a wraith of black smoke, the Shadow spun and tumbled around the room, desperately searching for a way out. There was nothing Alther wanted to see more than the Shadow leaving Marcia, and so he did something he did not often do—he Caused a thing to happen. A rush of air blew open the biggest window in the room, and the Shadow of Ellis Crackle flew out and vaporised in the clear summer air.

The brightness of the light surprised Jenna after the darkness inside the room, and it took her a few moments to notice that, silhouetted against the sun, there was someone— human—outside the window. Balancing precariously on a surprisingly large wooden platform that stuck out from the windowsill was Simon Heap.

Alther Caused the window to slam shut, but Simon pushed it open and leaped into the room. Jenna shrank back and Beetle, who had just emerged from underneath his cushion, put a protective arm around her. But this time it was not Jenna who Simon was interested in—it was the skeleton.

With the departure of Ellis Crackle, the haze of Magyk was clearing, revealing three figures, one of which, arm still out-stretched towards Marcia's throat, was disintegrating fast.

Simon ran towards the decomposing form. "I'm here, Master!" he shouted. "Your new Apprentice is here!"

So eager was Simon to claim his place as DomDaniel's Apprentice that at first he did not stop to consider that Marcia was still alive, which meant something had gone badly wrong with the Placement. But as he reached the last Magykal strands of purple, Simon stopped, an expression of dismay dawning on his face.

DomDaniel did not look good. Indeed, DomDaniel looked worse than Simon had ever seen him before, and that includ-ed the time when Simon had first encountered the muddy set of bones clambering out of the ditch. At least Brownie-picked bones were relatively clean and tidy. They did not melt and soften into a disgusting liquid mass, and they did not make a revolting squelching noise, either.

"Y-your new Apprentice is here . . . M-Master," Simon stammered, suddenly aware of Marcia and Septimus right there in front of him. Marcia was clutching Septimus's arm tightly, and their faces were ashen and wore identical expres-sions of revulsion mixed with relief as they watched

DomDaniel sink and begin to pool across the floor. The Identify was finally working.

Simon began to understand that all was not well.

A low, unearthly laugh filled the room. "You're no Apprentice of mine, you fool. I ask you to dispose of the Queenling—a simple task—and what happens? Not only does she escape from you three times, but she comes back here and *messes around with my bones*. Puts me together on the carpet like some child's jigsaw puzzle, in fact. And it is all *your* fault, you wretched Heap. Not that you ever *were* going to be my Apprentice—you were nothing more than a delivery boy. My Apprentice has been here all the time—Shadowing . . . Shadowing . . . Shadowing . . ." DomDaniel's voice faded away. A foul black mess spread out and collected around Simon's boots.

"You double-crossing fiend!" Simon yelled. "After all I've done for you and your revolting bones. You promised me!" Like a child kicking through a pile of fallen leaves, Simon kicked his way through the pool of sludge that was all that remained of DomDaniel, spraying it across the room.

"Don't do that!" shouted Marcia. "Get out, Simon—or do I have to make you go?"

Simon backed away. "Don't worry, I'm going. I wouldn't

want to stay here with all these *impostors*." He broke off and stared angrily at Septimus. "But you will not get rid of me that easily. I was promised the Apprenticeship. And I will have it. I *will*."

Simon ran to the window, pulled it open and scrambled on to the broad ledge outside. He stood for a moment, gathering his courage, then he threw himself off, scarcely caring whether the Flyte Charm would work—all his plans were gone, destroyed. But as Simon fell through the air, the Flyte Charm kicked in, and as he soared unsteadily over the Wizard Tower Courtyard (to the amazement of a group of Ordinary Wizards returning from a shopping trip) he knew that there was only one thing left for him—revenge.

Back in Marcia's room, the two thick silver bars slid back with a *clunk* and UnBarred the huge purple door, while the quiet whirring of the lock UnLocked it—and a faint tapping noise could be heard.

"Excuse me," came the tentative voice of Catchpole on the other side of the door, "er—are you all right in there? Need any help?"

✛ 43 ✛
FIRSTFLYTE

M arcia was sitting on Catchpole's chair on the landing, clutching *The Undoing of the Darknesse*. The purple door to her rooms was Barred yet again, but this time everyone, except for Spit Fyre, was on the other side of it, listening to the Deep Clean, Repair and Anti-Darke spells that were in progress inside Marcia's rooms. Marcia, worried by a large splotch of DomDaniel that Simon had kicked over the young dragon, had left Spit Fyre for the Anti-Darke spell to sort out.

Catchpole felt rather like the host at an awkward party.

Warily, he tried to make polite conversation. "Would this be a five-minute Clean, Madam Marcia?" he asked, trying to remember the Cleaning Schedules he had learned the previous week.

"Five minutes," Marcia snorted derisively. "It will take more than five minutes to get rid of all that Darke slime sprayed around the place. Not to mention the havoc wrought by a certain dragon. No, it's an infinite spell."

"Infinite. My goodness." Catchpole was lost for words. He had a vision of spending the rest of his life marooned on the landing trying to make polite conversation with Marcia Overstrand. It was not a relaxing thought.

"An Infinite spell will take as long as it takes," Marcia informed him. "It will not stop until the job is finished. Something that perhaps you could learn from, Catchpole—as I seem to remember that the section on Infinite spells is on the very last page of the Cleaning Schedules."

"Oh. Ah, yes. I do remember now, come to think of it, Madam Marcia," Catchpole gulped nervously, but Marcia did not seem interested. She had more pressing things on her mind.

"Alther, I want you to go and get Weasal and his ghastly housekeeper. I want them brought here right now. I shall be interested to hear what they have to say for themselves."

"Nothing would give me more pleasure, but I was Returned from the house." Alther shook his head dismally. "Marcia, I am so sorry for giving you such bad advice. I can't believe that after all Otto Van Klampff did for me, his son could turn out so wrong."

"I don't blame you, Alther," said Marcia. "I blame Una Brakket. And Hugh Fox. You warned me about Hugh Fox, and I wouldn't listen."

"You were affected by the Shadow," Alther replied. "You were not yourself."

"And I didn't listen to Septimus when Simon took Jenna, either," said Marcia. "All the signs were there but I wouldn't see them."

"*Couldn't* see them, Marcia, not wouldn't," replied Alther. "It's a terrible thing to be Shadowed."

Marcia stood up suddenly, and Catchpole leaped to catch the chair as it tumbled backwards.

"Well Alther, the Shadow's gone, and I see things clearly now. And even when I was being Shadowed, I knew well enough to keep an eye on the place where my ShadowSafe was being made. And one thing I know for sure is that although Simon must have been delivering those bones all through the year, he did not bring them through the front door of Weasal's house. None of my Watchers ever saw him—"

"Your Watchers?" asked Alther. "What Watchers?"

"The ex-Young Army Lads. The ones from the Resettlement Home. There are a few nice boys who want to be Wizards—"

"Nice!" snorted Septimus. "They were horrible. Every time I went there they called me names."

"Well, I told them to make it realistic. I didn't want anyone to get suspicious. They were very good. Out on the pier day and night in all weathers, quite dedicated, they were. They'll make good Wizards when they're older."

A sudden thought struck Septimus. "He went through the Ice Tunnels, didn't he? He's been doing that all the time."

"Shh!" Marcia looked shocked. "Not in front of— Catchpole, get down to Snake Slipway and bring Weasal Van Klampff and Una Brakket here. Put them in the Strong Room just off the Great Hall until I am ready to see them. Then you can go and get Hugh Fox and do the same. Understand?"

Catchpole bowed and headed for the spiral stairs, grateful to be spared any further duties as party host.

* * *

A few minutes later a soft whirring sound announced that the door was UnBarring. It swung open and everyone stepped into an immaculate room, Repaired, Cleaned and free of any lingering Darkenesse. Even Marcia looked pleased—for a brief moment—until she saw Spit Fyre sitting on her best Chinese carpet.

"It's fledged," cried Marcia in disbelief, "all over my best carpet. Wretched creature!"

Spit Fyre looked unconcerned; he was busy unfolding his wings for the first time. The soft down that covered them had fallen off, leaving a thick dusting of green fuzz on Marcia's carpet. Now Spit Fyre had an irresistible urge to open his wings and fly—and Marcia knew enough about dragons to know that there could be no stopping him.

"We'll have to get him out on to the launch pad," said Marcia. "I'm not having him trying his FirstFlyte in here."

"What launch pad?" asked Septimus, confused.

"Oh, the old one outside the dragon window," Marcia said, waving her hand at the window that Simon had Caused to open.

"Ah . . ." said Septimus, realising at last why there was a small carving of a flying dragon in the stone lintel above the window.

"Don't worry," said Marcia, "it's quite safe. All Extra-Ordinaries have to keep the launch pad maintained—you never know when you might need it—although unfortunately it does give idiots like Simon Heap somewhere to land."

Spit Fyre was enticed out on to the launch pad with a box of biscuits that Septimus found under the sink. They were a little damp and soggy but that did not seem to trouble the dragon. He sat contentedly on the wooden platform, chewing his way through the biscuits and surveying the whole Castle, which was laid out below him like a massive Counter-Feet board.

Inside the Wizard Tower a discussion was going on.

"Now, Septimus," said Marcia. "I don't want you doing anything complicated on your FirstFlyte. You are to fly around the Tower once and land in the courtyard. Do you want a Navigator?"

"A w-what?" asked Septimus, looking out the window and feeling his legs turning to jelly.

"*Draxx*, rule 16b, subsection viii states that: *a Navigator may only be used if he or she has participated in the FirstFlyte*. So if you want a Navigator, it's now or never."

"It's no good asking me, Sep," said Beetle apologetically, as he tried to help Marcia push the dragon's tail out the window.

"I'm indentured to the Manuscriptorium for five more years. Only get one day off a fortnight—if I'm lucky. Don't think I could fit in being a Navigator. Though I s'pose I might not have a job after all this . . ."

"Of course you'll have a job," Marcia told Beetle. "Which is more than can be said for Hugh Fox."

"Thank you," Beetle stammered.

"I'll do it, Sep," offered Jenna. "I'll be your Navigator. I mean, if you want one, that is."

"Would you really, Jen?" asked Septimus, brightening a little at the thought that at least he'd have some company when he was hundreds of feet above the ground.

"Yes, of course I would. I'd be honoured to."

Out on the launch pad, Spit Fyre finished the last biscuit and then, to avoid wasting any crumbs, the dragon gulped down the box as well. He sniffed the evening air. The thrill of electricity that all dragons get just before their FirstFlyte ran through him. He snorted loudly and smashed his tail down in anticipation. Marcia and Beetle leaped back just in time.

"You'd better hurry up and get on, Septimus," said Marcia. "You don't want him taking off without you—we don't want the Castle to be plagued with a riderless dragon for years to come."

Septimus forced himself to climb out the window on to the launch pad. You can do it, he told himself. You've been up a three-hundred-foot tree, walked across a rickety bridge at the top of a witches' house and flown a boat. You are *not* afraid of heights. Definitely not. But whatever Septimus told himself, his legs appeared to take no notice and still felt as if they were made of jelly that has been left outside on a hot summer's day.

"C'mon, Sep," said Jenna, scrambling up behind him on to the launch pad. She put her arm around his shoulders and guided him along the wide wooden platform. Septimus swayed for a moment as he felt the wind that blew around the top of the Wizard Tower ruffle his hair. "You're OK," whispered Jenna. "Look, Spit Fyre is waiting for you to get on."

Septimus had no idea how he managed it but a few seconds later he was sitting on the dragon's neck, in a dip just in front of the shoulders. It seemed to be the natural place to sit and he felt surprisingly secure. The dragon's scales, although smooth, had slightly rough edges that stopped him from slip-ping, and the broad spines running like a mane down the back of Spit Fyre's muscular neck fitted perfectly into Septimus's hands.

Jenna was less comfortable. "Budge up a bit, Sep," she said. "I'm right by the wings here." Septimus wriggled forward as much as he dared and Jenna dropped down into the space behind him.

"Right," said Alther, floating beside them. "Three things to remember. First—takeoff. When he jumps he's going to drop like a stone. But, trust me, it will only be for a second or two. That's how FirstFlyte always starts. Then you'll be off. Second—steering. Kick left for left turn, right for right. Two kicks left for down, two kicks right for up. Or you can just tell him. He's a bright dragon, he'll understand. Third—I'm right here with you. You'll be just fine."

Septimus nodded, anxious to start.

Marcia and Beetle looked out apprehensively. "Ready?" asked Marcia.

Septimus made a thumbs-up sign.

"Go!" yelled Marcia. "Go! Come on, Beetle, push!"

Together, Marcia and Beetle gave the dragon a hefty shove. Unfortunately, they had no effect whatsoever—Spit Fyre still sat firmly on the launch pad.

"Oh, for goodness' sake!" spluttered Marcia, giving the dragon another push. "Get *going*, you lazy lump!"

Like a high diver who is regretting his decision to climb to the topmost board, and knows there is only one way down, Spit Fyre shuffled forward and curled his toes around the edge of the launch pad. Hesitantly, the dragon peered out over the precipitous drop and gazed at the courtyard far, far below. Septimus closed his eyes and clung on tight. Behind her Jenna felt the fledgling wings twitch, but nothing happened.

"Look, you daft dragon, don't think you can come shuffling back in here, because you most certainly cannot!" Marcia shouted. "And if you know what's good for you, you'll get going right now!" Using all their strength, Marcia and Beetle heaved the rest of the dragon's tail on to the launch pad.

Spit Fyre's look of uncertainty changed to panic. Marcia may not have been a real dragon mother but she had many of the qualities that dragon mothers were renowned for, and Spit Fyre was finding it hard to tell the difference.

"Do as you're told and *fly!*" Marcia yelled, and slammed the window closed.

Spit Fyre did as he was told. He threw himself off the launch pad—and dropped like a stone. Down, down, down, past the nineteenth, eighteenth, seventeenth floors. Past the sixteenth, fifteenth, fourteenth they plummeted. At the thirteenth floor Spit Fyre realised what he had to do. At the twelfth he worked out how to do it. At the eleventh his wings were stuck. At the eighth floor he finally unfurled them and at the heart-stopping seventh floor Spit Fyre spread his wings into a huge green canopy, caught the air and glided up in a beautiful curve until he was once again level with the top of the Wizard Tower. Peering out from the Tower, Marcia's white face broke into a wide smile and Beetle whooped a cheer.

"Oh, thank goodness," muttered Alther, almost transparent with fear, swooping up to join the dragon and his shocked passengers. "All right?" Alther yelled, keeping pace with some difficulty—now that Spit Fyre had found his wings the dragon was reveling in the sensation of flying, and he was *fast*.

Septimus nodded.

"Once around the Tower, and land him in the courtyard," Alther shouted.

Septimus shook his head. In the distance he could see the uncoordinated black shape that was Simon Heap. Simon had just cleared the rooftops of the line of houses that abutted the boatyard wall and was dropping down to the other side.

"Go, Spit Fyre. Go get him," shouted Septimus.

⊹⊹ 44 ⊹⊦
LAST FLYTE

Down in Jannit's boatyard, work was beginning on the Dragon Boat. Jannit had towed her out of the Dragon House, turned her around and was about to reverse her back in so that she could face out on to the world. It was something that Jenna had asked Nicko to do the previous night, telling him that the dragon herself had requested it. Nicko, who still had trouble with the idea that the Dragon Boat was also a living creature, did not see why it mattered which way the boat faced, but Jenna had been insistent.

From her small tugboat, Jannit surveyed the Dragon Boat with a critical eye. She and Nicko carefully splinted the broken wing and fixed it to the hull, but the wing was badly smashed and a strange green fluid was oozing from it and dripping into the water. The dragon herself did not look well. Her scales were dull, her eyes were heavy and her head and tail drooped feebly. "She doesn't look good," Jannit called up to Rupert Gringe who, with Nicko, was on the deck of the Dragon Boat, directing operations.

Rupert nodded. "Don't see what we can do," he grunted. "If you ask me what she needs is some hocus-pocus rubbish."

Three Wizards, chosen by Jannit as the least bothersome from the thirteen that Marcia had sent to guard the boat, made disapproving noises. Hocus-pocus indeed.

Nicko said nothing. He didn't like the way Rupert had said it, but he thought he was probably right. What could an ordinary boatyard hope to do for a living, breathing Dragon Boat?

"What the—" Rupert suddenly exclaimed, catching sight of a movement far above him. "Some idiot's thrown himself off a roof. No he hasn't—Busted Barnacles, he—he's *flying!*"

With a sinking feeling, Nicko looked up. "Simon," he muttered. "It's Simon."

"What—your Simon?"

"He's not *my* Simon," said Nicko indignantly. "Quick, Rupert—he's dangerous. Get the Dragon Boat back inside."

But Rupert Gringe seemed mesmerised by the black figure

that had dropped down over the Castle walls and was flapping
about like a wounded crow, flying slowly towards them.

"It *is*. It's Simon blasted Heap." Rupert shook his fist and
yelled up into the air. "Get out of here, Heap. Or do I have to
come and make you?"

"Rupert," hissed Nicko. "Don't upset him."

"Upset him? I'll upset him all right." Rupert raised his
voice in Simon's direction. "Heap! Stop prancing about up
there like a girl at the MidWinter Feast. Come down here and
fight like a man."

"Rupert, *don't*," pleaded Nicko. "Just get out of the way.
He's got a Thunderflash."

"Oh, yes, and my aunt Gertie's the Queen of Sheba. Good,
he's coming over. Come on then, Heap. Don't be shy. Ha!"

Simon Heap was having a good deal of trouble with the
Flyte Charm. It was only once he was airborne and on his
way to the Wizard Tower that Simon had realised that the
Chief Hermetic Scribe had done nothing whatsoever to sort
out the Charm. He had not dared turn back and insist that
Hugh Fox repair it, for he could not possibly be late for his
appointment with DomDaniel and the beginning of his new
Apprenticeship. Little did Simon know that even if he had
returned, Hugh Fox would not have been able to fix the Flyte

Charm—for all the codes and encryptions had been in The Book, *The Undoing of the Darkenesse.*

Simon had only just made it over the Castle walls and he was using all his willpower to stay airborne. The Dragon Boat was in his sight and this time Simon knew that he would not miss—third time lucky, he muttered to himself, or third time *un*lucky if you happened to be a mutant mix of a boat and a dragon. As Simon flew awkwardly across the boatyard he took his very last remaining Thunderflash from his belt. He had had a recent run on Thunderflashes and Merrin had been worse than useless at preparing the new ones—but that didn't matter. The boat was a sitting duck; this time there was no way he could miss. That would teach the oaf Rupert to yell at him. He'd get two birds with one stone—even better.

Simon primed the Thunderflash.

A yell followed by two loud splashes rang through the air. Nicko had pushed Rupert Gringe into the Moat and jumped in after him. Cursing the fact that he had lost his chance to get even with Rupert Gringe, Simon hurled the Thunderflash. It flew off with a roar, rumbling and rolling through the air. With a surprising turn of speed, the three Wizards also hurled themselves into the Moat.

The Thunderflash hit the Dragon Boat square on the

stern, passed through the golden wood of the hull like a knife through butter and came to rest on the bottom of the Moat where it exploded, sending a spout of water shooting into the sky. In a seething mass of bubbles and steam, the Dragon Boat slowly disappeared under the water and sank to the bed of the Moat.

Jannit Maarten stood open-mouthed on the tugboat, horrified at what had happened. No one, but no one, messed with any of the boats under Jannit's care. She picked up the nearest weapon that came to hand, a large hammer, and hurled it up at Simon. Jannit had a powerful swing to her arm and the hammer flew through the air, only narrowly missing Simon. It flew on, curving upwards, and an oncoming dragon on its FirstFlyte just managed to avoid its first airborne missile (but not its last), thanks to a timely shout from its Navigator.

Simon had just caught sight of Spit Fyre. He could not believe his eyes—or rather his eye, as Simon was still wearing his eye patch after Wolf Boy's direct hit. What was it about this imposter brother of his? Why did he always turn up like a bad penny, just when he least wanted to see him? And what was he doing on a *dragon*?

Simon's success with the Dragon Boat had made him cocky. Even with no Thunderflashes left and a dodgy Flyte

Charm to contend with, Simon felt invincible. It was easy; he'd push one off the dragon, then he'd push the other one off the dragon and that would be that. Goodbye upstart Apprentice and little Miss Princess.

Simon hurled himself through the air, aiming first for Septimus.

The Navigator saw him coming and yelled, "Down, Sep, down!" Septimus kicked the dragon twice on the left and Spit Fyre began to drop towards a spiky forest of masts below.

"Turn right!" yelled the Navigator. "Land on the pontoon!"

Septimus kicked once on the right followed by two kicks on the left and Spit Fyre headed down towards the pontoon, where Jannit was bringing the tugboat alongside with three Wizards in tow.

Simon was not to be put off. He threw himself towards Septimus, only to discover that the Flyte Charm had developed an alarming bias to the right, and he was now heading straight for Spit Fyre's nose. A dragon's nose is a sensitive spot, especially on a young dragon, and Spit Fyre did not take kindly to being hit hard on it. Instinctively the dragon opened his mouth to take a large bite out of Simon, only to be overtaken by the most enormous sneeze.

"Aaah . . . aaah . . . *tchooo!*" Like a cork from an enthusiastically shaken bottle of fizz, a huge slug of warm dragon dribble slammed into Simon and sent him cartwheeling through the air. Dragon dribble is a corrosive substance; it hit Simon on the stomach, winded him and, in a few seconds, ate its way through his cloak, his tunic and the red belt with the three black stars of DomDaniel. Simon was on his third somersault when the Flyte Charm parted company with his belt and tumbled to the ground, landing in a toolbox that Jannit had been using earlier.

Simon fell out of the sky.

Without thinking, Septimus shouted his very first dragon order—"Save him!"

Spit Fyre knew what to do. He dropped like a stone, shot forward and caught Simon only seconds before he hit the ground. Then he landed with a jarring crash on the pontoon at the spot where the Dragon Boat's wing had been laid out only a few minutes earlier. The Navigator fell off with a bump and stood up angrily.

"What on earth did you do that for, Sep?" she demanded, jumping away from Simon, who was sprawled across Spit Fyre's back.

Septimus did not reply. He was staring at Simon.

"He—he's not dead, is he?" Septimus asked Jannit, who

had pulled Simon off Spit Fyre and was trying to get some response from him.

Simon lay white and still on the pontoon, his black robes full of holes from the acidic dragon dribble, his fair, curly Heap hair matted with sweat and his eyes closed. Jannit knelt down and put her ear to his chest.

"No," she murmured. "I can hear a heartbeat. He's just unconscious." At the sound of Jannit's voice, Simon's eyes flickered and he groaned. "Here, you lot," Jannit yelled at the Wizards, "come and make yourselves useful for a change."

Three dripping Wizards duly arrived at Jannit's side. "Help me get him over to the lock-up," Jannit told them.

Jenna and Septimus watched Jannit and the three Wizards each take an arm or a leg and carry Simon across the boatyard to the lock-up—a tiny windowless brick building beside the Castle wall that boasted a thick iron door complete with three heavy, well-oiled bolts.

"I still don't know why you did that, Sep," Jenna said grumpily.

"Did what?" asked Septimus, stroking Spit Fyre's bruised nose.

"Saved Simon."

Septimus looked up at Jenna, confused by her angry tone of

voice. "But what else could I have done, Jen?" he asked.

"Let him fall. *I* would have." Jenna kicked a pebble angrily into the Moat.

Septimus shook his head. "But he's my brother," he said sadly.

✛ 45 ✛
THE LOOKOUT TOWER

Nicko *had insisted on wearing the mask*—there was no way he was going to let Rupert dive down to the Dragon Boat without him. Jannit had taken some persuading, however, as Nicko had not used the mask before. Jannit had invented what she called the inspection mask so that she could check her boats below the waterline. The oval slab of glass was edged with soft leather so that it fitted closely to the face and tied around the back of the head with a leather strap. The glass was tough and thick. It was a deep greenish colour, which did not make for great visibility, but it was better than trying to keep your eyes open in the silt-laden water of the Moat.

Nicko was a good swimmer. When the boys were younger, Silas had often taken them out of the Castle to a sandy spot just past the One Way Bridge, which was where Nicko had learned to swim. But Nicko had never swum underwater before, and now, as he and Rupert struggled to lift the Dragon Boat's unwieldy head off the mud at the bottom of the Moat, Nicko was desperate to take a breath.

Rupert made a thumbs-up sign and together he and Nicko swam to the surface, bringing the dragon's head once more into the air. Jannit was waiting with a large canvas sling, which she quickly slipped under the head to take the weight.

"Well done, boys," said Jannit, gently bringing the limp head and neck down to rest on the side of the Cut, where she had laid her one and only Persian rug for the dragon's head to lie on.

Jenna watched. Septimus had taken Spit Fyre back to the Wizard Tower, but Jenna had refused to go with him. So Septimus—unwilling to fly without his Navigator—had walked Spit Fyre through the streets, much to the great interest of everyone he met.

Jenna knelt beside the muddy head of the dragon, searching

for signs of life—but there were none. The head lay motionless and the eyes were tightly closed under heavy green lids. Carefully, Jenna brushed the mud from the golden ears, and, with the hem of her dress, cleaned the silt from the dragon's smooth, scaly eyelids. She talked to the dragon as she always did, but there was no response. Only silence.

Jannit squatted down and looked at the head with a professional eye. There was no obvious sign of damage, but then what did she know? Was this a boat or a living creature? If it was living, could it breathe underwater? And if it couldn't, had the creature drowned—or been killed by the Thunderflash? Jannit Maarten shook her head. She was out of her depth here.

"Is she . . . dead?" Jenna whispered.

"I- I don't know, my lady," Jannit replied, a little ill at ease having the Princess kneeling beside her, covered in mud and with tears rolling down her face. "But we will have her out of the water in no time, once the boys get the sling underneath her hull. We will see what needs to be done, and then we will do it. We can make her hull as good as new."

"But can you make her open her eyes?" asked Jenna.

"Ah . . . that I couldn't say," replied Jannit, who never promised anything she was not sure about.

But suddenly there was something that Jenna *was* sure about.

She did not know how she knew, but she knew it was true—the dragon was dying and only Aunt Zelda could save her.

Jenna stood up. "There's something I have to do," she said. "Will you stay with her until I get back?"

Jannit nodded and Jenna was off, tearing across the boatyard. She flew through the dank tunnel and out the other side, into the sunlit streets of the Castle. She hurtled up the nearest flight of steps, which took her to the ledge on the inside of the Castle walls, and headed for the East Gate Lookout Tower. This was her last chance, she thought, as she sped along the broad ledge, oblivious to the sheer drop on one side. The dry stone of the ledge was well worn and smooth under her feet, and once or twice in her haste she very nearly slipped and fell. Slow down, Jenna told herself—you will be no good to the Dragon Boat if you fall.

The Castle wall twisted and turned along the higgledy-piggledy houses that clustered around it. Jenna kept her eyes firmly fixed on the Lookout Tower, which rose from the Wall some distance away and looked towards the Forest. She kept up a steady pace and before long found herself standing at the foot of the tower, hot, flustered and out of breath.

Jenna took a few moments to get her breath back, breathing in the sour smell of some overflowing rubbish bins lined up beside the small wooden door which led into the tower.

A faded notice hung on the door:

CUSTOMER OFFICE

MESSAGE RAT SERVICE

CHARTERED, CONFIDENTIAL, LONG-DISTANCE RATS AVAILABLE

OPEN ALL HOURS

Under the notice hung a much newer sign:

CLOSED

Jenna was not to be put off—she gave the wooden door a shove and almost fell into a small dark room.

"Can't you read? We're *closed*," a grumpy voice greeted her from somewhere in the gloom.

"The notice says OPEN ALL HOURS," Jenna pointed out.

"And the other notice says CLOSED," the voice retorted. "And closed is what we are. You can come back tomorrow. Now, if you'll excuse me, I'm about to lock up."

"I don't care," said Jenna. "I want a Message Rat and I want one *now*. It's urgent. It's a matter of life and death."

"Oh they all say that," said the rat dismissively, picking up a briefcase and making for the door. Jenna stepped in front of the rat, a rather portly brown creature. The rat glanced up and for the first time he saw properly who he had been talking to. He swallowed hard. "Oh," he said. "I. Um. I didn't realise it was you, Your Majesty. Very sorry."

"It doesn't matter. Just send the message, will you?" With Jenna still barring the door, the rat returned to his desk and opened his briefcase, looking through a list of names and shaking his head.

"Your Majesty," the rat said regretfully, "there is nothing I would like to do more, but all the Message Rats are unavailable. That's why I've closed up. The soonest I can get one for you will be tomorrow morning—"

"It will be too late tomorrow morning," Jenna interrupted.

The elderly rat looked worried. "I'm so sorry, Your Majesty. We've had a very difficult time recently what with the epidemic down by the sewer pipe which took out some of my best young rats, and now half of my staff are on holiday. And then we've had so many long-distance call-outs I've lost count—"

"I'll have a Secret Rat then," said Jenna. "Is Stanley available?"

The rat looked studiedly blank. "Secret Rat?" he asked. "I'm very sorry, but there is no such thing."

"Oh, don't be silly," snapped Jenna exasperated. "Of course there is. *I* should know."

The rat was stubborn. "I really don't know what you're talking about," he said. "Now I must be getting along, Your Majesty. I could send a Message Rat along to the Palace first thing tomorrow if that would be of any help?"

Jenna's patience was at an end. "Look," she said sternly, "I want a Secret Rat and I want one *now*. That's an order. And if I don't get one, there won't *be* a Secret Rat Service any more. Let alone a Message Rat Service. Got that?"

The rat gulped and shuffled his papers. "I-I'll just make a quick call," he said. Then, to Jenna's surprise he leaned out a small window beside his desk and yelled, "Stanley! Hey, Stanley! Get your tail down here. Pronto!"

A few moments later Stanley appeared at the window. "Keep your fur on, Humphrey, what's so important?" And then, catching sight of Jenna, he said, "Oh."

"Special request for you, Stanley," said the rat somewhat apologetically.

"Ah," said Stanley, sounding less than enthusiastic.

Jenna lost no time. "Stanley," she said, "I want you to take an urgent message to Aunt Zelda. She *has* to come here as soon as she can. She is my only hope for—"

In a familiar gesture, Stanley raised his paw. "No," he said firmly.

"What?" said Jenna. Even Humphrey looked shocked.

"I am sorry," said Stanley, stepping through the window on to the desk. "I am unavailable tonight."

"No, you're not," said Humphrey.

"Yes, I am," retorted Stanley. "Dawnie has asked me over for supper. I understand that she and her sister have had a falling-out. I have learned my lesson. In the past I have put my job first and Dawnie second. But no longer."

"But—" protested Jenna.

"I know what you're going to say, Your Majesty, and I am very sorry—but tonight Dawnie comes first, even if I do lose my job. Now if you'll excuse me, I want to pick up some flowers from the florist's garbage bin before it gets emptied." With that Stanley gave a small bow and walked past Jenna, head held high. Dumbfounded, Jenna held the door open for him and watched the rat jump down from the ledge and disappear over a roof.

"Well," said Humphrey, "I really don't know what to say . . ."

"No," said Jenna. "Neither do I. It was my last hope. But I don't suppose Aunt Zelda could have got here in time anyway. I don't think there is much time left. Goodnight."

"Goodnight, Your Majesty," said Humphrey, as Jenna quietly closed the door and made her way back to the boatyard.

✣ 46 ✣
THE LOCK-UP

Inside the *lock-up* Simon Heap opened his eyes and groaned. For a moment he thought he must be in Dungeon Number One, but then he realised that there was a small chink of light coming through a tiny barred window and he relaxed. Dungeon Number One was Sealed in darkness, and although wherever he was now smelled pretty bad, it smelled

nowhere near as bad as the dungeon. Simon had once been
shown Dungeon Number One by the Supreme Custodian,
and he had never forgotten it.

Very slowly, Simon sat up. His head hurt and his stomach
felt horribly bruised, but as far as he could tell there were no
bones broken. He was a little confused by the huge holes in
his tunic until, in a flash, it all came back to him. The dragon
. . . the brat . . . and the Flyte Charm—gone. Simon groaned
again. He was a failure. A terrible failure. Not only had Marcia
never asked him to be her Apprentice, but it now turned out
that DomDaniel had never wanted him either—and after all
Simon had done for him too. Picking up those horrible slimy
bones of his, taking endless trips to the Manuscriptorium with
them, having to deal with that snooty Hugh Fox who had
always looked down his long pointy nose at him, and worst of
all, making those bleak trips along the Ice Tunnels to deliver
the bones to that ghastly woman, Una Brakket, and making
sure that old Weasal never saw him. Sometimes he had even
ended up helping her put the wretched bones into the
Amalgam so that she could get off to her country dancing in
time. What a fool he had been. And then, to top it all, his
imposter brother turns up on a *dragon*. The boy was what—
only eleven—and there he was, not only the ExtraOrdinary

Apprentice, he now had his own blasted dragon. How did he
do it?

Simon sat on the floor of the lock-up in a cloud of self-pity.
No one wanted him. Nothing ever went right for him. Life
stunk and it just wasn't fair.

After a while a familiar feeling of anger stole over Simon.
He stood and began to look around his prison. He'd show
them they couldn't tame Simon Heap—he'd be out of here in
no time. Angrily, Simon pushed the door, but to no effect,
except he heard some frightened whispering.

"He's trying to get *out* . . ."

"What shall we do?"

"Is he very dangerous?"

"Oh, don't be such a baby, Brian."

"Stop bickering you two. The ExtraOrdinary will be here
soon."

Simon smiled broadly. Well, let her come, but he would not
be there to meet her. For Simon Heap had just realised where
he was.

Many years ago, Jannit had expanded her boatyard to take
in the derelict old Castle Customs Quay. The brick lock-up,
which had been used for drunken sailors and suspicious
characters landing at the Castle, was the only part of the old

Customs House left standing, and Jannit had kept it to store her more valuable tools in. It still had its heavy iron door with three massive bolts on the outside and the huge brass key in the lock. Simon was willing to bet it also still had its trapdoor leading into the Ice Tunnels.

Simon knelt and quickly set to work shifting the hundreds of years of accumulated dirt from the floor. Luckily, Jannit had thoughtfully provided him with a rather good shovel, and it did not take Simon long before the shovel hit metal about a foot beneath the surface.

The Sealed trapdoor easily swung open in Simon's practiced hands. A cold gust of air blew up to meet him, and Simon slipped through the trapdoor, down into the familiar chill of the Ice Tunnels.

The full complement of thirteen Wizards—for Jannit had speedily retrieved the other ten from the fishing jetty outside the boatyard—were dutifully encircling the lock-up when Marcia marched into the boatyard, accompanied by Sarah and Silas Heap.

Sarah and Silas had insisted on seeing their eldest son. Unable to believe what Marcia had told them, they had decided to confront him. "At least," Sarah had said, "he will have to sit and listen to us this time. He won't be able to run off like he usually does."

Jannit escorted the party to the lock-up, her small wiry figure somewhat dwarfed by Marcia in her purple silk robes, which billowed out around her in the summer evening breeze.

"Here we are, Madam Marcia," said Jannit as they stopped outside the circle of Wizards. "He's in there. We put him in a couple of hours ago and he should have come around by now. Had a nasty bump on the head from that dragon he attacked."

"Oh, dear," said Sarah anxiously, "I do wish he wouldn't do these silly things."

"I'm sure we all wish that, Sarah," said Marcia sternly. "But unfortunately he has progressed rather further than the silly stage now. Evil-minded-scheming stage is more what I would call it."

"Oh, Silas," wailed Sarah. "What *are* we to do?"

"We'll have a talk with him, Sarah," said Silas soothingly, "and see what he has to say. Now stop worrying; there's nothing we can do. Simon is grown-up now."

The two Wizards standing by the door stood back respectfully for the ExtraOrdinary Wizard to walk through. Jannit

shot the bolts, turned her heavy brass key in the lock and
pulled open the thick iron door.

"Simon!" said Sarah, rushing into the lock-up before anyone could stop her. "Simon . . . *Simon?*"

"Did *you* know about this?" Marcia demanded as Jannit
Maarten stared uncomprehendingly at the shiny metal trapdoor in the middle of the dirt floor of the lock-up.

"No," said Jannit curtly. She didn't like the way Marcia was
talking to her, and she certainly did not like having yet another thing in her boatyard that she knew nothing about.

"What—what *is* it?" asked Sarah, clinging to Silas for support, distraught that once again Simon had run away.

"It's nothing," said Marcia briskly. "Nothing that you need
to know about anyway. I want this trapdoor Sealed—now.
Where's Alther?"

Alther Mella wafted over to Marcia.

"Alther, are there any Ancients left who have walked the
tunnels? I want each and every trapdoor guarded until all Seals
are checked."

"The only suitable Ancient who is not completely gaga is
on the Wizard Tower trap, Marcia," said Alther. "I never
went down to the tunnels myself. No one ever did in those
days."

"No one should in these days either, Alther. Except for the Inspection Clerk. That Hugh Fox has a lot of questions to answer." Marcia thought for a moment. "Alther, please would you take a Wizard down to the Manuscriptorium and bring some SealingWax back? At least we can get this trapdoor Sealed."

"Excuse me," interrupted Jannit, "the Port barge has arrived. I'm expecting a delivery." With that Jannit was off to the pontoon to meet a long narrow boat piled high with boxes and baskets.

Jenna—who had no wish to go anywhere near Simon Heap—was back with the Dragon Boat, gently stroking her head and murmuring words of encouragement in her ear, looking desperately for a sign of life, while Nicko and Rupert struggled to place two huge canvas slings underneath the damaged hull. As the Port barge drew up to the pontoon, Jenna glanced up and saw Jannit catch the rope and secure the barge to a couple of large bollards. Then, to her horror, she saw something else or, rather, *someone* else—the dark stranger from the Port.

The tall man stood poised on the deck, watchful and waiting to jump ashore. His long dark hair was held in a silver headband and his red silk tunic looked crumpled and travel stained. Jenna froze. She ducked down behind the Dragon Boat's head and heard the stranger's low, slightly accented voice ask Jannit, "Excuse me, ma'am, but I understand that the Princess is to be found hereabouts. Would this be so?"

"And who might you be?" Jannit asked suspiciously.

The stranger was evasive. "Just someone seeking the Princess," he replied. Suddenly his eye caught the activity over at the lock-up. "Would that be the ExtraOrdinary Wizard over there, ma'am?" he asked.

"It might be," said Jannit, busying herself with a knot.

"Excuse me, I must go and see him."

"*Her*," corrected Jannit, unheard as the stranger strode off.

"Excuse me," the stranger raised his voice as he approached the group by the lock-up. "I wonder if I might speak to the ExtraOrdinary Wizard?"

Marcia turned around and the stranger looked confused. He stopped for a moment and fumbled in his tunic pocket, looking for something. "Alther?" he said. "Alther, is that *you*?"

Marcia did not answer. She looked white.

"Aha, found them." With an air of triumph, the stranger drew out a small pair of gold spectacles from his pocket and carefully put them on. His expression changed to one of amazement.

"Milo?" asked Marcia faintly. "Milo Banda? It *is* you, isn't it?"

"Marcia Overstrand," he said. "ExtraOrdinary Wizard! Well, well, well."

The stranger appeared a little overcome. He nodded wordlessly and to Jenna's horror, Marcia enveloped him in a huge hug. "Where have you been all this time?" she asked. "We thought you must be dead."

As Marcia let go of the stranger, a loud yell came from the Cut—Nicko had just dropped one of the canvas slings in the water.

For the first time Marcia saw the terrible state of the Dragon Boat. "Jannit!" she yelled. "Jannit—what has happened?"

Jannit was in no mood to reply. She was determined to raise the Dragon Boat before nightfall and she had had enough Wizards messing about in her boatyard to last a lifetime. Wearily she said, "Go get another sling, will you Nicko? Then we'll try again."

Jenna had been watching Marcia greet the dark stranger with mounting disbelief. Now, as Marcia set off across the boatyard towards the Dragon Boat, bringing the stranger with her, Jenna leapt to her feet. Before anyone could stop her, she was heading for the tunnel that led out of the boatyard.

✢ 47 ✢
THE QUEEN'S ROOM

J enna tore through the alleys and passage-ways, heading for the Palace. In her hand she clutched the gold key that Aunt Zelda had given her, the key to the Queen's Room. Too bad she had no idea where the Queen's Room might be, and too bad there would probably be nothing there to save the Dragon Boat. But it was the only chance she had, for Marcia was obviously in league with the stranger and could not be trusted.

Now Jenna knew how Septimus had felt when Marcia would not believe that Simon had kidnapped her. She hurtled around a corner and ran straight into Spit Fyre. "Ouch!"

"Jen!" said Septimus, surprised. "I thought you'd be down with the Dragon Boat. I was coming to see you. And then Spit Fyre wouldn't stay in the courtyard. Well, he ate most of the Dragon Kennel that the sub-Wizards were making for him and—" Septimus broke off, noticing Jenna's distraught expression. "Hey, Jen, what's the matter?"

"Oh, Sep, the dragon—she's dying. And now the stranger from the Port—he's *here*. He's come to get me!"

"What?"

"And what's worse, Marcia knows him! She was really pleased to see him. She *hugged* him."

Septimus was shocked. Marcia never hugged anyone. Ever.

"Sep, come with me. I'm going to the Palace. I'm going to find the Queen's Room. Maybe, just maybe, there'll be something there to save the Dragon Boat. A-a potion or something . . . I don't know."

"OK, it's worth a try. Come on, Spit Fyre. This way. No, *this* way. Hang on, Jen, you don't know where the Queen's Room is."

"I know, but Aunt Zelda said I would find it when The

Time Is Right. So maybe The Time Is Right now."

Jenna and Septimus made good progress until they were halfway down Wizard Way, when Septimus dropped behind to attend to Spit Fyre, who had just given Septimus an embarrassing moment. Jenna stopped to see what was keeping Septimus and saw him staring at a large pile of dragon droppings in the middle of Wizard Way, wondering what to do. He decided the best thing to do was to ignore it and keep going.

"Hey, you with the dragon!" a voice shouted after him. Septimus turned to see a thin, earnest-looking man in a striped homespun tunic chasing after him with a sack and a shovel. The man caught up with him and presented the two items to Septimus. "Wizard Way Conservation Society . . . Street Fouling Enforcement Officer," he puffed. "It is an offence to foul the Way. Please clean up your animal's mess and take it with you."

Septimus looked doubtfully at the large sack that the man had thrust into his hand. "OK," he said, "but I don't think it's all going to fit in there."

Septimus got busy with his shovel while Jenna impatiently held the sack open for him.

* * *

The sun was setting, and Billy Pot was wheeling away his Contraption at the end of a particularly trying day—the lawn lizards had been acting up again. His face brightened when he saw Jenna, Septimus and Spit Fyre coming across the lawn. Billy Pot had once smelled dragon droppings on his Lizard Keeping Diploma course and had never forgotten it—in fact most people, once they had smelled dragon droppings, never forgot it.

"Excuse me, young sir," said Billy Pot, running up to Septimus. "Please forgive me for being so presumptuous, but I wonder . . . well, I wonder if you would consider parting with the contents of your sack. I would be eternally grateful. There's nothing like strategically placed dragon droppings to keep the lizards in order. And I'm that desperate; ever since that horse ran over the Contraption they have been uncontrollable and—"

"Yes," said Septimus. "Take it. Please."

"You see, sir, I have dreamed of getting my hands on some. Dreamed of it, I have. But where can you find a dragon nowadays? It's a nightmare for a Lizard Keeper like myself. Nightmare." Billy Pot shook his head sorrowfully. "But of course if you don't want to part with it, I quite understand."

"No—please, *please* take it," said Septimus. He thrust the bulging sack at Billy Pot, who smiled for the first time that day.

As Jenna, Septimus and Spit Fyre reached the Palace door, Godric's thin voice drifted through the evening air. "Ah, good evening, Princess. How nice to see you. And good evening, Apprentice. How is the Transforming going? Have you managed the Transubstantiate Triple yet?"

"Nearly," said Septimus, dragging Spit Fyre behind him.

"Good lad," said Godric, and immediately went back to sleep.

In the turret at the east end of the Palace, Spit Fyre sat fretfully whining and scratching the bottom step of a flight of spiral stairs. Septimus had tied the dragon to a convenient ring in the wall and told him to *stay*.

"I'm sure it's up here," said Jenna, concentrating hard on the key to the Queen's Room as she led the way up the stairs. As she reached the small landing at the top of the turret, Jenna let out a triumphant whoop. "Yes! Hey, Sep, look at that—I've found it!"

"Where?" Septimus looked at Jenna, perplexed.

Jenna shot Septimus a quizzical look. "Very funny, Sep," she said. "You don't think it might be that gold door with all those patterns on it, and the big keyhole in the middle with an emerald set above it—just like the key?"

"What gold door?" asked Septimus.

Suddenly Jenna understood, and a thrill of excitement went through her. "You can't see it, can you?" she whispered.

"No," replied Septimus, a little overawed. "I can't. All I can see is a blank wall with lumps of plaster falling off it."

"Well, it *is* here, Sep. I can see it. I really can. I'm going to put the key in the lock now," said Jenna, hesitantly. "Will you wait here for me?"

"Of course I will."

"This is weird. I'll try the key then, shall I?"

"Yes. Go on, Jen. Oh, hang on—did you say the lock was in the middle of the door?"

"Yes, why?" Jenna looked concerned.

"Well, make sure you jump out of the way as soon as you've turned the key. The door will come down like a draw-bridge—it'll squash you flat if you don't."

"Will it? How do you know?"

"Oh, I just know these things, Jen," said Septimus airily.

"Silly boy," said Jenna fondly.

Septimus stepped back and had the strangest experience of watching Jenna push the key forward until the end of it disappeared. Suddenly she leaped back and smiled at him. Septimus smiled as well; then he watched her walk forward and vanish through the solid wall.

* * *

The golden door closed silently behind Jenna, and she found herself in a small and surprisingly cosy room. A fire was burning in the grate and a comfortable chair was placed beside it. Sitting in the chair, gazing at the fire, was a young woman wearing a heavy red silk tunic, with a gold cloak wrapped around her shoulders. Her long dark hair was banded by a gold circlet like the one that Jenna herself wore. At Jenna's sudden arrival, the young woman sprang to her feet, her violet eyes shining with excitement. She took a swift step forward, and in her eagerness to reach Jenna, she passed through the chair as though it was not there.

But Jenna saw nothing, which maybe was just as well. For as the ghost of the Queen stood before her, gazing at the daughter she had last seen as a day-old baby, Jenna would have found it hard to ignore the large bloodstain that was spread across the left-hand side of her mother's cloak—although she might not have noticed the jagged tear of the bullet hole, which was hidden in the folds of the dark red tunic.

The Queen stepped back to allow her daughter to wander around the Room. She watched Jenna gaze, puzzled, at the blazing fire and at the empty chair. She saw Jenna wrap her arms about herself and shiver slightly as she moved through the Room, glancing about as though she had caught sight of something out of the corner of her eye, and all the time searching desperately for something—*anything*—that would save the Dragon Boat.

Knowing that she must not Appear to her daughter, the Queen watched, willing Jenna to find what she had to alone. But Jenna had almost given up hope, for the Room was not the Magykal place she expected it would be; it was no more than an empty sitting room with a fire, a rug, a small table, a chair and—suddenly Jenna smiled—a cupboard, and not just any old cupboard either. For on the door of the cupboard was written: UNSTABLE POTIONS AND PARTIKULAR POISONS.

Jenna opened the door and walked inside.

The cupboard was as empty as the Room had been. Four intricately carved but completely bare shelves ran along the back wall, with no sign of the potion bottles, herbs or remedies, books of spells or Dragon Boat secrets that Jenna had longed to see. Desperately, she ran her hands over the shelves in case she had missed something, but there was nothing, nothing but dust. Then Jenna noticed a line of small drawers almost hidden in the dark mahogany panels under the shelves, and her hopes soared. She took hold of the small gold drawer-knob of the topmost drawer and pulled hard. The drawer slid out smoothly and Jenna smelled a musty combination of old mint chocolate and dust; she ran her hand around the inside of the drawer, but it was as empty as the shelves had been. Frantically, she pulled open each drawer in turn, but there was nothing to be found.

As Jenna reached the last drawer she felt desperate; she knew that this was her very last chance, for there was nowhere else to look. As she tugged it open, Jenna felt something inside the drawer move as if she had pulled a lever of some kind, and at the same time she heard a soft click behind her and the cupboard door swung shut. She was plunged into darkness.

Jenna pushed the door but it did not move. With rising panic she pushed harder, but the door would not budge—and something told her that it was locked. What was she going to do? She was trapped. No one except Septimus knew where she was, and however much he wanted to, he would not be able to help her. She would be there for ever, stuck in the dark . . .

It was then that Jenna realised that the cupboard was not as dark as it had been, that she could now see a thin strip of light under the door. Tentatively Jenna gave the door another push, and to her delight it swung open.

She stepped out on to the smooth flagstones of Aunt Zelda's cottage.

✠ 48 ✠
THE YOUNG QUEEN

Septimus *sat on the dusty landing* watching the peeling plaster on the wall, wondering when Jenna was going to reappear. He tried to imagine what she was doing inside the Queen's Room, and what was taking her so long, but he did not mind waiting. There was something Septimus had been longing to take a closer look at ever since Jannit had fished it out of her toolbox and handed it to him, saying, "Looks like something you could use, Master Septimus." He put his hand into his tunic pocket and took out the Flyte Charm.

The Charm felt oddly familiar to him, as though he had known it somewhere before. It was a surprisingly simple Charm, considering the power that it possessed, and the old, yellowish gold was scratched, the flights—such as they were—battered and bent. As the arrow lay quietly in his palm, Septimus felt a tingle run through his hand, and something made him reach into his Apprentice Belt and take out his own silver winged Charm, the one that Marcia had given to him when she had asked him to be her Apprentice. Septimus loved this Charm. With it—and a lot of concentration—he could hover about ten feet off the ground, but he could not fly. Not as Simon had done. Septimus had often dreamed of flying, and indeed had frequently woken up convinced that he could, only to be disappointed.

Sitting on the cold stone floor, with no sign of Jenna's return, Septimus held out his open hands, one Charm in each. He thought they were both beautiful in different ways—in his left hand he could feel the powerful spirit of the ancient golden arrow and in his right the delicate lightness of the silver wings. As he looked at them he could sense the Magyk from both Charms running over his skin and disturbing the air around him.

And then—something shifted, something *moved*.

Suddenly the wings were sitting upright in the middle of his palm, wafting back and forth like a small butterfly warming up in the sunlight. Enthralled, Septimus watched them as they fluttered from his right hand over to his left, where they landed delicately on the Flyte Charm. There was a Magykal flash of light, and the silver and gold of the two Charms melded together as the wings settled down and resumed their rightful place as the Flyte Charm's original flights.

Septimus picked up the completed Flyte Charm and held it between finger and thumb. It was hot—almost too hot—to the touch. A buzzing sensation ran through his fingers and Septimus suddenly found he had an overwhelming urge to fly. He leaped to his feet and went over the small turret window that looked out over the Palace gardens. He saw the long shadows of the midsummer evening and heard the rooks cawing in the trees, and all his dreams of flying came back to him—he imagined himself swooping across the lawns, scattering the rooks and skimming out low over the River . . . with some effort, Septimus shook himself out of his reverie. He was busy putting the Flyte Charm into his Apprentice Belt—out of temptation's way—when Jenna stepped through the wall.

Septimus leaped to his feet. "Jen—" he began, and then stopped in astonishment as Aunt Zelda and Wolf Boy followed her on to the landing.

"Oh, Septimus," said Aunt Zelda, as Septimus stared, open-mouthed. "It is so wonderful to see you safe . . . but there is no time to lose. Follow me. We must get straight to the Dragon Boat." Aunt Zelda clattered down the narrow stairs and Septimus heard a yell of surprise as Aunt Zelda bumped into Spit Fyre.

"Down, Spit Fyre. Yes, it's lovely to see you too. Now get off my foot, please."

Septimus had no need to untie Spit Fyre as the dragon had already chewed his way through the rope. They followed Aunt Zelda and Jenna out the side door at the foot of the turret and down to the Palace Gate. Aunt Zelda kept up a brisk pace. Showing a surprising knowledge of the Castle's narrow alleyways and sideslips, she hurtled along. Oncoming pedestrians were taken aback at the sight of the large patchwork tent approaching them at full speed. They flattened themselves against the walls, and, as the tent passed by with the Princess, the ExtraOrdinary Apprentice and a feral-looking boy with bandaged hands—not to mention a dragon—in its wake, people rubbed their eyes in disbelief.

Soon Aunt Zelda and her retinue emerged from the tunnel
that led under the Castle walls into the boatyard. They were
met by the sound of Jannit's voice echoing across the
upturned boats. "Heave . . . heave . . . heave . . ."

Aunt Zelda gave a scream of dismay—for slowly, very
slowly, raised by a gang of yard-hands pulling rhythmically on
a rope, the dripping, mud-caked hull of the Dragon Boat was
rising from the water. The green tail with its golden barb
hung down while the Dragon Boat's head was still slumped on
to the side of the Cut. Nicko sat cross-legged, slowly stroking
the dull green scales on the dragon's long nose.

Rupert Gringe was on the deck of the Dragon Boat. He was
caked in mud and soaking wet, having just dived into the Moat
and at last fixed the huge canvas slings in place beneath the
keel. With his mask pushed up out of his eyes, Rupert darted
from one side to the other, constantly checking the ropes.

Horrified, Aunt Zelda ran across the boatyard, dodging
between the ropes and anchors, discarded masts and stays,
and sat down with a bump beside Nicko.

"Aunt Zelda?" said Nicko, not quite believing his eyes.

"Yes—it's me, dear," replied Aunt Zelda, breathless, reaching out to touch the dragon's motionless head. She rested her

hand there for a moment, shaking her own head in disbelief. "Jenna, Septimus—quick. Come and sit here beside me. All three of us—the Keeper, the Young Queen and the Dragon Master—must do this," she said.

"Do what?" asked Jenna.

"The Transubstantiate Triple," said Aunt Zelda, ferreting through her many patchwork pockets.

"Hey—Sep can do that," said Jenna, excited.

"No, I can't," said Septimus.

"Yes, you can. Well, you nearly can. I've heard you tell Godric."

"Only because when he first asked me I said no, I couldn't, and he got really upset and started wailing. Then all the other Ancients in the Palace began wailing too. It was awful—and they wouldn't stop. I had to go and get Marcia, and she told me to stop nitpicking and humour the old fool for goodness' sake. But I read about it anyway, just in case Godric asked me questions. It's the four elements, isn't it, Aunt Zelda?"

"It is indeed, Septimus," Aunt Zelda replied, taking an ancient-looking leather pouch from one of her pockets. "This has been handed down from Keeper to Keeper for longer than anyone can remember. We keep it in a Locked box called the Last Resort. Every Keeper hopes that she will not have to use it, but every Keeper knows that one day the Time will Come. There's a prophecy written on the box—

The Time will Come, for it must be,
When She will Fly with Two of Three
For Then must Ye full Ready be,
And Keep the Triple Close to Thee.

"No one really knew what it meant, but when Septimus found the Dragon Ring, I realised that once again, for the first time since Hotep-Ra, we were Three—the Dragon Master, the Queen and the Keeper. And then when you and Jenna flew off with the Dragon Boat, I knew that the first part of the prophecy had happened, that the Time had Come. So I was ready for something, but when Jenna walked out of the potion cupboard, just as her dear mother used to do every MidSummer Day, I—well, I nearly inhaled my cabbage sandwich. Now let's see what we have here . . ."

Aunt Zelda tipped the leather pouch and three small hammered-gold bowls, with blue enamelling around their rims, fell on to Jannit's muddy rug. She gave the leather pouch a shake but nothing else fell out. She put her hand inside the pouch and felt around, but it was empty. Aunt Zelda's face fell. "There must be more than this, surely," she said. "No instructions—nothing. It's that Betty Crackle, wretched woman. She was so careless. What can we possibly do with three empty bowls?"

"I think I know what to do with them," said Septimus slowly.

Aunt Zelda looked at him with new respect. "Do you?" she asked.

Septimus nodded. "You place the bowls in front of the Being you wish to Restore . . ." he said, thinking hard. Septimus had read all he could find about the Transubstantiate Triple, but when he asked Marcia about the whereabouts of the Triple Bowls, she told him they had disappeared many hundreds of years ago.

"You do it, Septimus," said Aunt Zelda. "As Dragon Master it is only right that you should."

The dragon's eyes did not flicker as Septimus, Jenna and Aunt Zelda arranged themselves in a semicircle around her head. Nicko quietly got up and moved away, taking Wolf Boy with him. Nicko could feel strong Magyk in the air and he preferred to keep his distance. Wolf Boy looked scared; his eyes were open wide and his yellow teeth were bared as he watched his old Young Army comrade in his strange new role—weaving powerful Magyk.

"The four elements in this Conjuration," said Septimus in a low voice, "are Earth, Aire, Fyre and Water. But we choose only one of these to Restore the dragon. I think it should be Fyre."

Aunt Zelda nodded in agreement. "She has had too much of the others," she murmured.

"Jen?" asked Septimus.

Jenna nodded. "Yes," she whispered. "Fyre."

"Good," said Septimus. "Now each one of us must choose an element from the three that are left."

"Earth," said Aunt Zelda. "Good honest earth for growing cabbages."

"Water," said Jenna. "Because she looks so beautiful on the water."

"And I choose Aire," said Septimus, "because I flew the Dragon Boat today. And because I can Flye."

Aunt Zelda shot Septimus a quizzical glance, but he was too busy arranging the bowls to notice.

"Now," he said, "we each take a bowl and place our element in it."

Jenna scrambled up and dipped her bowl into the Moat. Aunt Zelda reached down from the pontoon and scraped up some dry earth. Septimus looked at his bowl and wondered what to do. As he looked and wondered, a purple mist appeared at the bottom of the golden bowl. Aunt Zelda gasped—she could see the signs of Magyk appearing around Septimus; his fair curly hair was outlined in a purple shimmering light, and the atmosphere felt charged, like the air before a thunderstorm.

Aware that Aunt Zelda and Jenna were watching him closely, Septimus gathered up all three bowls and, holding them tightly together, quickly turned them upside down. The earth and water fell straight on to the rug, but the purple mist sank slowly—its progress closely followed by one pair of green eyes, one pair of violet eyes and one pair of witch's blue eyes—until it met the muddy mess on the rug and exploded into flame. Septimus gulped; this was the bit he was dreading. He reached out to grab the flame, and a yell came from Wolf Boy, who had been watching with awe behind a boat. "412— no!" Wolf Boy cried out, feeling his hands burning all over again. But Septimus felt no pain as he gathered up the fire and placed it in the dragon's nostrils.

Suddenly there was a huge intake of breath, and the flames were sucked into the dragon's nose down deep within her. Moments later, the dragon reared her head, snorting, coughing and breathing out a bright tongue of orange flame, setting

Jannit's Persian rug on fire and sending Aunt Zelda, Jenna and Septimus leaping to safety. Nicko threw a bucket of water to douse the rug. The dragon opened her eyes for a brief moment and then, with a resounding crash, her great green head crashed back down on to the charred rug and lay as limp as before.

The whole boatyard fell silent. Even Jannit stopped her unloading and stood waiting uncertainly.

Jenna looked dismayed. She glanced at Septimus as if for reassurance but Septimus was staring unhappily at the Dragon Boat, convinced that his Transubstantiate Triple had failed. Aunt Zelda gave a small cough and was about to say something when Marcia's voice travelled across the boatyard.

"Will someone get this blasted bucket off my foot!" A yardhand rushed to her aid and pulled off a bucket that Marcia had inadvertently stepped into in her rush to return to the Dragon Boat. With her robes flying, Marcia continued her progress across the boatyard, and as she neared the dragon, Jenna, Aunt Zelda, and Septimus could see that she had a large green bottle in her hand.

Marcia arrived breathless at the pontoon and uncorked the bottle.

"Marcia, what are you doing?" asked Aunt Zelda crossly.

"Saving the Dragon Boat. I knew I had some somewhere. It's an ancient lizard-based Revive. I keep it under the floor-boards in the Library."

"Put it away," Aunt Zelda demanded. "Don't let that stuff near her. It will kill her."

"Don't be ridiculous, Zelda," Marcia retorted. "It's not for you to dictate what happens to the Dragon Boat any more. I am the Keeper now."

Jenna's and Septimus's eyes met. There was going to be trouble.

"You—" spluttered Aunt Zelda incredulously. "You—the Keeper?"

"Obviously," said Marcia. "The Dragon Boat is here now under my care. You are too far away to be able to continue with your duties as . . . how did you get here so *fast?*"

Aunt Zelda drew herself up to her full height—which was not much compared to Marcia, but it made Aunt Zelda feel better all the same. Her witchy blue eyes flashed triumphant-ly. "Keepers' secrets are not divulged to all and sundry, Marcia, and I am not at liberty to tell you how I got here. All I will say is that, as long as I live, I am the Keeper of the Dragon Boat and I shall remain so and be available to the Dragon Boat at all times. Now Marcia, this is a matter of life and death. The

Triple will take its time and nothing, particularly an ancient lizard Revive, must be allowed to interfere with it. As Keeper I am telling you to take that Revive away. Right *now*."

For the first time that Septimus could remember, Marcia was speechless. Very deliberately, she pushed the cork back into the Revive bottle and, with as much dignity as she could muster, she walked across the boatyard, studiously avoiding the bucket on her way out. It did not help her bad temper to discover that Milo Banda, plus Sarah and Silas Heap, had watched the whole episode from the shadows of the abandoned lock-up.

✢ 49 ✢
FLYTE

Marcia strode across the Palace Moat, her feet echoing on the warm planks of the old wooden bridge. At her side was Milo Banda who, on the brisk walk from the boatyard to the Palace, had had the task of calming Marcia after her encounter with Aunt Zelda.

Standing at the Palace door, beside the small gold chair on which the ghost Godric sat dozing, was a sub-Wizard, a smart young woman with brilliant green eyes.

"Good evening. Welcome to the Palace." The sub-Wizard smiled.

"Good evening, Hildegarde," replied Marcia.

Milo Banda hung back, standing uncertainly on the threshold. Marcia noticed that he was trembling slightly and there were tears in his eyes.

"Oh," she said softly, "I'm sorry, Milo. I didn't think. Would you like us to leave you alone for a few moments?"

Milo Banda nodded. He wandered off down the Long Walk, looking at the empty walls and shaking his head in dismay.

Suddenly Marcia felt weary—it had been a long day. The Identify had left her feeling curiously empty and, to top it all, her foot throbbed painfully from its encounter with Spit Fyre that morning. With a sigh of relief, she sat down heavily on Godric's chair and took off her shoe. The ghost leaped off the chair in alarm and fell on to the floor in a confused heap.

"Alther," said Marcia crossly, "I thought I told you to get rid of all the Ancients. We don't need them now that we have the sub-Wizards on door duty."

"Godric was very upset when I asked him to leave, so I told him he could stay. Anyway," Alther tutted, "you should have more respect for the Ancients. You'll be one, one day."

Alther dusted Godric off and wafted him over to a comfortable armchair in a quiet, dark corner of the hall. The old ghost immediately fell into a deep sleep and did not wake until many years later, when Jenna's own daughter ran into him with her scooter.

It was unfortunate that when Jenna returned to the Palace, she did not notice Alther and Marcia sitting quietly in the shadows cast by the rows of flickering candles placed around the hall. The first person she saw, as he emerged from the gloom of the Long Walk, was the stranger from the Port. At the sight of Jenna he gasped and stopped in his tracks. Jenna screamed.

Marcia jumped to her feet. "Jenna—what is it?" she asked, glancing around anxiously.

Jenna did not reply. She tore out of the Palace and headed for the safety of Septimus, Nicko, Aunt Zelda and Wolf Boy, who were making slow progress across the Palace lawns while Spit Fyre insisted on chasing a lawn lizard.

"He's here!" yelled Jenna as she reached Aunt Zelda. "That man—he's here!"

"What man?" asked Aunt Zelda, both bemused and amused at the sight of Marcia running across the lawn towards them, wearing only one shoe.

"Jenna," said Marcia breathlessly as she finally caught up with her. "Jenna, what's wrong?"

"That man—the stranger at the Port. The one who grabbed Thunder, the one who followed me, the one who's in league with Simon—you've asked him to *my* Palace. That's what's wrong!"

"But Jenna," Marcia protested, "that man has every right to be in the Palace. He's Milo Banda. He's—"

"I don't care who he is!" yelled Jenna.

"But Jenna, Jenna listen to me—he's your father."

Everyone stared at Marcia in shock.

"No he's not," stuttered Jenna. "Dad's down at the boatyard . . . with Mum."

"Yes, Silas is at the boatyard," said Marcia gently. "And Milo is here. Milo is your own father, Jenna. He has come to see you."

For a long time Jenna was silent. Then suddenly she said, "So, why didn't he come to see me before—when I was little?" And she took off across the lawns and along the path that led to the back of the Palace.

"Oh dear," said Marcia.

✳ ✳ ✳

Silas Heap did not take kindly to the arrival of Milo Banda either, especially when Sarah insisted on arranging a celebration supper on the Palace roof to welcome him home.

"I don't see how you can celebrate when our eldest son is stuck down in those awful Ice Tunnels," Silas had objected.

Sarah was busying herself with laying the table while Silas had plonked himself down on one of the Palace gold chairs and was staring gloomily at the darkening summer sky.

"I just don't want to even think about Simon," Sarah said briskly. "The Search Party will soon find him and then at least he'll be somewhere safe and warm."

"Safe and warm in the Castle jail is not what I wanted for him, Sarah," Silas muttered.

Sarah shook her head. "Silas, if you remember, yesterday we had no idea where any of the children were. We have three back today—four if you count Simon—and we should consider ourselves lucky. That's the way I am going to look at it from now on." She straightened the tablecloth and told the Supper Servant to go and see how the cook was getting on. "Anyway, Silas, we must make Milo Banda welcome. He is Jenna's father after all."

"Huh," said Silas grumpily.

Sarah carefully put her favourite candlesticks in the middle of the long table. "We knew this might happen one day. It's no good being funny about it."

"I'm not being funny," Silas protested. "I just think it's odd that he's turned up after all these years. I mean, where's he been all this time? Seems downright suspicious to me. Huh."

"Don't keep saying 'huh', Silas. It makes you sound so crotchety."

"Well, maybe I am crotchety. And I'll keep saying 'huh' if I want to, Sarah. Huh."

Supper went on late into the night. Sarah had put Milo Banda at the head of the table simply laid with a white cloth. It reminded Jenna of the morning of her tenth birthday, which now felt like another lifetime. Jenna had sat as far away from Milo Banda as she could get—at the other end of the table— but it wasn't until she sat down that she realised she was now opposite Milo, and every time she looked up she saw him trying to smile at her or catch her eye. Jenna spent most of the meal staring at her plate or making pointed conversation with Aunt Zelda, who was sitting next to her.

As the torches burned down and midnight approached, the summer air cooled and people began to yawn. Aunt Zelda leaned over to Jenna and said in a low voice, "Your father is a good man, Jenna. You should hear what he has to say."

"I don't care what he has to say," Jenna answered.

"A wise Young Queen listens first. Then she judges."

Supper was finished. Marcia, Septimus and Spit Fyre had gone back to the Wizard Tower. Nicko was off with Silas, who wanted to show him a new colony of Counters he had found behind a pipe in the Palace attic. Sarah was tending to Wolf Boy, who had fallen asleep at the beginning of supper, and Aunt Zelda was down in the kitchens trying to get the night cook to boil a cabbage for breakfast the next morning. Alther Mella sat quietly in the shadows, musing on the events of the day.

And Jenna was listening to Milo Banda.

"You know," Milo was saying, "your mother and I were so pleased when we knew we were going to have a child. We both hoped for a girl so that she could become Queen. Of course, I was never King; it is not the way you do things here, unlike many of the Far Countries. There, would you believe, they pass the succession down through the boy children—very strange. But I was glad not to be King, for although I was just an ordinary merchant, I loved my job. I loved the excitement of travelling and the possibility that one day I would make my own fortune. Then six months before you were due to be born, I heard of just such an opportunity. With your mother's blessing, I chartered a ship at the Port and set off. My luck was in and before long I had a ship full of treasure to bring back to you and your mother. All went well, I had a good crew and fair winds all the way home, and I arrived in Port on the very day you were due. Everything, I thought, was perfect. But then . . . when we docked . . ." Milo's voice faltered. "I-I remember it as though it were yesterday . . . a deckhand told me the news, the terrible news that was all over the Port . . . that my dear Cerys—your mother—had been killed. And my little daughter, too."

"But I wasn't killed," whispered Jenna.

"No. I know that now. But then— I didn't. I believed what everyone said."

"Well, they were wrong. Why didn't you come to the Castle and see if it was true? Why didn't you come to find me? You ran away."

"Yes. I suppose it seems so. But at the time I could not bear to stay. I left on the next tide and wandered wherever the winds took me—until I was captured by Deakin Lee."

"Deakin Lee!" Jenna gasped. Even she, who was not at all interested in pirates, had heard of the dreaded Deakin Lee.

Milo risked a rueful smile in Jenna's direction. She gave him an uncertain half smile in return.

"I will never forget those seven long years in Deakin Lee's hold," he said in a low voice. "All the time I thought of the terrible thing that had happened to you and your dear mother. . . ."

"How did you escape?" asked Jenna.

"One night, in the spring of last year, the ship came upon tumultuous waves. I've heard it said they were the swell from a Darke storm thousands of miles away, but they were good waves for me. Deakin Lee was washed overboard and his crew freed me. I took over the ship. Some weeks later we put in to a small port and I heard the rumour that you were alive. I could hardly believe it—I felt my life was beginning again. We set sail immediately and had fair winds all the way to the Port. We anchored offshore and raised the Yellow Duster to alert Customs, and the Chief Officer was rowed out to us the next morning. She took one look at the treasure onboard and told us we had to wait until the main bonded warehouse was free—she was a tough one, that Officer Nettles. But I am grateful to her, for had she not done so I would not have seen you that night."

Jenna remembered the scene at the warehouse. It all made sense now.

Milo continued, "When I looked up and saw you sitting on that horse, just the way your mother used to, and then I saw the circlet around your head, I knew you were my daughter. But I am sorry, Jenna, I think I frightened you that night. I wasn't thinking—I just wanted to talk to you. Jenna . . . Jenna?"

Jenna had spun around and was gazing into the shadows cast by the torches guttering on the Palace roof.

"Jenna?" Milo repeated.

"I can feel someone watching me," she said.

Milo shifted uncomfortably. "So can I," he said. Milo Banda and his daughter stared into the shadows but neither saw the ghost of the Queen watching her husband and daughter talk together for the first time in their lives.

Alther wafted up to the Queen. "It's good to see you venturing out of the Queen's Room at last," he said.

The Queen smiled wistfully. "I must return at once, Alther, but I could not resist seeing my dear Milo just once again—and with our daughter too."

"You can tell they are father and daughter," observed Alther.

"Yes, that's true," the Queen nodded slowly. "There is something about the way they stand, is there not?"

"Yet she looks like you—remarkably like you."

"I know," sighed the Queen. "Goodnight, Alther."

Alther watched the Queen drift silently past Jenna and Milo Banda, both of whom looked straight at her but saw nothing. Soon the Queen reached the turret and delicately stepped through its thick stone wall. Inside the Queen's room the fire burned as brightly as always and the Queen sat quietly in her chair, remembering the events of the day—the day she had awaited for so many years.

Septimus, Marcia and Spit Fyre walked slowly along Wizard Way. The torches blazed in their silver posts, and Spit Fyre kept pouncing on the flickering shadows cast on the pavement. It was now after midnight and all the shops were closed and dark, but as they walked past the Manuscriptorium, Septimus thought he glimpsed a light behind the great piles of books and papers. But when he looked more carefully he could see nothing.

Marcia limped painfully up the marble steps to the Wizard Tower. Septimus settled Spit Fyre into the dragon kennel for the night.

"Make sure he can't get out, Septimus," Marcia told him as the great silver doors of the Tower opened for their

ExtraOrdinary Wizard. "And don't forget to double bolt the door."

"All right," he said, and Marcia tottered gratefully inside.

Spit Fyre settled down surprisingly easily. Septimus shot the two massive iron bolts across the door and tiptoed away to the sound of the dragon's snores shaking the kennel.

It was a beautiful night. The Wizard Tower courtyard was deserted; the Magykal torches placed along the tops of the courtyard walls cast a soft purple light across the old flagstones, dim enough for Septimus to still see a myriad of stars in the night sky.

Septimus was reluctant to go inside. He looked up at the stars and all his old dreams of flying came back to him. He knew he could resist no longer—he took out the Flyte Charm. The golden arrow with its new silver flights sat buzzing in his hand, and Septimus felt a thrill of Magyk go through him. As the flights began to flutter, Septimus felt himself lifting off the ground, up, up, until he was as high as the Great Arch. Holding the arrow between finger and thumb he pointed it towards the Palace, then he spread his arms out as he had once seen Alther do—and he flew.

He swooped down Wizard Way, low and fast just as Alther liked to, sped over the Palace Gate, and then soared up on to the Palace roof, just as he had always done in his dreams. Below him he saw Jenna and her father leaning over the battlements, talking quietly. Unsure whether to interrupt them, but longing to surprise Jenna and show her how well he could Flye, Septimus hovered for a moment waiting for a break in Milo's ramblings. Then something caught his eye.

On the other side of the river, a horse galloped through the Farmlands. Riding the horse—newly stolen from outside the Grateful Turbot Tavern—was a familiar figure. Simon.

Septimus pointed the Flyte Charm towards the shadowy figure of his eldest brother. "Follow," he whispered to the Charm. The next moment he found himself hurtling away from the Palace and swooping across the lawns that led to the river. Soon damp smells of the river filled his nostrils as he skimmed low across the cool night-time water, startling a few ducks on the way. As the ducks' angry quacking subsided, Septimus reached the far bank; he flew above the thatched roof of a lone farmhouse and hovered for a moment, searching out his brother. Sure enough, in the distance along the dusty road that wound through the Farmlands, Septimus saw a horseman spurring his horse into the night. A final, breathtaking turn of speed brought him level with Simon, and Septimus flew—unseen at first—alongside him, easily keeping pace with the sweating horse.

At last Simon became aware that all was not well. "You!" he yelled, skidding to a halt in a cloud of dust.

Septimus landed lightly in front of the horse.

"You—you've got my Flyte Charm," Simon spluttered, seeing the golden arrow in Septimus's hand.

"I do have the Flyte Charm," Septimus agreed, neatly flying out of reach as Simon lurched forward to snatch it. "But the Flyte Charm is not mine. The Flyte Charm belongs to no one, Simon. You should know that an Ancient Charm is its own master."

"Pompous prat," Simon muttered under his breath.

"What did you say?" asked Septimus, who had heard perfectly well.

"Nothing. Get out of my way brat, and don't think you can try any Transfixing rubbish this time."

"I'm not going to," replied Septimus, hovering in front of the horse. "I've just come to tell you to get out of here."

"Which was exactly what I was doing," Simon growled.

Septimus held his position, blocking Simon's path. "I also came to tell you that if you ever try to harm Jenna again, you will have me to deal with. Understand?"

Simon stared at his youngest brother. Septimus returned

the stare, his brilliant green eyes flashing angrily. Simon said nothing, for there was a feeling of power about Septimus that he recognised—the power of a seventh son of a seventh son.

"Understand?" Septimus repeated.

"Yeah," muttered Simon.

"You can go now," Septimus said coolly and dropped to the ground, standing to one side so that Simon could pass.

Simon looked down at the defenceless boy in green in the dark, deserted Farmlands, way past midnight. For a brief moment he considered how easy it would be to make Septimus disappear; no one would know what had happened. No one would ever suspect . . . but Simon did nothing. And then suddenly he kicked his horse into action and galloped off, yelling over his shoulder, "I wish you *had* been dead when the midwife took you away!"

Septimus flew slowly back to the Wizard Tower with Simon's words echoing in his head.

He smiled. The last of his brothers had accepted him.

WHAT HAPPENED
BEFORE . . .

BILLY POT

Billy Pot once had a pet shop that specialised in reptiles. Billy loved lizards and snakes, and he specialised in breeding purple pythons. The biggest python that Billy Pot had ever bred lived in the backyard of Terry Tarsal's shoe shop. Terry, who did not like snakes, very reluctantly used their sloughed skin for Marcia's pointy snakeskin shoes.

When the Supreme Custodian bought a colony of snapping turtles from Billy and then ordered him to move to the Palace to look after them, Billy did not dare refuse. Billy's niece, Sandra, took over the pet shop and to Billy's great disapproval started selling fancy hamsters and fluffy rabbits. Sandra's new line in cuddly animals proved very popular, and she soon offered to buy the pet shop from Billy.

With the money Sandra had given him for the pet shop,

Billy set up the lizard lodges down by the river, built the Contraption and embarked on his never-ending quest for the perfect lawn. When the Heaps moved into the Palace with Jenna, Silas asked Billy to stay on and help them get rid of the snapping turtles. Billy agreed, but the job proved impossible and he gave up after he nearly lost a finger to a particularly aggressive turtle.

UNA BRAKKET

Una Brakket was housekeeper at the Young Army Barracks when Septimus was a toddler. Una did not like boys, even subdued and scared Young Army boys; she soon got a transfer and became housekeeper to the Hunter and his Pack. Una admired the Hunter very much indeed, although it is doubtful whether the Hunter even noticed her. He once asked her where his socks were, and Una went around in a daydream for days afterwards. After that she took to hiding the Hunter's socks so that he might ask her again, but he never did.

When the Supreme Custodian fled and Jenna came back to live in the Palace as Princess, Una took advantage of Marcia and Alther's Second-Chance Scheme. She applied for a job as Palace housekeeper, which she did not get as Sarah Heap thought she was scary. The Scheme eventually referred her to Professor Weasal Van Klampff, who only took her on because he was too frightened to refuse.

However, Una's sympathies still lay with DomDaniel, and she joined the Restoration Unit, a secret network of people who wished to see him return. They met every Saturday night under the pretence of country dancing classes. It was through them that Una was put in touch with Simon Heap.

PROFESSOR WEASAL VAN KLAMPFF

Weasal Van Klampff came from a long line of Professors. Many hundreds of years ago, Professor Doris Van Klampff had worked out a secret and very complicated formula for getting rid of Hauntings. This included Shadows, such as Marcia's, and Spectres like the one that had Waited for Alther when he was Apprentice to DomDaniel. Although the Van Klampffs had great mathematical ability, they tended to be rather gullible and extremely forgetful; Weasal was no exception.

After Weasal's father, Otto, blew himself up—along with the original Van Klampff Laboratory—while mixing some volatile Amalgam, Weasal decided to give up experimenting and live a quiet life beside the Moat. On moving into his house

on Snake Slipway he was dismayed to find an ancient laboratory tucked away at the end of a warren of tunnels. Weasal
spent many years trying to ignore the laboratory, but in the
end the temptation was too great and he decided to carry on his
father's work. He perfected Otto's Amalgam so that it acted as
a highly efficient screen for Darke energy, thus unwittingly
providing an ideal hiding place for DomDaniel's bones.

Weasal Van Klampff was a trusting man and had no idea
that Una Brakket belonged to the Restoration Unit.

BEETLE

Beetle was an only child. He grew up in The Ramblings—his
parents had two large rooms on the floor immediately below
the Heap family. One of Beetle's earliest memories was his
mother banging on the ceiling with a broom handle, yelling,
"For heaven's sake *be quiet!*" His parents refused to let Beetle
have anything to do with the Heaps, which only made them
more attractive, and he soon struck up a friendship with Jo-Jo
Heap, who was the same age.

At the age of eleven, Beetle passed the highly competitive
entrance test to the Manuscriptorium, much to his mother's
delight. He started as General Dogsbody, and after the

Inspection Clerk fell off the sledge and broke his ankle, Beetle was trusted enough to take over the weekly inspections of the Ice Tunnels.

Beetle liked Septimus a lot; he reminded him of Jo-Jo, but he also shared Beetle's interest in Magyk and his liking for weird fizzy drinks. Beetle shared Septimus's dislike of Darke Magyk for, as he once said to Septimus over a mug of FizzFroot, "All that Darke stuff is depressing. When that awful old bloke came back to the Wizard Tower my hamster died, my mum got a huge boil on the end of her nose and the cat ran away. All because Darke stuff stuck to me at work, and then I brought it home. Horrible."

Septimus liked Beetle a lot too. He trusted him completely.

BORIS CATCHPOLE

Ever since he could remember, Boris Catchpole had been known by his last name. His mother had tried her best to call him Boris, but by the time he had started toddling she, like everyone else, had given up and reverted to plain Catchpole— somehow Boris seemed just too familiar.

Catchpole's ambition was to be a Hunter. He had run away from home and joined the Hunting Pack in the Badlands while DomDaniel had been preparing the assassination of the Queen. Catchpole had trained hard with the Pack, but he was not popular. He had given up cleaning his teeth as a boy and had no intention of starting again now that he did not have his mother telling him to. He had a nervous habit of clicking his tongue against the roof of his mouth that made people feel snappy, and, to top it all, he was growing fast and was soon too tall to make a good Hunter.

Catchpole, true to his name, became Deputy Hunter but progressed no farther. After the overthrow of the Supreme Custodian he joined the Second-Chance Scheme and was accepted as a sub-Wizard—a new trainee Wizard post for those of more mature years or no Magykal background.

Catchpole's ambition was now to be a proper Wizard. At the very least he wanted to be an Ordinary Wizard, but he had decided that he would not turn down the job of ExtraOrdinary Wizard if it were offered to him. It never was.

JANNIT MAARTEN

If you asked Jannit Maarten to describe herself, she would say, "boat builder." And that is all she would say. Jannit had little time for politics and even less time for Wizards. Whatever went on in the Castle was of no concern to Jannit, whose whole world consisted of her boatyard just outside the Castle walls. She slept soundly in her hammock at night, rose at dawn and spent all daylight hours happily building, mending, painting and scraping—and all the other hundreds of wonderfully time-consuming fiddly things that boats require.

Although Nicko found it hard to believe, Jannit had once been a little girl, but she had forgotten all about it—possibly because she had grown up on a small farm in the middle of the Farmlands and had disliked chickens, hated cows and loathed pigs. Her parents never understood why, at fourteen, Jannit had dressed as a boy and run away to sea. At nineteen she returned with a ship of her own and set up the Jannit Maarten Boatyard next to the derelict Castle Customs Quay. Jannit was entirely happy with her life and set foot outside her beloved boatyard with great reluctance.

SLEUTH

Sleuth had once been a tennis ball. It had spent two years lying in a damp ditch beside the Port Municipal Real Tennis House after someone had hit it out the window in a fit of temper; it had been seriously nibbled by mice and was slowly falling apart, until one day Simon Heap picked it up, put it in his pocket and took it back to the Observatory.

Over the next few months, Sleuth lay in a Sealed box, which Simon Heap carefully tended. He regularly filled and refilled the box with gases and potions, chanted over it for long hours and encircled it with Reverse Charms. As Sleuth gradually became conscious, it heard incantations muttered over it at midnight and smelled the Darke fumes that Simon wafted through the box. It had lain there, confused but excited, waiting to see what was going to happen.

Then, one night, at the Dark of the Moon, Sleuth was let out of its box and saw the world for the first time. It liked what it saw and Simon Heap was equally pleased with his creation. Sleuth glowed brightly and seemed intelligent; it was obedient and quick to learn. Soon it followed its Master everywhere and became Simon Heap's most loyal and faithful servant.

NURSE MEREDITH

Nurse Agnes Meredith, ex-Matron Midwife, ex-baby snatcher, made her way to the Port after being released from the Castle Asylum for Deluded and Distressed Persons. She walked the streets looking for her son, Merrin, but she had no luck. Eventually she ran out of the allowance the Asylum had given her and found a job as a cleaner in a seedy lodging house in the Rope Walk, next to the Port Witch Coven.

The owner of the lodging house was a Mrs Florrie Bundy, a large woman of short temper and long memory. Florrie had numerous ongoing feuds with her neighbours, the Port Witches, and it was a heated argument over a used teabag—which Florrie claimed had been deliberately aimed at her head—that led to her demise. Linda, who one day for want of nothing better to do had indeed thrown a teabag at Florrie's head, eventually got tired of being yelled at and placed a Shrink Spell on Florrie. Over the course of a few weeks the Shrink Spell gradually reduced Florrie to the size of a teabag herself, and one frosty morning she slipped on some ice, fell down the drain outside the backdoor and drowned.

Agnes Meredith had watched Florrie Shrinking with great interest. One day, when she could no longer find the diminutive landlady, Nurse Meredith took over the lodging house as though nothing had happened. She soon made it her own—hanging flock wallpaper, writing whimsical messages to stick on the walls and filling the house with dried flowers and dolls. She enjoyed the company of her dolls, and after a while she stopped looking for Merrin. At least you knew where you were with dolls, she told herself.

MAUREEN

Maureen had run away to the Port with the Chief Potato Peeler after an incident in the Palace kitchens. Maureen and the Chief Potato Peeler, Kevin, were saving up to buy their own café. When Kevin was taken on as cook on a large merchant ship on a round-the-world voyage, Maureen took the only job she could find at the time, working in the Doll House. It was not ideal but she managed to save the tips she was given by grateful guests, and at least living in the cupboard under the stairs meant she did not have to pay for lodgings. She longed for the day that Kevin would return and they would find a little place of their own down by the harbour.

PORT WITCH COVEN:
VERONICA

Veronica had been in the Coven for the longest of all the witches, but she did not hold the post of Witch Mother on account of her forgetfulness and tendency to sleepwalk out of the Coven and get lost for days on end. Veronica loved rats, something she had inherited from her father, Jack, who lived out on the reed beds near the Marram Marshes. Like her father, Veronica had a large collection of caged rats in various stages of decay.

LINDA

Linda was the youngest of the witches and was, as she put it, "up for anything, me." The other witches enjoyed her company but not her practical jokes. Linda had a fiery temper and a penchant for very nasty spells if anyone crossed her. But after the incident of Dorinda's elephant ears, none of the witches did. Pamela, the Witch Mother, saw that Linda had potential and was secretly grooming her as her successor.

DAPHNE

Daphne was the quiet one of the Coven. She bumbled around amiably and kept to herself, happily nurturing a colony of giant woodworms, which were slowly eating their way through the house. Daphne loved her woodworms and kept most of her conversation for them.

PAMELA

Pamela was the Witch Mother and the Darke one of the Coven. Of course all the witches thought they were Darke Witches, but Pamela was the real thing. She had spent some years with DomDaniel at the Observatory and had returned with many Darke tales to tell, which had frightened the other Coven members, even though they would rather drink rotten frog juice than admit it. Pamela had her own Locked room, which the other witches kept well away from, and at night, when bloodcurdling shrieks echoed from the room, the rest of the Coven stuffed their fingers in their ears and tried to sleep.

DORINDA

Dorinda had not been especially concerned about her appearance until the terrible night of the elephant ears. She knew she was not particularly good-looking, for her nose was slightly crooked after an argument with a fire escape, and she had never liked her hair. But Dorinda gave up any attempt at personal grooming after Linda accused her of eavesdropping on a private conversation with a young Warlock she had brought home. Dorinda had strenuously denied it—even though the whole Coven knew she crept around listening at keyholes.

Linda was furious and Bestowed upon Dorinda a pair of elephant ears (African elephant ears—the really big ones), saying that "if she was going to go flapping her ears around the place, she may as well have some decent ears to flap." Since that night Dorinda had worn a large towel swathed around her head and kept up the pretence to the rest of the Coven that she had just washed her hair, even though they knew—and Dorinda knew that they knew—that underneath the huge towel lay a pair of neatly folded African elephant ears. It was a permanent spell, and not even Pamela could get rid of it.

Hugh Fox, Chief Hermetic Scribe

Hugh Fox had been a lowly scribe in the Manuscriptorium for twenty-five years when he was Picked to become the Chief Hermetic Scribe.

When DomDaniel had lured Marcia back from the Marram Marshes, he had snatched the book she had with her, *The Undoing of the Darkenesse*. The Necromancer had taken the book to Waldo Watkins, who was the Chief Hermetic Scribe, and told him to use the Darke Hermetic Powers that are always available to a Chief Scribe to Unlocke its secrets.

Watkins had refused, and that night on his way home Waldo
Watkins vanished, never to be seen again.

DomDaniel insisted on an immediate replacement and the
Draw was made. The Draw was a ceremony: each scribe
placed his pen into a large ancient enamelled Pot. The Pot was
taken into the Hermetic Chamber and left overnight. The
next morning one pen would always be found lying on the
table, while the rest would remain in the Pot. Traditionally the
youngest scribe would be sent in to retrieve the chosen pen.

However, when Hugh Fox was Picked, DomDaniel insisted on going into the Hermetic Chamber himself to get the
pen. When he brought out a much-chewed black pen belonging to Hugh Fox, no one could believe it. Not even Hugh Fox.
There were rumours about the Pick not being fair, but nothing could be proved.

The truth of it was that DomDaniel had put back a pen
belonging to Jillie Djinn, a talented and well-read scribe, and
pulled out Hugh Fox's pen—because he reckoned that Hugh
Fox was a pushover.

And so Hugh Fox was instructed in the Cryptic Codex, hand-
ed the Official Seals and duly installed as Chief Hermetic Scribe.
To DomDaniel's disgust, Hugh Fox had great trouble
Unlocking the secrets of Marcia's book, but he did manage to

find the Flyte Charm—Concealed in the cover—just as DomDaniel became a bundle of bones in the Marram Marshes.

After DomDaniel's demise and Marcia's return to the Wizard Tower with Septimus, the Restoration Unit threatened Hugh Fox with the same fate that had befallen poor old Watkins if he did not give Simon Heap access to the Ice Tunnels. Hugh Fox agreed. And when Simon Heap demanded the Flyte Charm, he handed it over without a murmur. DomDaniel had been right—Hugh Fox was, indeed, a pushover.

PARTRIDGE

Colin Partridge had once been a Custodian Guard. He had been unwillingly recruited from a small village on the edge of the Sheeplands. Partridge was a dreamy child whose days were spent minding his father's sheep. Partridge had lost more sheep than his father cared to think about, and his father despaired of him ever making a good shepherd. So when the Custodian Guard Recruiting Party promised to "make a man of him," Partridge's father had young Colin packed and ready in no time at all, much to the horror of his doting mother.

Luckily for Partridge, he arrived right at the end of the Supreme Custodian's regime, and within a month of joining, he had signed up for the Second-Chance Scheme and been snapped up by the Manuscriptorium. Partridge had never been happier.

THE ICE TUNNEL GHOSTS

Eldred and Alfred Stone were brothers. They, like many other stonemasons, had been brought in at the time of the Great Catastrophe underneath the Castle. They had worked long hard hours to try to repair the breach in the tunnels but to no avail. They were among the thirty-nine people who were trapped by the Emergency Freeze and never again saw the light of day. Along with their companions, they continued to walk the tunnels, unaware that many hundreds of years had passed since they were Frozen. Both brothers were convinced that their lives still awaited them, if only someone would tell them the way out.

ELLIS CRACKLE

Ellis Crackle had been DomDaniel's Apprentice when the Necromancer was first ExtraOrdinary Wizard at the Castle, many years ago. Ellis was a slow, ungainly young man with little aptitude for Magyk, but DomDaniel did not care. He chose Ellis because he was Betty Crackle's brother. At that time, Betty Crackle was Keeper of the Dragon Boat. She was a disorganised White Witch who meant well, but she always left a trail of trouble behind her, due to her absentmindedness and general untidiness. Aunt Zelda eventually took over from Betty after she wandered off to the Port one winter's night and got caught by the Big Freeze.

Ellis Crackle was even more forgetful than Betty was, but DomDaniel had guessed that there might be something very important at Keeper's Cottage—something that stopped him from getting complete control of the Castle—and he wanted to find out what it was. Employing Betty Crackle's brother seemed like a good way of worming his way into the secret.

Unfortunately for DomDaniel, just after Ellis took up his Apprenticeship, Betty and Ellis had a huge row. Ellis boasted once too often about his important new post and Betty, who was very jealous, could stand it no more. She put an Enchantment on Keeper's Cottage to keep Ellis away and never spoke to her brother again. And so it turned out that DomDaniel never discovered the Dragon Boat at Keeper's Cottage—or even where the Cottage was.

When Aunt Zelda took over from Betty Crackle, Ellis was

of no further use to DomDaniel. He took on Alther Mella as a new Apprentice and Ellis was Suspended—a long and nasty Darke process of Reducing someone to a Shadow. DomDaniel then Kept the unfortunate Ellis for further use. He came in very handy later, as Marcia's Shadow.

HILDEGARDE

Hildegarde had worked for the Council of the Custodians in the accounts department, which had spent most of its time trying to curb the lavish spending of the Supreme Custodian. It was an impossible task. Later Hildegarde had been transferred to the Sales Force, which forced the sale of all the Palace treasures. Hildegarde grew to love the old pictures and furnishings she had to sell, but she drove a hard bargain and got a good price for them.

Hildegarde was very pleased when the Second-Chance Scheme helped her get accepted for training as a sub-Wizard. She was a little uneasy at being on door duty at the Palace, and when she looked at the empty places where all the treasures had once stood, her conscience troubled her. She was determined to become an Ordinary Wizard and make any amends possible.